BEST
AMERICAN
FANTASY

BEST
AMERICAN
FANTASY

Guest Editors
**ANN & JEFF
VANDERMEER**

Series Editor
**MATTHEW
CHENEY**

PRIME BOOKS

BEST AMERICAN FANTASY 2007

Prime Books
www.prime-books.com

ISBN: 978-0-8095-6280-0

TABLE OF CONTENTS

PREFACE: BEST AMERICAN FANTASY

Matthew Cheney

THE THREE WORDS IN OUR TITLE DO NOT HAVE STABLE DEFINI-
tions. Instead of a cause of frustration, this lack of stability can be
a source of wonder.

Best. According to whom? Under what criteria? Relative to what?

American. Where? Is it a geography or a mindset? Is it governments
or landscapes? Is it a history or a bunch of histories or the eradication of
history? Is it by birth or choice? Is it more about *and* and less about *or*?

Fantasy. Swords and dragons? Dreams and portents? Nonsense?
Does fantasy have to include magic, or can it simply hint at strangeness? Is it a genre or a lens? Is it subject or object? Can it live within the
structure of a story, or must it emanate from the content? Where does
fiction end and fantasy begin?

To explore these instabilities and pose impermanent answers to the
questions, we have settled on two principles for this series: after the
second volume, each book will have different guest editors; and every
editor will be encouraged to search as broadly as possible for stories that
fit within their conception of what *best, American,* and *fantasy* mean. If
there is one prejudice at the heart of these anthologies, it is a prejudice
in favor of the theory that great writing does not show up only in predictable places, under predictable labels, in predictable forms—great
writing is, in fact, the least predictable.

You could be excused for wondering why the world needs yet another best-of-the-year collection when dozens are published annually by big and small publishers alike.

I can only answer by telling a story.

More forcefully than any other books, a series of best-of-the-year anthologies edited by Judith Merril in the 1950s and 1960s taught me how limitless and powerful short fiction can be. I discovered a few of these anthologies in a used bookstore when I was in my teens, and for some reason or another I bought them and read them. Though at first they challenged and frustrated me, soon I found those books to be among the most thrilling collections of short fiction I ever read.

The first of Merril's anthologies came out in 1956, was titled *The Year's Greatest Science Fiction and Fantasy*, and had an introduction by Orson Welles. The last came out in 1968 and was titled *SF 12*. Merril had always had eclectic taste, but the last few volumes of her series are monuments to diversity. That last volume puts Donald Barthelme's "The Balloon" beside J.G. Ballard's "The Cloud-Sculptors of Coral D"; it puts a short-short story by Günther Grass beside a novella by Samuel Delany; it puts writers generally considered traditional genre writers (Katherine MacLean, Fritz Leiber, Charles L. Harness) beside writers who skirted the boundaries of genres (Sonya Dorman, Thomas M. Disch, Carol Emshwiller) beside writers generally seen as "literary" writers (William S. Burroughs, John Updike, Hortense Calisher).

What is most remarkable to me now when I look at Merril's last few annuals is that they represent the fiction of their time so well. Many of the writers she included are writers who have, for one reason or another, maintained strong reputations for decades. Certainly, there are stories and authors that have lost their appeal over the years, and stories that do not hold up well when read now, but the contents of those books still, forty years later, impress. (Consider, for instance, the authors listed on the cover of the beat-up old Dell paperback of the eleventh volume that I have: Arthur C. Clarke, Alfred Jarry, Isaac Asimov, J.G. Ballard, Roald Dahl, Thomas M. Disch, Gerald Kersh, Donald Barthelme, Jorge Luis Borges, John Ciardi, Harvey Jacobs, Fritz Leiber, and Art Buchwald. "And many more." Indeed.)

Best-of-the-year collections today sometimes make an attempt to add writers of a variety of styles from various types of publications, but none to my knowledge make it part of their purpose the way Judith Merril did. That is the gap we seek to fill, because we believe the world of fiction is as diverse and exciting as it was when Merril was compiling her collections, and there should be one anthology, at least, to chronicle such diversity.

Why have any limits, then? Why *best*? Why *American*? Why *fantasy*?

One of the reasons we set limits is that we do not have time to read everything written everywhere in any one year. There are tens of thousands of short stories published annually in big and small magazines, in anthologies and single-author collections, on websites and via email subscriptions. We searched high and low and far and wide for every sort of fiction we could find, and yet we know there are great swathes we never even glimpsed.

I am haunted by all the stories I know we missed, the gems we never discovered, the masterpieces that got away. Nonetheless, I was amazed by the quality of writing we encountered—stories of vivid imagination, stylistic brilliance, narrative power, and personal vision. Every one of the dozens and dozens of stories I recommended to Ann and Jeff was one I thought would do the book proud if included. The stories we settled on including were the ones that we couldn't forget, the ones we couldn't bear to let go, the ones that held our interest even after we had read them again and again.

The list of Recommended Reading at the back of the book is a list of stories we seriously discussed including. We're not lying when we say we recommend them. Seek them out. Support the publishers of these stories, because it is their efforts that allow quality writing of all types to thrive.

We have planned from the beginning to have Ann and Jeff VanderMeer as guest editors for two volumes, because we want to establish as solid a foundation for the series as possible, and I don't know of anyone better qualified than the VanderMeers to help make this anthology vibrantly unique. Indeed, the project was their idea originally, and it would not exist without their vision and effort. Working with them on it has been both an honor and a joy.

For guidelines on recommending or submitting material to be considered for *Best American Fantasy*, visit our website and blog:
http://bestamericanfantasy.com.
http://bestamericanfantasy.blogspot.com

INTRODUCTION: FANTASY AND THE IMAGINATION

Ann & Jeff VanderMeer

I N HER EXTRAORDINARY CREATIVE WRITING BOOK *THE PASSIONATE, Accurate Story*, Carol Bly presents a hypothetical situation. One night at dinner a girl announces to her father and mother that a group of bears has moved in next door. In one scenario, the father says (and I paraphrase), "Bears? Don't be ridiculous," and tells his daughter to be more serious. In the other scenario, the father says, "Bears, huh? How many bears? Do you know their names? What do they wear?" And his daughter, with delight, tells him.

The imagination is a form of love: playful, generous, and transformative. All of the best fiction hums and purrs and sighs with it, and in this way (as well) fiction mirrors life. This is how we think of the fiction collected in this first volume of *Best American Fantasy*. There's a flicker, a flutter, at the heart of these stories that animates them, and this movement—ever different, ever unpredictable—makes each story unique.

Does it matter if the imaginative impulse is "fantastical" in the sense of "containing an explicit fantastical event"? No. It matters only that, on some level, a sense of fantastical play exists on the page. *Bears have moved in next door.*

We often disregard this sense of play. Why? In part, the idea of "play" seems immature or frivolous, especially in a society still blinkered by its Puritan origins. However, we also tend to discount play because it speaks to an aspect of the imagination that defies easy measurement. It brings yet another level of uncertainty to an endeavor already supersaturated with the subjective.

During Medieval times, the imagination was often associated with the senses and thus thought to be one of the links between human beings and the animals. Only with the Rennaissance was the imagination firmly linked to creativity and thus the intellect. Both views, however, and modern ideals of *functionality* and *utility*—even, sometimes, the idea in modern fiction of *invisible prose*—ignore or have no place for the sense of play that precedes and infuses creative endeavor.

This is perhaps no surprise, given that you cannot teach imagination in a creative writing workshop. As Bly explicitly states in *The Accurate, Passionate Story*, by the time a person reaches the age where they want to write and be taught to write fiction, that particular muscle, that particular manifestation of the soul, is firmly locked in place. A good instructor can perhaps draw out an imaginative impulse in a timid student but cannot instill it as other, more empirical aspects of fiction can be instilled with patience and a firm hand.

And yet, how *critical* a sense of play can be in great fiction. The first story in this anthology, "A Hard Truth About Waste Management," whose title cheekily maintains a professional demeanor, embodies the importance of that which may seem frivolous. In "A Hard Truth," the absurd, the surreal, the playful, is ultimately put to the service of something more profound that rises from the depths of the story. This "something," which will always remain partially undefined even as it resonates, could not exist without the unique quality of imagination that gives it voice.

To pull out a hoary old quote, Jung once wrote: "The dynamic principle of fantasy is play, which belongs also to the child, and as such it appears to be inconsistent with the principle of serious work. But without this playing with fantasy no creative work has ever yet come to birth. The debt we owe to the play of imagination is incalculable."

In the stories contained in this anthology, events continually challenge and surprise our own imaginations. A rock thrown in "The Stolen Father" changes context completely by the time it lands at a man's feet. In "The Chinese Boy," hyenas and elephants and savannah sanctify an extended metaphor put to the service of exploring profound loneliness. "Bit Forgive" features letters that relate fantastical events in a context where the truth of them is unimportant, and yet, again, they resonate, they illuminate; there is something beyond and behind them bigger, darker, and wiser than what appears to be on the page.

These are not isolated incidents. In *Best American Fantasy*, you will find unexpected alligators, a man as big as a county, baboon playwrights, a flying woman, sordid superheroes, men who marry trees, the fragments of a storyteller, and the very edge of the world. You may even find the end of narrative.

What you will not find is a set definition of "fantasy." If you enter into reading this volume eager for such a definition or searching for the fantastical event that you believe should trigger the use of the term, you will overlook the many other pleasures that await you. These are the same pleasures you can find in non-fantastical stories: deep characterization, thematic resonance, clever plots, unique situations, pitch-perfect dialogue, enervating humor, and luminous settings. The extraordinary depth of imagination in the best stories affects not merely their content but their form, the form shaping the content, until we realize the two are not separate, that they are, in the best writing, united by the same imaginative act.

In a sense, defining "fantasy" in the context of fiction is a losing proposition—simply not worth the effort. Every setting of every piece of fiction ever written is fantastical in some way because it is impossible to truly replicate reality. If we are truthful, then we must acknowledge that even realistic fiction is not all that realistic. We do not really talk like people talk in fiction. Lives do not have the kind of narrative arc or denouement often found in fiction. Therefore, we should not look askance at writers who change the paradigm, who have no interest in replicating reality if it does not suit their purposes. At the same time, we should also remember that fantasy can operate at the level of metaphor alone. When Ann Stapleton overlays images of Africa onto a more prosaic setting in "The Chinese Boy" she is engaging in an act of transformation no different on one level from that engaged in by the writer of secondary world Fantasy.

In all of this, it is important to remember that even flights of fancy must have anchors to be successful. That rock landing in "The Stolen Father" has no meaning without its connection to the character. The alligator knows the plot of the tale better than anyone. The man as big as a county is weeping for a reason. The flying woman has an admirer. The failed superhero has bills to pay. The edge of the world isn't the end of *everything*. Even baboon playwrights and men who marry trees may have hidden depths. The fragments of the storyteller collect themselves long enough to tell one last story.

There's no *real* end to narrative, just as there is no real end to the ways in which "fantasy" elements can be put to use in the service of narrative. Every time someone reads Bly's *The Passionate, Accurate Story* and comes to the part where the father asks his daughter about the bears, there's the tantalizing possibility in the reader's mind that she'll say something different—something wonderful or horrible or bittersweet.

There's every possibility that what she says will *be* different for every reader, depending solely on the generosity of the individual imagination.

When we came up with the idea for *Best American Fantasy* with assistance from publisher Sean Wallace, we hoped it would be one of those transformative acts of the imagination. However, we couldn't have guessed how much pleasure we would get out of the experience. Any project of this nature starts out as an act of faith: that what you believe to be true—the diversity and quality of American fantasy—is actually true. In this case, our faith was rewarded. In addition to being able to read and select so many wonderful stories, we also had the pleasure of working with Matthew Cheney, an excellent and demanding series editor. In the conversations, email discussions, and, yes, arguments during the process, we all learned something. Thanks also to Sean for taking a chance on this project. Although one of the other main reasons for creating *Best American Fantasy* was to set up a fantasy best-of with rotating guest editors, we both know that once our time is up we will miss not only the experience but the people involved in that experience.

A HARD TRUTH ABOUT WASTE MANAGEMENT

Sumanth Prabhaker

from Identity Theory (online)

THE FAMILY LIKED SO MUCH TO FLUSH THEIR TRASH DOWN THE toilet that they sold their TV and used the money to buy three chairs to arrange in their upstairs bathroom. This was a time when flushing trash down the toilet was not uncommon, but this particular family's enjoyment was rare. Where most families who resorted to trash-flushing were ashamed and frustrated, this family looked forward to the sight of their trash bins filling up. They would sit in their three chairs and watch their trash get sucked down into the hole at the bottom of the toilet, which had a permanent black ring smeared around it, and they would cheer and punch their fists together.

None of the three chairs in the bathroom matched in size or color or shape or texture. The family had driven to the shopping mall and split up, and one hour later each member returned to the parking lot, carrying a chair that cost roughly one-third of the price the pawnshop had paid for their TV. The father's chair was dark brown with an electrical cord coming out the back. When he plugged his chair into the bathroom wall and sat down, he would feel small vibrations all over his shoulders and even around his knees, and he would wonder how he would ever manage to leave such a comfortable chair.

The mother's chair was more like a swing than a chair. It hung from the ceiling like a swing and it swung like a swing, but it was very comfortable as well. The cushion was made of a mixture of gelatin and polycarbonate, so every time she sat down it would shift around to make space for her, like a mold. The mother loved her mold cushion because she often carried a portable whiteboard in her pocket, which made her pants stick out in a direction most normal cushions couldn't accommodate. She used the whiteboard to write what she wanted to say, having lost the ability to speak as a child.

The son's chair was made of gingerbread, graham crackers, gum drops, licorice ropes, jawbreakers, chocolate bars, bubble gum sticks, candied fruits, lollipops and suckers, nougats, caramel cream cubes, honey roasted cashews, peanut butter cups, and a long crunchy board that tasted like balsa wood, not toffee. The cushion was cotton candy. The chair was covered in hairs and strings of dust and all sorts of sticky papers, but the boy sat in it every day and picked off little bits to eat while he watched loads of trash sink down the toilet and occasionally used the X-Tend-O plunger to unclog the drain without having to get up.

At first the family had simply tried to cut down on their waste by recycling it; they used banana peels as dishrags and plastic wrap as kindling, which turned the fires in the fireplace a blue-green hue they liked especially to make s'mores over. The mother began to use hot glue to string together small wreaths from the trash that accrued naturally in their home. She also tried cooking the pieces of paper they used to throw away. For herself she shredded the newspaper and mixed it into chicken broth. For the father she fried old post-it notes and grated asiago cheese over them to hide their messages. For the son she made unflavored chewing gum by churning tampon boxes and corn syrup, but he never chewed it, preferring instead to lick his graded homework assignments up and down, pour sugar and melted butter over every inch, and crumple the sheets into a ball that he would freeze and later eat for a snack on a hot afternoon.

The father finally put this diet to a stop when he noticed a Christmas card stuck inside a leftover flan. He called a family meeting that night.

"I'm putting this diet to a stop," he said.

"It's not our choice," the son said.

He's right, the mother wrote. Trash has to go somewhere.

"I don't care. We'll do what we have to do, but there will be no more eating of trash in this home. This is lower than dogs," the father said, holding up the Christmas card on his fork.

They searched their home that night, looking for any holes or crannies to pack their trash into, but they quickly gave up and reconvened around the kitchen table; there was too much trash, and not enough space for it. The mother looked helplessly at her checkbook. Seeing this, the son decided to confess a habit he'd slowly picked up since the waste management tax increase was instituted.

"Sometimes," he said, "when I don't like dinner, I flush it down the toilet."

He showed his parents how he would scrape his food off his plate and into the toilet, and how easily it was taken away from him. The mother put her checkbook back in her purse and began to cry.

"I don't know where it goes to," the son said, "but it's free."

"You've saved us a lot of grief," the father said.

I've never been more proud of you, even if you sometimes don't like supper, the mother wrote, wiping at her tears.

The family began trash-flushing the next day. They were the first in the city to try it in such a large scale. They gathered uneaten food and grocery bags and the bag from inside the vacuum cleaner when it got filled up, and they piled everything up to the rim of the toilet. The son pressed the flusher and watched the trash spin around in a circle, and then slowly lower. The father felt his stomach pull at its center; if the toilet broke because of this, he would have to buy a new one, which would cost at least twice as much as a forty-gallon garbage bin ticket. But the trash went down just like the son said it would, and they all clapped in surprise.

Look at it spin, the mother wrote.

Trash-flushing soon became a habit for the family; when they no longer needed something, it went into the toilet, and was taken immediately away. They felt this process bore an uncanny resemblance to the way their bodies functioned, which made it vaguely Native American-feeling to them.

But their toilet was not designed for such large amounts of waste, and when the son complained that he was tired of having to crush his Diet Coke cans every time, the father went to the hardware store and made up a disease called Excretory Elephantitis; he came home that day with a wide-mouthed specialty toilet that could flush a low-top shoe with no jiggling. It was a pricey investment, but the son pointed out how much fun it provided, aside from its convenience.

"I'd do this even if we could afford garbage tickets," he said.

To keep the water bill from going up, the family used public restrooms when they could, and they agreed to flush their trash only twice a day, once at 4:00 and once at 10:00. This way they had something to anticipate all afternoon and all evening, and they could all share in the flushing together, which only seemed appropriate to them.

The 4:00 flush was the louder of the two. This was partly because the afternoons tended to collect louder sorts of trash, like cardboard slats and empty cans of hairspray, and partly it was because the family had been thinking of nothing but this 4:00 flush all day, and so they cheered rather loudly for it. They cheered when trash piled up so high they had to balance it by poking it with brooms to keep it from tipping over. They cheered when the mother got so sick from the combination of trash smell and a lavender Glade plug-in that she leaned forward and vomited in the soggy toilet bowl; she cheered this as well, writing out the sounds of her vomit on her portable whiteboard, and then clapping along with her son and husband. And they all three of them cheered when the toilet shook and made a wet belching sound after sucking down the afternoon's trash, and a small gray animal popped out from the toilet and landed on the bathroom rug.

The animal shivered as the family cheered it on. It shook its leathery skin and curled around the graham cracker leg of the son's chair.

The family agreed to adopt it as their new pet. They named it Bleachy, after the way it smelled. Bleachy was more beautiful than anything that had ever gone into the toilet, but no one knew what it was. After much consideration, the son decided that it was a small male cat.

When the family took Bleachy on walks around the neighborhood, other families stared and pointed at them. Trash-flushing had grown more widespread by then, due to the steep price of garbage tickets, but no other family bragged about it the way this particular family bragged about it. They outlined all the grease stains on their T-shirts with magic marker and group-hugged every time Bleachy coughed up a ball of their old trash. This was something Bleachy did very often, so the family trained him to cough into the toilet when he needed to.

The son suspected that Bleachy was beginning to understand how much fun putting trash in the toilet could be; even though he knew his pet cat had no concept of how much money they were saving with this new habit, he could see the way Bleachy grinned every time he hacked a Popsicle stick or poker chip into the toilet, and he cheered loudly for this as well.

But Bleachy soon grew to be emotionally needy in ways the family couldn't satisfy. He ate all their food and cried all night. He constantly napped in the father's massage chair, which caused the electric bill to go up, because he never remembered to turn the massage function off. He even borrowed the son's sweaters without asking, which stretched them in strange shapes as Bleachy grew larger and longer.

One day, the son came home from school with a backpack full of pencil shavings to flush, only to find his mother perched on her gel swing in the bathroom, crying.

I've done a terrible thing, she wrote. I flushed Bleachy back down.

"Well, he was very codependent," said the son. "He was also too big for a cat."

It was so strange. He told me that he missed his home. He asked me to flush him back down, so I did, but I think the toilet broke.

The son tried pressing the flusher, but it flipped down without the friction and resistance of a healthy flusher. The X-Tend-O plunger didn't help, nor did the Ultra Sonic Air Hammer plunger that the family reserved for emergencies. The mother and son sat on their chairs and discussed how to lie to the father.

The bathroom smells so bad, the mother wrote when the father came home from work that day.

"Yeah it's like toxic, none of us should go in for a few days at least," the boy said. "Also Bleachy got hit by a car. You missed the funeral because you were at work."

"Well, these things happen," the father said. "Only it's a shame that the bathroom's gotten toxic."

The father liked trash-flushing as much as his wife and son did, and he loved his brown vibrating chair and how it felt like small voices against his back, but more than either of these he valued his family's safety. By dinnertime that night, he had locked the bathroom door and stuffed towels in the cracks, except where in the corner under the hinges he had inserted a flexible rubber tube, so they could occasionally check the air inside.

The door remained locked for eleven days.

When the father finally agreed to venture into the bathroom again, the family's trash bins were hidden under triangles of trash. Spider webs netted the hallways and maggots took up the fridge's crisper drawers. The family had dug a small outhouse in their backyard while the bathroom was indisposed, a four foot hole covered by the son's Batman tent. Two neighbors had already moved away because of what the family's reputation had done to the subdivision's property value; one more had moved this past week, seeing the family's trash pile up so fiercely against the living room window that the glass actually fractured, leaking out a black oil.

The father first strapped oxygen masks on all three of them. He then opened the door two inches and released a canary tied to his wrist, and shut the door. He counted to twenty and opened the door again, tugging his wrist back. The other end of the string had only the canary's foot attached to it.

The son shrugged and opened the door.

Inside, lying across the counter, was a gray crocodile wearing a tan sweater.

Bleachy, the mother wrote.

"Motherfuck," the father said.

"I knew you weren't a cat," the son said.

The mother stared at the wet pencil shavings littered along the crocodile's skin and tried to understand.

"I got stuck halfway," Bleachy said. "I had to come back or I would drown."

I'm sorry, the mother wrote. I know how you feel.

Bleachy lurched forward and locked his jaws around her throat and pulled up, dislodging her head. The son ran downstairs, listening from under the trash stocked in the kitchen corner as his father screamed, and then gurgled, and then fell silent.

The son eventually fell asleep in his pile of trash, still wearing his oxygen mask. He dreamed of stepping on dry leaves, when actually his brain was trying to warn him that Bleachy was munching his way toward the son. When Bleachy had eaten all the trash in the corner except for the credit card bill folded on the son's head, he stopped and put his nose on the son's bent knee.

The son gasped when he woke up.

"Don't worry," Bleachy said, "I'm not going to kill you."

"Don't kill me," the son said.

"Listen to me. I'm not going to kill you. You've made some bad choices, but you're young. You still have time to change."

"Where's my dad?"

"How would you like it if there was a big tube that poured someone else's trash in your house? How would you like it if I took you away and made you cough in my toilet?"

Bleachy placed his teeth around the son's calf and bit down as hard as he could, until he felt the bone underneath. The son cried out, looking at the new holes in his leg, his eyes cracked like crayon. The jaws came unclamped without a sound, and Bleachy turned and crawled away, out of the house, still wearing the son's tan sweater. Filled with a feeling that was almost sorrow, he lifted his long gray head and breathed in deep, hoping to find a scent that would remind him of home.

THE STOLEN FATHER
Eric Roe

from Redivider

WHEN MY FATHER RETURNED FROM THE EDGE OF THE WORLD, hundreds came to greet him. He had been gone twenty-five years. Behan, my sister, had planned a small welcoming dinner at her house. I helped set a table for seven while my nephew, Linus, assailed me with questions: "What's he like? Does he go to church? What does he do? Why did he go away? Why's he coming back?" That last was easiest to answer: "Because he was invited," I said. I glanced at my mother, who sat waiting in a corner chair, but she had turned her head to a murmuring from outside. Behan's dog started barking, and the cat flattened itself and slunk underneath the couch. Outside, car horns trumpeted and voices whooped with good cheer. My mother stood up, straightened her dress, and flung the door open to a landscape eclipsed by eager faces.

"Who's that?" Behan called from the kitchen. "Is it him?"

My mother stepped out onto the stoop, and I followed, surveying the crowd. Every member of our family had come. Every friend my father had made before his departure was there. All of our childhood friends, Behan's and mine, had arrived with curiosity. "We want to see your *real* father," one of them explained. "We want to understand what you've been missing all these years."

"Who's here?" Behan asked, stepping out behind me.

"*Every*one," I told her.

"Is he here yet?" the multitude wanted to know. "When's he arriving?" they clamored.

I turned to my sister, who stood gaping at the faces. "The word must be out," I said.

"I only bought one bottle of wine," Behan mumbled. "I only have a ham in the oven. And some mashed potatoes."

My mother raised her arms to the crowd for quiet. "He'll be here soon!" she announced. Then, without a glance at Behan, "You're all welcome here!" A breeze caught my mother's hair and spun it into gold, and her eyes brimmed with joy. An elixir smile from a summer night at the dawn of first love rejuvenated her by twenty-five years. I thought I'd never seen her so lovely as in this moment.

"Does she ask me?" Behan complained. "When does she ever ask me?"

The crowd was grateful. They spilled over the yard and onto the street. They trampled the flowerbeds, the garden, the swing set, the pets, and they didn't realize what they were doing. They were so happy for us. They just didn't realize.

When my father returned from the edge of the world, he pulled up in a hulking, barnacle-covered truck, the doors rusted paper-thin from twenty-five years of sea salt. Strapped to the top in a tub of melting ice was a gargantuan fish, its mouth gaping at the masses that waited. The truck shuddered to a stop, and a familiar whistled tune drifted out from behind the dusty windows, bringing with it phantom smells: garage mildew, car oil, mechanic's hand-cleaning solvent, pipe tobacco, old-fashioned shaving cream. The truck door swung open with a creak. My father stepped out, and the waiting crowd engulfed him with delight.

Linus was on my shoulders. We had not been able to penetrate the mob, so we watched from the distance of the side porch. "I can't see him," he said. "I can't see what he looks like."

I had to admit that I couldn't quite see him either, but I assured my nephew that we would soon.

For dinner, we cooked the fish strapped to the truck. It took ten of us to pull it down and clean it. We chopped it into pieces and cooked it on ten different grills. When their parents weren't looking, children climbed within the fish's bare ribs to play. Linus watched but wouldn't join them. "The ribs look like a jail," he said. So they did, and so this was what the children were pretending: that some of them were kings and queens sending the others off to jail. When they felt gracious enough, they would let certain ones come back out from their banishment.

There was enough fish for everyone. My father told Behan to hand out wineglasses. "Okay," she said. "To which people? I have six glasses."

"Just hand them out," my father said, smiling. So Behan handed out the six glasses, and then she looked into the cupboard and saw there were more after all, and so she handed these out as well, and she kept handing the glasses out until everyone had been supplied and the cupboard was finally empty. My father poured the one bottle of wine, and there was enough for everyone. So we toasted a health to my father, all of us at once, seven hundred wineglasses raised to the sky, a sea of wine doled out into glasses. The glasses clinked together all at once, and the sound was of a shattering glass tower, and it could be heard fifteen miles away.

"You can't tell it that way," Behan says. "That's not how it happened."

"Stories are never told just how they happened. But it's my story. I'm the one telling it."

"It's *our* story, and you can't tell it that way." Behan is insistent.

"What do you want me to do?"

"Answer the questions Linus asked you. And say why we couldn't see our father when he returned. It wasn't because of any crowd."

"The crowd made it difficult. They had their own ideas. It was hard to see around them."

"But what about the shadows?" Behan asks.

Oh. Right. The shadows.

When my father returned from the edge of the world, shadows clung to him so that we could not see for certain who he was. I saw the shape of a hero, disgraced into wrongful banishment, now returning into the arms of clumsy, embarrassed clemency. Behan, as the shadow figure approached, saw a ball of rage bent on conniving revenge. "It's a trick," she said. "He's only pretending not to hold a grudge." Our mother had been the one to send our father away; now she had invited him back, simultaneously exiling the impostor who had taken his place. Behan watched our father's approach with a confused scattershot of trepidation and misgiving.

"We prayed for this to happen," I reminded her.

"It's been twenty-five years, Keith."

"We weren't specific enough."

"Don't you have any feelings for Trent?"

Trent was the impostor, a blank-faced Frankenstein's monster who pounded on the walls when he wanted something. Behan and I had grown up dreading his return from work every day—not because of any abuse, but because of the way his dour, unforgiving presence permeated the house. My relationship with him had been one of carefully planned distance, and so this was what I knew of father-son relationships: distance. "I never really cared for Trent," I told Behan.

"What about all the things Mom has said about Dad over the years?"

"Now she says she was wrong."

"Which really means she lied to us. For twenty-five years. To keep us from our own father."

So even now Behan felt the compulsion to choose, where I wanted to accept them both, my mother and father together as a couple again. Behan's struggle—as it had been for us both during the past twenty-five years—was deciding where her sympathies should lie: With our mother, who had sent our father away in the first place and then lied about the reasons? With our father who, after all, had left too easily and then stayed away from us for twenty-five years? Or with the impostor, who in a certain light could be made to seem the true victim in this scenario? The solution lay beneath the shadows that cloaked our father. We would have to carefully peel away the shadows so we could see exactly who he was after all this time.

When our mother told us that our father would be leaving for the edge of the world, it was like this: I remember coming through the kitchen and turning into the living room and seeing my mother and Behan on the couch, Behan crying and my mother's eyes solemn and red. I remember that she called me over and gave me the news, too, but that is where my memory of the moment stops, with the words, *Your father and I.* For twenty-five years after that, our mother told us who our father was, and so he became, in our minds, someone different from the father we thought we had known. He became a man dark and threatening in his mystery. His eyes turned to angry coals, and his black beard became a manifestation of the darkness that seeped from a twisted soul. He was not with us to show us any different.

But before he left for the edge of the world, my father came to school one morning and talked to my teacher in the hallway and then called me out of my class. He drove me to Oak Openings, my favorite park, and he rented bicycles for us so that we could ride the trails through the woods together. Usually we didn't get to ride bicycles here, but this time we did, and it was just my father and me, and I was supposed to be in school but wasn't, and so the forest that day became a magical wild wood that had been hiding here all this time, that my father alone had been able to reveal. We rode silently through the woods, sharing this secret, and deer darted across the trail in front and behind of us, and a horse of air thundered through the trees, racing us, and cardinals exploded like roses from the leaves, and faeries rode the tufts of milkweed seeds that floated through the air as the trees curtsied and opened up for us a path that no one else could follow. At the end of the day, as we sat on swings and ate ice cream cones, my father asked, "Did you have a good day, Keith?" and I told him that I had. He reached over and put his hand on my shoulder, and the strength and hugeness of it was warm and comforting, and he said, "You're my only son, and I'm very proud of you."

I kept this day secret, and my mother's stories of my father were never able to touch it.

In the weeks before I learned that my father would be returning from the edge of the world, I had been anxious in my sleep. Mischievous whispers in my ears had given me unquiet dreams. For instance: A leviathan-sized fish arose from a mist-swirled sea of black ink, yawning with a great intake of breath that sucked into its mouth the sea, the land and mountains, the cities and their crowds of people. Among the people was my father, who seemed merely preoccupied and melancholic. Then—*schloop!*—down the fish's slippery throat he went. In variations of the dream I was there with my father, and I could feel my feet losing their grip on the earth. Sometimes I could see Linus on a golden beach, building a sandcastle. The sand around him was sifting away toward the gaping mouth, but he did not realize what was happening.

Julia, my wife, shook me awake, again and again, each time the dream came. "*Who* is whispering to you?" she wanted to know. "What are they whispering?"

The words perpetually escaped me. But one morning the dream was cut short by a brief, suffocating catch in my chest that forced me awake—and the whispered words were fresh enough for me to recall. I refused to tell Julia. I took comfort only in her insistence that she had not heard the words, she had not heard anything at all.

The whispers were these: *Come away, come away, come away.*

I had heard them before.

When we were preparing for my father's return from the edge of the world, I visited Behan's house. She met me at the door and asked if I might be so kind as to climb the sugar maple in the backyard to retrieve her son, who had been up there for an hour with no inclination of coming back down. "What's he doing up there?" I asked.

"He says he's trying to see the edge of the world," Behan told me. "Please go get him, Keith. Uncles are good for that sort of thing."

Linus had climbed close to the top of the tree, and it took me awhile to scale my way up to where he sat straddling a branch, his back to the trunk. A pair of binoculars hung around his neck. He looked dejected. "Any luck?" I asked, trying to catch my breath and not look down.

"Nope," Linus said.

"Not even with the binoculars?"

He shook his head. "When Grandma Evey sent Grandpa Addison to the edge of the world, did you look for him?"

"Yeah, I looked pretty hard."

"Did you think that if you found a tree that was high enough you might be able to climb all the way to the top and look for him?"

I had thought exactly that, and I'd tried it many times. Climbed all the way to the top, up beyond the trunk to where it was all limbs and twigs and air. Peered through a plastic telescope from a cereal box until I could see the curve of the world disappearing into haze, but that was all. I'd cupped my ears and listened for my father's whistle, but there was not even an echo carried back by the lonesome wind.

"It's never high enough," I told Linus. "There's never a tree high enough for that."

"That's what I thought," he sighed.

"My father—Grandpa Addison—he'll be here soon. You'll be able to see him then."

"What about Grandpa Trent? Where's he going?"

It wasn't a question I wanted to try to invent an answer for. I didn't really care where Trent the impostor wound up. The *other* edge of the world would be just fine. I didn't want to try to assure Linus that his Step-Grandpa Trent would still be around, because I didn't *want* the impostor to still be around when my father returned from the edge of the world.

"Your mom's worried about you," I said instead. "She sent me up to bring you back."

A gust shook the tree and my guts teetered around each other for an instant. I started down, hoping Linus would take the hint. When I looked up I saw he hadn't moved except to turn his head, brow furrowed in thought. I followed his gaze to the window of his parents' bedroom.

"Sometimes I can hear them calling to my dad," Linus revealed. "At night. And I can hear them whispering to my mom, too."

I gritted my teeth. "What do they say?"

"To my dad they say, 'Come away.' And then they tell my mom, 'Send him away.'"

Linus took the binoculars from around his neck and handed them down to me. He pointed at the window, so I put the lenses to my eyes and looked. There were tiny handprints on the pane, and the paint was scratched and the wood slightly indented where, perhaps, the window had been pried open. A dead limb of the maple formed a crooked bridge between tree and house. The handprints were smaller than a child's. When I took the binoculars away, Linus was watching with resignation. "Stay there a minute," I said, "and hold on." I tightened my grip on two strong branches and kicked at the dead bridge limb until it finally cracked loose and clattered against healthy branches on its way down to where it thudded on the ground. Linus's eyes were on me, wide and amazed. "Maybe you won't hear any whispering tonight," I said and shrugged. Uncles were good for that sort of thing.

Come away, come away, come away, the whispers went, *to where waves of moonlight gloss the dim gray sands.* My bedroom, twenty-five years

ago, was the upstairs family room at the head of the stairs and outside my parents' bedroom. I lay awake and heard the temptations
that slithered into my parents' ears as they slept. A fluttering of black
wings for an instant against the ceiling. The creak of a window, tapping on the pane. Smoke-like mist seeping from underneath the door.
Send him away, send him away, send him away with us, the whispers
went. An evil titter, a beetle-like scuttling on the stairs. A tiny visage
leering from the foot of my bed, disappearing when I sat up with a
horrified gasp.

Behan doesn't have these memories. What she remembers is when
our parents' voices supplanted the whispers. Angry words, bitterness,
weeping, frustration. A heavy boot stomping once on the floor to cut
off a spiraling argument—I remember that, and how all the glasses
and plates in the cupboards and all the pictures on the walls shook. I
remember thinking of Rumpelstiltskin stomping his foot through the
floor and ripping himself in two in his fury. Tears next—lots of those.
At one point, a violent scuffle and then a scream from our mother upstairs, screaming for Behan to run across the street and bring back our
fireman neighbor. This moment would define Behan's life. This decision: help our mother or protect our father. Behan ran across the street,
and in her mind she was still running across the street for the next
twenty-five years, and every time she ran it was in search of a father
figure that could replace the one she had betrayed. Every time she ran it
was to reinforce her belief in the horrible things our mother said about
our father that could justify such a betrayal

I had not been called on to run across the street. I had been spared
that decision.

When my father went away through the water and the wild, I
chased after him on my bicycle. I rode out into the country, out among
windswept fields of corn. I rode into my teenage years, fast and hard,
accustomed to the salt of sweat drenching my face. I rode past silos
and mills, through small towns, past crumbling schools and useless

churches, across bridges, along rivers. I couldn't reach the edge of the world. I rode into adulthood, trading the bike for a motorcycle, and I extended the sweep of my search. Rolling hills, hairpin curves, a white-walled mosque incongruous with its surrounding wheat fields, mountains of jagged granite, a city where lightning etched the sky and set tall buildings aglow. I couldn't find the edge of the world. I couldn't travel in one direction long enough to reach it. My signals got crossed, my fancies waxed and waned, I took roadside rests that became extended stays.

My father became a memory, and the memory became clouded with my mother's stories.

"Am I telling it all right now?" I ask Behan.

She doesn't answer immediately. "I didn't know he took you to Oak Openings," she says. "I didn't know you remembered when I had to run across the street."

"Did he take you anywhere before he left?" I ask.

Behan shakes her head slowly, as if searching her memory for some hidden, forgotten event. "No," she says. "He just left. Mom took us away to live with Trent, and Dad sold the house. The next time we saw it another family was living there, and they'd taken out the front porch and paved the driveway and cut down the tree out back. And Dad was gone."

I remember this, too, seeing the house and the stump out back, and how I wanted to throw rocks through the window and, like a wrathful ghost, chase out this usurping family. But then it was off to a church and a wedding, and then our mother was holding Trent's hand and telling us, *You can call him Dad now*, and everything in our world became a kind of unreality.

"Do you think," I ask, "that I'm being too hard on Mom?"

"Mom lied to us," Behan says. "But."

"But. If you were going to tell this story."

"It would start like this: 'When our father left for the edge of the world, he didn't *have* to go so far away. He didn't *have* to go so far out of reach that our mother's stories could reconstruct him so completely in our minds.'" Behan tilts her head, looking at me. "You're not going to skip to the end now, are you?"

"Isn't that pretty much all that's left?" I ask.

"Not quite. You have to tell about that morning first. You can't leave that out."

She's right, of course. Again, she's right.

The morning of my father's return from the edge of the world, I walked into Behan's house to find her dining room table covered with wrinkled-up scraps of paper. She was laying each one out and pressing it smooth. I didn't have to read the words to know what notes these were. After she sent him to the edge of the world, our mother sometimes hurled stones after my father. She had a good arm, my mother, and the stones seemed to know where to fly. Sometimes she wrapped words around the stones she threw. The words might be: *Remember, this was your own doing!* Or: *Because I wouldn't want you to "worry," we're getting along just fine without you.* Once in awhile my father would return a volley of stones, but the effort always seemed half-hearted. Out of a blue sky, a pebble would *plink* against the windowpane, or a stone would bang harmlessly on the roof and roll down to drop into the hedges. Once in awhile my father's stones would also be wrapped in words. These stone-notes of my mother's and father's were the scraps that Behan was laying out across her table.

"You collected all these," I said, amazed.

"I have these and I have their wedding photos," Behan replied.

"What are you going to do with these?"

"Sort through them for awhile."

I surveyed the words spread across the table, concentrating on hand-writing instead of content. But then I saw that some of the handwriting was Behan's, and looking closer I saw that some of the handwriting was my own, and I felt my face redden.

Behan watched me carefully. "We have to sort through all of this," she emphasized.

"We didn't throw any stones on our own," I said. "We had to be taught how. We had to be forced to do it at first."

"All of it has to be sorted through, Keith."

"Can't we just take these out back and burn them all?"

"No." My sister held my gaze, wads of yet more words in her fists. "Mom and Dad have to show us that these don't mean anything anymore. I won't get rid of these notes until they've proven that."

"Then let me take mine out, at least."

Behan considered this, then swept her hand over the table, over all the words, inviting me to take mine back.

I couldn't do it.

When my father returned from the edge of the world, there were six of us waiting at Behan's house to greet him. Behan had planned a small welcoming dinner. She cooked a ham and made mashed potatoes. Julia helped me clear the stone-notes from the table, and we placed them back in the trunk where Behan had kept them all this time. Julia wanted to read the notes out of curiosity, but I said it was probably best if she didn't. Behan's husband, Rick, helped me carry the trunk to the basement. "We used to keep this in the attic," he told me as we plodded down the stairs, "but the box got too heavy and I was worried the ceiling wouldn't hold."

Back upstairs, Behan complained that Linus had climbed the sugar maple again. I offered to bring him down, but Rick said that Linus could come down on his own when he was ready.

"He doesn't want to meet Dad," Behan confided to me a bit later.

"Who—Linus or your husband?"

"Both. All they know is all I've told them. They're both attached to Trent. To them, our dad is the impostor coming to replace Trent. Linus has been asking me why Grandpa Addison has to come back if he's been gone all that time anyway."

"Because he was invited," I said, shrugging. I glanced at my mother, who paced in the living room, chewing her fingernails. Julia tried to engage her in conversation. She complimented my mother on the pies she had made for this occasion, and my mother became animated in her concern that her pies wouldn't be good enough, that they wouldn't be as good as my father remembered them, that maybe he had found someone at the edge of the world who could make even better pies than my mother's and maybe he would miss that person's pies, and maybe he would want to go back to the edge of the world. Maybe he wouldn't want to stay here after all. Julia was trying to assure my mother of her singularity in the field of pie-making when we all heard the rumble of the truck from down the street.

When my father returned from the edge of the world, he pulled up in a barnacle-covered truck, the doors rusted paper-thin from twenty-five years of sea salt. Strapped to the top was the gargantuan skeleton of a fish. He would tell me later about that fish, how it had emerged from the gray soup at the edge of the world and scooped him up from the mist-threaded shore, and how it had carried him around in its belly for a length of time he didn't know—it could have been three months or three days; it sometimes felt like three years. Finally the fish spit him back up on shore. It haunted him for a long time after that, as if constantly warning him that he was in a place where he shouldn't be. What finally killed the fish, my father would tell me, was a rock that fell from the sky. When the fish washed ashore, my father found the rock embedded in its skull. When he pulled the rock out, he found it wrapped in a note in my mother's handwriting: a plea for forgiveness, a promise of clemency, an invitation.

The truck in Behan's driveway shuddered to a stop. Julia squeezed my hand, excited for us all. Behan and our mother stood together, also holding hands, wide eyes already glistening with tears. Nearby stood Rick, squinting at the truck, putting on a welcoming face in spite of all the words he'd been storing in the basement of his house. I glanced to see Linus high up in the tree, straddling a branch and watching the truck through his binoculars. He was, I thought, in a better position to see than any of the rest of us, who were too close to know just what we were seeing. The truck door swung open with a creak, and my father stepped out of myth, out of memory, out of absence, out from the water and the wild, out of twenty-five years and into our lives again.

THE SAFFRON GATHERERS

Elizabeth Hand

from Saffron & Brimstone (collection)

H E HAD ALMOST BEEN AS MUCH A PLACE TO HER AS A PERSON; the lost domain, the land of heart's desire. Alone at night she would think of him as others might imagine an empty beach, blue water; for years she had done this, and fallen into sleep.

She flew to Seattle to attend a symposium on the Future. It was a welcome trip—on the East Coast, where she lived, it had rained without stopping for thirty-four days. A meteorological record, now a tired joke: only six more days to go! Even Seattle was drier than that.

She was part of a panel discussion on natural disasters and global warming. Her first three novels had presented near-future visions of apocalypse; she had stopped writing them when it became less like fiction and too much like reportage. Since then she had produced a series of time-travel books, wish-fulfillment fantasies about visiting the ancient world. Many of her friends and colleagues in the field had turned to similar themes, retro, nostalgic, historical. Her academic background was in classical archeology; the research was joyous, if exhausting. She hated to fly, the constant round of threats and delay. The weather and concomitant poverty, starvation, drought, flooding, riots—it had all become so bad that it was like an extreme sport now, to visit places that had once unfolded from one's imagination in the brightly-colored panoramas of 1920s postal cards. Still she went, armed with eyeshade, earplugs, music and pills that put her to sleep. Behind her eyes, she saw Randall's arm flung above his head, his face half-turned from hers on the pillow. Fifteen minutes after the panel had ended she was in a cab on her way to SeaTac. Several hours later she was in San Francisco.

He met her at the airport. After the weeks of rain back East and Seattle's muted sheen, the sunlight felt like something alive, clawing at her eyes. They drove to her hotel, the same place she always stayed; like something from an old B-movie, the lobby with its ornate cast-iron stair-rail, the narrow front desk of polished walnut; clerks who all might have been played by the young Peter Lorre. The elevator with its illuminated dial like a clock that could never settle on the time; an espresso shop tucked into the back entrance, no bigger than a broom closet.

Randall always had to stoop to enter the elevator. He was very tall, not as thin as he had been when they first met, nearly twenty years earlier. His hair was still so straight and fine that it always felt wet, but the luster had faded from it: it was no longer dark-blonde but grey, a strange dusky color, almost blue in some lights, like pale damp slate. He had grey-blue eyes; a habit of looking up through downturned black lashes that at first had seemed coquettish. She had since learned it was part of a deep reticence, a detachment from the world that sometimes seemed to border on the pathological. You might call him an agoraphobe, if he had stayed indoors.

But he didn't. They had grown up in neighboring towns in New York, though they only met years later, in D.C. When the time came to choose allegiance to a place, she fled to Maine, with all those other writers and artists seeking a retreat into the past; he chose Northern California. He was a journalist, a staff writer for a glossy magazine that only came out four times a year, each issue costing as much as a bottle of decent sémillon. He interviewed scientists engaged in paradigm-breaking research, Nobel Prize-winning writers; poets who wrote on their own skin and had expensive addictions to drugs that subtly altered their personalities, the tenor of their words, so that each new book or online publication seemed to have been written by another person. Multiple Poets' Disorder, Randall had tagged this, and the term stuck; he was the sort of writer who coined phrases. He had a curved mouth, beautiful long fingers. Each time he used a pen, she was surprised again to recall that he was left-handed. He collected incunabula—*Ars oratoria*, Jacobus Publicus's disquisition on the art of memory; the *Opera Philosophica* of Seneca, containing the first written account of an earthquake; Pico della Mirandola's *Hetaplus*—as well as manuscripts. His apartment was filled with quarter-sawn oaken barrister's bookcases, glass fronts bright as mirrors, holding manuscript binders, typescripts, wads of foolscap bound in leather. By the window overlooking the Bay, a beautiful old map chest of letters written by Neruda, Beckett, Asaré. There were signed broadsheets on the walls, and drawings, most of them inscribed to Randall. He was two years younger than she was. Like her, he had no children. In the years since his divorce, she had never heard him mention his former wife by name.

The hotel room was small and stuffy. There was a wooden ceiling fan that turned slowly, barely stirring the white curtain that covered the single window. It overlooked an airshaft. Directly across was another old building, a window that showed a family sitting at a kitchen table, eating beneath a fluorescent bulb.

"Come here, Suzanne," said Randall. "I have something for you."

She turned. He was sitting on the bed—a nice bed, good mattress and expensive white linens and duvet—reaching for the leather mailbag he always carried to remove a flat parcel.

"Here," he said. "For you."

It was a book. With Randall it was always books. Or expensive tea: tiny, neon-colored foil packets that hissed when she opened them and exuded fragrances she could not describe, dried leaves that looked like mouse droppings, or flower petals, or fur; leaves that, once infused, tasted of old leather and made her dream of complicated sex.

"Thank you," she said, unfolding the mauve tissue the book was wrapped in. Then, as she saw what it was, "Oh! *Thank* you!"

"Since you're going back to Thera. Something to read on the plane."

It was an oversized book in a slipcase: the classic edition of *The Thera Frescoes*, by Nicholas Spirotiadis, a volume that had been expensive when first published, twenty years earlier. Now it must be worth a fortune, with its glossy thick photographic paper and fold-out pages depicting the larger murals. The slipcase art was a detail from the site's most famous image, the painting known as "The Saffron Gatherers." It showed the profile of a beautiful young woman dressed in elaborately-patterned tiered skirt and blouse, her head shaven save for a serpentine coil of dark hair, her brow tattooed. She wore hoop earrings and bracelets, two on her right hand, one on her left. Bell-like tassels hung from her sleeves. She was plucking the stigma from a crocus blossom. Her fingernails were painted red.

Suzanne had seen the original painting a decade ago, when it was easier for American researchers to gain access to the restored ruins and the National Archaeological Museum in Athens. After two years of paperwork and bureaucratic wheedling, she had just received permission to return.

"It's beautiful," she said. It still took her breath away, how modern the girl looked, not just her clothes and jewelry and body art but her expression, lips parted, her gaze at once imploring and vacant: the fifteen-year-old who had inherited the earth,

"Well, don't drop it in the tub." Randall leaned over to kiss her head. "That was the only copy I could find on the net. It's become a very scarce book."

"Of course," said Suzanne, and smiled.

"Claude is going to meet us for dinner. But not till seven. Come here—"

They lay in the dark room. His skin tasted of salt and bitter lemon;

his hair against her thighs felt warm, liquid. She shut her eyes and imagined him beside her, his long limbs and rueful mouth; opened her eyes and there he was, now, sleeping. She held her hand above his chest and felt heat radiating from him, a scent like honey. She began to cry silently.

His hands. That big rumpled bed. In two days she would be gone, the room would be cleaned. There would be nothing to show she had ever been here at all.

They drove to an Afghan restaurant in North Beach. Randall's car was older, a second-generation hybrid; even with the grants and tax breaks, a far more expensive vehicle than she or anyone she knew back east could ever afford. She had never gotten used to how quiet it was.

Outside, the sidewalks were filled with people, the early evening light silvery-blue and gold, like a sun shower. Couples arm-in-arm, children, groups of students waving their hands as they spoke on their cell phones, a skateboarder hustling to keep up with a pack of *parkeurs*.

"Everyone just seems so much more absorbed here," she said. Even the panhandlers were antic.

"It's the light. It makes everyone happy. Also the drugs they put in our drinking water." She laughed, and he put his arm around her.

Claude was sitting in the restaurant when they arrived. He was a poet who had gained notoriety and then prominence in the late 1980s with the "Hyacinthus Elegies," his response to the AIDS epidemic. Randall first interviewed him after Claude received his MacArthur Fellowship. They subsequently became good friends. On the wall of his flat, Randall had a hand-written copy of the second elegy, with one of the poet's signature drawings of a hyacinth at the bottom.

"Suzanne!" He jumped up to embrace her, shook hands with Randall then beckoned them both to sit. "I ordered some wine. A good cab I heard about from someone at the gym."

Suzanne adored Claude. The day before she left for Seattle, he'd sent flowers to her, a half-dozen delicate *narcissus serotinus*, with long white narrow petals and tiny yellow throats. Their sweet scent perfumed her entire small house. She'd emailed him profuse but also wistful thanks—they were such an extravagance, and so lovely; and she had to leave before she could enjoy them fully. He was a few years younger than she was, thin and muscular, his face and skull hairless save for a wispy black beard. He had lost his eyebrows during a round of chemo and had feathery lines, like antenna, tattooed in their place and threaded with gold beads. His chest and arms were heavily tattooed with stylized flowers, dolphins, octopi, the same iconography Suzanne had seen in Akrotiri and Crete; and also with the names of lovers and friends and colleagues who had died. Along the inside of his arms you could still see the stippled marks left by hypodermic needles—they looked like tiny black beads worked into the pattern of waves and swallows—and the faint white traces of an adolescent suicide attempt. His expression was gentle and melancholy, the face of a tired ascetic, or a benign Antonin Artaud.

"I should have brought the book!" Suzanne sat beside him, shaking her head in dismay. "This beautiful book that Randall gave me—Spirotiadis' Thera book?"

"No! I've heard of it, I could never find it. Is it wonderful?"

"It's gorgeous. You would love it, Claude."

They ate, and spoke of his collected poetry, forthcoming next winter; of Suzanne's trip to Akrotiri. Of Randall's next interview, with a woman on the House Committee on Bioethics who was rumored to be sympathetic to the pro-cloning lobby, but only in cases involving "only" children—no siblings, no twins or multiples—who died before age fourteen.

"Grim," said Claude. He shook his head and reached for the second bottle of wine. "I can't imagine it. Even pets . . . "

He shuddered, then turned to rest a hand on Suzanne's shoulder. "So: back to Santorini. Are you excited?"

"I am. Just seeing that book, it made me excited again. It's such an incredible place—you're there, and you think, What could this have been? If it had survived, if it all hadn't just gone *bam*, like that—"

"Well, then it would really have gone," said Randall. "I mean, it would have been lost. There would have been no volcanic ash to preserve it. All your paintings, we would never have known them. Just like we don't know anything else from back then."

"We know *some* things," said Suzanne. She tried not to sound annoyed—there was a lot of wine, and she was jet-lagged. "Plato. Homer . . ."

"Oh, *them*," said Claude, and they all laughed. "But he's right. It would all have turned to dust by now. All rotted away. All one with Baby Jesus, or Baby Zeus. Everything you love would be buried under a Tradewinds Resort. Or it would be like Athens, which would be even worse."

"Would it?" She sipped her wine. "We don't know that. We don't know what it would have become. This—"

She gestured at the room, the couple sitting beneath twinkling rose-colored lights, playing with a digital toy that left little chattering faces in the air as the woman switched it on and off. Outside, dusk and neon. "It might have become like this."

"This." Randall leaned back in his chair, staring at her. "Is this so wonderful?"

"Oh yes," she said, staring back at him, the two of them unsmiling. "This is all a miracle."

He excused himself. Claude refilled his glass and turned back to Suzanne. "So. How are things?"

"With Randall?" She sighed. "It's good. I dunno. Maybe it's great. Tomorrow—we're going to look at houses."

Claude raised a tattooed eyebrow. "Really?"

She nodded. Randall had been looking at houses for three years now, ever since the divorce.

"Who knows?" she said. "Maybe this will be the charm. How hard can it be to buy a house?"

"In San Francisco? Doll, it's easier to win the stem cell lottery. But yes, Randall is a very discerning buyer. He's the last of the true idealists. He's looking for the *eidos* of the house. Plato's *eidos*; not Socrates'," he added. "Is this the first time you've gone looking with him?"

"Yup."

"Well. Maybe that *is* great," he said. "Or not. Would you move out here?"

"I don't know. Maybe. If he had a house. Probably not."

"Why?"

"I don't know. I guess I'm looking for the *eidos* of something else. Out here, it's just too . . . "

She opened her hands as though catching rain. Claude looked at her quizzically.

"Too sunny?" he said. "Too warm? Too beautiful?"

"I suppose. The land of the lotus-eaters. I love knowing it's here, but." She drank more wine. "Maybe if I had more job security."

"You're a writer. It's against Nature for you to have job security."

"Yeah, no kidding. What about you? You don't ever worry about that?"

He gave her his sweet sad smile and shook his head. "Never. The world will always need poets. We're like the lilies of the field."

"What about journalists?" Randall appeared behind them, slipping his cell phone back into his pocket. "What are we?"

"Quackgrass," said Claude.

"Cactus," said Suzanne.

"Oh, gee. I get it," said Randall. "Because we're all hard and spiny and no one loves us."

"Because you only bloom once a year," said Suzanne.

"When it rains," added Claude.

"That was my realtor." Randall sat and downed the rest of his wine. "Sunday's open house day. Two o'clock till four. Suzanne, we have a lot of ground to cover."

He gestured for the waiter. Suzanne leaned over to kiss Claude's cheek.

"When do you leave for Hydra?" she asked.

"Tomorrow."

"Tomorrow!" She looked crestfallen. "That's so soon!"

"'The beautiful life was brief,'" said Claude, and laughed. "You're only here till Monday. I have a reservation on the ferry from Piraeus, I couldn't change it."

"How long will you be there? I'll be in Athens Tuesday after next, then I go to Akrotiri."

Claude smiled. "That might work. Here—"

He copied out a phone number in his careful, calligraphic hand. "This is Zali's number on Hydra. A cell phone, I have no idea if it will even work. But I'll see you soon. Like you said—"

He lifted his thin hands and gestured at the room around them, his dark eyes wide. "This is a miracle."

Randall paid the check and they turned to go. At the door, Claude hugged Suzanne. "Don't miss your plane," he said.

"Don't wind her up!" said Randall.

"Don't miss yours," said Suzanne. Her eyes filled with tears as she pressed her face against Claude's. "It was so good to see you. If I miss you, have a wonderful time in Hydra."

"Oh, I will," said Claude. "I always do."

Randall dropped her off at her hotel. She knew better than to ask him to stay; besides, she was tired, and the wine was starting to give her a headache.

"Tomorrow," he said. "Nine o'clock. A leisurely breakfast, and then . . ."

He leaned over to open her door, then kissed her. "The exciting new world of California real estate."

Outside, the evening had grown cool, but the hotel room still felt close: it smelled of sex, and the sweetish dusty scent of old books. She opened the window by the airshaft and went to take a shower. Afterwards she got into bed, but found herself unable to sleep.

The wine, she thought; always a mistake. She considered taking one of the anti-anxiety drugs she carried for flying, but decided against it. Instead she picked up the book Randall had given her.

She knew all the images, from other books and websites, and the island itself. Nearly four thousand years ago, now; much of it might have been built yesterday. Beneath fifteen feet of volcanic ash and pumice, homes with ocean views and indoor plumbing, pipes that might have channeled steam from underground vents fed by the volcano the city was built upon. Fragments of glass that might have been windows, or lenses. The great pithoi that still held food when they were opened millennia later. Great containers of honey for trade, for embalming the Egyptian dead. Yellow grains of pollen. Wine.

But no human remains. No bones, no grimacing tormented figures as were found beneath the sand at Herculaneum, where the fishermen had fled and died. Not even animal remains, save for the charred vertebrae of a single donkey. They had all known to leave. And when they did, their city was not abandoned in frantic haste or fear. All was orderly, the pithoi still sealed, no metal utensils or weapons strewn upon the floor, no bolts of silk or linen; no jewelry.

Only the paintings, and they were everywhere; so lovely and beautifully wrought that at first the excavators thought they had uncovered a temple complex.

But they weren't temples: they were homes. Someone had paid an artist, or teams of artists, to paint frescoes on the walls of room after room after room. Sea daffodils, swallows; dolphins and pleasure boats, the boats themselves decorated with more dolphins and flying seabirds, golden nautilus on their prows. Wreaths of flowers. A shipwreck. Always you saw the same colors, ochre-yellow and ferrous red; a pigment made by grinding glaucophane, a vitreous mineral that produced a grey-blue shimmer; a bright pure French blue. But of course it wasn't French blue but Egyptian blue—Pompeiian blue—one of the earliest pigments, used for thousands of years; you made it by combining a calcium compound with ground malachite and quartz, then heating it to extreme temperatures.

But no green. It was a blue and gold and red world. Not even the plants were green.

Otherwise, the paintings were so alive that, when she'd first seen them, she half-expected her finger would be wet if she touched them. The eyes of the boys who played at boxing were children's eyes. The antelopes had the mad topaz glare of wild goats. The monkeys had blue fur and looked like dancing cats. There were people walking in the streets. You could see what their houses looked like, red brick and yellow shutters.

She turned towards the back of the book, to the section on Xeste 3. It was the most famous building at the site. It contained the most famous paintings—the woman known as the "Mistress of Animals." "The Adorants," who appeared to be striding down a fashion runway. "The Lustral Basin."

The saffron gatherers.

She gazed at the image from the East Wall of Room Three, two women harvesting the stigma of the crocus blossoms. The flowers were like stylized yellow fireworks, growing from the rocks and also appearing in a repetitive motif on the wall above the figures, like the *fleur-de-lis* patterns on wallpaper. The fragments of painted plaster had been meticulously restored; there was no attempt to fill in what was missing, as had been done at Knossos under Sir Arthur Evans' supervision, to sometimes cartoonish effect.

None of that had been necessary here. The fresco was nearly intact. You could see how the older woman's eyebrow was slightly raised, with annoyance or perhaps just impatience, and count the number of stig-mata the younger acolyte held in her outstretched palm.

How long would it have taken for them to fill those baskets? The crocuses bloomed only in autumn, and each small blossom contained just three tiny crimson threads, the female stigmata. It might take one hundred thousand flowers to produce a half-pound of the spice.

And what did they use the spice for? Cooking; painting; a pigment they traded to the Egyptians for dyeing mummy bandages.

She closed the book. She could hear distant sirens, and a soft hum from the ceiling fan. Tomorrow they would look at houses.

For breakfast they went to the Embarcadero, the huge indoor market inside the restored ferry building that had been damaged over a century before, in the 1906 earthquake. There was a shop with nothing but olive oil and infused vinegars; another that sold only mushrooms, great woven panniers and baskets filled with tree-ears, portobellos, fungus that looked like orange coral; black morels and matsutake and golden chanterelles.

They stuck with coffee and sweet rolls, and ate outside on a bench looking over the Bay. A man threw sticks into the water for a pair of black labs; another man swam along the embankment. The sunlight was strong and clear as gin, and nearly as potent: it made Suzanne feel lightheaded and slightly drowsy, even though she had just gotten up.

"Now," said Randall. He took out the newspaper, opened it to the real estate section, and handed it to her. He had circled eight listings. "The first two are in Oakland; then we'll hit Berkeley and Kensington. You ready?"

They drove in heavy traffic across the Oakland-Bay bridge. To either side, bronze water that looked as though it would be too hot to swim in; before them the Oakland Hills, where the houses were ranged in un-dulating lines like waves. Once in the city they began to climb in and out of pocket neighborhoods poised between the arid and the tropic. Bungalows nearly hidden beneath overhanging trees suddenly yielded to bright white stucco houses flanked by aloes and agaves. It looked at once wildly fanciful and comfortable, as though all urban planning had been left to Dr. Seuss.

"They do something here called "staging," said Randall as they pulled behind a line of parked cars on a hillside. A phalanx of realtors' signs rose from a grassy mound beside them. "Homeowners pay thousands and thousands of dollars for a decorator to come in and tart up their houses with rented furniture and art and stuff. So, you know, it looks like it's worth three million dollars."

They walked to the first house, a Craftsman bungalow tucked behind trees like prehistoric ferns. There was a fountain outside, filled with koi that stared up with engorged silvery eyes. Inside, exposed beams and dark hardwood floors so glossy they looked covered with maple syrup. There was a grand piano, and large framed posters from Parisian cafés—Suzanne was to note a lot of these as the afternoon wore on—and much heavy dark Mediterranean-style furniture, as well as a few early Mission pieces that might have been genuine. The kitchen floors were tiled. In the master bath, there were mosaics in the sink and sunken tub.

Randall barely glanced at these. He made a beeline for the deck. After wandering around for a few minutes, Suzanne followed him.

"It's beautiful," she said. Below, terraced gardens gave way to stepped hillsides, and then the city proper, and then the gilded expanse of San Francisco Bay, with sailboats like swans moving slowly beneath the bridge.

"For four million dollars, it better be," said Randall.

She looked at him. His expression was avid, but it was also sad, his pale eyes melancholy in the brilliant sunlight. He drew her to him and gazed out above the treetops, then pointed across the blue water.

"That's where we were. Your hotel, it's right there, somewhere." His voice grew soft. "At night it all looks like a fairy city. The lights, and the bridges . . . You can't believe that anyone could have built it."

He blinked, shading his eyes with his hand, then looked away. When he turned back his cheeks were damp.

"Come on," he said. He bent to kiss her forehead. "Got to keep moving."

They drove to the next house, and the next, and the one after that. The light and heat made her dizzy; and the scents of all the unfamiliar flowers, the play of water in fountains and a swimming pool like a great turquoise lozenge. She found herself wandering through expansive bedrooms with people she did not know, walking in and out of closets, bathrooms, a sauna. Every room seemed lavish, the air charged as though anticipating a wonderful party; tables set with beeswax candles and bottles of wine and crystal stemware. Countertops of hand-thrown Italian tiles; globular cobalt vases filled with sunflowers, another recurring motif.

But there was no sign of anyone who might actually live in one of these houses, only a series of well-dressed women with expensively restrained jewelry who would greet them, usually in the kitchen, and make sure they had a flyer listing the home's attributes. There were plates of cookies, banana bread warm from the oven. Bottles of sparkling water and organic lemonade.

And, always, a view. They didn't look at houses without views. To Suzanne, some were spectacular; others, merely glorious. All were more beautiful than anything she saw from her own windows or deck, where she looked out onto evergreens and grey rocks and, much of the year, snow.

It was all so dreamlike that it was nearly impossible for her to imagine real people living here. For her a house had always meant a refuge from the world; the place where you hid from whatever catastrophe was breaking that morning.

But now she saw that it could be different. She began to understand that, for Randall at least, a house wasn't a retreat. It was a way of engaging with the world; of opening himself to it. The view wasn't yours. You belonged to it, you were a tiny part of it, like the sailboats and the seagulls and the flowers in the garden; like the sunflowers on the highly polished tables.

You were part of what made it real. She had always thought it was the other way around.

"You ready?" Randall came up behind her and put his hand on her neck. "This is it. We're done. Let's go have a drink."

On the way out the door he stopped to talk to the agent.

"They'll be taking bids tomorrow," she said. "We'll let you know on Tuesday."

"Tuesday?' Suzanne said in amazement when they got back outside. "You can do all this in two days? Spend a million dollars on a house?"

"Four million," said Randall. "This is how it works out here. The race is to the quick."

She had assumed they would go to another restaurant for drinks and then dinner. Instead, to her surprise, he drove to his flat. He took a bottle of Pommery Louise from the refrigerator and opened it, and she wandered about examining his manuscripts as he made dinner. At the Embarcadero, without her knowing, he had bought chanterelles and morels, imported pasta colored like spring flowers, arugula, and baby tatsoi. For dessert, orange-blossom custard. When they were finished, they remained out on the deck and looked at the Bay, the rented view. Lights shimmered through the dusk. In a flowering quince in the garden, dozens of hummingbirds droned and darted like bees, attacking each other with needle beaks.

"So." Randall's face was slightly flushed. They had finished the champagne, and he had poured them each some cognac. "If this happens—if I get the house. Will you move out here?"

She stared down at the hummingbirds. Her heart was racing. The quince had no smell, none that she could detect, anyway; yet still they swarmed around it. Because it was so large, and its thousands of blossoms were so red. She hesitated, then said, "Yes."

He nodded and took a quick sip of cognac. "Why don't you just stay, then? Till we find out on Tuesday? I have to go down to San Jose early tomorrow to interview this guy, you could come and we could go to that place for lunch."

"I can't." She bit her lip, thinking. "No . . . I wish I could, but I have to finish that piece before I leave for Greece."

"You can't just leave from here?"

"No." That would be impossible, to change her whole itinerary. "And I don't have any of my things—I need to pack, and get my notes . . . I'm sorry."

He took her hand and kissed it. "That's okay. When you get back."

That night she lay in his bed as Randall slept beside her, staring at the manuscripts on their shelves, the framed lines of poetry. His breathing was low, and she pressed her hand against his chest, feeling his ribs beneath the skin, his heartbeat. She thought of canceling her flight; of postponing the entire trip.

But it was impossible. She moved the pillow beneath her head, so that she could see past him, to the wide picture window. Even with the curtains drawn you could see the lights of the city, faraway as stars.

Very early next morning he drove her to the hotel to get her things and then to the airport.

"My cell will be on," he said as he got her bag from the car. "Call me down in San Jose, once you get in."

"I will."

He kissed her and for a long moment they stood at curbside, arms around each other.

"Book your ticket back here," he said at last, and drew away. "I'll talk to you tonight."

She watched him go, the nearly silent car lost among the taxis and limousines; then hurried to catch her flight. Once she had boarded she switched off her cell, then got out her eyemask, earplugs, book, water-bottle; she took one of her pills. It took twenty minutes for the drug to kick in, but she had the timing down pat: the plane lifted into the air and she looked out her window, already feeling not so much calm as detached, mildly stoned. It was a beautiful day, cloudless; later it would be hot. As the plane banked above the city she looked down at the skein of roads, cars sliding along them like beads or raindrops on a string. The traffic crept along 280, the road Randall would take to San Jose. She turned her head to keep it in view as the plane leveled out and began to head inland.

Behind her a man gasped; then another. Someone shouted. Everyone turned to look out the windows.

Below, without a sound that she could hear above the jet's roar, the city fell away. Where it met the sea the water turned brown then white then turgid green. A long line of smoke arose—no not smoke, Suzanne thought, starting to rise from her seat; dust. No flames, none that she could see; more like a burning fuse, though there was no fire, nothing but white and brown and black dust, a pall of dust that ran in a straight line from the city's tip north to south, roughly tracking along the interstate. The plane continued to pull away, she had to strain to see it now, a long green line in the water, the bridges trembling and shining like wires. One snapped then fell, another, miraculously, remained intact. She couldn't see the third bridge. Then everything was green crumpled hillsides, vineyards; distant mountains.

People began to scream. The pilot's voice came on, a blaze of static then silence. Then his voice again, not calm but ordering them to remain so. A few passengers tried to clamber into the aisles but flight attendants and other passengers pulled or pushed them back into their seats. She could hear someone getting sick in the front of the plane. A child crying. Weeping, the buzz and bleat of cell phones followed by repeated commands to put them all away.

Amazingly, everyone did. It wasn't a terrorist attack. The plane, apparently would not plummet from the sky; but everyone was too afraid that it might to turn their phones back on.

She took another pill, frantic, fumbling at the bottle and barely getting the cap back on. She opened it again, put two, no three, pills into her palm and pocketed them. Then she flagged down one of the flight attendants as she rushed down the aisle.

"Here," said Suzanne. The attendant's mouth was wide, as though she were screaming; but she was silent. "You can give these to them—"

Suzanne gestured towards the back of the plane, where a man was repeating the same name over and over and a woman was keening. "You can take one if you want, the dosage is pretty low. Keep them. Keep them."

The flight attendant stared at her. Finally she nodded as Suzanne pressed the pill bottle into her hand.

"Thank you," she said in a low voice. "Thank you so much, I will."

Suzanne watched her gulp one pink tablet, then walk to the rear of the plane. She continued to watch from her seat as the attendant went down the aisle, furtively doling out pills to those who seemed to need them most. After about twenty minutes, Suzanne took another pill. As she drifted into unconsciousness she heard the pilot's voice over the intercom, informing the passengers of what he knew of the disaster. She slept.

The plane touched down in Boston, greatly delayed by the weather, the ripple effect on air traffic from the catastrophe. It had been raining for thirty-seven days. Outside, glass-green sky, the flooded runways and orange cones blown over by the wind. In the plane's cabin the air chimed with the sound of countless cell phones. She called Randall, over and over again; his phone rang but she received no answer, not even his voicemail.

Inside the terminal, a crowd of reporters and television people awaited, shouting questions and turning cameras on them as they stumbled down the corridor. No one ran; everyone found a place to stand, alone, with a cell phone. Suzanne staggered past the news crews, striking at a man who tried to stop her. Inside the terminal there were crowds of people around the TV screens, covering their mouths at the destruction. A lingering smell of vomit, of disinfectant. She hurried past them all, lurching slightly, feeling as though she struggled through wet sand. She retrieved her car, joined the endless line of traffic and began the long drive back to that cold green place, trees with leaves that had yet to open though it was already almost June, apple and lilac blossoms rotted brown on their drooping branches.

It was past midnight when she arrived home. The answering machine was blinking. She scrolled through her messages, hands shaking. She listened to just a few words of each, until she reached the last one.

A blast of static, satellite interference; then a voice. It was unmistakably Randall's.

She couldn't make out what he was saying. Everything was garbled, the connection cut out then picked up again. She couldn't tell when he'd called. She played it over again, once, twice, seven times, trying to discern a single word, something in his tone, background noise, other voices: anything to hint when he had called, from where.

It was hopeless. She tried his cell phone again. Nothing.

She stood, exhausted, and crossed the room, touching table, chairs, countertops, like someone on a listing ship. She turned on the kitchen faucet and splashed cold water onto her face. She would go online and begin the process of finding numbers for hospitals, the Red Cross. He could be alive.

She went to her desk to turn on her computer. Beside it, in a vase, were the flowers Claude had sent her, a half-dozen dead narcissus smelling of rank water and slime. Their white petals were wilted, and the color had drained from the pale yellow cups.

All save one. A stem with a furled bloom no bigger than her pinkie, it had not yet opened when she'd left. Now the petals had spread like feathers, revealing its tiny yellow throat, three long crimson threads.

She extended her hand to stroke first one stigma, then the next, until she had touched all three; lifted her hand to gaze at her fingertips, golden with pollen, and then at the darkened window. The empty sky, starless. Beneath blue water, the lost world.

THE WHIPPING

Julia Elliott

from The Georgia Review

IN ONE HOUR AND FORTY-FIVE MINUTES MY PUNISHMENT WILL *transpire*. That's how Dad, who sits in the kitchen flicking ash on his greasy plate of pork crumbs, always says it. After putting on a rubber glove, stealing a pack of cigarettes from the snot-yellow depths of his handkerchief drawer, getting caught, taking advantage of this opportunity to insult his cheap brand (Doral), and then hovering around the breakfast table pronouncing the similarities between the intestinal tube of liver pudding he was eating and a turd, I was told that I would receive a whipping, in my parent's bedroom, in exactly two hours.

My father, an elementary school principal who paddles kids for a living, has several lines on his résumé devoted to his whipping expertise. Because summer school is packed with retards and delinquents, he's developed whipping into a high art form. Just last week I overheard him tell my mother about a nightmare he'd had in which an endless line of bad boys stretched down the central hallway of the school, wound through the hot hell of the playground, and then snaked up the hill toward the poultry processing plant, where the angry gong of the sun clanged over the horizon. The boys he whipped were blond Aryan imps like the children of the damned, and they taunted him with the high tinkle of their laughter. Dad finally discovered that he'd been beating them with a dead chicken, and he woke up, had a cigarette, and did not get back to sleep.

It's Saturday, late morning, and the dog breath of summer pants from the windows. Cicadas scream. T.W. Manley's go-cart keeps ripping through our back yard, where my twin brothers are boxing with the gloves Dad bought them so they won't bash each other's faces in. Mom's taking a nap upstairs. My huge father hunches at the kitchen table in his red velour bathrobe, working on his novel about King Arthur, and I'm not allowed to say one word to him. I creep around the table, every now and then freezing into the position of a hideously deformed mutant and flashing him fake sign language. He's trying to act mature, frowning thoughtfully, scribbling notes in the margins of his manuscript. But the knuckles of the fist grasping his pen are white.

The best way to delay a whipping is to keep my parents angry. They won't whip us when they're mad. That would be abusive. So now I'm gargling grape Kool-Aid and spitting long spumes of it into the sink. I've already blown my chance to get a home perm, so I'll be ugly for the rest of the summer, and one of my little boobies has grown an alien lump down in it that hurts. A massive zit festers in my nose like a parasite; I've spent the morning picking at it with a needle. I shaved my legs without Mom's permission, and the tiny cuts where I sliced off my mosquito bites sting. The sour chunks of food I keep sucking from my braces symbolize something—I'm not sure what. And this makes me think about the night Dad told me about *Turdus philomelos*, the songbird who lines its nest with mud, dung, and rotten wood. *Walling itself in a domestic prison of its own crap* was how he put it. *That could be a metaphor*, Dad said, lighting his zillionth cigarette and scowling at my mother.

And now, exactly one hour and forty minutes before my scheduled beating, Dad splashes Jim Beam into his glass of Coke. If he gets drunk, he won't be able to *administer* the beating. Then my mother will lash me with one of her colorful belts.

I'm thinking that this time I'll run away. I'll get my best friend Squank to swing by on his moped, and we'll ride all the way to the beach. We'll build a fort and live off fish and candy. But my bathing suit is hideous, my boobs are deformed, my freckles have darkened into an ugly swarm, and I don't feel like creeping out of the hot dark house today. So I slump against the desk where Mom's bloated purse holds court amid unpaid bills, an empty cheese puffs bag, a broken sandal she's been meaning to have repaired, several of Dad's prescriptions, a bottle of Mercurochrome, a catcher's mitt, a corroded battery, and an empty basket adorned with dusty plastic magnolias.

One hour and thirty minutes before my appointment with the whipping expert, the twins come scrambling through the back door, Little Jack clutching a bulging *Star Wars* pillowcase spattered with blood, the Runt toting their BB guns. I wonder what it'll be today, and Dad, into his second whiskey Coke, perks up at the smell of game.

"What you got there, boys?" he asks, pecking at the bag with his long gray nose, pinning it with his good eye and licking his lips.

"Robins," the twins squeal.

"Robins don't have much meat, but we'll cook up a huntsman's feast."

Sputtering happily with nervous tics, a fresh drink tinkling in his hand, Dad leads the boys out to the picnic table. As he spreads newspaper, he babbles on about survival in the wilderness, how a true man must learn to live off the fruits of forest and lake, how he could gut a hummingbird with a toothpick before he was potty trained. I sit down at the kitchen table, light one of Dad's butts, and suck the sweet smoke down. Poison frolics through my bloodstream. I drip some Jim Beam into my Kool-Aid and guzzle it. I eat a Tic Tac. Enjoying a second cigarette butt, I watch Little Jack pick over the pile of robins as emerald flies cavort and my baby brother Cabbage strolls over in his tinfoil loincloth to aim his laser gun at Dad's head. Our obese Boykin Spaniels have crawled from their holes, and they waddle and grunt at my father's feet, drunk on the delicious musk of dead animal.

"Chew chew," says Cabbage. "You dead, Daddy."

A cat skull dangles from a filthy shoelace tied around Cabbage's neck. He's wearing Dad's yellow jock strap on his head, long gloves made of pantyhose, and two plastic RC bottles strapped to his back with a Cub Scout belt. Born premature, Cabbage lived in a tank for three months, and he still looks like a bleached frog.

"I kilt you," Cabbage says. Dad slumps at the table, then twitches back to life.

"I'm immortal," he says, grabbing a bird.

Dad plucks feathers and demonstrates how to singe the remaining fluff off the scrawny carcass with his cigarette lighter. He decapitates the robin with one strong chop of his rusty hunting knife, then hacks off its wiry reptilian claws. He slits it open and picks out a wad of dainty guts, cupping the gleaming wine gem of the animal's heart in his hand for the twins to examine. Cicadas pulse their mystical chants. The sun beats down, and my father's great and noble nose gleams with manly oils.

"This is the heart, sons," says Dad, "the pouch containing the animal's soul. We'll dice it up and put it in the gravy, and it'll give us the keen eyesight of the bird. Indians said a prayer for the beasts they killed, thanking them for their sacrifice."

Dad closes his eyes, and the idiot twins copy him; Dad mumbles something and then drops the giblet into a bowl.

"General Richard Heron Anderson lived an entire month in the wild on pokeweed salad and fried lizards," Dad says.

"Gross," says Little Jack, "I'd starve."

"If we ever suffer a nuclear holocaust," says Dad, taking a sip from his blood-smeared tumbler, "you might have to live off the flesh of radioactive dogs."

"I would eat stuff out of cans first," says the Runt, trying to saw through a robin's neck bone with his pocketknife.

The twins make a mess of cleaning their robins. They can't find the guts. They slump in the heat, glancing hungrily at the shrubbery when

T.W. Manley's go-cart engine revs up again. Dad hurls a cluster of intestines at the Runt's cheek and scowls at him when he squeals.

Fifty-five minutes before my scheduled punishment, my mother's still taking a nap, and Dad's manning the kitchen in his red bathrobe, cooking up a huntsman's feast of robins and grits and gravy, sloshing golden drink from his Jim Beam bottle without bothering to screw the cap back on. The grimy ceiling fan churns the muggy air. The twins hunch at the table, drinking pickle juice from shot glasses. Cabbage lurks in the dim roachy realm of the pantry, clanking metal cans together and muttering.

I'm eating stale cheese puffs while reading random snatches from Dad's novel:

> And so Merlin became a hawk and flitted through the green velvety forest; When Sir Lancelot gazed into the deep pools of Gwenevere's eyes, fires flickered within him, terror and joy commingling in the hot cauldron of his soul; From a shroud of white mist Morgan Le Fey slipped naked and laughing, her alabaster breasts adorned with twin rosebuds, her long raven locks dancing about her taut buttocks.

Say what? With his huge greasy hand, Dad snatches the pages just when the reading looks promising. He stashes his novel atop the refrigerator and stomps back to his pale pile of birds. The robins look fetal. They might be frogs or mice or fatty little moles. He rolls the dead things in flour and drops them one by one into the spitting skillet. Rich marrowy smells float from the pan, and Cabbage emerges to take a sniff. His rabbit nostrils quiver, and his eyes screw up with thinking.

"It smells like a rusty hamburger out here," Cabbage says, disappearing back into the dark of the pantry. Dad chops a purple onion and sautés it in the charred grease, adding flour, sloshing milk from the gallon jug, spattering Worcestershire sauce and bright red drops of Texas Pete. On a silver platter pulled from the dusty depths of the china cabinet, he piles the fried birds and smothers them in gravy. He sets a plate of grits before each twin and positions the platter in the center of the table, beside Mom's diseased cactus plant.

"Eat up, boys," Dad says.

The twins pick at their robins, fidget, and take iddy-biddy baby bites. They hold their noses and squirm. Into the stubble-fringed shredding machine of his mouth, our father slowly inserts a whole bird carcass, grinds it into gamy gruel, and swallows.

"Delicious," he says, bathing us in the glow of his ghoulish grin.

"Among the Indians it is a sacrilege to let the sacred flesh of an animal go to waste," Dad informs us. "You must eat, boys, or the spirit of the robin will haunt you. The spirit of the robin will fly around your room at night, slither into your ears, and peck your brains until you go crazy."

Each twin lifts a bird to his lips, sighs, and licks it clean of gravy. Each twin removes the burnt, scabby film of fried breading from his respective dead animal, wads it into a ball, places it on his tongue like a holy wafer, closes his mouth, and waits for the substance to dissolve. Tears drip from their eyes as they swallow.

"That doesn't count as the animal itself," says Dad, biting a robin into two pieces. Delicate bones snap as he chews. He gulps as he swallows, and his tongue slithers out to dab grease from his lips. "The flesh is the thing," he says. "The transubstantiated spirit of the robin will fill you with the bird's power."

The twins pinch tufts of meat from their carcasses and line them up like pills to be swallowed whole. Little Jack eats one first.

"It tastes like pesticides," he says.

The Runt copies Little Jack.

"It tastes like toads," says the Runt.

According to the twins, the robins taste like hair spray, ammonia, and chicken-necks. The robins taste like greasy grasshopper meat dipped in gasoline. They taste pee-sautéed and weird. According to the twins, because the robins they slaughtered spent the morning pecking pesticidal pellets from old Mr. Pricket's mouthwash-green lawn, the birds are probably lethal.

"Get out of my sight, you ungrateful wenches," Dad says, banging his tumbler on the table. "You better prepare yourselves for a visit from the Great Robin. It will flap into your window tonight and fill your room with feathers. The Great Robin will terrify you with its rotten worm breath. The Great Robin will drop turds the size of shoes. Calling upon the nobility of its bird genealogy, the Great Robin will sprout the atavistic claws of the pterodactyl and tear your soft, womanly bodies into bloody confetti."

Dad grins until his mandible vanishes. The twins scramble to their feet. Dad lights a cigarette and flicks ash into the ribcage of a half-gnawed robin. A sunbeam shines directly onto the ashy carcass and lights up stained cracks in the ceramic plate.

On a rancid summer dog day, when you're dirty and scrawny and ugly and poor, when your fingernails sting from too much biting, when the kitchen stinks of unclean plates, when there's nowhere to go, when punishment awaits you, when swarms of gnats flicker beyond bright windows, when heat sinks your mind into the syrupy filth of boredom, when you are disgusted by the sight of your own stubbed toes, when the glimpse of an ancient neighbor drifting across the green void of his lawn fills you with a new species of sadness, a screen door slamming can shoot straight to your heart, sinking it deeper than you thought it would go.

I hold my breath for as long as I can. I exhale noisily. Father sneers at me and pours himself another drink.

Even though my father may whip me in twenty-five minutes, I feel abandoned when he staggers off to the living room, snatching his manuscript from the top of the refrigerator. He closes the sliding wooden door behind him. I mope around in the kitchen, plucking crusted bowls from counters, sniffing them, putting them back down. I hear a creak on the stairs, and my mother steps into the greasy light of the kitchen. Her face looks puffy. Her nylon housecoat sticks to her sweaty spots. She plods to the stove where Dad has left the heap of fried robins covered with a dented pizza pan. She lifts the pan and sniffs. Slowly, with blank black eyes, she fixes herself a plate of robin and grits and gravy and sits down under the stale bluster of the ceiling fan. She nibbles a chunk of robin from its carcass, and only after she has chewed and swallowed and made a bitter face does she see me, lurking behind her.

"What are these—quail?" she asks.

"Robins," I say.

"Quit being a smart-ass; they must be quail; they're just freezer-burned."

My mother will not believe that the robins are robins, and she eats several bites of grits and robin gravy before putting down her fork. Her mind is sunk deep beneath her chewing, but eventually she registers the taste.

"They're robins, I swear to God," I say.

"Who would cook robins?"

"Dad, of course. He would cook anything. He would cook an iguana or a monkey or a cat."

"I don't believe you."

I take Mom out back where bright guts and rusty feathers have been strewn across the table by the scavenging dogs. Flies crawl on the waxy shreds of organs.

My mother glances around the world she has made for herself.

"Get away from that filth," Mom says, and she runs inside. I trudge after her.

She's retching over the trash can but can't bring anything up. My father appears in the kitchen doorway, crouched in drunken ogre mode, his sarcastic smile fluttering with repressed giggles, and I slip into the shadows of the hallway. Dad lunges at my mother, staggering and twitching in his old madman routine, spraying drink upon the grimy linoleum. I've seen him dig his false teeth vampirically into her neck. I've seen her, bursting with animal happiness, gasping for kisses. But this morning Mom jumps and wrings the damp neckline of her housecoat. She rolls her eyes, mutters the word *idiot*, and heads for the stairs.

"Wait," says Dad. "You've got to spank Kate."

My heart sinks. My ears become the equipment of a bat, huge and intricate, keening in the shadowy emptiness.

"What did she do?"

"She stole cigarettes. And she almost made me throw up."

"Why don't you do it?"

"As you can see, I've been *partaking*."

"Don't you think she's getting too old for spankings? She's about to grow breasts for God's sake."

"What?" says Dad. "This is news to me."

"Well, maybe not breast breasts, but something. And even if she's not physically mature, she's at that age."

"She tried to make me puke my breakfast," whines Dad.

Mom laughs.

"That's not funny. And she attempted to make off with a whole pack of cigarettes this time."

"OK," says Mom. "I'll do it, only because you already told her, and if we don't do what we say we're gonna do, they'll walk all over us. But this'll be the last time. When school starts, we need to come up with a new kind of punishment."

"She's got about thirty minutes, I think," says Dad, squinting at the place where his wristwatch usually is. "I'll send her up." My parents depart, each to his respective lair, and I stumble into the bright chaos of the back yard, where the twins are boxing amid a throng of screaming boys. The fat, matted dogs grunt beneath our clothesline, where yellow nylon panties and linty boxer shorts flutter in a sunny dust cloud. And

Cabbage squats on the picnic table, picking through robin guts with a pair of tweezers, a white dust mask covering his nose and mouth.

"What the hell are you doing?" I scream at him. Cabbage jumps, which makes me smile.

"Playing operation," he says.

"Those guts are contaminated," I say. "You're gonna get a disease just from touching them."

"Disease? Like what?"

"Leprosy, AIDS, epilepsy, hemophilia, diabetes, or the elephant man disease."

"Oh my God, no way!"

"Yes way. If you don't do something fast, your muscles are gonna puff up like biscuit dough and bust right through your skin. You're gonna bleed all over the fucking place, Cabbage. Green fungus'll grow in your nose and mouth, and your eyes are gonna turn black and shrivel up like frostbit toes."

"Shit," says Cabbage, dropping his tweezers. He removes his dust mask and thrusts his thumb into his mouth. He tries not to cry.

"You fool!" I shriek, jumping up and down for emphasis. "What the hell are you doing sticking that filthy thumb in your mouth? Do you actually want to die?"

"Damn," hisses Cabbage. He pulls his thumb from his mouth and spits on it.

"Here's an old Indian cure that might just save your life," I say solemnly. "You've got to wash your hands in milk and peroxide. You've got to eat an ant and pray to the god of the underworld and the god of the moon. Then you've got to find a toad with orange eyes and a stinky stomach. Lick the toad belly six times while chanting prayers to the stars, and maybe, just maybe, you'll live."

I follow Cabbage inside. In the kitchen he pulls the milk jug from the refrigerator and fills a large steel bowl. He sets the bowl on the floor and sits Indian style over it. He mumbles some creepy baby gibberish and plunges his little hands into the cold, white, animal fluid. Leaving the bowl on the floor, Cabbage heads for the bathroom, where he finds a brown, economy-sized bottle of peroxide under the sink. He splashes the sizzling medicine into his palm and rubs it over both hands, making a retard face and muttering. He dries his hands with toilet paper, sniffs his fingers, and runs outside. I follow him around as he lifts bricks and rocks in search of ants.

"Don't want no fire ant," he says.

"It's got to be a fire ant, or the spell won't work, and you'll die and go down under the ground."

"What gone happen down there?"

"Little slimy creatures are always fluttering against you, nibbling you and sticking their needle teeth down in your skin. And there's nothing to eat but canned spinach and nothing to drink but cough syrup, and the place smells like the Devil's farts, which is like burning plastic and rotten catfish and Mr. Pricket's denture-breath mixed. And there's no windows and there's bright florescent hospital light and nothing to watch on TV but the news."

"Shit," says Cabbage, dashing for the anthill at the edge of Mom's okra patch. Like a little monkey, he sticks a twig in the hill, gathers a few furious insects, and lifts the utensil to his grimacing lips. Cabbage mashes an ant between two fingers and pops it into his mouth, screams, swallows, then flings the stick far from him. He drops to his knees. He thrusts his nose into the grass and gabbles a prayer to the underworld; then he lifts his head up and scans the sky.

"Ain't no moon up there," he says, fixing his harrowed frog eyes upon me.

"The Devil has the moon down in the ground. It's like a helium balloon. He lets it go each night, and it floats up into the sky."

"He got a string tied to it?" Cabbage asks.

"Yep."

"Thought so."

"The moon is made of green cheese, which stinks, and that's another bad thing about hell. There's no one to play with down there, except retarded kids with vampire teeth. There are no toys, of course, so you'll have to play with dried dog turds."

Cabbage shudders and starts digging a hole in the ground with his knobby tree-frog fingers. Then he lowers his face to the mouth of the hole, cups his lips with his palms, and in a deep croaky voice recites his prayer to the moon.

"Jibba jibba, regog mooga, onga poobah, salong teet."

"In hell you don't have a family," I tell him, "but sometimes, when the Devil's bored, he'll make a fake family with the skins of dead animals and old hair he's pulled out of hair brushes, just to trick you. You'll think you have your family back, but then you'll notice that the puppets are hollow and filled with dust, and when the Devil laughs at you he sounds like TV static and screaming rabbits."

I look up to see my father standing on the back stoop, eating a Little Debbie Star Crunch and staring up into the trees. He looks like he wants to sprout feathers and a beak and flutter up there to romp in the branches with some sexy medieval witch who's turned herself into a hawk. A warm breeze flutters his comb-over, and longing oozes from him, but all he can do is chomp a huge bite out of his Star Crunch and close his eyes as he chews the sticky sweet gunk. When he opens his eyes, he catches me looking. He winces. He grins. He tries to look sober.

"Upstairs, young lady," he says in his professional voice, "on the double."

The moment has come. The underbellies of sluggish clouds glow a sickly green. My boxing brothers, who are now trying to kill each other, look like poisonous elves. All around them, half-naked boys with bent spines hoot and leer.

"Good left hook, Bill," yells my Dad. "You better watch out Little Jack."

Dad slips on his glasses to watch the boxing match, and I trudge upstairs.

Unlike the rest of our house, my parents' bedroom is cold. The window unit, going full blast, leaks picklish chemicals; the room smells like boiled peanuts and Listerine. My parents' bed looks damp and lumpy, as though stuffed with dead rodents, the mattress battered and drenched by the throes of my father's gigantic, nightmare-wracked body. Mom's crusty breakfast plate sits on the dresser, between two perfume bottles, reflected in the stark sadness of the mirror. In the dingy roots of the baby-blue shag carpet, boogers and dead skin and disintegrated hairs have settled with roach legs and paper bits, dried bodily fluids and particles of scratched off scabs.

My parents like to keep us waiting in the alien chill for at least five minutes to heighten the horror of the punishment. I usually use this time to pick through their drawers and closets. Behind a dusty vaporizer and several cartons of Dorals, I discover an old pack of Pampers from Cabbage's babyhood. An idea so brilliant I slap myself in the face for not thinking of it sooner pops into my head. My heart gets that belchy feeling as I hop out of my shorts and panties. I take a Pamper from the plastic package and unfold it. I pull it up to my crotch and fasten the adhesive tabs. The Pamper fits tight like puffy bikini bottoms. I check myself out in the mirror, and the sight of my scrawny, diapered frog body is like a sip of vinegar. I turn my stinging eyes away and pull on my underwear and shorts. After checking my figure for conspicuous lumps, I try out different facial expressions until I settle on a Joan of Arc scowl, the haughty look a beautiful virgin fastened to a stake would give her bitter old executioner when he struck the match.

Mom strides in at this moment, trying to look professional. She's changed into a matching floral shorts-and-top set and curled her limp bangs into two crispy cylinders that frame her little cat face. My lips tremble with a burning smirk as Mom fishes through her belt collection, choosing a pink leather number with fake rubies encrusting the big brass buckle. Mom doubles the belt and lashes at a pillow to test its power. She gives me a firm look, and I bend over the bed, gripping the bedpost hard.

The worn floral bedspread smells of sweat and dust and fabric softener. Chill bumps prickle my limbs. I close my eyes and listen to Mom's delicate grunting as she whips me. The lash striking my butt is a mere flick of pressure on the puffy padding of the Pamper, but I scream and flinch as though I'm about to fall into a seizure.

"Quit exaggerating," Mom hisses. "It doesn't hurt that much."

"It does," I bellow, realizing that I'll have to make myself cry. I feel like an idiot for not stashing a chunk of onion in my pocket. I try to think of sad things—my parents dying, for example—but generic fantasies don't cut it. I picture little Cabbage struggling to breathe in the humid tank of his incubator, his lizard ribcage rising and falling in the acidic light of the hospital. I think of T.W. Manley, waving the little fish-fin hand he was born with, driving by on his beloved go-cart. I consider Duncan, a fat retarded man in our neighborhood whose mother always dresses him in brown polyester slacks. I recall the night that Dad, upon receiving a phone call informing him that his mother was dead, shook the house with the earthquake of his weeping. I remember the day our neighbor's daughter drowned, and the drunk old woman spent the afternoon winding through her rose garden in a slip, cutting roses until she had nothing left but tangles of thorny vines. I think of hungry African children and Hiroshima body shadows and Soviet teenagers who spend their whole youths in hideous jeans. I think of filth-packed vacuum cleaner bags and closets crammed with ugly Christmas sweaters and the way the inside of a church smells when a hundred bored people with bad breath open their mouths to sing.

At last the tears start trickling, and the sadness of the world courses through my scrawny body, hurling me into the musky nest of my parent's bed, where I give in to the delicious abandon of weeping. My mother hangs her belt on its hook and slips out of the room. I start feeling sorry for myself. I'm an ugly runt, breastless and knobby-kneed, writhing on a cheap bedspread, wearing a Pamper under my linty shorts. My hair won't hold a curl, and I've blown my chances for a home perm. My nose won't stop growing. I'm a peeling, sunburned, freckled monster who'll never know the casual beauty of glowing, sun-kissed limbs. My mouth is scrap heap of bitter metal. School will start soon, and I'll have to face my class without breasts, without a tan, without a perm.

By the time I'm done wallowing, it's late afternoon, and I'm overjoyed to discover, on the dresser, an open pack of cigarettes. I figure I deserve at least six after what I just endured, so I slip the cancer sticks into the empty cups of my training bra. Then I tiptoe down the stairs, through the dark living room, and out into the yard, where dark birds churn the sky. The twins have put down their boxing gloves. They're sitting in the long grass, taking turns scratching each other's back. And Cabbage walks toward me in the balmy air, cupping something in his hands.

"Got him," says Cabbage, opening the cage of his palms.

Cabbage cups a toad, belly down, in his fist. A tiny head pokes out, nostrils quivering, goggle-eyes glowing in the sulfur light. The beauty of the toad's eyes shocks me—rich and marbled gold. I lose myself in their intricacies, breathing in smells of warm pine straw, metallic boy-sweat, the crisp, dusty gaminess of the bones around Cabbage's neck. The sky flushes pink. A breeze, light as a genie, swirls through the thick air.

Cabbage sticks out his creepy little tongue, turns the toad belly-up, and licks it.

"What does it taste like?" I ask.

"Rain," he whispers, "with Lysol and ham."

"Now chant," I say.

"O Gobwe gammu," says Cabbage, "hep me not die. Gwabu, gwabu, gwabu."

He licks the toad solemnly and closes his eyes in prayer. When he opens them, the yard fills with the moist whistling of the blackbird flock. The air has darkened.

"Gwabbu monsoon ubu booboo," says Cabbage, holding the toad high in the air. Lightning bugs rise from dusky shadows. Cabbage marches with his toad to the picnic table.

"Belteety momamabu," he says, blessing the piles of robin guts with his toad. The moon has floated to the top of the sky like a bubble of golden grease. Gardenias perfume the deadbird stench. Flies walk around on the robin guts like delicate and mysterious robots. Cabbage moves off chanting in the darkness, and I feel the back yard expanding around me, glowing with stars and bugs, crawling with strange beasts. And Dad is in the kitchen smoking, a warm light illuminating his bald spot. Mom laughs at something he has said—they must be in love again. Some kind of stew boils on the stove, crickets are singing, and the twins are humming the Donkey Kong theme. I light a cigarette, lie on my back in the pine straw, and take a deep, sweet drag while staring up at Venus, which pulses in the sky.

A BETTER ANGEL

Chris Adrian

from The New Yorker

"I WOULDN'T DO THAT IF I WERE YOU," SHE TOLD ME THE FIRST time we met. Six years old, I was digging under a log, looking for worms. This was back when my father still had all his property, and I could walk for the whole afternoon without leaving his orange groves. I spent a lot of time amusing myself that way, making up games, inventing friends to play with, since I really had none of my own, or looking for buried treasure. My sisters were all much older and hated to have me underfoot, so they'd draw fake maps, age them by beating them in the sand with a baseball bat and burning them around the edges, then send me off on quests. I fell for this sort of thing for years.

She was sitting in a tree, gently tapping an orange that hung near her face, making it swing. My imaginary friends were not the kind you could see. I figured her for a smart-aleck picker's daughter, since it was nearing the end of the season and the groves were full of Guatemalans. She wore a sleeveless yellow dress with a furry kitten face on the front— I remember that very clearly, and remember wondering later how, if she didn't exist, I could have made that up. Her skin was very dark. Her hair hung past her lap. She looked to be about my age. I ignored her.

Lifting the log up, I disturbed a nest of yellow jackets, which flew out, stinging my face and my neck and my hands. I could see her watching me while I slapped at them and yelled and cried. She said nothing but stood up on the branch and spread her wings out behind her, which amazed and frightened me. I tried to run home but could hardly breathe. I found a group of pickers having their lunch in the grass, and collapsed in front of them, swollen and squeaking.

She came to see me in the hospital. High on I.V. Benadryl, I told anyone who would listen that there was an angel in the room, and the doctors and nurses found that charming. Even back then I was a quick and subtle thinker when I was stoned, and by the time my father asked me about it I had figured out that it would be best to pretend not to know what he was talking about. But when we were alone, and she stood silently at the foot of my bed, looking strange not just on account of the wings but because she was dressed as a doctor, with a white coat and a stethoscope and her hair done up in a smart bun, I asked her why she hadn't warned me about the wasps. "I'm not that kind of angel," she said.

Though my father only ever knew a tenth of the trouble I've been in, I was still his least favorite child, and the last person he wanted taking care of him when he got very ill. But every one of my sisters was pregnant—one very much augmented and on purpose, and the other two accidents of fate. How they celebrated the coincidence, and then rued it when it forced them to bully me back to Florida from San Francisco. I was in clinic when they called, and it's a testament to their power-of-three invincibility that they were able to blow through the phone tree and the two receptionists who routinely deny my existence when patients try to find me.

"Dad is sick," Charlotte said.

"He's been sick," I said, because this had been going on for a year, and though nobody gets better from metastatic small-cell lung cancer, he'd been holding his own for months and months.

"Dad is sicker," Christine said, and Carmen added, "Much sicker!" She is the eldest and the (barely) most pregnant.

"He's in the hospital," Christine said. "There's an infection."

"In his bladder," Charlotte said. There are two years between each of them, but they've always seemed like triplets, all with their furrowed brows and disapproving hatchet mouths, all as tall and fair as I am short and dark, all with the same blue eyes that seem just the right color for staring a person down. My eyes, like my father's, are nearly black, and Carmen says I can hide anything in them.

"A little cystitis," I said. "So what?"

"Dr. Klar says he's very ill," Christine said.

"She doesn't know if he'll come out of the hospital," Charlotte said.

"She always says that," I said. "She never knows. She's an alarmist. She's a worrier."

"You have to go!" they said all together.

"*You* have to go," I said. "You go, if it matters so much."

"We're pregnant!" they said. And then the individual excuses: mild preëclampsia for Charlotte and Christine and a clotty calf for Carmen. They can't travel from New York, where they live within waddling distance of one another.

"People travel when they're eight months pregnant," I said. "People do it all the time!" Though I knew that they didn't, and now the angel was sitting on my desk and shaking her head at me.

"You're a doctor," they said, as if that should settle it, and I wanted to say that I'm impaired, and a pediatrician to boot. I could have confessed right then, to them and to the whole world—*I am an impaired physician*—and then started down the yellow brick road to rehab.

Instead, I quietly hung up on them. The angel was still shaking her head. She was dressed to shock, in a filthy housedress, with a plastic shopping bag on her head and a dead cat wrapped around each foot.

"I barely know him!" I shouted at her, but she didn't respond. Then I told her I had a patient waiting, which she already knew, because there is nothing I've ever been able to hide from her.

"Put that lady and her evil children behind you," she said, not looking up as I swept by her. She did not like Mrs. Fontaine for the obvious reason, but what she had against her two kids I could not figure out, though she has always done that—pointed out the ones that would grow into car thieves or lottery fixers or murderers, as if I were supposed to smother them with the great pillow of righteous prevention when they were six months old.

The Fontaines were waiting patiently in the exam room, Zebadiah splashing in the sink while his mother fed his sister and his aunt read *Highlights*. I locked the door, and Zebadiah toddled over to check it, an innocent part of our enterprise. "Baby," Mrs. Fontaine said, meaning me and not her son, "how you been?"

"It's been a rough day," I said.

"Well, your friend has got just the thing for a rough day," she said, and took a little foil-covered package from her diaper bag and laid it on the counter near the sink, and that is all we said about it, because one of our terms of business is a nearly silent sort of discretion. I put down my envelope and she took it, and when her package was in my pocket we talked about her babies.

I examined Zebadiah and then his sister Lily, who was four months old, fat and happy and singing wordlessly as I listened to her heart and fiddled with her hips. The angel paced in the confines of the room, the cats going *squish* and *squash* as she stepped, and Lily seemed to be watching her. "A fire from Heaven should come down right now," the angel said. Though the medicine was only in my pocket, just having it in my possession made it easier to ignore her.

"She's beautiful," I said to Mrs. Fontaine.

"She's all right," she said, ducking her head and smiling, and her sister reached out to take the baby and hold her for a moment and proclaim that she was indeed a beautiful girl, and then she handed her to her mother, who handed her to me, and then, without knowing why, I handed her back to the sister. Sometimes it happens like that, something entirely bearable, the baby smiling and laughing and going round and round, from hand to hand to hand, and her brother shouting "I'm beautiful, too!" and lifting his arms to be picked up, and all five of us laughing while the angel scowled impotently. I wanted it to go on forever.

"Does everybody get an angel?" I asked her one day, about a month after I met her, when it finally occurred to me to wonder if every boy and girl had a guiding spirit that was invisible to me. I looked around my first-grade class, squinting to see them, the girls in plaid jumpers, the boys in blue pants, looking so ordinary except for their immaculate posture and drooping folded wings.

"Only the ones who will be great or do great things. And sometimes being great is enough. The great things go out, generated as easily as thought or love. Do you understand?"

I cannot describe how gentle her voice could be in those days.

"No," I said. So when we got home she took me into my father's library, ignoring my pleas not to enter without his permission, and sat me down in front of the encyclopedia. I opened a volume at random, and she marked with her finger the men and women who had warranted an angel to guide them into their greatness. There were fewer than I'd expected, and as many who were greatly bad as greatly good. I flipped backward through the A's, familiar with only one in ten of the names she touched, making the letters shine in a way I could see forever after. Attila I knew, having just heard of him in history class, and taken part in a little skit for which I dressed up in my mother's furs and shouted in front of the class with five other boys and the girl whose long black hair had landed her the part of the Hun. "But he was bad," I said, and she said that not everybody listened to his angel.

In medical school, I could not wait to get away from adult hospitals and adult medicines and adult patients, from their aching lower backs and chronic depression and get-me-out-of-work-related injuries. I hated especially the little old ladies with their parchment faces and frail broken hearts, who'd die if you so much as frowned at them. Even a half-dead preemie is more resilient. And I hated the smell—children are not so smelly to begin with, and as they get sick or die they do not give off that odor that fills up adult hospitals and blows out of the angel's wings when she shakes them in agitation. It always seemed to cling to me after a particularly egregious fuckup in medical school, so for days afterward, just by sniffing my fingers, I'd be reminded of how I had almost killed this or that poor old zombie with my bad math.

The angel seemed to like the hospital where my father was staying, but then she enjoyed death, or at least it seemed to excite her. She was always making a show of smelling people and predicting the hour of their demise. It became the only thing I was good at, distinguishing the really sick ones in the midst of the confusing daily crowd of patients that were presented to me as a student and then as a resident, though I never could remember how to save them. As we entered my father's Florida hospital, she had a spring in her step, and though she was dressed as a bag lady once again, she'd exchanged her cats for tissue boxes and shined her wings and put on an elegant, if very dirty, hat. To her mind, I was doing the right thing, and so she had taken it easy on me during the trip, and now she bounced along like a schoolgirl. I think she would have been happier only if I had killed myself.

The nurses did not look up when I walked past their station to the end of the hall where my father had his room, or when I hurried by in the opposite direction, fleeing from him. "Here he is," the angel said when I walked in—she'd run ahead the last few feet and passed through the wall. She gestured toward him as if he were a new car or a sexy motorcycle in a showroom. When I'd last seen him, he was the same dour black-eyed man I'd known all my life, my six-foot-four, imperious, responsible reflection, a man who I always knew should have had an angel of his own. Now he was laid out diapered in a filthy bed, as bald and toothless and somehow as grand as Aslan on his table. He looked up at me when I walked in and said by way of greeting "You!" and managed to invest the word with equal measures of disappointment, accusation, and surprise. I dropped my book and candy box and ran out.

Some nights as a resident, I would withdraw into the bathroom and leave the intern to flounder and drown, later claiming that I'd never got the frantic pages when in fact I had turned off my pager and was sitting on the toilet with my face in my hands or taking little hits of whatever I was really into that month. There was a bathroom near the elevator on my father's floor of the hospital, a nice one-person arrangement with a lock on the door.

The angel was there in just a few moments—I never know what delays her, when she can travel at the speed of guilt and sometimes seems to be everywhere at once. She berated me while I hid my face, her voice making the little room seem very full, all the "What do you think you're doing?"s and "You get back there"s seeming to bounce off the white walls in discrete packages of sound. I am not this sort of doctor, I said to my hands. I am not any sort of doctor and I don't know what to do about what's back there in that room. And she said that even if you are the sort of doctor who doesn't know anything about medicine, and even if you passed your certifying exams only because you paid a certain Dr. Gupta to bypass the pathetic security measures taken against cheats and impostors by the American Board of Pediatrics, you can still recognize a patient at the extremes of abandonment and grief, and even you can do the smallest human thing to improve his lot.

In answer, I gave her a little toot. Not Mrs. Fontaine but another supplier, someone who had been a sort of girlfriend, though only snortable heroin had brought us together, had had a little horn on her key chain which she would bring out in the face of any sort of adversity—a flat tire or a broken foot or syphilis, syphilis being a two-toot trouble. "Toot them away!" she'd say, and laugh really quite innocently. She was beaten by a boyfriend more passionate but less gentle than me, and died one night in the E.R. at the General Hospital while I was on duty seeing children. I recognized her worked-over corpse when I went into the trauma room to fetch a warm blanket for a cold baby.

With just the smallest hit the angel changed. She'd barely warned me not to do it before she was stretching and shaking her wings, and there was that awful stench for a moment, and then there was another odor, fresh grass and cookies and new snow on the sidewalk. And she cast off her haggery with a few shakes of her head, her eyes bright now but not icy like my sisters', and with several sweeps of her fingers—it's always as if she were primping for me—she combed the tangles out of her hair. Three times she shook her hips and the housedress became a lovely blue sari, and her pretty feet were naked.

"Take that!" I stuttered at her.

"Better have another," she said, and I did. Then she stood in front of me with her hands on my shoulders, steadying them while they shook. It wasn't the first time that I'd felt as if I were flying backward: the toilet was a vessel in the air propelled by weeping, and with her hands she was steering me.

"Do I have to go back there?" I asked her, when I was feeling better.

"Not yet, my love," she said. "Not until you are good and ready."

When I was a child, she was always good, but this is not to say that she was never awful. Though many days she was so ordinary a tagalong that I hardly thought of her as an angel, every so often she would put on such majesty that it made me cower. One day in fifth grade, I was half listening to Mrs. Khemlani's talk about cowboys and Indians. "History always moves west," Mrs. Khemlani said, because that was one of the truisms she announced at the beginning of the semester, and she liked to point out how right she was about things at some point in every lesson. Books will always be burned, she said, and women are always second-class citizens, and history from the dawn of time has always swept in a westward circle around the globe.

I was daydreaming about Chinese ladies and their very small feet, about which we'd just been learning in social studies. I was fascinated by the pictures we'd seen, and had held on to the little cardboard shoe I'd made, though it was supposed to be drying on the windowsill with the others, so that I could turn it over and over in my hand. The angel was done up that day in the dress and skin of a Chinese girl—sometimes her form obliged my fancy, though I knew I could not control it, having tried to make her take on the shape of a dog or a corncob by staring at her and concentrating until she told me to stop it.

On little feet, crippled feet, she hobbled up to the front of the class when she heard Mrs. Khemlani talking about the grand sweep of history, a look on her face that I had learned to associate with anger over something stupid she'd just heard. I was used to getting lectures that no one else could hear, or having her place a hand on a book I was reading to say, "Listen, it was not so."

"Once, the most important city in the world was Nanking," Mrs. Khemlani was saying. "Then it was Athens and then it was Rome. Later it was Vienna and after that it was Paris and then London and then Boston and then New York. But, look here, now San Francisco is becoming most important, and where will it be after that? My husband says outer space, because he is an engineer and has a very scientific mind, but I say west, and so back to the East!"

Cindy Hacklight, my neighbor across the aisle, asked what this had to do with cowboys or Indians, but Mrs. Khemlani's response was drowned out for me by the angel's voice.

"Not so!" she shouted, stamping her foot at the head of the class, standing behind Mrs. Khemlani and growing out of her child's form. It was the first time I'd ever seen her in the guise of an adult, and she made herself huge. Her head scraped the ceiling and her wings spread from one end of the class to the other. "Not west!" she said, and pictures started to flash in her wings, men whispering in dark rooms, and soldiers at war, and tanks rolling through villages as they did in old newsreels, and people sitting quietly together. She had stopped saying words but her wings were certainly speaking to me, images were blazing out of the white depths and, more than that, feelings were radiating off them, so that I knew sadness and joy and rage and sourceless love together and in succession, the images and feelings a speech through which she communicated to me the true sweep of history. "It's toward you!" she said, unnecessarily, because she had already made me see myself as riding an enormous tide. Sitting at my desk, I could feel the relentless pressure of history under my feet, pushing me up through some mysterious medium toward a goal I could not describe except by its brightness, but I could see it in that moment very clearly. I leaped up from my desk, dropping my little torture shoe, and threw my hands above my head and gave my best up-with-people "Hooray!" I was eleven years old and thought I understood what the angel had in store for me, and felt sufficient to it in a way I can't comprehend now.

"Yes," said Mrs. Khemlani, who thought I was applauding her theory. "Hooray! Hooray for history!"

Better to be a garbageman than a doctor when your father gets sick. If I were a tree surgeon or a schoolteacher or a truffle-snuffler, or even a plain old junkie, then sickness would just be sickness, something to be borne and not something I was supposed to be able to defeat. For months, my sisters had wheedled me into meddling telephone consultations with my father's doctors, and I had pretended to understand what they were saying, and offered ungrounded opinions to them and to my sisters and my father. Even if I hadn't cheated my way through medical school, the task of recalling whatever I'd learned of pathology in my second year would have been beyond me. I make my living praising the beauty of well children. I love babies and I love ketamine, and that's really why I became a pediatrician, not because I hate illness or wanted to make anybody better, or believed that I could.

But nobody deducts the credit I deserve for being impaired and a fake. The doctors hear that you are a doctor and they enlist you in their hopeless task, forking over the greater portion of the guilt that is packaged with that hopeless task. The nurses hear that you are a doctor and immediately hate you for judging their work.

As it became more and more obvious day by day that my father was going to die, the angel, who has catalogued my every failing and should have known better, berated me for failing to save his life. It was the least I could do, she told me, because even this miracle is nothing compared with what I was supposed to grow up to achieve. And if I could do this then everything else would turn around. It was the first hope, besides death, she'd offered in a long time.

"He is not an enemy you can outwit," Mrs. Scott, one of my father's Tuesday chemotherapy buddies, said. He had got out of the hospital a week after I arrived home, and for another month I brought him back every week for his infusions. He would fall asleep during the infusion, and leave me alone to talk to her. He had told me that he hated the way she whored after hope—every week something else was going to save her life—and I'd have thought he was faking it just to escape her if I hadn't known firsthand the beautiful thick sleep that I.V. Benadryl can bring. Every session, she began by telling him about her latest discovery in the pages of *Prevention* or *Ayurvedic Weekly* or *High Colonic Fancy*, and five minutes into it he'd tell her that he felt oblivion pressing on his face, and five minutes after that his chin was on his chest and he was snoring more softly than he does in natural slumber. And, because I could not shut her up, I always suggested a game of checkers or cards or backgammon. Dr. Klar's infusion salon was packed with those sorts of diversions.

Most often, we played chess, a game that usually generated a lot of thoughtful silence—she'd put a finger to her temple and stare so hard at the board that I expected it to start vibrating in sympathy—but today she was distracted and a little agitated, maybe because she was getting steroids, or maybe because my angel was sitting so close to her, and despite her optimism she was getting sicker from week to week, and I swear that as they get closer to death people can start to feel the angel's ugly emanations.

"It's not a game of chess, you know," she continued, when I said nothing. "I think I just fully understood that right now."

"What's that?"

"You know," she said, putting her hand on her chest. Like my father, she had lung cancer. "Oncoloqatsi," she whispered. That was the name she had assigned to her disease, and she always whispered it, as if to speak his name too loud would be to summon strength to him.

"Oh, him," I said.

"I know it suggests a game, how you move and then he moves—you pick a chemo and he counters with a mutation, or you find the perfect herb to overcome him and he produces another measure of resistance, and the doctors play the game from organ to organ until your whole body is a board. They even doodle you up like one." She pulled down the neck of her blouse to show a piece of skin below her collarbone—it was just a cross to mark a target for radiation. "But this is only the surface. Look deeper, like I have, and you will see the truth."

"I think I've got you," I said, moving my bishop illegally. She didn't even look down.

"How often have I heard that from him? But he never has got me, and it's not because of my disciplined mind. It's because I have learned to resist him in the very marrow of my being. The very marrow, Doctor. It's not a lesson you would have learned in school, but I want you to learn it. I want your father to learn it. I have disciplined my soul against this enemy, and he must do it, too."

The angel sidled closer while Mrs. Scott was talking. She leaned over and took a sniff of the lady's turbaned head. "Three weeks," she said. And then she put her nose close to the shining skin of my father's forehead—every day his skin seemed to get a little thinner or stretch a little tighter, until I was sure that just the faintest rubbing pressure would reveal the dull white bone underneath—and said the same thing.

"Shut up!" I told her.

"It's hard to hear," Mrs. Scott said. "I know it's not your common wisdom, but you don't have to be rude." Dr. Klar came in before I could answer or apologize.

"Hallo, everybody!" she called out. Thirty years in southeast Florida had not dulled her accent much. This appealed to my father, who liked the fact that she was German, order and discipline having always added up to success in his life. Just being in sight of her immaculate white coat I felt accused of slovenliness and failure. "Here is the grandma of your better nature," the angel said the first time she saw her.

My father woke at the sound of her voice and smiled at her. "Charlotte?" he said. Soon after I took him home from the hospital, he started mistaking people and places, thinking that a nurse or some solicitous church lady was one of my sisters, or thinking that he was in his childhood home, in Chicago, calling out for a dog who had died sixty years ago. Me he never mistook for anyone else, though he often seemed surprised to see me. "Still here?" he said some mornings.

"It's Dr. Klar!" she said brightly. She said everything brightly, even things like "What's the use?" or "If he's alive in a month it will be a miracle." She was one of those oncologists who speak life out of one side of their mouth and death out of the other. For my father she had only good news, for me only bad.

"Darling," my father said, closing his eyes again and still smiling. "When is the baby coming?"

"Soon," she said. "The baby is fine. Everything is fine!" She reached out to pat his shoulder, but I caught her hand.

"The bad shoulder," I said. He had metastases all over his body, but his shoulder and his back bothered him the most. He nodded his head and fell back asleep.

"How is the pain, then?"

"Worse. And we're out of Percocet. He's out of Percocet."

"Easy enough to fix," she said.

"An ounce of meditation is worth a pound of Percocet," Mrs. Scott said.

"In certain traditions!" Dr. Klar said brightly, then she beckoned me out into the hall. "I think it's time to stop," she said.

"Stop what?"

"Stop hiding!" the angel shouted.

"Stop the chemo," Dr. Klar said. We had this conversation every week. "What are we doing? What good is coming of it? Why are you coming here every week, when he could be at home?"

"He doesn't want to stop. He wants to keep going."

"Just put out your hand to him and he will be healed," the angel said. "Just put out your hand to him and you will undo all the pain you've caused me."

"Does he know what he wants?" Dr. Klar asked.

"He's always confused here. You keep it too cold. And the Benadryl before the infusion makes him sleepy."

"Carl," she said, putting her hand on my shoulder the same way she did with him, comfort for someone who is already dead. "It really is getting to be time."

And the angel said, "It has always been time!"

Things started to go wrong between the angel and me after Cindy Hacklight showed me her pooty in seventh grade. Cindy had made a sort of cottage industry of showing her pooty to anyone—girl or boy—who would give her five dollars, a large sum back then, before high-school inflation. You got the sense that she didn't really care about the money but understood that what she had wasn't something to show for free.

"Go not that way," the angel said. She saved onerous fancy-speak like that for her most serious moments, for things she really meant, for things that really mattered. But I went with Cindy into the woods behind the gym, where she leaned against a narrow poplar and swore me not to secrecy but to respect for what she was about to show me. It was the one promise I've managed to keep all my life—I maintained my reverence for her bald little pooty then, in seventh grade, and ever after, even when I met it again one summer when we were both home from college. "Turn your face!" the angel shouted as Cindy lifted her skirt. And the angel was ugly for the first time, having put on the apricot face of our headmistress, Ms. Carnegie. I looked back and forth between them, startled by the contrast, how beautiful was the one and how ugly the other, until Cindy, holding her skirt up with one hand, put the other on my head and turned my face to her. "If you're going to respect it, you've got to look at it," she said.

The angel berated me for days afterward—how mild it seems in retrospect, compared with what she dished out in later years. "How is a seducing pooty like a grand destiny?" she kept asking me, and then she'd answer her own question, and eventually she trained me to give the right answer. "Exactly not at all," I said. Yet awakening lust wasn't the problem, though eventually the lust that had awakened made me a monster and a fiend, and I would waste, and still waste, half my life in thrall to it, screwing whoever would hold still for me in high school and forever beyond, to the exclusion of work and food and sleep, though never drugs. I think it was the first time that something so ordinary had been as attractive to me as the extraordinary things the angel said I must dedicate myself to. When I lay with Cindy on the scented ground in my father's orange groves, what I experienced was a very ordinary comfort, and when she raised her skirt in the woods I understood that I could want—so badly—something the angel thought I shouldn't.

My father had a little bell that he rang when he wanted something. Mornings, I would hear it and rise from the single bed I'd slept in when I was a boy, and go downstairs to see what he wanted. At first, after he came home, it was to be helped out into the yard to sit in the sun, and then it was coffee or breakfast when he could not get those for himself, and then it was just to be turned or to retrieve a blanket that had migrated past his hips, and then finally he would just ring it and ring it as constantly as a beggar Santa, not knowing what he wanted, in which case I gave him a pain pill (and took one myself, always supremely faithful to my rigorous policy of one for you and one for me), and that would settle him.

Janie Finn was our hospice nurse. I always hated hospice and hospice people, nurses with smart heels and smother pillows, and the women in charge of the palliative-care programs, who seemed universally to be dark-eyed and dark-haired and very tall. They dressed like nineteenth-century Jesuits and cherished their crushes on death. But Janie brought me liquid morphine and Ativan—and either of those would be enough to make me forgive anybody a mere crime of being. "Your jab and your hook," she said in the kitchen the day she met us. She had placed the bottles in my hand. I hadn't even had any yet and already I could feel a lovely warmth coming out of them; they seemed to catch the afternoon light in a very special way. Janie set her feet and threw out two quick punches. "A one-two against the pain," she said. "One-two! Give it a try." With a bottle in each hand, I gave it a try, and, yes, my fists seemed to have a certain heft to them. I threw a punch at the angel and she actually ducked.

I made a lot of trips back and forth to the pharmacy, and imagined the little man in the back filling the bottles from two big coolers of bright, pure drug, and dreamed of following him back there to put my mouth to the spigots, because I was sure that if I could just ingest enough then the angel would be permanently transformed—and if it happened also to be enough to kill me, so be it. I was sure that she would take me someplace bearable. How she hated those little bottles.

"Just put out your hand," the angel kept telling me. "Touch him and make him well." Though she had hardly screeched at me in those last few days, it seemed like an even worse torture to have her demand the impossible of me so consistently, and to blame me for the fact that my father was getting sicker every day. It made me feel worse than anything she'd ever said to me. I could not ignore a homeless person on the street without her detailing the ways in which I was responsible for his misery, all those missing policies and initiatives, as if the hundred thousand sins of omission that were my unfulfilled destiny added up to national as well as individual catastrophe. It was easier to bear when she blamed me for the woes of strangers, even when those strangers fell out of the sky or burned in their churches. I could make little children faceless, but my father could never be anonymous to me, and as the weeks went by in Florida I believed her more than ever when she told me that every wrong thing I'd done could be redeemed in a single miracle, and that if I could make my father well with one hand then with the other I could do the same for the whole world.

"Make me dinner," my father said, so I did. It was only three in the afternoon, but no matter what time of day it was, the meal was always dinner, and dinner was always the same thing: a chocolate milkshake with a banana and a raw egg and a little Ativan in it. When I brought it to him, he took a sip and he was done. He turned his head and opened his mouth like a baby bird—this was the signal for pain medication, so I took the morphine out of my pocket and squeezed in a few drops. He smacked his lips and turned back to the television, then closed his eyes. "Now I'll take a nap," he said. "Go to your room."

I went outside instead. It was another brilliant blue afternoon. He kept saying he wanted a storm. We mostly watched television when he could stand to have me in the living room with him, and we always watched the weather. It was hurricane season, but all we'd had was near-misses. "Look at that!" he'd say, pointing at a gigantic storm swirling across the Atlantic, or he would shout "Fool!" at the hapless reporters clinging to light poles and declaiming the magnificently obvious. Hurricanes had been the enemy when I was a child—they tore up our trees and scattered the fruit. But now he spoke the names of the female hurricanes with great fondness.

Our nearest neighbor was a mile away, so nobody asked what I was doing when I hung the hurricane shutters on the living-room and kitchen windows, and my father asked no questions from inside. He slept so heavily now that a few times I thought he had already died. I nozzled up the hose and propped it so that it would spray on the shutters, and at dusk I turned it on. The angel was half ugly and half kind, because I was half stoned. "You play tricks on him when you should be calling him out of his bed."

"It's not a trick," I said. I spent another few moments watching the sky and taking just the smallest nip of morphine and then went in. When I came into the living room with a candle, he asked what was going on. "A big storm," I said.

"Finally!" he said.

We had a party during the storm, two more dinners and Ativan and morphine all around, and he was more alert for a while, telling me stories of hurricanes past, of ruined crops and toddlers surviving miraculously when a tornado stole them from their homes and deposited them in the next county.

"I know you have secrets," he said suddenly. And then he said, "Your sister tried to drown you when you were two—do you remember?"

"No," I said, and asked him to tell me more. But then he thought I *was* my sister Carmen.

"How could you hurt a little baby like that?" he asked, and I said I'd done a lot of bad things.

"Tell me about it!" the angel said. I took another drop of morphine, right in front of my father, because his eyes were closed, but then as if he could smell it he opened his mouth, so I gave him some, too. And then I took some more, and gave him some more, and then switched to the Ativan. But still the angel was a harpy. "Put out your hand!" she said. "Another angel is coming!"

"It's all right," my father said. And then he whispered, "Your mother tried to smother him once. Just a little, with a blanket, and she told me about it right away. But she was depressed, and that's what you do when you're depressed."

"If you were a great man," the angel said, slurring now, "if you were President—and you could have been President—then I would be a national conscience!"

"Shut up," I said quietly to her, thinking that I had pitched my voice so that she'd hear it and he would not.

"Don't tell me to shut up, sassy girl!" he said, and I gave him some more morphine. Though he hadn't asked for it, he sucked at the dropper when I put it in his mouth.

"You can do it," she said, her face flashing beautiful for a moment. And she showed me how, putting out a hand that was soft and white on one side and hairy and rough on the other. She held it over his chest. "All you have to do is finally stop fucking up."

"You're ruining it," I told her, and took a swig of the Ativan, just a nip, really, but you are supposed to take it drop by drop and I knew why as soon as I took the swig. It was too good, and it made everything too beautiful, not just the angel, whose ugly skin flew off as if blown by a real hurricane, so that her wings were clean again and her naked face and body were open and compassionate. Even my father's face became beautiful, still yellow and sunken but now utterly lovely, and how strange to see a beautiful face that looked so much like my own. The room shone with something that was not light, and there really was a thrilling storm blowing outside and shaking the walls. Every so often, he would reach blindly for something not there in front of him, and he did this now, so I reached with him, and the angel reached, too, all three of us reaching out our hands together.

"You have to be ready at any time to have the conversation," Janie Finn had told me, meaning the conversation where you sorted everything out and said your goodbyes, and the dying person sorted everything out and lost all his regrets. "You talk about things and then you let go," she said, making an expansive gesture with her hands, as if she were setting free a bunch of doves or balloons. It was just the sort of thing hospice people always say.

Suddenly I thought that this must be the conversation, as we opened our mouths in turn and shared something important and lovely, and the whole room seemed like a great relief to me and I knew it must to him, too. The angel was struggling, though, seeming to wrestle with herself. Her face was beautiful but her body was ugly again, and my bottles were almost empty. My father's mouth was open, yet I took the last of the morphine myself and gave him a drop of water. He opened his eyes and looked at me and said it again—"You!"—and he shook his head, then closed his eyes again. But when I put my head on his chest he didn't push it away, and though one hand was reaching out blindly above him, he let me put the other on my neck. "I want a better angel, Dad," I told him. "That's all I need."

"I'll take a nap now," he said. "Batten down the hatches and go to your room." But I stayed where I was and took a nap myself. I woke up the next morning on the couch, the fake rain still drumming at the shuttered window, with no recollection of how I had got across the room. The angel was in the corner, her face ugly, but only in that way that all weeping faces are ugly. I sat down next to my father, who must have died very recently, because though his face was cold and his open eyes already had the look of spoiling grapes, his chest and his belly were warm. I put my hands on his chest, and my head on my hands, and stayed that way for a long time before I called Janie to tell her that it had happened.

I.

THE MUSEUM OWNS EIGHTY-NINE SPECIMENS OF THE GENUS *Draco*. It is unlikely that there will be any additions to the collection, for the adit to the array of arcs in which dragons are found has become increasingly unstable in the last two centuries. For that same reason, very little work has been done with the specimens since the last of the great dragon hunters willed his collection to the Museum one hundred thirty-two years ago. They were once a prized exhibit, with their own salle, the Salle des Dragons, but after the great taxonomic scandal under the previous Director, they became an embarrassment rather than a glory, banished to a cavernous hall in the sublevels of the Museum where they stood, shrouded in layers of yellowing plastic, their great eye sockets full of darkness deeper than shadows, unvisited, unwept, unheeded.

But not unremembered.

II.

The Lady Archangel was no longer in favor with the Empress.

That much was certain, and the Museum buzzed and rustled with the rumors that strove to create the story around that fact. The visitors chattered of it while the tour guides looked remote and superior and squirreled away every tidbit to be shared later over tea. The curators speculated, in slow, disjointed conversations; the visiting academics asked nervously if there was any danger of an uprising, for the Lady Archangel was popular, and the papers reported unrest in those parts of the Centre where her charity had been most needed and most freely given.

No, said the curators, the tour guides, even the custodians. There had been no uprising in the Centre since the short and bloody reign of the long-ago Emperor Carolus, and there would not be one now. But when the academics inquired as to the probable fate of the lady herself, they were met with grim headshakes and the sad, gentle advice to concentrate on their research. Whether it was sin or treason the Lady Archangel stood accused of, if she could not prove her innocence, she would be beheaded at the culmination of Aquarius. Such was the penalty for falling when one climbed as high as the Lady Archangel had climbed, and though the Empress was just, she was not merciful. She could not be, and still hope to maintain her rule.

It was not for mere poetry that her throne was called the Seat of Dragons.

III.

The Director has a dream. So she says, and no one in the Museum would dare to say otherwise, no matter how much they may doubt her ability to dream. Everyone knows she does not sleep.

Perhaps it is only a metaphorical dream, but even so, her shining coils are restless with it, her great yellow eyes (which only blink when she remembers that they ought to) hypnotizing. There are rumors that they were the eyes of a basilisk, and somehow that seems more likely than the idea that the Director can dream. Her metal claws score gouges in the vat-grown teak of her desk, and when she leaves her office, the tithe-children come creeping to sand and polish, as they have been doing for years, so that no unwary visitor may catch a splinter in the soft pads of his or her fingers.

She has a dream, a glorious dream; she dreams of making the Museum ever more magnificent, ever more an empire unto itself. She dreams of making the Museum worthy of the Empress.

Her dream begins with the dragons.

IV.

Visitors come to the Museum from all arcs of the Circumference. It is the second most popular tourist attraction of the Centre, after the Empress's palace (and that only in the summer months, for in the winter the Gardens of the Moon are closed to the public), and far ahead of such delights as the Tunguska Robotics Works and the People's Memorial of War. Visitors come on two legs, on four, on the sweeping sinuosity of scaled, legless bodies. There are perches in front of every exhibit for those who come by wing, whether feathered or membranous, and the Museum does its best to accommodate those whose habitual method of locomotion is aquatic. Parties of schoolchildren are allowed, although they are expected to be clean and quiet and capable of obeying the Museum's rules.

The most popular exhibit in the Museum is the mechanical orchestra of the Emperor Horatio XVI, bequeathed by him to the Museum on his deathbed. His deathbed is also an exhibit, though few visitors penetrate far enough into the Domestic Arts wing to find it.

Horatio XVI's mechanical orchestra is kept in perfect working condition by the curators, although it has not been played in over a hundred years. The sixteen rolls of its perforated paper repertoire—imported, like the orchestra itself, from arc ρ29—stand in a glass cabinet along one side of the orchestra's specially built hall. Each is five feet long and, mounted on its steel spindle, heavy enough to kill a man.

Nearly as popular as the mechanical orchestra is the Salle des Joyaux, where the Museum keeps—along with a number of stunning examples of the jeweler's art—the Skystone, sacred to the aborigines of arc v12; the black Blood of Tortuga from arc κ23; the cursed Hope Diamond from arc σ16; and the great Fireball Opal, donated to the Museum by the Mikado of Hekaiji in arc φ05.

Many visitors spend hours enthralled by the illuminated manuscripts of the Pradine Cenobites, brought out of arc τ19 mere days before the eruption of Mount Ephramis closed that arc permanently. Others marvel over the treasures of the Arms and Armor Wing: the armor of the spacefarers from arc θ07; the porpentine gloves characteristic of the corsairs of Wraith (ξ22); the claymore of Glamis (σ03); the set of beautifully inlaid courtesan's stilettos from the Palace of Flowers (α08).

It is considered advisable to purchase a map at the ticket window. Assuredly, the stories of visitors becoming lost in the Museum, their desiccated corpses found years—or decades—later, are merely that: stories. But all the same . . . it is considered advisable to purchase a map at the ticket window.

V.

He was the greatest taxonomist of twenty arcs. His enemies said bitterly that formaldehyde ran in his veins instead of blood. Unlike the stories whispered about the Director, this was a mere calumny, not the truth.

He was pleased and proud to be part of the Director's dream (he said at the Welcome Dinner organized by the Curators' Union), and if there was any irony in him, the curators did not hear it.

All that season, the taxonomist, impeccable in suit and crisply knotted tie, assisted by a series of tithe-children, none of whom he could distinguish from any of the others, clambered among the bones of the eighty-nine dragons, scrutinizing skulls and teeth and vertebrae, recovering from the mists of misidentified obscurity *Draco vulcanis, D. campestris, D. sylvius, D. nubis*; separating a creative tangle of bones into two distinct specimens, one *D. maris*, the other *D. pelagus*; cleaning and rewiring and clarifying; entirely discrediting the identification of one specimen as the extinct *D. minimis*. It was merely a species of large lizard, said the taxonomist—any fool could see that from its teeth—and should be removed from the collection forthwith.

Meanwhile, the Director ordered the Salle des Dragons opened and cleaned. The tithe-children worked industriously, washing and polishing, commenting excitedly among themselves in the sign language that no outsider has ever learned. They found the armatures where they had been carefully stored away, found the informational placards, beautifully written but entirely wrong. They found the tapestries, artists' reconstructions worked in jewel-colored yarns by the ladies-in-waiting of the current Empress's great-grandmother. These, they cleaned and rehung, and the Director gave them words of praise that made their pale eyes shine with happiness.

Swept and garnished, the Salle was ready for its brides, and as the summer waxed and ripened, the taxonomist and the tithe-children brought them in, one by one, bearing them as tenderly across the threshold as if they came virgin to this marriage.

VI.

The dragon lies piled like treasure on the sweep of the West Staircase, cold and pale and transparent as moonlight, its milky eyes watchful, unblinking. It is visible only on rainy days, but even in full sunlight, the staff prefer the East Staircase.

The tithe-children, though, sit around the ghost dragon during thunderstorms, reaching out as if they could touch it, if only they dared.

VII.

Once, as the taxonomist was making comparative measurements of two *D. anthropophagi* skulls, a tithe-child asked, "Are there any dragons still alive, mynheer?"

The taxonomist was surprised, for it was not customary for the tithe-children to speak; he had not even been certain that they could. "Perhaps, although I have never seen one."

"I would like to see a living dragon."

The taxonomist looked at the tithe-child, its twisted body, its pale, blinking eyes. He said nothing, and the tithe-child turned away from his cold pity. It would never see a living dragon, would never see anything that was not catalogued, labeled, given a taxonomy and a number and a place in the Museum's long halls. But it had dreamed, as every living creature must.

The taxonomist returned to his measurements; the tithe-children, watching, wondered what *he* dreamed.

VIII.

One does not wander in the Museum after dark. Even the tithe-children stay in their rookeries; the security guards keep to their narrowly prescribed paths, traveling in pairs, never any further from each other than the length of a flashlight's beam. And of all the Museum's staff, it is the security guards who are hardest to keep. For they, who see the Museum's night-veiled face, know more clearly than any of the daytime staff the Museum's truth, its cold, entrapping, sterile darkness. They know what its tall, warped, and shining doors shut in, as well as what they shut out.

In the reign of the Empress Heliodora, a security guard committed suicide by slitting his wrists in the main floor men's bathroom. No one ever knew why; the only suicide note he left, written in his own blood across the mirrors, was: *All things are dead here.*

Later, the mirrors had to be replaced, for although the tithe-children cleaned and polished them conscientiously, the reflection of those smeared letters never entirely came out.

IX.

It was a sultry afternoon in mid-August when the taxonomist descended the ladder propped against *D. campestris*' horned skull, turned, and found the lady watching him.

She was a tall lady, fair and haggard, dressed with elegant simplicity in gray. The taxonomist stared at her; for a moment, recognition and memory and pain were clear on his face, and it seemed as if he would speak, but the lady tilted her head infinitesimally, and he looked over her shoulder, seeing the two broad-shouldered men in nondescript suits who stood at the door of the Salle, as if waiting for someone or something.

His gaze met hers again, and in that glance was exchanged much that could not be spoken, then or ever, and he bowed, a formal, fussy gesture, and said stiffly, stiltedly, the pedantic mantle of his profession settling over him, "May I help you, mevrouw?"

The lady smiled at him. Even though she was haggard and no longer young, her smile was enchanting, as much rueful as charming, and heart-breakingly tired. "We loved this room as children," she said, lifting her eyes to gaze at the long, narrow wedge of *D. campestris*' skull. "I remember coming here with my brother. We believed they were alive, you know." She waved a hand at the surrounding skeletons.

"Indeed."

"We thought they watched us—remembered us. We imagined them, after the Museum had closed, gathering in a circle to whisper about the people they'd seen that day and make up stories about us, the same way we made up stories about them." Her face had lost some of its haggardness in remembering, and he watched her, almost unbreathing.

"Indeed."

"Tell me about them. Tell me about this one." She pointed at *D. campestris*.

"What do you wish to know?" he said, his gaze not following the graceful sweep of her arm, but remaining, anxiously, on her face.

"I don't know. We never read the placards, you see. It was so much more interesting to make up stories in our heads."

Their eyes met again, as brief as a blow, and then the taxonomist nodded and spoke: "This is *Draco campestris*, the common field dragon. This specimen is an adult male—you can tell because his wings are fully developed. He is thirty feet long from snout to tail-tip and would probably have weighed well in excess of three tons. The wings are merely decorative, you understand, primarily used for display in mating rituals. The only dragon which can fly is *Draco nubis*, the cloud dragon, which is hollow boned—and much smaller than *campestris* in any event. Contrary to popular belief, *campestris* does not breathe fire. That would be *vulcanis*"—he pointed at the magnificent specimen which dominated the Salle—"which must breathe fire because it cannot physically move its bulk fast enough to catch its prey."

"Yes," the lady murmured. "It is very large."

"*Campestris*, like the other dragons, is warm-blooded. They are egg-layers, but when the kits hatch, the mother nurses them. It is very rare for there to be more than two kits in a *campestris* clutch, and the sows are only fertile once every seven years. Even before that arc was lost, sightings of them were very rare."

"Yes," the lady said sadly. "Thank you."

He took a step, almost as if he were being dragged forward by some greater force. "Was there something else you wanted to know?"

"No. No, thank you. You have been very kind." She glanced over her shoulder at the doors of the Salle, where the men in suits still waited. She sighed, with a tiny grimace, then straightened her shoulders and defiantly extended her hand.

The taxonomist's startle was overt, but the lady neither flinched nor wavered. Slowly, gingerly, he took her hand. He would have bent to kiss it, if she would have allowed him, but her grip was uncompromising, and they shook hands like colleagues, or strangers meeting for the first time.

Then she released him, gave him a smile that did not reach the fear and desolation in her eyes, and turned away, walking down the Salle toward the men who waited for her.

The taxonomist stood and watched her go, as unmoving as the long-dead creatures around him.

At the door she paused, looking back, not at him, but at the great skeleton towering over him. Then one of the men in suits touched her arm and said something in a low voice. She nodded and was gone.

X.

Even the Museum cannot preserve everything, though it is not for want of trying. The Director is vexed by this, perceiving it as a failing; tithe-children and curators are allied in an unspoken conspiracy, tidying the riddles and fragments out of her way on her stately progresses through the departments and salles of the Museum.

But always, when she has gone, the riddles come out again, for scholars love nothing more than a puzzle, and the tithe-children have the gentle persistent curiosity of *Felis silvestris catus*, as that species is classified in those arcs to which it is native, or to which it has been imported. It is as close as they come, curators and tithe-children, to having conversations, these attempts to solve the mysteries left by the receding tides of history and cataclysm:

A fragment of a ballad from arc ψ19: *The Dragon Tintantophel, the engine of Malice chosen* . . . But arc ψ19 has been lost for centuries, and no one from that array has ever heard of Tintantophel.

A pair of embroidery scissors, sent to the Museum by one of its accredited buyers in arc ρ29 with a note saying *provenance to follow*. But the buyer was killed in the crash of the great airship *Helen d'Annunzio*, and the provenance was never discovered.

Two phalanges from the hand of a child, bound into a reliquary of gold wire. This object was found in one of the Museum's sublevels, with no tag, no number, no reference to be found anywhere in the vast catalogues.

And others and others. For entropy is insidious, and even the Museum's doors cannot bar it.

XI.

The tithe-child said in its soft, respectful voice, "I saw in the papers today that the Lady Archangel was beheaded last week."

The taxonomist's face did not change, but his hands flinched; he nearly dropped the tiny *D. nubis* wing bone that he was wiring into place.

"They say she came to the Museum last week. Did you see her, mynheer?" There might have been malice in the great pale eyes of the watching tithe-children; the taxonomist did not look.

"Yes," he said, the words grating and harsh, like the cry of a wounded animal. "I saw her."

Then the taxonomist *did* dream, the tithe-children saw, and they did not speak to him of the Lady Archangel again.

XII.

You who visit the Museum, you will not see them. They are not the tour guides or the experts who give informative talks or the pretty girls in the gift shops who wrap your packages and wish you safe journey. They are the tithe-children. Their eyes are large, pale and blinking, the color of dust. Their skin is dark, dark as the shadows in which they live. The scholars who study at the Museum quickly learn not to meet their eyes.

They might have been human once, but they are no longer.

They belong to the Museum, just as the dragons do.

GEESE
Daniel Coudriet

from Mississippi Review

THE GEESE IN THE POND TOOK ME FROM MY STROLLER, THEIR horrible bills pinching and mangling my flabby toddler arms, my soft belly. I kicked them like hollow watermelons when they snapped at my genitals.

The woman in the paddleboat with her two little girls. The smallest one's head turned to a balloon, sprouted a string (which her tiny fingers slid quickly around) and she floated away.

"You're too young to be worried about a family," the woman said. I could feel pondwater soaking through my overalls. She tried to load me into her boat. "This water we can use to grow more skin, to make a new sister," she said to her one little girl, watching her old sister float.

"I didn't get to attach a note to her with our address," the girl pouted, "in case she gets found."

"She no longer has all of her parts," the woman said.

Another woman spreading bread crusts into the edge of the water. Her family is laying a path of stones out into the pond, leaping from one stone to the next. I want her to be mother.

I raise my arms, but the geese have taken them. I raise my legs, but my skin has already drained out of my pants with the pondwater. I cannot find my genitals without the geese, honking all around me, and because there is language spilled everywhere, I am touching nothing.

THE CHINESE BOY
Ann Stapleton

from Alaska Quarterly Review

S CAFF IS PASSING THROUGH THE DRIVE-THRU BANK WITH HIS daughter when he first sees the Chinese boy, and the love that has stalked him silently all his life and until now has only come upon his dried footprints many years old (*ah, Scaff was here*) finally catches up with him. The boy's face inside the little bank building comes up suddenly, blooms in the light and dies away, smooth and pearlescent, with that look of belonging somewhere else Scaff will never get to, in an element he cannot breathe. The shadows there are so heavy Scaff can barely see. The pressure in his chest is unbearable.

October closes around him, floats him, almost weightless now, along its shining edge, the light so beautiful as it recedes into winter that the trees are trying to hoard it, *mine*, in their own black hands. But it only breaks apart wherever they try to touch it. Brightness disintegrates, the one trick it always knows.

On this day, Scaff sighs into the cool air and sees his own breath disappearing ahead of him, he cannot stop it. O, wait for me, he wants to say, but to what? To whom? So through his front window he watches the sun go down, blood-faced and bucking in the evening's arms, *not now!, not yet!*, until whatever it wanted so badly to finish is ended by the black hills beyond the town. All night long Scaff picks up the bits of what it said to him alone, though he only stares into the darkness, the stars collecting in his palm, a tiny mountain of light that shifts and cuts him as he tries to climb.

At dawn, Scaff is still in his chair with the rubber wheels, Scaff the difficult, the unlikable, the failed, watching the black birds mock his life, whatever corn all eaten now but one scant, yellow handful. The bentness of his wings is evident in how easily the birds put him behind them, hundreds at a time, lifting up lightly into the air as if they are glad to see the last of him, acute with love as he is. Burdened so late. A lapful of leaves. His hands do not know what to do with themselves. His yearning can assure him of nothing at all.

Behindhand friend to a zealot of loneliness, he bangs the bars of morning with the tin cup of his brooding. He is trying to bend the steel of circumstance with his small hands, but it will not bend. Everything from out of nowhere looking in the window, he rocks himself in the outgrown cage of his life, the same leaf falling just beyond his reach, over and over, like the smudged, red key to everything he needs.

Scaff's daughter Tonya is the Elephant Girl of Littleton. Six and a half feet tall at least, and big as all grief, with rings of pale skin that bulge up and back along her arms as she lifts them up or hangs them down. Every day she climbs the red and orange circus stool, stickered with every A from school, though she is forty-six years old now, and does tricks for her father. A cup of tea. A bath. A trip through the town in the sunshine. *Papa, look at the leaves. Look at the moon, so full.* But her tricks are just the same old same old—he has seen them a thousand times—and Scaff only stares out the window, his crooked little shoulders saying *enough.*

Scaff at the age of eighty-three has recently begun to look back upon his life. *Ah, Scaff! Who knew that everyone who can't die young will arrive at this one day?* His soul in jeopardy, he has begun to try to say to his daughter some few nice things. One pleasantry a day because it is the right thing to do, like a terrible green medicine, sour in his mouth: *that soup was not bad; a hot bath can't be beat.* Scaff writes these on an erasable message board; since his stroke, he cannot speak. He pushes the board toward Tonya to say *I have traveled through the world on business all these years, and yes, of course, I have brought you a present, you can open your eyes now.* But Tonya does not profit from this as you might think, for she was trained with the hook of indifference, and over time the reward becomes the reward, whatever it is, and when Scaff scrawls his kind word, she only looks at him questioningly, as if he is not himself today, as if she should put her hand up to his forehead and match his temperature against hers. As if the stroke was a whirlwind through the very core of his personality and she is patiently stooping and lifting beams away with her trunk, trying to find him as he was, bitter and slight and familiar. *Papa, I see your hook! Here it is.*

Scaff's blue house is poked into a hillside on a corner, the grass bending backward because it must, the little serviceberry tree leaning in to hold on as something rocks lightly in its branches. Before the stroke, Scaff was an agile-footed mountain goat flying up and down the sheer drop of the steps. But now there is now, and then has gone away for good. They do not have the money for a ramp, and at the angle of Scaff's yard, it would be like the Terror Slope anyway, no telling where he would end up. So Tonya stands behind and holds the arms of the chair, and her enormous bulk, quivering and steady at once, balances everything, everything, like a red and blue ball with shining gold trimmings. And Scaff goes from the top of the steps to the bottom on the lightest of bump, bump, bumps, Tonya's troubled breathing saying, *It's OK, Papa, I've got you,* to the top of Scaff's bald head.

Somewhere there is an Africa, but they do not know where, and so must believe this is home. Taken as infants in the black bag of the world, they have all but forgotten freedom. Out on the plains of some Serengeti, a little tickbird perches on an elephant's back and the wind blows and symbiosis becomes almost the ordinary trick of happiness. An elephant will not tolerate a tickbird. But these two are so lonely;

life asks what it asks. Sometimes love is only this dark perch of regret on a gray cloud of longing. But no matter, for it is nearly time for everything left alive, so full of thirst, so hungry for anything green, to commence its great migration somewhere else. It is nearly time now, as the twilight begins its slow unwinding over each and every one, stroking their faces so gently, a familiarity they hardly notice. See how the grass waves gold into the deepening evening, how love sometimes looks, so late on its way.

But Scaff and Tonya are in a little house on a little corner of a little town in the Midwest. With one foot taking up the whole front yard, Tonya does not even wonder anymore if there is a place where she would fit the scale, if somewhere there is a blue mountain so massive it could shade her happiness as she snorts in the grass beneath it, the wind's hands warm against the small of her back. No, she is where she is, the jackals of paltriness slicing into her giant legs, the insufficiency of it all inescapable with its brilliant teeth, or so she has come to believe. But see how the bright grasses of the plain are beginning to stir, the horizon restless with so many beating hearts, all of them dreaming at once. Grass, in its bid to go along, cresting and cresting with so much hope, who could imagine it? Where does it come from? And still the light goes wandering off on its own as it always does; all the dreamers can do is follow it into the dusk. That is their mission, and they are always true.

Scaff's neighborhood has been purchased by a grocery chain, his neighbors disappearing one by one in the night, popping up in better parts of town without him, their sleek new cars parked self-consciously along the curb. But Scaff said, "No!" and "The thieves!" His arm crooked around the serviceberry, something holding tightly to a limb overhead, he smacked his cane against the fence like this till the whole thing trembled, and now he and the Elephant Girl are almost alone here behind the mega store, peeking over it toward the cornfield and the river, keeping a solid eye on the drive-thru bank just across the street to the right, where the Chinese boy swims in his tank, down to the end and back, down to the end. Sometimes he moves his hands slowly over the glass as if he is feeling for a crack in its smoothness, a breach that could lead to an exit, a sky, a bubble of air. The light is like the beloved in jail; he puts his hand up to match the shape of his fingers to another's, but there is only the hard, bright density of everything beyond his reach.

Every afternoon the sun sets again like a swollen fruit no one can eat, bitter and green-rimmed in the shadows' cupped hands. The Chinese boy can see through everything, but only all the way into darkness. The light comes for him repeatedly, *I am here*, but he is forbidden to open the door of the bank. The key in his pocket burns his thigh. The cornfield waits, drumming its fingers, bits of light trampled and strewn. A crime scene where victim and perpetrator are one and the same, where the search dog just goes round and round in confusion.

Only Scaff the unconscious can see now, the sunset fierce in his keeping, singeing his small, empty fingers. A boy who gives his books to the river, one by one. A black-haired boy who watches the light on the water, how something gives up again and again at the top of the spillway, chained forever to its own descent. A cormorant's neck makes a single black loop in the middle of the lake, but it is not enough to hold on to. Danger swoops in the chill air, does backflips, hangs upside down by its hard, yellow nails. The world swings toward and away. Scaff's scalp prickles as he looks on. Someone should be notified, but what would he say? What would he request? *The Chinese boy is lonely; he walks beside the river in desperation. He is the son I will never in a million years beget and do not deserve, come to weep me out of the world, and in the sadness of his face, in the grief of his wrists as they twist so lightly to accommodate nothing, all has been revealed.* How can such things be explained? How can they be said aloud? Tonya brings a dish of hot peaches with brown sugar on top, his favorite, but he only grimaces and sets them aside, the juice making a tiny water hole, dim and undrinkable, in the green shallows of the bowl. Something shivers in the serviceberry, freezes as he turns to look.

The first snow flurries are enough to push the Chinese boy down on his knees, but he cannot think of anything to ask for. The river in blackness is pulling him down; the cornfield and sky in their bright-ness are stunning him, over and over, warm fingers stroking his eyelids shut. The drive-thru is dimming so much that he can barely discern its gray outline, his own thoughts like insects straight out of Africa, like six inch flying ones that smack against his neck and shirt front in the middle of a long, long party. He cannot look at them or he will scream the guests away, never to return. *Yes, sir. Would you like that in ones?* He hears the birds diving above his head, feels their rigid claws graze his hair. Scaff, for his part, has things he needs to give away. Like the bright clouds over the field, they are crushing his life, they are so heavy, and he must hurry, hurry to divest himself.

The Chinese boy used to read books on his breaks. Scaff could see him at the window or cross-legged in the grass behind the drive-thru, each volume a buoy bearing him up in the blue day, long hands opened around a fragile way forward. But lately the boy walks over the road to the cornfield beside the river. A rectangle of green once, now a pale, pink-tinged gold, all tattered and flapping, like Scaff looking out the window. He sees a human figure drafted in dark-ness, a smear of light for a human face. The Chinese boy sits in a tire swing hung from the tallest tree, a sycamore enamored of the water, saying and saying with its days *I will come to you, some night soon, expect me.* Little scrolls of bark, smooth and blank, lie at his feet. He smokes a cigarette and watches the birds turning above the river, spelling *Scaff loves you* with their ardent black bodies, though he cannot read the words.

One day as the Chinese boy is closing up, Scaff, as he spies for love, sees this: a brown shadow breaking through the drive-thru chain as if it is made of paper, a lion bounding toward its living supper as it runs ahead, its small heart beating so heavily. Eyes find the boy in the sunlight and their brightness smashes against the window; darkness like water rushes over him, though he is dry inside. Across the road a man, a woman, and a small child try and try to climb up the river-bank to reach him, but are swept back down. A heaviness like stone strikes the glass where his face floats, then bounces away. The shadow prowls around and around the drive-thru, motions for the Chinese boy to come out, but he waits, perfectly still, until it finally goes. He takes off his sweatshirt and slowly wipes the river water from the glass, though it is dry, carries the jacket by one sleeve as if he is hold-ing hands with something that can hurt him terribly. And Scaff, who has lived a long life with only a black cavern in his chest, filled with tiny bats everywhere all upside down, and a small, sulfurous trickle of water no one could drink from and live, that same Scaff, a little monkey pelting the sky with peanuts, guards the Chinese boy against the autumn afternoon as best he can. He is the only one to see. The boy hurries up the street and into the late sun, but it is the boy who sets, going down behind the hill, a small, dark streak disappearing from Scaff's intent eyes. Something, only a trace or a half-thought, covers itself in the leaves.

Scaff's daughter prepares for everything, Tonya the Elephant Queen with her little blue walkie talkies. (*You take one and I'll take one. This button right here if you need me, Papa.*) Tonya, the toast of the Serengeti, with her big button phone and her instantaneous tie-in to the EMS. (*Just push this, Papa. I already gave them the name and address.*) Scaff half listens, his eye on the drive-thru bank, his heart where, after all these years, it suddenly must go. A herd of elephants could not stop it. The golden afternoons pull his sparse hair, prick his thinned, ashen flesh like burrs.

Scaff is troubled. The Chinese boy never reads anymore. He walks in little circles at the edge of the cornfield, stares up at the autumn birds going over, pure belonging right in his face like that. Too big, too small, no wings, he flaps his arms once as if to lift off, but he is too heavy for the sky. Out of the darkness of the Chinese boy's hair, Scaff's heart comes shooting up in his throat. The world that just weeks ago had laid him aside, a finished tale, arises again beyond THE END to want something now, its fingers clutching his life as he tries to pull it away. The light on the field rakes his eyes. The Chinese boy puts both hands up and dances lightly with the sun-warmed glass, nothing holding him as close as it can.

Balanced on the trunk of his daughter, the Elephant Wonder, Scaff enters the drive-thru. He scribbles, "Let me," on a piece of paper and puts her check in the pneumatic tube, hiding beneath it a peppermint from lunch, a gift for the Chinese boy, who looks up in confusion, only seeing Scaff's daughter, Scaff is so small, slumped down in the seat.

The Chinese boy says, "Would you like that any special way, ma'am?" holding his breath, as if he is lying on the ground beneath her for a trick and he is relieved she isn't stomping him to jelly while the crowd looks on. Tonya smiles in her beneficence, her fleshy face red and bland and kind. The mint comes back (*shoop!*) and Tonya thinks the bank is having a giveaway. She smiles and says thank you, offers it to Scaff, who just scowls and looks out the window. She pops it into her mouth, the taste like an old forgiveness, frozen hard.

The Chinese boy and the river, the cornfield and the birds dip crazily away from Scaff as his daughter turns the car uphill toward the house, a little blue Tibet above the mega store, the autumn light an intense, crystalline gold on dust-colored snakeroot racked to seed. Tonight is hot soup and television, everything on a tray with a cornucopia napkin. Tonight no man will sink his teeth into the soft folds of Tonya's belly once again, though up on her stool washing dishes she has done every trick she knows. Her loneliness will find her later, coming through the dark at breathtaking speed. *Ah, there you are, my sweet one. How are you? Did you think I could forget?*

Tonya, with little Scaff walking beneath you past all lions, what is it like to take up so much of the horizon? You sit down on the edge of everything and the legs of the world smash beneath you, small splinters of good intention everywhere. You live in a house built for vervets, your clothes hung at an angle because there isn't enough room for them front to back, the usual way, in the tiny closets. Men look at your thighs and picture their own faces on milk cartons all across the land: last seen on the outskirts of the Serengeti, holding one red rose. You think there must be someone in town named Lardass who looks exactly like you, you have been mistaken for her so many times as the cars go by, one after another, beeping their horns! Love looks at your kind, pink face, as big as a cake plate, and sighs with happiness. Beautiful! So beautiful. But Scaff is small; he cannot peak up over his own life to see it. A good father should carry his girl child to safety on his shoulders. The whole world knows. But you are just another mirror everywhere for Scaff to look into and see his own failures. You say "Papa" dozens of times a day, as if to invoke someone dear and devoted, conjured wrongly out of Dickens. And in his sharp monkey eyes you see you are a mistake to be repented of and nothing in this world can unmake you. With your own hand, each day you paint the bull's-eye on your soft, warm belly, a rhino horn inexorable on its way. As if they will remember you, you look up at the stars, expecting someday even now. Distracted by their closeness, you do not try to move. There is nothing at all you cannot forgive.

The Chinese boy opens a box of paper clips the sun shines on, a tiny silver bridge cracking apart in his hands, a little figure falling, disappearing into dark water. He looks out the window of the drive-thru and sees his joy growing smaller and smaller, a black bird no one notices leaving the world, the fringe of a sore wing brushing the sun so far away. The cornfield calls his one true name; his head jerks hard in response, he feels such longing. *Lie down with me*, say the broken stalks. *Right here, right here. Whatever you need.*

Tonight when the Chinese boy is floating alone in his bed, ice will be trying to tell the river something, but the water will have its hands over its ears. A man, a woman, a little girl are huddled there, unable to reach up to the light, waiting and waiting in the green-brown water. It has been years, and still they are looking up with so much love. They hold out their hands to the Chinese boy, but he rolls over and closes his eyes, mistaking their voices for the cries of birds in his dreams.

Scaff, my old friend, at last I have found you, says love, putting its arms around him, kissing him MWAH! MWAH! on both cheeks like a European, ignoring his look of discomfort, pushing him up and down the hall all night while he tries to fall asleep. *Please forgive my tardiness, a hazard of my profession, sometimes.* Scaff looks out at the yellow lights of the drive-thru as if love is not standing there beside him, telling him, belatedly, everything it knows, and yet the stars in the background are wobbling and splintering, rocked with his longing. Everything he sent away, its hands empty, is crossing the bright plain now, hoping somehow to reach him. The lions are watching from the edge of his dream, the evening sun stroking their manes, licking their peppermint paws. They have eaten his old life down to the last knucklebone, a thimbleful of blood and dust and things he could not say. Eyes peer in at him from the serviceberry, but look down before he can read their expression.

Though she swears she will never, in bed at night, the Elephant Girl's heart rushes to the window when the bad boy death throws his little rocks. She climbs down the swaying darkness right into his arms, smokes cigarettes and hurls the holes of light from the car, lies down on her back in the grass, a girl named Apnea with her elbows up over her head, her fingers in the yellow weeds, his hands all over, almost his. Tonya wakes up gasping for breath. Ba BOOM BOOM b bbb b ba BOOM! She slows her breathing as she has taught herself to do, *in, out, you're OK, you're OK,* her finger and thumb pushing deep in the dough of her wrist to feel her pulse kick and fade and then grow regular again, as death laughs and peels off without her one more time. All this happens in silence so that Papa will not wake, but he is up on his palms in the front window, having it out with the stars. *What do you want of me?* He begs for an answer, but they are silent. They only move closer when he looks away.

The late rains return and the cornfield floods. The Chinese boy looks down at the trees and the sky and his own puzzled face, pierced by the stubble there next to his shoes. A bird retreats with his heart, a dim, dried berry, his *help me* scrawled in mold unreadable. Tonya flips a grilled cheese sandwich over and back again, both sides done brown, and Scaff's chair rolls inexorably toward the window's light.

The hyenas show up in the daytime and the Chinese boy must wait on them, he cannot avoid it. The lion circles the drive-thru, its long tail lashing the air. Laughing in the sunlight, they are putting something into the pneumatic tube container. Scaff refocuses his binoculars. The darkness of their gift comes shooting in, an arrow of hate, straight toward the Chinese boy, who cannot move from its path. It finds him there as they flee into the afternoon. *Asante sana.* Thank you very much, he says, his hands so afraid to unlatch the little silver door.

Scaff writes on his erasable message board that there should be bullets for his gun. Tonya says, "Papa," (in Swahili, "throb of a heart or pulse") and goes on slicing carrots with her puffed out balloon fingers. She is singing a John Prine song to herself, and Scaff scowls, caught like a stunned bird—he never even saw the glass—in the hands of love. But who will blow into his mouth to keep him from going into shock? Who will open these fingers and fling him again toward the sky? He is an old man, wretched with sudden, perhaps final, feeling. He is sitting in a chair with rubber wheels, looking out over the river, where the Chinese boy is spinning slowly in the swing, the birds all around him like the notes to a love song he cannot hear.

He looks far into the river and cannot even glimpse his homeland anymore, the world formed of four faces nowhere now; there is only the darkness moving over him, why does it take so many years? Could his family find a hole to America? Could a river flow so far across the world that he might come upon them here on these deserted banks, his mother's beautiful hand clutching a brown reed? He is the only one left, his whole body encased in glass like water he can see through but not break. His mother and his father. His baby sister. He used to see their faces, but now the water is only dark. He is the failure of the family, who goes on floating and floating forever after the others who had such a talent, all of them but him, such a talent for drowning. He wants to enter the river that has been calling to him for so long, can think of nothing else to try, but fears the world will only swim away as it always does. He sifts the water with his fingers, but there is no trace. The wind blows and his hand dries.

He had climbed up the hill, so far and fast, so proud and glad that he could do it, to free their kite, the pleased face of the dragon on it suddenly so confused as it said, *Follow me home*—And then the impossible waters had broken over the world and rushed down the narrow valley below him and taken them away forever. Left him behind, his hand severed from the kite string slipping upward out of the branches. For a moment, from high above in the sunlight, it could see their heads—and then not, the little sister, unable to struggle, even, afloat the longest like a small hole of light moving away on what became of his love. The dragon tried to tell the clouds as he traveled on, but they were restless, always changing, and could not pay attention. The moon came and went.

And then the occluded days of the orphanage with its handless, armless caretaking. And then America and the little room the boy shared with his twin brother, the brazen idiot loneliness, wailing and clutching at his clothes when he came in, putting its hands in his pockets, greedy for whatever nothing it could find, biting his forearms if he tried to stroke its cheek.

He left his family to the river that day; he did not have the strength to search for the grace of their bodies as it wandered off, he did not have the courage to find them and look into their open eyes. And if his love climbed out somewhere downstream, the shoe of a baby sister, its mouth broken by mud, he looked beyond it to the red pines as he lived daily onward and did not stoop to pick it up, so that it followed him at a distance wherever he could not go.

The trees give up, set free, finally, the beautiful light, what choice do they have? Their branches let in the wind like any cage in its cruelty. The winter will come, though it is always so hard to believe. Scaff and his daughter enter the drive-thru, big Tonya, serene and massive in the lead, with little Scaff intense beside her, missing only the tiny bellman's uniform with its golden braid, with its flat red cap. Scaff tries a follow-up to the peppermint. An inspirational message. His fingers fly over the scrap of paper: *You must hold on tight. You must never give up. Please.* It's all he has time for as Tonya retrieves the container from the pneumatic tube to put her check inside. She looks over just at the wrong moment, sees him still writing, assumes the note is for her.

As she has done a thousand times, she reaches over and takes the paper from him to see what it is he wants. A styptic pencil, perhaps. A boiled egg for dinner. She blushes with surprise as she reads and the Mara grasses tremble ever so slightly as a hungry snake is thwarted somehow and turns back into its own coming. Is it possible? Can he have seen her sadness, after all? She turns her head away from him, chin trembling like the soft mud at the edge of the water in spring. The Chinese boy looks down to scatter the birds from his sight (they are so insistent now), then takes another customer.

"I— I will, Papa," she says. "I mean, I won't." So simply, she takes the grail into her hands. Heart of an elephant, this woman. Scaff looks agitated, but less stern than usual, surprised himself. Distractedly, his eyes still fierce, he smiles a stern little monkey smile, meant somehow to be reassuring, and, wonder of wonders, it actually is. Hesitantly, shyly, almost, Scaff puts his pale monkey hand on the high gray boulder that is his only child and pats lightly, two times, then turns to fiddle with his seatbelt, already fastened correctly. Tonya looks out the windshield over the plains of the Serengeti, the wind blowing her giant ears back like lilies as she moves along. She must cross the Mara after the sun sets. This is all her life. "I promise," she says, putting each foot down so carefully, walking on a road of crocodiles over the twilight.

Scaff is afraid for the boy, a one-man autumn, letting everything go. Scaff can see it in his posture, the way his books have molted into cigarettes, the lack of fight in him when the wind turns against the swing. Though he does not know it, there is only one thing holding him now. There is only Scaff in his little chair, balanced on Tonya's broad back. In some Africa, the stars are everywhere, so close you can taste them on your lips, but she does not know there is a land of others just like her where the wind could explain to her how she could be free. *Jambo, rafiki. Unatoka wapi? Hello, friend. Where are you from?* This greeting starts toward her on its own sometimes, but is stopped in darkness somewhere along the way, who knows how, her loneliness swelling what contains it so that it cannot move forward or backward, like love, still alive, grown huge in a snake's cold belly. She brushes crumbs from the tiny kitchen counter, hits her elbow on the low door frame as she clumps slowly off to bed. The escarpment is aflame with light. *Oloololo.*

Scaff is usually asleep by now, down in a little ball of flannel, his arms and legs a few bent twigs protruding. But tonight he is agitated. Tonight he is on fire with eighty-three years' worth of human feeling, and he is sitting up straight under the strain of it, is sitting up as high as he can in his chair, staring out the front window at the yellow lights of the drive-thru, his wasted life a *moto* (a hot object) he tosses from hand to hand, but cannot hold. The serviceberry vibrates in the wind.

And then suddenly they are there, bad intentions swirling like bats from the cavern of how he never cared, swooping and diving now on the Chinese boy, who has his hands up to his face, the river in darkness, the bare trees full of black birds gone completely silent, as if they aren't even there, then, as one, streaming all together out of the world. But Scaff catches their black tail feathers in his fingers, drags them back with both hands, no!, as he feels himself lifted from his chair. He tries to call out (*hatari!*), but he cannot speak. By habit, he starts to scribble on his message board, but Tonya the Elephant Girl is far up the stairs, and fast asleep.

Under the yellow lights, the Chinese boy is pushing a box into place. He is climbing up in clarity, the world ambling off through the darkness, moving away from him. Behind him the man, the woman, the little child are trying so hard to climb up the riverbank, they are begging the mud and the slimmest of grasses for help, but the Chinese boy will not turn to look at them and their knees slip down and the water closes over their grief.

Scaff screams without a sound, his message hurtling upward in urgency, only to stop halfway up the stairs and slide back down. His heart is bursting as he sees the necklace. The hyenas have brought a white necklace for a present and are putting it around the neck of the beautiful, far-off-eyed Chinese boy, proudly and carefully, as if he is their bride. They are using his own hands.

The lion puts its paws up on Scaff's chest and holds him. He looks wildly around his little chair with the rubber wheels, looks for anything at all. And then he remembers. The African Queen has prepared him! He grabs the one blue walkie-talkie off the nightstand and jabs the button over and over. A little alarm goes off in front of him, and he can hear its counterpart upstairs like an owl answering from a nearby tree. *Nisaidia!* (Help!)

The Elephant Girl comes out of her sleep in a roar, her heart lurching and skidding. *Papa!* She stamps down the stairs of the tiny house, her feet so big they hang over each step and almost trip her, the little purple birds on her pajamas swollen and pulsating. *Papa!* She sees Scaff by the window, his face frozen in horror, both hands pointing toward the terrible dream he cannot stop the world from having. From the serviceberry a face in terror looks back into his.

The Elephant Girl follows his gaze, after all these years sees exactly what he sees, as he sees it. And then she goes roaring out into the night, she doesn't stop to think, and an enraged elephant is a terrible sight to see, Scaff up on his hands on the arms of his chair, the whole golden plateau of the Masai Mara stretched out before him. He hangs from the moon by one finger, trying to see it all, whatever he once was moving off into the night on its own, so small and stiff-legged. Love looks on in pity, silent now that it has finally had its say.

She crosses the road and the field in seconds, a curtain of love sweeping across the darkness straight toward the Chinese boy who was so certain any more that he had no one at all. It is the great migration of herds across the vastness of the Serengeti plain, the zebras and wildebeests, gazelles and elephants, swarming over the grass with their very bodies toward something they cannot name but must do, toward their own survival and the way the water will taste on their lips when they finally come to it, to the way the wind will blow over their backs, and something—the singing of the grass, the angle of the sun, the hard taps of a tickbird over their neck bones—will mean they can live. It is their own darkness over the plain that will link the horizons together, light and light. Do you see how death, for a while, is crushed beneath so many hooves, so many gray and wrinkled pounds? So many hearts headed off in the same direction, how can it ever be? Even the stars do not know.

And then in only seconds, the lawn still quaking from the approach, she reaches them, trumpeting and swinging her trunk wildly every which way, her shadow over them enormous. And the brutal ones, stunned by the strangeness of her arrival, the moon obscured entirely by her bulk, let go of the Chinese boy just like that, and the circle of hyenas around him breaks apart and wheels away, their laughter blowing off like dust, leaving the cornfield whispering of the brown lion's disappearance, the slinking away of the shadows. And then the Chinese boy himself, his whole body and all he thinks about and everything he hopes for, the way the whole world turns slowly around him as he sits in the swing, so lonely and so loved, though he does not know, careers into the darkness.

But Tonya is there to receive this time. She takes out of the blackness as it moves so quickly toward her the little striped candy of this one chance and puts it in her mouth. *I will. I mean, I won't. I promise, Papa.* She catches the Chinese boy in her arms, as he starts to shoot through them, like a tunnel down to the bottom of the river, a little skier smacking straight into Kilimanjaro, sure to die. But the mountain is not made of stone and ice as some might think. And the skier hits hard against only a wide expanse of human flesh and the reverberation of an oddly beating heart and is saved. And Tonya the Elephant Girl goes up on her toes on her stool of blue and red with the golden trimmings and does the most wonderful trick imaginable, a trick she has been doing forever for Scaff, but which he has never noticed. The trick called holding up the world. And then she is balancing the Chinese boy on her trunk, light as a feather, light as a human breath. And she can see across the dark field, across the road, her Papa's face like a monkey's in the window of their house, and yes, he has seen the trick finally. He is clapping his hands in joy over it; he is swinging by his tail around the room. He is ringing and ringing the little bell of happiness.

And then Scaff sees the dilemma. She can hold the boy up, but she can't take off the necklace. She could loosen the necklace, but the boy would hurtle alone into darkness. The trick does not encompass both acts. And so, as good as she is, his daughter, as much of a Colossus as his Tonya is proving herself to be under the yellow lights of the drive-thru, it is up to Scaff now. *It is time*, says love, after eighty-three years, now putting its hand on Scaff's, so warm he jumps. And in his weeping and his fear and his feelings of devotion so intense that he cannot move, Scaff knows what to do, for Tonya is helping him. She has prepared him long ago, just for this night. *Just push this button, they will be here in minutes, Papa.* And Scaff's crooked little good for nothing fingers, stiff from their withholding everything so long, so long, bear down on the button, and the cry for help goes out through the darkness and someone opens the container immediately and they come shooting right back through the night on the stream of light that is human love, through the tall black grass, never still in its yearning. The serviceberry stays motionless, a being holding its breath.

Scaff rolls out on the porch, tiny sallow-faced monkey in flannel, to point them where to go, and they see in yellow light an Elephant Woman raising a Chinese boy in her trunk above the river of hurt that has come flowing toward him on this night. Scaff has never seen anything so beautiful as this. His heart is fractured in a million pieces, the whole field glittering with grief, rustling where the lion moves off through the dried cornstalks, dragging his helpless life.

And then in seconds everything comes down, the boy and Tonya like some temporary installation as the circus moves on, and the boy funneled away to the hospital right up the road. And Tonya's odd heart goes on beating, the circus drum now inside her chest somehow and the drummer drunk again on so much sadness, the leaves of Ohio saying his name against a window open since the day he left. She shuffles back across the road toward the house lit with Scaff's tardy love, a dusty candle flickering in the cup of his need. She goes back to her own loneliness that no one can see like a vast, grass-filled plain with its herd of one, goes back dragging her stool that feels so heavy now. She steps into the cage and closes the door with her own trunk, as she has been taught to do.

When she comes through the door, she sees Scaff writing on his message board. *Thank you. Thank you. Asante sana.* As if she is a surgeon who has saved the most important person in the world to him. She is amazed, her heart calming down a little, and turns to look down into his face. *Papa.* And then, through the darkness, so sudden in its arrival, after forty-six short years, though the man's heart is too small to contain it and the plain of loneliness too wide for the daughter to be found, despite the lions and the crocodiles so hungry, and the buzzards that follow like the first sadness wherever they go, still it comes for them. Still love comes, though no one can say how he got there and even after so much time they are not prepared, embarrassed as they are, looking down so intently at nothing. Though all they know to do is to have a cup of tea in silence and look out over the empty drive-thru. Though they cannot stay long like this, but wander off from the waterhole toward dawn, the same world before them.

And you may think that the Chinese boy would be so grateful he would become one of the family, *tatu* (three), and move right into the little house in the hill where such love has been waiting for him all along, like a set of beautiful clothes that fit perfectly, all laid out on the bed. And you may even picture them at the dinner table together: Scaff passing the *wali* (rice) and the *kuku* (chicken), Tonya the Elephant Girl bringing more water for the Chinese boy, who is smiling as he begins to tell them all he has read today and how it has moved him, as he tries one of the sweet, bitter stars (Nina njaa!) from the plateful set before him.

But this is life we are talking of, and what happens at the end of the migration is only a retracing, after all, is only a massive turning around to go back, and so the Chinese boy, though he is partly—yes, only partly—glad not to be dead, is mortified by the way in which he was saved, cannot agree to though it is already over. He remembers being scooped up out of his tank, held forever where he could not breathe. He swims around that every day and cannot break out of the tiny current of it. The flesh on the woman's arms engulfing him. The little man's burning eyes. How their love shamed him in its strange clothing, with its hair all up on end so that the world wanted only to laugh.

And so one day soon after, he takes his books under his arm and rides away on the bus to the world that has not read the paper, gets off where it looks straight into his eyes and does not know him, to become, of all things, a writer. And here you would think he might immortalize his two friends who watched over him so well from their cramped perch above the mega store, though so often the light across the Mara burned their eyes. But for now, he is too ashamed to think of them. His hands are flown too far away from his heart to write the story. His life is the birds over his head, one darkness massing above him at evening, the scraps wafting in loneliness from a hundred different trees. The serviceberry adjusts and adjusts again to the slight weight in its arms.

And Tonya the Elephant Girl, who might have lain down and died that night, her oddly booming heart saying *enough*, a sacrifice to the yellow light, does not do it. She simply lumbers home again and climbs from the golden valley up the stairs too small for her feet, her toes gripping tightly, her heels on nothing but air. In a way, she does become rich for what she has done, as her Papa has thanked her and she has heard. And she does become famous, in a way. After the incident, the local paper carries this headline, repeated in slightly varying forms around the state: *400 Pound Woman Saves Boy*. The editor led with the four hundred pounds, he could not resist, and the saving part shrank down to a nubbin as a consequence. But she would change nothing about that night, nothing at all. She does not begrudge the stars a single thing, they themselves would tell you if they could.

What will happen now anyone can guess. The life that Scaff and Tonya have on the hill will continue to erode, a day here, a lifetime there, a clod of dirt hitting the sidewalk and bouncing away, until the death of one or the other of them stoves the hillside in for good. The other will lumber or wheel along as best he can for a while and then follow. The house is already headed downhill. Perhaps the day it takes the Thrill Ride to the curb will be the day the Chinese boy takes up his pen and begins to write. Or perhaps he will only walk along the same water, watching the same birds as they go, not knowing, still, how he belonged to someone once, how tenderly the cornfield meant to hold him in its dying arms. Maybe he will go on waiting—it takes forever sometimes. The little tree can show him.

But perhaps an elephant, a wild elephant moving across a plateau of brightness, far out on the edge of what the boy can feel, and the tickbird riding lightly on its head, parting the whole sky so bravely with its small, brittle wings, will, just for a moment, just in one patch of light at sunset, enter the heart (for where else can they go?) of a Chinese boy turning in a swing, his feet writing nothing in the dust. A boy who was cherished, though he did not know, and will not be remembered forever. A boy impatient for the birds to tell him what they saw: love as it came slowly along the riverbank, shoes caked with mud, its arms full of light—

So that the woman comes to find him, arrives somehow with her long hair following after her like the wings of black birds flying homeward, negotiating his future with the wind along the river, paying the long ransom with her dark eyes and her calm hands, exchanging all she has, her life alone, for his. So that one night in spring he comes hesitantly across the sighing bridge of her body to safety, leaving the old days and who he was then, so delicately made and unsure, so hastily sketched in, behind the smooth bars of glass: the black curve of a cheekbone, hands unable to reach the light. And love, thinking he is safe now, finally, love, who makes mistakes sometimes, even after so much experience of humankind, goes hobbling away, goes hurrying onward into the cooling afternoon, he has so much to do, and he is so old now, as old as the world.

But the Chinese boy is still in danger—if Scaff were alive, it would be so easy to see. But he is dead, a little puff of hope for the end to be different from the rest, swirling down slowly for a while, then hitting the ground, dispersing again into the brilliant light of another life. The danger now is subtle, is small and unaccounted for, the way a man can look at his wife and see her unhappiness, an unhappiness he might turn to dust so easily between his first two fingers and his slender thumb, if he wished. But instead he looks past her, out the window, and yearns for the river's body he has never held, that has never held him, and lets his wife go so quietly up the stairs she almost disappears into the twilit carpet. He feels her footsteps like his heartbeat going away, but he does not move. The serviceberry sighs so sadly.

And then the child is born to them, flies straight into their hours with his arms outstretched just as he is supposed to do, and everything changes and nothing does, and they are happy for a good part of each day and they are only sometimes alone. But the Chinese boy has no past at all, and though the woman looks for it all over the house and sometimes when he sleeps she sees it vanish in the window of his face, it is not to be found. He does not wish to speak of it, and after enough of that, she does not ask.

And so the boy, who has eyes like his mother's, looks for it too, after a while, holds out his hands to be picked up by it, but never is, crawls on the floor, putting his tongue on everything he comes across, so close he can almost taste it, but never finding it. He says *Dada!* every afternoon when the Chinese boy arrives at the door, with such great joy, as if he has never seen him before, as if he could never have imagined anything so wonderful! But the Chinese boy is frightened of his son, of the way he calls the past into being in his small eyes, and though he lifts him up in happiness, there is always space between them, a separating light because the father has no before and so the son has no after. And things go on like this, sometimes for a lifetime, they can.

And then the baby catches a cold, no—the flu, no—they do not know what it is. *A hundred thousand viruses out there*, the young doctor says, and smiles and smiles in trying to be kind, like a hyena slowly and quietly tearing the legs off of language. It will either burn itself out, or—He does not finish and does not have to. The Chinese boy's whole body shakes with sudden cold. His wife is perfectly still, like a beautiful statue crazing in every part, small cracks opening from within her, releasing the black birds that whirl and whirl around their heads. Take him home, they say. An instruction sheet. Nothing more to do now. Nothing more.

The Chinese boy holds the baby to his chest, as if his own heart has fled outside his body suddenly, like this. Crossing a small strip of green grass, suddenly the space of light between him and the child is absorbed into the darkness. Between them now is only energy, pure and black, that enters both beings freely as if there were no such thing in the world as a wall. Later in the night he lets his wife sleep a little while he keeps holding the boy, little hot coal of his life, of all their lives, the father's arms curved perfectly to the small shape, his shoulders and wrists frozen in pain for he cannot dare to move.

"Dada, do you see them running?" the boy cries out. "Do you see them all?"

And the Chinese boy says, "Yes, I see. I see."

And the birds keep trying to come into the room and the father shoos them off by closing his eyes so tightly. The baby is stiff-backed and burning hot, a smell of singed feathers in his father's nose. And the wife reaches in with a cool sponge in her hand and her eyes catch her husband's and they are the same person now in two incapable bodies. Nothing comes between them this time, their one heart hoarding the baby's small shrieks, strangely like delight, like amazement: "Oloololo!" Ears in the serviceberry strain to hear.

He is standing deep in the river with a book, the one book of everything he ever did not understand, clasped hard against his chest and the sycamore yearning so far toward the one it loves that the whole world is almost pulled down with it, and the empty cornfield calling and calling his name. And then he looks up over the small head of all his hope and love and sees them again, after so many years, the behemoth woman and the fierce-eyed little monkey man who shamed him once with their love, what did they mean by it?

Why was he saved? Their faces are so beautiful, he wants to laugh, to cry out. Why did he not see? What could they have meant but this? The birds fill the field before him, it is black with them suddenly, completely, and the dark waters as if they had his hands to use, finally, wash over the fever with their cold, cold grief. The baby relaxes against him, still alive! Alive! The white necklace, worn and cracked now, so tight around his neck, breaks apart and his small, regular breathing fills the world. The hyenas slink away into the cornstalks, into the tall grass bright with fear. The lion climbs the sycamore to sleep, still hungry. And he is trying to touch them, but they are fading, shimmering like the oldest light in the world, and blending into this day as it is, as it must be, and then they are gone, and he cries out NO!, for the pain is so terrible that he must bring them back. He must find them somehow. He commands and he pleads, calls out to the tree to help him, but the tree loves only the water and they do not return. While he is still holding his son, and with his wife's hands so lightly on his back as if they are his own wings budding, the father, though he is standing still, starts running, runs and runs, far back through his own life as if he is following a white string, so far into an old, old light that kept trying to show him his life. His wife and son with him now, he runs until he comes to the little blue house on the hill, gone for years and yet still waiting there. And though there is no blue house to be found anymore—only a chain drugstore all orange and silver, though he does not know it—the Chinese man cannot stop. He runs up the stairs anyway, runs three at a time.

"I'm here! I'm here!" he screams. He bangs on the door with both hands. He looks in every window, sees in each one his own face weeping, and his own eyes, the eyes of his father looking up at him on the hillside, safe in the sunlight, so afraid and wild with love, and behind him the empty river, and in his hand the baby's shoe.

In the top of the serviceberry tree, bulldozed years back on a bright blue day, is the dragon, so thin now and old he is almost clear, so tired and ready, finally, to become a part of the sky. Though he wishes for it, he has no way to tell the Chinese man how he remembers Scaff, his lonely face looking out into the light, his hands, so stiff and awkward in their mission, holding tightly to the string.

1. THE FLYING WOMAN IN PROFILE

The flying woman is just a little bit glamorous. I don't know if the flying came before the glamour or vice versa, but her beauty is airy, and her flying has style. In this picture, she wears her hair long and wavy. Her nose flips up at the end, like a ski jump, and her skin is ruddy from the wind. She's a more beautiful woman than I am. I don't mind.

If the image were a daguerreotype, she would seem mysterious. If it were a bust, she would seem noble. If it were a holy card, she would be a saint. But the image is a photograph on my wall, and when people see it, they all say, *Who is that? She looks so far away.*

2. THE FLYING WOMAN IN FLIGHT

The flying woman didn't fly above the clouds. "It's cold up there," she'd say, "and there's not enough air." She skimmed the roofs and treetops. Her legs dangled behind her, and she wore her wheelchair strapped to her back. "It's hard work," she'd say. "It takes focus." But she needed to fly every day. Otherwise, she had trouble falling asleep.

She used to solve this problem by taking trips. She strapped on her wheelchair and a backpack and flew to a new town every day, then camped there for the night. She covered a lot of ground—she made it to Ohio and back—but she got lonely. To combat this, she decided to start from the same place every day, and gave herself projects. She sat on top of every water tower in the tri-county area. She saw the top of every courthouse. She had been very close to balancing on top of every car dealership flagpole, wrapping herself in the massive American flags, and sinking slowly to the ground.

Sometimes the flying woman invited me over to get drunk. We sipped beer and sparkling wine and talked about our jobs. The flying woman was a supermarket checkout girl. I worked at a beauty salon. Then the flying woman would announce that she felt airy. She'd burp, and suddenly she'd rise an inch off the couch. She'd burp again, and she'd rise a foot. We'd put music on, and soon she'd be burping, spinning, floating in the air as I danced on the ground. I got rug burns on my feet; she got a headache from bumping her head on the ceiling.

At that point, we'd decide to go to bed, and she'd ask me to sleep over, to hold her down for the night. I slept with her coiled in my arms, this close to happy. When her body floated up, I held her closer, and dreamt of the moment when I would sit up and cover her lips with my own.

3. The Flying Woman in High School

When the flying woman went to high school, she did not know she could fly. She did not know many things about herself. But she did have desires, nagging fantasies that seemed as impossible as marrying a European prince or traveling back in time. Especially during liturgy, she used to look up at the ceiling and wish to float up there, right in front everyone, like the host the priest held above his head. And then, one day, she did.

The entire auditorium gasped as the flying woman, then more of a flying girl, rose towards the ceiling. When she reached the top, she panicked. She wanted to fall, like things were supposed to. With that simple shift, the moment broke; she plummeted and crashed on the seats below. Something in her body broke, and she passed out from the pain.

When she returned to school in a wheelchair, no one could decide: had it been a miracle, or a sin? The priests, sent from around the world to examine her, treated her with wonder and condescension. For a short time, letters poured in, asking would she pray for peace, speak to angels, send a scrap of her clothes? Her classmates shunned her. Eventually, the priests determined that her flight had been a miracle of faith, but, like Peter, who first walked on water only to sink into the sea, she had failed to believe.

Privately, they warned her never to try that sort of thing again, at least not within the house of God.

4. The Flying Woman in Love

One day, I went to the flying woman's house for dinner and found her talking to a man. He wore bicycling gear. He left as soon as I arrived. The flying woman told me nothing about him, and we ate our spaghetti in peace. Then, the next day, after work, she told me she was in love.

She had met the bicyclist as he was cresting a hill on his bike, right as she was flying over it. She had surprised him so badly he fell over. They laughed about it for a long time, and the bicyclist invited her out for a drink. They discovered that they shared a love of gin and tonics, shark movies, and historical fiction set in the Renaissance. They both hated Catholicism, and cars.

I said that the bicyclist sounded pretty nice. For a stranger.

I saw less of the flying woman after that. The bicyclist could do many flying-friendly activities, it turned out. He could hanglide with her. Mountain climb. Skydive. She could follow him for hours on his bike rides, like some sort of private superhero, warning when hills, children, or cars approached. After a day of perfect compatibility, they would go back and drink gin and tonics, watch shark movies, or read historical fiction set in the Renaissance. At night, they'd have sweaty, passionate sex. I knew the last part was true, anyway, because I went by her apartment one night, as a surprise, and heard moans through the door. My face flushed with shame, and I left without knocking.

I'm sure afterwards they fell asleep in each other's arms, no longings unfulfilled, no one floating away, or left behind.

One day, the flying woman called me, sobbing. He had gone, just up and left a note saying he had decided to bike across the country. He had promised to return, but he didn't say when, if ever. I held her, let her wipe her nose on my shirt, and hoped he'd find another flying woman. Or get hit by a truck.

5. The Flying Girl in Peril

After the accident at school, the flying girl kept flying, despite the priests' warnings. More than once her mother found her sprawled on the floor, a bump on her head from having shot up to the ceiling too fast. She would punish the flying girl, call her prideful, but the flying girl never gave up. Soon she could do a lap around the top of her room. Then two. Then ten. Then a hundred. And then—she went outside.

In those days, she didn't have her compact chair, just a standard folding one that was too big to carry on her back, so she never went far. But she maintained a small patrol route around our town. She even gave herself a superhero name. She refused to tell me what it was, but I saw the shirt she wore. She had written a huge "A" on it with permanent marker. I asked her if it was for "Angel," and she laughed. Hard.

I was the first, and last, person the flying girl ever saved. For me, it started in church. The saints in stained glass windows talked to me. Not about God. They wanted candy. *Something sweet,* they'd say, *something small.* Every week, they kept it up, begging me for Hershey's, Reese's, M&Ms.

They told me about the other girls who had brought them cakes, chickens, paintings, and even armies. They never called me the right name, just kept saying, *Please, Regina, Joanie, Catherine, Ann. Kit-Kat, Milky Way, Mars. Something blest. King Size bag of something good.*

Finally, on All Saints Day, I gave in. Before the first Mass, I placed my pillowcase full of Halloween candy at the feet of a small, unpainted statue of Mary that stood beneath the stained-glass windows. I think the saints had been expecting this (they kept reminding me about Halloween), but they acted completely surprised, like a small child's parents opening a gift they had helped pick out. They sang my praises during the entire service, blazing sunlight even as, outside, it rained. I thought I was free. Then came their reward.

They wanted to teach me to fly. But nothing they taught me made any sense. They whispered about teenagers and jumping fish and a girl who couldn't walk. I tried to fight it, but the whispers won.

One night, they got me to climb to the top of our town's parking garage. It was winter, and I had to clamber up drifts of snow to get to the edge. *Now*, they said. I jumped.

For a minute, I swear, I hovered. That's why she saw me. Why she had time. The flying girl rocketed towards me, screaming, and caught me just before I hit the ground. The impact shattered her wrist, and she dropped me. I fell with a thud, and she crumpled into a ball beside me, crying. When my heart stopped pounding, I looked over and saw her shirt with the "A," her cape. I picked her up and carried her to the hospital. We trudged through the empty streets in the wee hours, the wind so cold our tears burned our faces, and in that silence we became lifelong friends.

I never heard the saints again. But sometimes, the flying woman told me she heard whispers urging her, "Higher. Higher." I like to think I was the voice that whispered, "Come back."

6. The Flying Woman in Transit

Last fall, the flying woman decided to migrate. I offered to come with her. I had taken up cycling during the bicyclist incident and had gotten pretty good. We bought matching bicycle clothes (she had discovered they were very aerodynamic) and set off for Miami, or some equally warm place with a preponderance of grocery stores and hair salons. We figured it was three weeks down to Florida, maybe longer if we decided to take breaks from traveling. We took back roads, and the flying woman flew high enough overhead to see around the next bend, but low enough to shout down to me, "Look at those cows!" or "What a pretty house!" Most of the stuff was too far away for me to see; two minutes later I'd spot a cluster of cows or a white and yellow farmhouse and yell back, "Oh, yeah!"

We took turns carrying the wheelchair, which was a little heavier than usual because we had fitted it with off-road tires for camping. At night we roasted cheap hot dogs and talked about old memories, small things we had left behind. Now that we were on the road, we felt like we had stepped out of our lives and finally become important.

We made it all the way down to Savannah this way. We thought about staying there until one of the locals told us sometimes they got snow. We were disappointed, but we decided to celebrate getting so far south. We got a motel on the edge of town and bought two bottles of cheap champagne. We had no music, so we sang, and the flying woman bounced against the ceiling. I held her hands and pulled her around the room, smiling up at her in drunken bliss.

Eventually, she asked me to pull her down, and after some jumping, I grabbed her leg and got her onto the bed. My nose brushed her cheek. She turned to look at me, and before I could think I kissed her. Her mouth was warm and wet. It tasted like bubbles. She pulled me on top of herself to keep from drifting. We kissed again. I felt her body rising beneath mine, in danger any moment of floating away.

We got our shirts off without incident, and with practiced hands unhooked each other's bras. I took her nipple in my mouth and felt her rise slightly, press her skin to mine. I grinned at her with unabashed happiness, and she pulled my mouth back to hers.

Even with her hands hooked behind the headboard, getting our pants off was a bit more of a challenge. We giggled raucously as I pulled jeans and panties off of her thin, tiny legs, which were already floating towards the stucco ceiling. I pressed my palm against her hip and kept her centered. I worked my way slowly, made her sigh in the ways I'd always imagined while tracing the contours of my own body. I traced the soft crevices of her lips, pressed my tongue into the deep, wet center. I heard her moan, and her whole body pushed against my grip. I kept my hand steady, held her back. Then she cried out, deep and unrestrained, and I felt her sink. I lifted my head and kissed her. She held me and whispered over and over, thank you thank you, oh god, you saved me.

7. The Flying Woman in Memory

I made a lot of plans that night, or at least I started to before I passed out. But when I woke in the morning, she was gone. I didn't believe it at first. I lay in bed, smiling, waiting for her to come back with breakfast, a map, a car, a home, anything, as the hours wore on. Finally I went to the front desk, and they told me she had checked out hours ago, paid our bill. I must have looked the way I felt, because the clerk touched my hand and asked if I was okay. I rode my bike in circles all day, asking about a woman who could fly, or perhaps one in a wheelchair, but no one had seen her. I stayed in the motel till my money ran out, but she never came back.

I don't know what happened. Maybe she was ashamed. Maybe she met the bicyclist at the Waffle House next door, on his way back to find her. Maybe migration is a solitary thing. I still live in Savannah. I still cut hair. Now I watch the sky. And sometimes I even go to church, and pray for that elusive miracle, not just the touch of lovers, but love.

FIRST KISSES FROM BEYOND THE GRAVE

Nik Houser

from Gargoyle Magazine

M Y MOTHER SAYS I'M HANDSOME. I BELIEVE HER. IT'S SOME-
thing she's always said and it's always done me, more or less,
the same amount of good.

"You're so lucky to be so smart and handsome!" she hollered from
the porch as I waited for the bus to my new school. I remember the
air was drastically cool for the tail end of summer, but I didn't want
to go back in that house for a jacket and risk a second hug, a second
kiss goodbye. I'd lost track of how many times Mom had said, "Don't
worry, you'll make friends in no time!" but I could stand no more of
those either. It was one of her favorite phrases, as though the clay of
creation was mine to shape and mold into a brand-new clique of ostra-
cized freaks with whom I had nothing in common save the fact that the
social trapeze had snapped between our fingers somewhere between
our eleventh and twelfth years.

So I stood at the curb, freezing like an idiot. I looked back at my
mom standing in the open doorway, unwavering optimism painted
over her face in great broad strokes. One of her legs hovered at a forty-
five-degree angle from the other, so that Mouselini, our cat, wouldn't
bolt out the door.

I smiled thinly, then looked back across the street where my best
friend Art White snickered as he waited for our bus. At the sight of

him, my head snapped back like a spider had swung in front of my face. I squished my eyes shut, then opened them, like a cartoon, which is what I must have looked like to the casual passerby, staring in astonishment as I was at the empty sidewalk across the street where my dead friend had stood only a moment before.

The morning after Art let all his blood run down the bathtub drain (rumor has it his mom kept running into the bathroom with cups, pitchers, and ice cube trays, trying to save some of it, some of him, before it all got away), the school bus stopped in front of his house. For years it had always stopped in front of his house and I'd always crossed the street to get on, just as I did that morning. Like always, I lurched to the back row of seats and propped myself against the window, reflexively leaving room for my pal, though I knew he would not be joining me.

The bus driver idled in front of Art's house. An uncomfortable silence fell over the crowded transport, something my English teacher Ms. Crane might refer to as a "pregnant pause." The driver was the only one on board who didn't already know. Everybody else had seen it on the news the previous night, had spread word via email and cell phones, text messages for the dead. Ask not for whom the cell tones, the cell tones for thee.

Gus the Bus looked up at me through the broad rearview mirror.

"I'm only waitin' another minute."

A month later, when I got the notice in the mail which informed me that I would be spending my latter three years of high school away from the boys and girls I had grown to love and loathe respectively, my mother was as positive as ever. It was June by then. School was out and Art was in the ground, missing his finals by a week.

"What a great opportunity!" Mom said when I was done reading the letter aloud at the dinner table. "You can meet new people and . . ."

I glared at her across the table as she struggled to maintain her unwavering optimism " . . . make new friends."

"You said the same thing to your cousin when he was sent to Riker's Island," Pop reminded her, looking over his glasses at the seven o'clock news on mute. My old man was nearsighted, but he loved the condescending erudition of looking over his tortoise-shell rims at whatever questionable piece of Creation happened to fall under his scrutiny.

"And he was so smart and handsome, too," Mom replied absently.

When the ghost of Art White had come and gone, I pulled the Notice of School District Transfer out of my pocket. It read like a draft notice, or one of those letters you get with a folded American flag to inform you that your child has been killed in action:

> Dear Mr. Henry,
> As superintendent of the Northside Public School District, it is my responsibility to inform you that as of September 1st, 2004, in an effort to further integrate our public schools, your street address will no longer be included in our district's educational zone roster and will henceforth be transferred to the Middle Plain School District. I apologize for any inconvenience this may cause.
> Sincerely,
> J.R. Sneider, Jr.
> Superintendent, Northside Public School District

No sooner had I finished reading my own death sentence than the familiar, noisome expulsion of school bus air brakes sounded off at the far end of my street. I looked up for the bus, but saw nothing—only the familiar line of SUVs parked along the curbs and in driveways. A stiff breeze picked up and made me shiver with cold for the first time since last April when the previous winter exhaled its death rattle. Or maybe it was the sudden silence that ran that chill up my spine. The street was dead quiet, a far cry from the familiar din of leaf-blowers, garbage trucks, and protein shake blenders that usually accompanied Monday mornings on our fair boulev—

CREEEEEE-SWOOSH!

The door to the school bus swung open in front of me, coming within an inch of my face and exhaling a cloud of dusty, tomb-like air.

Startled by its sudden appearance, I backpedaled on the wet grass, tripped on a sprinkler, and fell flat on my back.

I lay there for a second, staring up at the overcast sky, trying to breathe. It had been a long time since I'd had the wind knocked out of me, and for a second I thought I was dying. At last the airlock in my chest opened up and I sat bolt upright, panting, and stared up at the great black school bus humming cantankerously in front of my house like a hearse built for group rates.

Where the fuck did that come from?

I looked up through the open door, at the driver staring ahead at the road, black jeans and a gray hooded sweatshirt draped over his wire-hanger frame. The sweatshirt's hood covered his eyes as he slowly turned his head toward me. The rest of his body remained frozen in place, both hands glued to the steering wheel.

I stood up, grabbed my sprinkler-soaked backpack, and looked back at my house, an are-you-seeing-what-I'm-seeing? face pointed at the empty doorway. Mom was gone. Only Mouselini stood on the front step, eyes wide and tail shocked-up, a tremulous rumble sounding from the depths of his twelve-year-old gut like a drawstring dolly that's been buried alive.

Behind me, the bus's engine revved, once. I turned and started up its steps, heard the door close behind me while the driver's hands remained on the wheel. At the top step I paused and stared down at my chauffeur, at the empty black space where the shade of his hood covered his eyes.

"Morning." I slipped on the thin, polite smile I saved for teachers, strangers, extended family.

I looked back at the empty bus. The seats and windows were in decent condition, but dusty and tired-looking, as though the great vehicle had only just been called back into service after decades of neglect.

"First to get on, last to get off, I guess." Again that thin smile, more for myself than the driver now.

The driver turned his pale, expressionless face back to the road as the houses, cars, and trees began to slip slowly past the windows. The bus betrayed no perceptible shudder or lurch when we pulled away from my home, as though we remained still while the stage set of the neighborhood was drawn back to the flies.

When I first received the notice of transfer, I thought my folks were responsible. I wasn't exactly inconsolable after Art leapfrogged over his elders into the Great Beyond, but I wasn't the same either. I lost weight, stopped sleeping, stopped jerking off. I think the fact that I put down my penis worried the 'rents more than putting down my fork. They'd read that loss of libido was a common part of the grieving process for any close friend or relative. But they also knew that he was my *only* close friend, and that I was dreading the fall. More than any summer before, the phonetics of the forthcoming season sounded to me, and to them, like some dramatic plunge I was about to take, a forty-foot dive into a glass of water.

Mom and Pop were both teachers at my school. Having them with me at home, with their lingering smells of chalk dust and textbooks, the tiny snowflakes of spiral-bound notebook paper torn from its binding caught unmelting in the hems of their clothes, was like bringing the funeral home with me. It was because of this that I started to wonder if maybe the transfer wouldn't be so bad.

Strangely enough, however, it was when I suggested this very notion, and the uncharacteristically positive outlook inherent therein, that my folks started worrying, in earnest, about my mental well-being.

As the bus drove on, the sky grew dark. My surroundings grew increasingly unfamiliar as we passed into a stretch of suburbs which had taken an early turn toward fall and even winter. On the street below, the bus's enormous tires scattered decay-colored leaves across sidewalks that crumbled into the road like rows of rotting teeth. It soon became apparent that we would be making no other stops.

Jesus Christ, I thought as we passed into the overcast farmlands beyond the city—a bleak stretch of wild, untended wheat interrupted only by the occasional skeleton of a burned-out barn, *I've been transferred to Deliverance High*. The sky was nearly black. The sight of it took me back to the tornado drills we practiced on days like this in the second grade, when we would duck under our desks with our thickest textbooks held tight over our heads, a mere three hundred pages of long division standing between us and total, whirling annihilation.

Eventually, the rolling fields gave way to a vast stretch of incinerated woodlands—black, emaciated cedars reaching out to the day-for-night sky like the arms of the damned on Judgment Day. I opened my mouth to holler down the row of seats, to casually inquire about the fire which had apparently torn through this area. But when I opened my mouth, the nervous vacuum inside me would let no words escape. I looked up at the mirror suspended above the driver, at the yawning sweatshirt hood which now absorbed his features entirely, then at the massive fog bank rushing toward us as we began to accelerate.

The landscape was quickly erased by the fog, as though we'd traveled beyond the borders of Nature's grand composition and were barreling toward the edge of God's very canvas. I closed my eyes, felt the bus shimmy and shake as it continued to accelerate. Every bump in the road felt like the one that would dislodge a wheel, every turn was the road ending at a thousand-foot cliff.

"Please, God," I muttered to myself, a knee-jerk theological reaction. "Please."

The word itself was the prayer, not so much asking for a safe arrival, but to simply let me *keep* everything that I had and was, to finish the things I'd planned to do. The bus shook and shivered, tires screaming against the road. All my blood pressed against the surface of my skin in a centrifuge of fear. Everything that had ever happened to me: birth, laughter, friends, growing up, jerking off, Christmas, was boiled down to one word—

"PLEASE!" I screamed, my cry punctuated by the sound of the bus's door folding into itself as we came to a gentle stop. We were there.

I marched down the aisle on wobbly sea legs, bracing myself on the rubbery, crimson seatbacks. When I came to the driver I stopped to say something nasty, or sarcastic, or grateful, but when I saw his hands gripping the wheel, knuckles pressed against their gloved surfaces like only bone hid beneath, I thought better of it and climbed down the stairs to the curb.

"A fucking cemetery?" I asked myself aloud.

I surveyed the endless rows of tombstones to which I'd been delivered. No school. No students. Nothing but graves, trees, hills, fog.

I turned around to get back on the bus and ask the driver wh—

The bus was gone.

I looked down either side of the empty road, swallowed entirely by mist after ten yards in either direction. The driver had taken off as silently as he had arrived at my house that morning.

"Great. So what the fuck am I supposed to do now?"

As if in response, a lone crow cackled down at me from a nearby tree and took off over the stones. I watched him glide, then turn to croak at me again. A third time I watched him cruise out a dozen yards, double back, and let out another sonorous cackle.

"I'm already looking back at this and wondering what the fuck I was thinking," I said. I hopped the low wooden fence and followed the old black bird into the cemetery.

Most of the headstones were for people who'd died before I was born. Some dated within the year. Covered with moss and undergrowth, the sweat stains of finality and neglect, grave markers of every size and shape, from hand-carved mausoleums to wooden planks nailed together in cross formation, covered the surrounding hills in rows so crooked the caretaker had to be either cross-eyed, blind, or both.

When the old crow and I crested the last hill I looked back at the boneyard, at so many stones like goose bumps running up the spine of some tired leviathan.

I turned around to see where the crow had led me—a vista no less gloomy and depressing than the graveyard.

My new school was flat and broad and as featureless as it was silent. With a resigned sigh, I crossed a field of knee-high weeds, at either end of which stood a tall, crooked football goal, and hiked up the parking circle to the empty campus. The building itself was gray and unremarkable. The front door was unlocked. Inside, the lights were out. The only light came from the windows that lined a hallway to my right. The other side of the hall was lined with blue lockers, with the occasional break where a classroom door could be found. The tiled floor was white and clean. I started walking to see if anyone was home. All in all, it looked like your basic high school on a still, overcast Sunday afternoon. It was, however, Monday morning, and by now I was more annoyed than intimidated. I could be at my old school now, getting depressed, getting bored, getting horny. But instead I found myself wandering the empty halls of a forei—

What the fuck was that?

I whirled around, heart suddenly racing, more nervous than I'd let myself believe, and spied a tall locker door hanging halfway open a few yards away.

Whatever.

I turned back to where I was headed an—

"Who the fuck is there?!" I shouted, spinning around when the locker slammed shut behind me, its flat echo continuing past me down the hall.

"WHO—"

The locker creaked halfway open, slowly.

Someone's in there.

I took a step back with one foot, a step forward with the other, half brave and half smart. The front foot won. Slowly, I made my way toward the locker, sliding along the windows that lined the opposite wall to try and get a peek around the open door. The combination latch was missing. Only two rough screw holes remained where the lock had been torn off. I opened my mouth to say something to whoever was inside, some idle threat, but the vacuum inside my stomach had started up again, so that all I could manage was to slowly reach out, curl my fingers around the rusty locker door, and—

BA-RIIIING!!! went the homeroom bell. I jumped, slipped, cracked my head on the floor.

I stared up at the ceiling. The homeroom bell rang in my ears, bounced off the tile under my head. My first reaction was to panic that I was late, but once the combination of shock, terror, and pain had ebbed to a dull throb between my ears, I asked myself, "Late for what?" I didn't expect an answer.

Then the sounds came.

Something stirred outside.

I stood up and looked out the window at the hideous, skinless face staring in at me.

"Late," moaned the walking corpse on the opposite side of the glass. He looked about my age, his face puffed out in gaseous boils of decomposition. The flesh of his jaw hung loose, exposing a bloated green tongue laminated in pus and mud. He wore blue jeans and a varsity letterman's jacket. A backpack hung from his right shoulder. Dirt littered his unkempt hair, filled the spaces between his teeth.

I didn't even know I was screaming. The sound of my terror echoed down the hall, harmonizing with the great earthy rumble rising up from the ground outside as the tiled floor beneath my feet began to quake. Scared beyond coordination, I stumbled back on stilted legs and crashed into the wall of lockers behind me. My eyes stayed glued to the window, growing ever wider. Scores of rotten, worm-riddled bodies staggered from the cemetery beyond the football field, dusting the consecrated earth from their team jackets and cheerleader uniforms as they stalked en masse toward the school. No sooner had the first of the walking dead reached the parking lot than a ghostly white school bus pulled into the parking circle and expulsed a swarm of iridescent vapors who drifted toward the school dragging their souls and sack lunches behind them.

Thisisadreamthisisadreamthisisafuckingnightmare, I chanted in my head, pinching myself over and over until a trail of stinging, bloody fingernail marks lit up my arm like Christmas tree lights.

"You'll want to get those looked at." A voice from inside the locker behind me.

Again I shrieked, turned around, staggered into the middle of the hallway, surrounded by drifting, translucent ghouls from the white school bus. Twenty yards to my left, the front doors of the school opened, admitting the horde of teenage undead as they made their way inside like a river of coagulating blood. I looked back at the talking locker, which was now open. A tall, pale kid stepped out from within. He stretched out his folded arms and yawned, exposing two rows of healthy white razor-sharp teeth.

"Hey, watch it!" warned a female voice. The tall boy's clothes wavered in an unseen breeze.

"Fuckin' vapors." A second kid emerged from the next locker down, his face as gaunt and bloodless as his neighbor's. Beside him, one of the walking dead from outside bumped into a locker and fiddled clumsily with its combination.

"Next one down, you *moron!*" hollered a voice from inside the locker. The zombie moaned, lurched one step to the left, opened his locker, and pulled out a spiral notebook riddled with teeth marks.

"Hey!" yelled the voice from the locker. "That bonehead locked me in, you guys!"

The two boys in front of me snickered.

"You guys suck!" The voice banged on the inside of the locker.

"Yeah," the tall one chuckled. "That's kind of our thing."

The two vampiric jocks stalked down the hall, laughing wildly. By now the hall was swarming with rotten, lurching corpses, pale red-eyed kids staring ravenously at the cuts on my arms, and a gaggle of ghostly, transparent figures drifting over and through the meandering rabble. Wolf-men, swamp things, and hellhounds ambled to and fro, chatting briefly with each other as they parted ways to head to class.

"Come on, you guys!" pleaded the voice from inside the locker. "Lemme out!"

By the time the second bell rang, I was on my feet and the rest of the hall was empty. Well beyond shock, my heartbeat returned to normal. Calmly, I surveyed my surroundings. The occasional puddle of blood and ectoplasm notwithstanding, the loose bits of paper and scattered contraband cigarette butts at my feet gave the impression of a typical, harried Monday morning at Average Joe High School, USA.

"Hey," came the sad voice from the locker in front of me.

I turned to look at the three dark slats at the top of the locker door.

"Hey, new kid, lemme out or I'll suck the jelly from your eyeballs."

I stood there, staring blankly at the locker, slightly perplexed and, perhaps as a result of previous exposure to the relentless bullying I'd witnessed at my old high school, slightly amused. He clearly wasn't one of them. Just trying to fit in.

"Please?" the voice said, pitiful now, drained of all pretense of malice or ferocity.

I stepped up to the locker and tapped the combination lock. I always felt sorry for geeks and nerds, always helped them pick up their books while they dug wedgies out of their lower intestines.

"What's your combination?" I asked the locker.

"Six . . . six . . . five," the voice muttered hollowly.

At last the locker opened and out spilled the lanky, woe-begotten creature inside.

"You'd think with all the brains they ate, those fucking zombies would be like, geniuses, right?"

The kid bent down, dusted himself off. His voice sounded familiar. At first I was unsure. It sounded deeper and farther away than when I'd last heard it, a certain knowledge of things beyond haunting its cadence. But the sarcasm was unmistakable, and when he finally straightened himself up and showed me his bloodless, trademark smirk, all doubt vanished.

"Art?" I gasped, dropping my backpack into a splat of green, luminous jelly at my feet. I looked down at the long, deep canyons he'd cut into his arms only three months before. "Is that you?"

"Holy shit, man," my friend laughed, dead eyes wide with friendly astonishment. He leaned forward, pressed his cold, stiff chest against mine and hugged me. "Welcome to Purgatory High!"

"English, History, Health, Woodshop, Geometry, P.E.?"

Behind the registrar's desk, a skeleton in a moth-bitten sky blue pantsuit stared blankly up at me through a pair of faded pink reading glasses as I read my schedule aloud. Behind me, Art sat reading an old newspaper.

"Would you look at that," he muttered to himself. "Ollie North sold guns to Iran. Wait a minute . . . " He flipped over the newspaper, examined the date, then shrugged. "News to me," he obliged, and continued reading.

"Is that it?" I looked up from my schedule to the registrar, at the heavy layer of foundation mortared evenly across the surface of her skull, punctuated by two slashes of red-light-red lipstick, explosions of rouge, and neon-blue eye shadow, all watched over by a magnificent, Babel Tower beehive hairdo. A regular Bloomingdale's Day of the Dead Special.

"Is there a problem?" the secretary asked. Her rusty screen-door voice rose up from the center of her rib cage and escaped through two empty eye sockets adorned by a set of outrageously long false eyelashes.

"What do dead people need Geometry for?"

"You're not dead."

"I know. And yet I find myself asking the same question. I mean, come on, Health? You don't *have* health. You're dead!"

"This is Middle Plain High, young man. *Purgatory High*, if you will. *Good* little boys and girls, who die the *right* way, aren't sent here."

"Wait a minute. You mean I got transferred to like, Juvenile Hall for the Damned?" I threw up my hands. "That's great! Fantastic! Whatever. Doesn't matter." I leaned on the counter. "The point is I'm, you know, *alive*. Right? So obviously there's been a mistake. I shouldn't be here."

"That's what they all say."

By the time we got back to first period, Homeroom was over and English class had begun.

"Ah, Mr. Henry, welcome to our class." Mr. Marley stood in front of the blackboard, dressed in a turn-of-the-century waistcoat, dusty gray pantaloons and a powdered wig lying limp over his scalp, as though it had been ridiculed and debased by larger, more imposing wigs until all sense of pride or decorum had been wrung from its monochrome curls. Draped across the pedagogue's chest, over his arms, and around his legs was a seemingly endless length of rusty chains from which a series of padlocks and strong boxes rattled and clanged with his every movement.

I stood at the head of the class, staring at the erudite, emaciated apparition. He returned my gaze with polite impatience, no doubt accustomed to new students gawking at him.

"Chains you forged in life?" I asked casually.

He nodded like I'd asked if he'd gotten a haircut.

"Okey-dokey," I replied and turned to search for an empty seat.

As Mr. Marley began the lecture, I surveyed my classmates from the back row. I watched a gargoyle pass notes to a drowned drama queen covered over with seaweed and bright patches of dried brine. A studious nerd, the noose with which he'd hung himself still hanging around his neck, took notes while a bright red she-devil in a cheerleader's uniform giggled behind him.

Not much different than a regular high school, Art scribbled on a scrap of paper and passed to me. *Right?*

In the exact moment I finished reading the note, an anonymous spitball slammed into the five-inch-tall aborted fetus taking notes in front of me. He was dressed in a tiny basketball jersey and warm-up pants.

"What up, nigga'?!" the tiny voice hollered up at me, mistaking me for the perpetrator of the spitball. "You got a muthafuckin' problem!? You wanna piece a'this, son?!"

"No thanks," I said in the distracted fashion that warded off most every gangster and jock at my old school. I jotted down my response to Art's note: *Not as such.*

History class, as it turned out, was History of Everything. Purgatory High, apparently, had dug its foundations outside of the conventional space-time continuum, and could look at the history of the universe from a fairly objective vantage.

"Dude." Art put a hand on my shoulder, "I don't think it's a good idea for you to go in there."

"You mean about me gaining potentially hazardous foreknowledge of mankind's future which I could use to alter the course of human events?"

"Huh? No, I mean I got this joint from Lenny Baker and we should go smoke it."

"Nah, I'll pass, this whole day's been like one long, bad trip anyway."

"Suit yourself."

Over the next forty-five minutes I learned that (a) I would never be famous, (b) mankind would never be conquered by super-intelligent robots of our own design, and (c) ipso facto, my lifelong ambition of being the leader of the human resistance against their titanium-plated tyranny would never be fulfilled.

Such is life.

Next was Health Class.

On my way into the classroom, Missy Nefertiti, a hot little mummified number shrinkwrapped in a layer of Egyptian cotton no thicker than an anorexic neutrino, stumbled behind me in the hallway, spilling the contents of her purse at my feet.

"Thanks," she said absently as I knelt to help her.

I picked up a small, pearly jar which contained her brain, then another for her liver, and a third for her lungs.

"Where's the one for your heart?" I asked as we stood up together.

"No room," she replied. "I'd have to carry a bigger purse."

Five minutes into Health Class Ms. Tenenbaum-Forrester, a decomposing zombie, announced that this week would be Sexual Education and Awareness Week. It was at this point that I raised my hand, looked into my teacher's deflated, rotten-tomato eyes, and respectfully asked to be excused.

Lunch was no better.

"You gonna eat those brains?" Art asked from across our table. Roland, the gangster fetus from first period, sat to my left, poised on Missy Nefertiti's lap and free-styling to all who would listen, most notably, her big round gazungas.

"Ask George." I pointed to the towering zombie in a Middle Plain High basketball jersey sitting beside me. "They're his anyway."

Without a word, Art reached over the table and speared a forkful of gray matter from my tray.

"So what do you think so far, man?" He gestured at our surroundings with his fork.

I turned around, glanced back at the lunch line where a tall vampire dressed in fishnet tights and a Joy Division T-shirt leaned over the serving area and sank his teeth into the lunch lady's neck. I looked back at my friend sucking the dendrites from an oblongata kabob.

"I think you should chew with your mouth closed."

That afternoon, when the last horn of the apocalypse rang out the end of the school day, Art and I wandered back through the cemetery as our fellow students made their way to their graves, loaded up with that night's homework.

"Hey, Art," I said. "I've been meaning to—"

"Think fast!" interrupted a distant voice.

I turned around in time to throw up my hands and block a dive-bombing football before it spread my nose over my face like a warm pad of butter.

"Sorry about that, new guy!" From the direction of the dive-bombing pigskin, a burly, middle-aged man as wide as he was tall, dressed in a shimmering red leotard, hurdled a nearby tombstone and landed in front of us.

"You teach my gym class." I spoke to his huge, waxed handlebar mustache.

"That's right," the strong man agreed. "I was watching you today. You looked good. You've got good moves."

"I sat in a tree while everyone else ran around the track."

"Yeah, well, you've got to be in good shape to climb trees, right?"

"I was smoking two cigarettes at once."

"And *that's* the kind of go-getter attitude we need on our football roster, son! That little sneak attack earlier was my subtle way of testing potential new recruits!"

"There's a football team here?"

"Of course!"

"Do you get hoarse very often?"

"Excuse me?"

"Nothing. Besides, I didn't even catch the ball."

"But you managed to block it, which is better than most, let me tell you. So whad'ya say, son?"

"Um, no thanks. I'm not really what you'd call a team player."

There was a pause here, where I could almost hear the magnetic tape inside the coach's head reach the end of its reel and start rewinding itself for the next recruit.

"Well hey, no hard feelings!" he said and patted me on the back. He scanned the horizon and found his mark.

"Hey, DeMarco! Think fast!"

We turned and kept walking.

"Isn't Tim DeMarco deaf?" Art asked.

I shrugged, stared at my feet. We walked in silence for a time, weaving around the tombstones. Angels etched in granite stared up at us from stones marking the graves of children. Dead leaves pressed into the ground underfoot.

"I dunno," Art said at last.

"Huh?" I looked up at my friend.

"I don't know why I did it." My friend stared down at the dark little rivers running up the topography of his forearms, the barren, tilled flesh. "You know how, like, when you're trying to do something that takes a long time, like fixing something, or balancing something, and after a bunch of tries you finally just throw it at the wall because you're so frustrated? I don't know—that was how I felt about pretty much everything, I guess. I just sort of threw my life at the wall. I was tired of trying to fix it. Of course, it was only after I showed up here that I realized it wasn't *broken* to start with, just not *finished* yet. I dunno. That's what the school counselor told me. I guess that makes sense."

I didn't know what to say. It had been a long summer, during which I'd developed a staggering resentment for my best pal and his cowardly exit. I was angry at how selfish he could be, leaving me alone with this fucked-up world.

At last we came upon the road which had led me from my front door to Death's door that morning. The sky was overcast and still, as it had been all day.

"I was pretty mad," I said at last, staring down at the uneven pavement.

Art let out a long breath, like he'd been holding it in for a while.

"I'm sorry, man," he said. He looked wistfully up at the treetops across the street. "If I could change anything . . . If I could go back and change *anything* I'd *ever* done, or left *undone* . . . I'd have felt up Suzie Newman at the Freshman Homecoming Dance."

I laughed and punched his shoulder as hard as I could, heard something crack under the putty-like flesh.

"Had I but known she'd become the biggest slut in our fucking class!" he entreated the clouds overhead, throwing his head back melodramatically and clenching his fists until the squeal of air brakes snatched the laughter out of our throats and tossed it on the ground like so much loaded dice.

We stood at the edge of the road, staring up at the hooded driver ᵇis great black bus idling restlessly.

"Well, uh," Art backed away slowly. His eyes never left the driver. "I'll see you tomorrow man."

"Dude, wait!" I jogged a couple of steps to where my friend stood poised to sprint back through the boneyard. "You should come back with me," I whispered, and reached out for his shoulder. No sooner had my hand touched him then a bolt of lightning screamed out of the sky and seized my forearm in a cataclysmic Indian burn. The shock of the bolt knocked me back six feet through the dazzling, electrified air. I landed at the edge of the road, the wind knocked out of me, head buzzing like a pressure cooker full of hornets. I stood up slowly, gasping, reaching for the stars that swirled around my smoking head. By the time the Big Bang orbiting my head had dissipated in the encroaching dusk, my friend was gone.

I looked down at my arm, which was turning green, then up at the sky. Broad, rumbling thunderheads stared back at me like a reproachful parent. I remembered my uncle telling me about the time he was struck by lightning during his barnstorming days. He said it was like "God put a hand on my shoulder." He also said it "hurt like a motherfucker."

I craned my neck for a last glance at my friend, but there was no one, not even a crow.

"See you tomorrow," I said to cemetery, the vast stone harvest.

My only assignment that night was to memorize a poem of my choice, which I did, while nursing my fried appendage back to life and listening to my folks converse politely about their student, Ginger Banks, who had been brutally slain at school that afternoon. The cadence of John Donne bounced around my brain, playing tag with phrases like "teeth marks," "massive trauma," and "still at large."

Once my homework was done I could eat, as had been the rule of my family since my first day of kindergarten. The table was set with the summer dishes, though the brisk, teasing breath of fall could be felt in the breeze coming through the propped kitchen door. Autumn was my season—so haughty, yet sexy, it always reminded me of an aloof librarian with a brain full of Hawthorne and rabid, sexual fantasies.

Both my parents had a habit of reading at the table. You could always tell what kind of mood they were in by what they were reading. Grading papers meant they didn't want to talk. A newspaper meant they wanted to talk, but not about themselves, that the outside world would do just fine. A novel meant they were feeling romantic, while poetry meant I was going to sleep in the garage if I didn't want to lie awake to the sound of groans, spanking noises, and all manner of nauseating aural hullabaloo. Dr. Mengele, for all his crimes against nature and man, unknowingly left one form of torture untapped throughout his long years of evil: the sound of your own parents talking dirty to each other.

When I sat down at the table that night, I saw a folded *New York Times* beside my mother's plate, and a book of two thousand crossword puzzles adorning my father's place setting. I was safe. The table was set with two polite candles, three steaming chicken potpies, a bowl of green beans, and news of a bloodbath.

"I don't know what this world is coming to," my mother said, one hand on her paper, the other around her fork. "That poor girl."

"Didn't you used to have a crush on her, Zack?" My father glanced over the rim of his glasses at my blurred visage.

I shrugged and blew on a spoonful of thick, under-salted chowder. My mother was allergic to salt.

I thought about Ginger Banks, about her fiery red hair, and the first time I'd ever whacked off. She was the one I'd thought about on that distant autumn afternoon not so dissimilar from the evening we were presently enjoying. I'd always imagined her pubic hair as a tiny, quivering lick of flame where her warm, rosy thighs came together. I remember ejaculating far less than I thought I would.

"And in the women's lavatory of all places," my mother continued.

I held my spoon in front of my mouth, stared down at its congealing contents while my mother described the state in which Ginger Banks had been found—her head bashed in, with little bits of bone and brains scattered across the floor like the dashed dreams of every boy who'd ever dreamed of standing below her in a pep rally "cheeramid."

"Bruce Salinger is beside himself," my mother informed us. "I understand they had quite a thing."

"I thought she was dating George Dickson."

"Hmm, not sure. She could have been dating them both, for all I know, and for all either of them would care."

"She took quite a reputation with her when she went. Ms. Knotsworth was talking about it in the lounge."

"Speaking of the lounge, that new boy Pennybaum wandered in today while I was pouring myself a cup of java. What an odd young man, so pale and quiet. I think he was rather shaken up about what happened to poor Ginger. He was just wandering around in a daze. When I asked him what was the matter, all he could say was 'Brains.'"

"I think he's from Slovenia. Or is it Pennsylvania? Some vania or another. Which reminds me, your Aunt Ruth from Fairbanks called."

"Now why would Pennsylvania remind you of Fairbanks?"

"Oh, I don't know, it's just one of those things. Actually, I think I was at the supermarket today and I saw this can of tuna from Fairbanks right next to . . . "

Listening to my folks, I felt my appetite burn up and vanish, like my stomach was made of bright, flashing magnesium. I couldn't eat, but couldn't excuse myself from a full plate. So I sat there and watched my parents eat, in awe of these dull, lifeless creatures.

"I'm a nobody.

"Who are you?

"Are you a nobody too?"

"So let me get this straight," Art whispered from his desk. At the front of the class, Missy Nefertiti recited Emily Dickinson with all the passion and understanding of an empty Gucci shoebox. Tucked under her arm was a pearly, hand-carved jar adorned with the head of Anubis, in which she kept her brain. "You're saying that if *you* were the one that found Ginger Banks' corpse, you *wouldn't* sneak a peek before you called the cops? I'm sorry—which one of us is dead again?"

"All I'm saying is that it would depend on how gross she was," I hushed back. "I mean, her freakin' head was bashed in."

"So," Art replied. "You've *seen* her *head*."

Missy Nefertiti finished her poem and took her seat in front of Art.

"I heard she was already dead by the time they found her," Art informed me as I stood to walk to the front of the class, "before her last rites could be performed. Her soul's lost, dude! She's totally transferring here!"

I stood before my classmates, scanned their eyes, horns, and globules of protoplasm. I thought about Ginger Banks, and about her transferring to our school. I thought about cold pussy.

"Death be not proud," I began.

"Mr. Henry," the skeletal registrar addressed me as I waited to see Principal Grimm, "it appears that you were just dying to come back and see us."

"Was that supposed to be funny?" I asked from my chair.

"Do I look like I know funny?"

I glared at the tacky, painted skull glaring back at me with all the knowledge of the grave, then at the great wigwam of coiled, purple locks festooned on top of it.

"So, care to explain why you're here?"

I thought back to Mr. Marley interrupting my poem, waving his iron-clad arms in embarrassed indignation. As I'd gone back to my desk to collect my things, Roland the gangster fetus had offered me his condolences.

"Shit, son," he'd said, holding up a tiny fist for my fist to bump. "Grimm's secretary is scary, yo. They call 'er the muthafuckin' Clown of Dachau. Good luck."

At first I'd felt apprehensive about seeing the principal on my second day of school. But when an aborted fetus feels sorry for you, you have nowhere to go but up.

"So," I asked the neon skull to pass the time, "how did you die?"

There was a moment's pause, statistically long enough for someone to die in a car accident.

"A fanatical cultist blew himself up in the drive-thru where I worked. He was protesting the Korean War. He wasn't even Korean."

I paused a moment to reflect on the suddenness of it all, at having no time to say goodbye, to leave so many things left undone.

"Did you have to wear roller skates at work?"

"Yes."

"Mr. Henry, we have a problem."

Principal Grimm sat behind his tidy, faux-wood desk in a brown suit with a green tie. The pinstripes of his suit were the same width as the wood grain running along his desk. My first impression was that he was growing out of his furniture.

"You know, sir," I began casually, with just a hint of condescension. I've always found the best way to deal with authority figures is to talk to them like they're delivering your pizza. "I'm sorry if the poem offended anyone. I thought it was apropos."

Of course I knew perfectly well that my poem might offend the teacher. That was the point—the point of the poem and of high school in general, it seemed: Four years of sailing as fast as we could toward the edge of the earth to see if it was round.

"There's no need for an insincere apology, Mr. Henry. That's not what I need from you." Mr. Grimm gripped the surface of his desk and wheeled his rolling chair around to my side as all sense of subtle mockery was wrung from my guts like a sponge full of blood. I stared down at his lower half, or lack thereof: His brown blazer ended in a bloody tangle of bone, sinew, and strips of torn flesh. Averting my gaze to let the nausea pass, I looked up at the surfboard mounted on the wall behind him. An elliptical path of two-hundred-some-odd teeth marks ran up the middle of the board where a massive chunk was missing. "You see, the same clerical error which was responsible for your transfer here, transferred one of our students to your old school, and apparently, there's been some sort of incident."

I recalled poor Ginger Banks and her bashed-in brains.

"Is she coming here?" I asked, perhaps a little too eagerly.

"Excuse me?"

"Ginger Banks. Is she transferring here, now that she's, you know, dead?"

Mr. Grimm's face looked somewhere far off, as though called by a bell only his ears could hear.

"I really couldn't say," he began tentatively. "What I can say is this: you can't go back to your old school while Mr. Pennybaum is enrolled there. However, if he were to somehow meet an untimely *end* in your world, perhaps through the sudden rupture of his cranial cavity, you would be able to resume your place at your former alma mater."

"You're saying I have to kill this guy to go back to my old school?"

"Well, technically, he can't be *killed*, per se, because he already died. He's undead. A zombie, in the popular nomenclature."

"You want me to *kill* this guy?"

Mr. Grimm sighed and wiped a layer of ectoplasm from his perspiring brow.

"As of . . ." Mr. Grimm looked at his watch, held up an index finger. He opened his mouth, made ready to bring his hand down, then paused, and spoke quietly to his watch. *"What are you waiting fo*—NOW! Paul Pennybaum has killed three more of your former classmates."

"So you want me to stop him before he kills again."

"Mr. Henry, with deaths so sudden, the victims are bound to end up here. If this continues, our student-to-teacher ratio will be drastically upset. We're underfunded as it is. Lockers, desks, and food will start to run low."

I looked up at a corkboard mounted under the surfboard. This month's cafeteria menu was pinned to it by a single black thumbtack. I perused today's menu.

"So you want me to stop him before you run out of meatloaf?"

A long pause. Long enough for someone to realize that someone else has loved them all along.

"Yes," the principal nodded, and rolled back behind his desk. His stomach rumbled. Behind the desk a dripping noise pricked the momentary silence. "That sounds about right."

When I left Mr. Grimm's office she was there, standing in profile, looking down at her new class schedule, just as I had done nearly twenty-four hours earlier, with equal amounts of disbelief and anger. I imagine it sucks finding out you're dead, especially when you were so popular. Ginger Banks was tiny, pale, her head shaved where they'd cleaned up the wound for her autopsy. She wore the cheerleader's uniform in which she'd died. Long, dark blood stains ran down the back of her white top.

I approached and opened my mouth to say something clever or sarcastic to the secretary to show Ginger how funny I was, how alive and breathing I was. But when I got close and felt all the boy in me flare up my front in a wave of campfire warmth, the speech centers of my brain stalled out. I tried to talk, to say something casual yet enigmatic. But I couldn't form a coherent sound, frozen in a mute, awkward panic,

mouth open and eyes wide, like a wax museum dummy getting mo-
lested by a lonely security guard.

I came to my senses when she turned toward me and reflexively
drew a wave of nonexistent hair behind her ear. She'd been crying.
Watercolor veins of tear-diluted eye shadow ran down her cheeks. I
closed my mouth, kept staring.

I love watching people cry. Maybe I shouldn't, but I do, and I've
done nothing to change.

Still, I wanted to say something nice, something cool yet empa-
thetic. But the problem was that I'm none of those things, really. Well,
maybe I'm nice, but I'm too selfish to call myself a nice *person* and still
be honest. Either way, I wanted to make her feel better about being
dead. But how?

Say something, I thought to myself. *Make it good. Show some insight
into the human condition that will lessen the blow of eternity rolling out
before her.*

"Hey, at least now you can eat all you want and never get fat."

"Excuse me?" Ginger sniffed, wiped her nose on her bare forearm.

*Oh God, just keep going you idiot. Don't stop till you can end on some-
thing good.*

"Uh . . . you'll never get a pimple again?" *Never mind. Stop now.*
"And you can smoke all you want."

"Who *are* you?" she asked.

"Plus, you died when you were still totally hot." *Please stop. For your
own good.* "Just let that little nugget sink in."

For the love all that's holy . . . STOP!

She paused. Let it all sink in. More mad. Less sad. I have that effect
on women.

"What are you, kidding?" she replied. "I'm freakin' *bald* you
moron!"

From behind the counter, Ms. Needlemeyer, the Clown of Dachau,
cleared her throat.

"Mr. Henry—"

I held up a single index finger, finally feeling the residual ire of Principal Grimm's admission that my transfer here had been a clerical error.

"Can it rollerball?" I snapped, still locking eyes with Ginger, who flinched a little and smiled. Now that I'd made a complete fool of myself and had no chance of her being attracted to me, I could actually relax, be myself, and say something interesting. "Look, Ginger, the most popular kid in school is an aborted fetus. I think bald's gonna work."

"Are you like, retarded or something?" Missy Nefertiti asked. Roland sat on her lap, leaning back against her tightly wrapped midriff. Missy took a jiggly bite of blood-flavored Jell-O.

"No doubt, son," Roland concurred. "You gotta be outta your goddamn mind."

"Whatever," I said absently. Across the cafeteria, Ginger ate alone at her table. "She looks alive."

"She dead, son," Roland said.

"So are you."

"But you're *not*," Art chimed in. "There are like, *laws* against that shit. Not like, *don't smoke pot laws*, but, you know, *real* ones."

I thought back to the previous day, to the lightning that had struck me when I suggested Art return with me to the land of the living. My arm was still a faded shade of aquamarine, and twitched when I tried to make a fist. What would become of my soul if I made it with Ginger Banks? Would it turn blue and feel fuzzy for a week? I could live with that.

"There's more than one high school for people like us, dude."

I glanced up at Art.

"What do you mean?"

"I mean stick around for the football game after school."

"*Football game?* Who the hell are we playing?"

Roland, Art, and Missy exchanged a look. Across the cafeteria, a pair of she-devils from the Spirit Squad sat down at Ginger's table and said something that made her smile.

"Why isn't anybody cheering?"

"What's the point?" Art asked. "It won't make any difference."

Even the cheerleaders sat on the sidelines watching the slaughter in total silence.

"The sun ain't even set yet, son."

I looked down at Roland sitting between me and Missy on the decrepit wooden bleacher. All around us the students and faculty made polite conversation in the packed stands, rarely watching the game as our hometown boys, the Middle Plain Lost Souls, were taken to school by the Inferno High Horsemen. Our players, a group of small, unassuming squirts with all the fighting spirit of a euthanized tree sloth were squaring off against the greatest generals of Satan's Legions. On the opposing sidelines, the Dark One himself sat in the bleachers, a great swirling mass of flame and agony contained in an old ratty letterman's jacket.

The grassy plain before us looked like a minefield in which every bomb had been detonated, so many times had our poor, brave lads been driven face-first into the sod. The score was thirty-six to zero. The opposing team had already rushed five hundred yards. A buzzer rang out to end the first quarter as the surrounding hills slurped down the last rays of sunlight. I edged my way to the stairs and stepped down to the sidelines where Ginger sat with the Spirit Squad.

"Hey, Zack!" She waved me over and scooched to make room for me on the bench. That one gesture made my heart beat so fast that every Christmas morning, every birthday I'd ever had, was instantly put to shame and forgotten. My whole life added up to that little space on the bench next to her teeny-tiny skirt.

"This is Misty and Twisty." Ginger waved to the two devils I'd seen in the cafeteria. The twins gave an upward half-nod that meant they'd seen me before, had scraped me off their shoe, and kept walking.

"Can you believe this game?" Ginger said.

"Yeah, I know. Why aren't you guys cheering?"

From the other side of the bench, Misty and Twisty sighed and rolled their eyes.

Ginger shrugged and bunched up her shoulders in a chilly gesture, leaning into me. She rubbed her hands up and down my bicep for warmth. Casually, I looked over my shoulder at Art, who studiously ignored me as the moon slowly hoisted itself over the field and the buzzer for the second quarter sounded.

"Come on, Ginger." Misty and Twisty stood with the rest of the squad and led Ginger before the crowd. I suddenly noticed that I was the only spectator still sitting. The entire crowd began to stamp and holler. The cheerleaders twirled and spun and ground their palms into their hips, spinning their heads around three-hundred-sixty degrees, whipping their hair in every direction. Too bad the crowd wasn't looking at them. All eyes were on the field as the home team broke their huddle, newly transformed into a raving band of howling wolflike demons. Matted black fur bristled through every seam in their uniforms. They howled up at the full moon blazing down on them.

The Middle Plain Lost Souls scored seven touchdowns in six minutes, plus seven two-point conversions, chewing their way through the opposing line until Inferno High didn't have enough players on the field to continue.

Ginger never stopped looking at me while she cheered. When it was all over I sought her out before the lightless vacuum of victory and popularity sucked her down for the rest of the evening. Misty and Twisty glared at me, my social ostracism forming a hideous, invisible hunch on my back which only they could see.

"Hey, can I walk you to your grave?"

Ginger stood at the stands, smiling broadly, out of breath. The air must have been gloriously thin at the top of a cheeramid. I imagined that when it dispersed and Ginger fell from the top and was caught, it must have been like the whole world was reaching out for you, wanting to make sure you're safe.

"Sure." Ginger's dead, glassy eyes caught the light of the full moon and swallowed it. Behind her, the other cheerleaders scratched behind the victorious players' ears. The crowd began to disperse.

As we left the field, Ginger put her arm around mine and put her head on my shoulder. I felt her cheek muscles tense with a smile.

"You're so warm," she said.

I looked back at the stands, at my friends studiously ignoring me, at Principal Grimm shaking his head. Across the field, someone else watched me. Though I didn't dare look back, I could feel a dark smile fix on me from the opposing sidelines, as the visiting team was carried off the field in defeat.

"I'm surprised you remember me, from when you were alive."

Ginger and I walked side by side through the rows of tombstones, fingers intertwined.

"Of course I remember you. Just 'cause you weren't popular doesn't mean you weren't cute." Ginger spoke to the moon, to the dead leaves at her feet.

"But I'm still not popular."

"So what?"

"So why do you like me?"

"Does it matter?"

"Not in the slightest. Just wondering why aren't you ignoring me now?"

"I don't know. Maybe vampires and ghosts don't have like, pheromones or something. And besides, you're *way* cuter than an aborted fetus."

"Awe shucks," I replied. "You're too good to me."

"You ain't seen nothin' yet, honey."

I could tell she'd said it before, with other guys, and that she re-cycled the phrase because she knew it was sexy. And it was sexy.

For a second, before her cold, dead tongue slid between my teeth, I thought, *maybe this isn't a good idea. What about the rules of Heaven and Earth?* But then my hand slid under her shirt, cupped her firm, icy breast, and I didn't care.

Let me tell you something you already know:

A polite girl or woman, with whom you've never spoken of sex, suddenly telling you where to go, grabbing your hand, and sliding it between her legs, admitting that she wants to feel good—in the years after that night, such a thing wouldn't seem like a big deal. Grown women can talk about what they want, what they need from you. But in high school, when girls are supposed to be ladies instead of human be-ings, hearing such things from a total hottie like Ginger Banks, when all I'd dared to dream of was first base and a decent view of second, was like looking for trace elements of fossilized bacteria on Mars and find-ing the Miss Hawaiian Tropic competition camped out at your landing site.

Her skin was achingly cold.

"You're freezing," I said.

"I get goose bumps all the time."

She stood there with her top off while we kissed. She kept her skirt on, her socks and shoes too. Half-dressed like that, that strange com-bination of nudity and modesty, was an intoxicating cocktail of dream life and daily life. I'd only ever seen one or the other. In movies, they always cut from the kissing to the sex montage. In pornos, "actors" peeled off their own clothes like layers of useless, dead skin. But when Ginger lay back on a patch of hallowed earth overrun with clover, grabbed my hips, and guided me into her hidden, frozen pussy, it was as though we'd fallen into the crack between fantasy and reality, into that twilight of sensuality which you can visit once, the first time, but only in dreams thereafter.

Plus, I'd always thought people called out each other's names when they did it. I've since learned that this is seldom the case. I've also learned that people seldom even think of each other when they're fucking each other. But back then, that night, I could only think of Ginger—and not even all of her, just her breasts, or her eyes, or how we tried to keep it in when we turned over so she could be on top. One thing at a time. I didn't even know my name.

She came when I came, *because* I came, I would later find out. Apparently, what I left in her was hot and anxious and she had only the chill of death to fill her insides the rest of the time. I haven't made many women cum since then.

"It's so weird just sitting here," she remarked afterwards, propped against the base of a towering, angelic grave marker. "I used to have to, you know, button up while my boyfriend defrosted the windshield so he could drop me off before curfew." She sighed. "It's so weird being dead. You know?"

"Not really."

"You will."

"Thanks."

She smiled at me, straightened her clothes, and reached back to try and tuck her buzzed-off hair behind her ears.

"I heard your hair keeps growing after you die," she said. "I hope it's true. You know—" She sounded serious all of a sudden (something else I would have to get used to, and dread—a woman getting a serious tone after a sound shag). "How do you know, for sure, that you shouldn't be here?"

"What do you mean?"

"I mean, think about it," she said.

But I didn't have to. Already my heart started rattling in my chest like a punching bag. She meant *how did I know I wasn't dead*. Did I know?

I started talking fast. More to myself than the dead girl scrutinizing my dazed expression.

"But I've gone home to my house and seen my parents and—"

"Did they talk to you? Did they acknowledge you?"

"No, but they usually don't. They—"

I stopped when I saw it. By the light of a lightning flash, I saw it staring back at me, unassuming, defiant, smug.

"Ohmigodimdead." I knelt in front of my grave, stared down at my name and the date underneath. July fourth. I died on Independence Day. I thought back to a firecracker nearly going off in my hand. It must have gone off too soon. I must have bled to death.

"I'm dead?" The world went quiet. Long enough for a light to turn red too soon.

The cool earth snuck up and cold-cocked me from behind. I was on the ground. Somewhere beneath me, I was *in* the ground. The transfer wasn't a mistake. I was supposed to be here in the land of the dead, haunting my parents at night, unable to let g—

"PSYYYYYYYYYCH!"

The call resounded through the boneyard. Disoriented from my fall, I tried to stand, tried to use my own tombstone for balance as it crumbled into a lumpy mass of gray, standard-issue, sophomore Art Class self-hardening clay and I fell into it on my way back to Earth.

From behind the nearest mausoleum, Art, Roland, and Missy Nefertiti leapt into the moonlight, the surprise causing my heart, my still-beating, magnificent, most all-important muscle to batter against its calcium housing, threatening to stop, but persevering nonetheless.

"Sha-ZAAM, son!" Roland called out, laughing hysterically before Missy nearly squashed him as she doubled over in hysterics.

"You guys are so fucking dead!" I swore to Art as he helped me to my feet. Had they been there listening to us the whole time? Did I care? No! I was alive! I was laid! It was funny, too—I'd equated those two states of being for so long, now that I got both at once, they seemed completely different.

I grinned at the smug bastard, punched him in the shoulder as hard as I could, which wasn't very hard. "You are so *fucking* DEAD!"

"I know."

Nobody parties like the dead. The damned have rhythm. The entire school celebrated our victory in the cemetery that night, stamping their feet, howling at the moon loud enough to wake the dead and serve them up a tall one from the keg.

Ginger stayed close to me, getting drunk and clingy as the night spiraled down into the rosy abyss of bad breath and good vibes. Living in Limbo, a place to which God apparently turned a blind eye, was like your folks going away for the weekend and leaving the keys in the ignition and the liquor cabinet unlocked. The idea of bashing Paul Pennybaum's skull in was as distant and meaningless as Monday morning seen from the observation deck of Friday night.

"Listen!" Ginger said to me over the music sometime after midnight. She was sweaty from dancing and talked right into my face with a boozy lack of depth perception. "I don't want you to think I'm a slut or anything because we fucked!"

"But *aren't* you kind of a slut?!" I howled and lit a cigarette.

"Well, yeah, but I don't want you to think of me that way!"

"I don't!"

"Good!" she proclaimed, then climbed on top of a broad, flat grave marker, took off her shirt, and started to dance. It was at that moment that I knew I was falling in love.

Just before dawn, things started to slow down, and my new girl-friend started to cry.

"I was sooooooo fucking popular!" she lamented, tears streaming down her face. The moon was down and all was dark. All around us, drunken kids and bilious abominations stumbled back to their graves.

"I was about to get my *license!* And just 'cause that dumb-ass zombie ate my brains I wound up here. I should *totally* be in *Heaven!*"

"At least you didn't wind up in Hell."

"My cell phone doesn't get *any* reception here!" she shouted to the black sky. "I *am* in Hell!"

She sobbed. I held her close. Her nipples were hard under her shirt. Her tears were cold.

"What the fuck is a *last rite* anyway? Is that like, the directions to Heaven? They couldn't give me directions before I died, so I got lost and ended up here? I don't even believe in God!"

I struggled to find the right thing to say that would either make her feel better or at least make her stop crying.

"Yeah, but, you know, *He* believes in *you.*"

"Really?" she asked, teary-eyed and hopeful. "You think so?"

"Um . . . not really. Sorry. I just said that to make you feel better. I stopped believing in God before I stopped believing in Santa Claus."

In the next plot down, Brutus Forte, our school's star quarterback, slid down into his grave, drunk with victory, beer, adoration of the masses. Peering over the lip of his grave, I watched him fluff up the dirt where his head would rest, then reach up to the surface, and in a single, sweeping motion draw a pile of loose earth on top of him as he fell back, already sound asleep before his head touched the cool, wormy terra firma.

"Do you love me?"

"Huh?" I turned back to Ginger. She propped herself against a headstone, watching me like a mirror while she wiped away her smeared eye shadow. Dead leaves clung to her scalp and clothes. The last of the alcohol had left her body, leaving her more sober than she was before she started drinking, the way you get when you've stayed up late enough for the booze to find its way back out, temporarily flushing out the drunkenness of everyday self-denial.

"I know they want you to kill Paul Pennybaum," she continued. "If you do, you won't ever come back."

"Well, I could come back," I swallowed. "I mean . . . I'd have to do it like Art di—"

"But you wouldn't." She looked up at the moon, saw herself in it, pursed her lips, drew a finger around them to erase a smudge. "You're not that kind of person."

"What do you mean?"

"You're the kind of person that makes good decisions. That's why girls don't like you—as more than a friend I mean." She sighed, eyes focused on a leaf stuck in the front clasp of her bra. "You'll never break my heart," she said. She sounded a little surprised, and a little disappointed.

She looked up at me, caught my expression.

"I'm not stupid," she replied to my thoughts. "Girls understand boys. It's just that most of the time, we don't have to, or we don't want to."

"I don't wanna kill Paul. I want to keep coming to see you."

"Then *don't* kill him," she pleaded softly. "He'll probably get killed some other way, anyway. People die all the time. Look at *me*."

A cold wind rustled through the cemetery, a parent checking up on their child after lights-out. It found us and we huddled together. Ginger's skin made me even colder, but I didn't want to let go.

"I should get to bed," she said at last, and lowered herself into the empty grave beside us. Once in, she paused and peered up at me. Her head just barely came up above ground level. "Will you tuck me in?"

"Sure," I replied, and got down on my knees. As I worked the dirt into her grave, I thought about the times my father would wake me up and tell me I was having a nightmare. I never remembered having a bad dream, but I believed him and felt better with him there.

"When you're done," Ginger said before I covered her face, "you have to go."

"What do you mean?"

"You can't spend the night here, or you can never leave again."

"How do you know?"

"I don't know, I just know. It's just one of the rules. Your parents are probably worried sick."

"But I wan—"

"Nobody worries about me anymore," she interrupted.

She leaned forward, crawled her fingers through the hair on the back of my head, kissed me, then fell back to the dark earth, the dirt around her body caving in as she fell. Behind me, I could already hear the black bus idling at the side of the road.

"Where have you been?"

"Have you been drinking?"

"We've been so worried!"

"You have no idea!"

It's funny how quickly relief can turn to anger. It's like we keep both emotions spring-loaded inside the same little tin can inside our chests and when we let one feeling out, the other must inevitably follow.

"Did you drive drunk?" my father demanded to know, rubbing the sleep from his eyes. "Who have you been out with?"

"Zombies."

"Zombies? What is that, some kind of gang?" the old man inquired, exasperated from running every drug overdose and child-kidnapping scenario imaginable through his head while waiting to hear my key in the door. "Are you in a fucking gang now?"

My father rarely cussed at me. It was one of those rare glimpses I ever caught of his non-father personality. I rarely liked what I saw.

"Oh my God." My mother sat down at the table, her face in her hands. She looked up at her jailbird son. "Are you dealing drugs?"

I wanted to tell them to get real, to remember that the best lessons they ever learned were from the mistakes they made, that the first step in becoming your own person is to make a conscious decision *not* to become your parents.

But I didn't know how to say all that, to articulate what I would only learn years later when I yelled at my own kids, because the only way to grow old is to forget what it's like to be young. And besides, they didn't *deserve* a response, or so I believed. They'd never been this mad before, never talked to me like this. It made all their love, all their kind words and tender moments seem totally and unforgivably conditional.

"Yeah," I replied coldly. If they needed to blame everything on changes in the world outside, instead of changes in their son, I wouldn't stand in their way. "That's it." I started up to my room, spoke over my shoulder, let my words tumble down the stairs behind me. "The big bad wolf made me do it."

"That must be his supplier," I heard my father explain to my mother. "They all have nicknames. It's all—"

The door SLAMMED! on his words, caught them and held them like fingers in a car door.

I collapsed on my bed, listened to my parents fighting downstairs, turned on the ten o'clock news. Channel 4 was running an exposé on the deaths at my old high school. A young, statuesque, serious-minded telejournalist reported that students were living in a state of mourning, that grief had struck the school "like a brick through a stained-glass window." As she said this, a man with a clipboard stepped behind her, into frame, and waved off the mob of students mooning the camera and flashing middle fingers and gang signs.

"Excuse me, young man." The reporter snared a passerby and aimed the camera at him. It was Paul Pennybaum, lurching to class. Flies orbited his tilted head, alighting on his rotten fruit face and taking off again. His clothes were tattered and sullied from his time in the grave. His eyes looked at the world like a retarded monkey would look at a banana painted on a brick wall.

"Young man," the reporter began again, "how does it feel going to school under the shadow of Death?"

"Brains," Paul droned, with great effort, as he stared straight through the reporter.

"Yes," the reporter responded, "the victims have all suffered severe trauma to their craniums. How does that make you feel?"

"Feel . . . dead."

The reporter turned back to the camera.

"As you can see, some of the students here already consider themselves future victims. Back to you, Bob and Alice."

I changed the channel, tried to pick up some scrambled porn, but nothing was on. So I sat there in the dark, weighing the gravity of so much death against the weight of Ginger's body on top of mine. I supposed it was partially my fault. If I whacked Paul, got rid of him somehow, the killing would stop. But I would never see Ginger again. Thus, the combination of my lust for her and my loathing for my former classmates was enough to persuade me, before I whacked off and fell asleep, that most of them were better off dead anyway. Paul Pennybaum was by no means the only zombie at San Los Pleasovale High.

By the following Saturday, five more students and three teachers were dead at school. My parents spoke as though I was one of them. Good riddance. And don't give me that look, either. How many times have you looked around a room and, however fleetingly, wished half of them would just disappear?

At the table that morning, my father spoke of days gone by, when he and I would barbecue burgers in the backyard and play catch. My mother made no reply. Tears welled up in her eyes as she hid them behind that day's crossword. Sitting between them at the table, I wanted to remind my father that he was a vegetarian, and that we had played catch once. Neither of us liked it. We both hated sports. And while I couldn't claim to like the jocks at my school, I couldn't blame them for being what they were. After all, if I had the choice between being a moderately clever writer, amusing himself alone at his computer, or being a Neanderthal in a football jersey at a blowjob buffet (or so I have to imagine them), I'd have to think about it.

Leaning over his bowl of cereal, my father flipped to the business section, exposing the front page to the rest of the table. The headline read that both the FBI and the Centers for Disease Control and Prevention had been called in to investigate the series of deaths at my old high school.

I got up to leave when I heard my bus arrive to take me to the Homecoming pep rally and game. We'd been prepping for it all week—hanging streamers in the hallways at school, pinning up signs so parents and alums wouldn't get lost when they arrived for the game from their various planes of existence. I'd stayed late every day to help decorate and then fuck my girlfriend. Every day was Christmas. Then I would come home and see my parents asleep on the couch, in the armchair, at the kitchen table, dreaming in uncomfortable positions. First I'd be mad. Then I'd be sorry. Then I'd go to sleep feeling mad that they made me feel sorry.

I paused for a second at the door, looked back at my parents looking down at their papers and plates, not so much looking at these items of interest as not looking at me.

For all they know, I am *in a gang. This could be the last time they see me, and they don't care.* They *wouldn't care if I was next.*

Going out the door, I thought about what Ginger said every night when I tucked her into her grave and I always asked to stay a little longer. *If you stay,* she'd invariably warn me, *you can never go home.*

I thought about that as I got onto the bus, and about how little home felt like home anymore.

Well, maybe I will *be next.*

As we pulled away, I looked back at the house I'd grown up in. It felt like I hadn't been there in years, as though it had been sold long ago and that I'd only just returned for nostalgia's sake, but had changed my mind when I drew close, and decided to keep driving.

"Where are they?"

"They'll be here."

The air was cold and electrified, the sky black. It was two minutes till game time and the opposing team still had yet to show, as had their fans. The bleachers opposite ours were bare, the sidelines equally so.

"If they don't show, do they forfeit?"

"They'll show."

I sat in the top row of bleachers with Art and Roland.

"I need a smoke," Roland said. He and Art, along with the rest of the hushed crowd, watched the field intently. The players on our side had already made their big entrance and were sitting on their benches, waiting and watching the field. "Wish I could hold a cigarette."

That afternoon, the pep rally had proceeded as all such events do—cheering, clapping, yelling, clapping some more and yelling louder, followed by more cheering, and, time permitting, more yelling and clapping. All throughout, however, there had been something in the air between the fans and the players, something in their distant smiles that made our good wishes sound almost mournful—some unacknowledged dread, as though our boys were going off to war, that we might not ever see them again.

"But if they don't show up," I repeated.

"They'll show up."

My breath came out as a fog. Nobody else's did.

"But if they d—"

A sound rang out from On High—a lone trumpet echoing down from the cloud cover. I looked up at the sky, as did everyone, and felt fear choke my heart. The horn sounded once more, like a distant cavalry charge. As it did so, a solitary ray of golden light, no wider than a child's arm, pierced the clouds and focused on the fifty-yard line. A third time the trumpet sounded. My breath caught in my throat. I wanted to hide, to cover my face, so terrible was this sound that said *your dreams are over*, a sound that told you, convinced you, that *every-*

thing you thought you would become you will never become; all the plans you have laid for yourself, will never come to pass. It was the bang of an unseen gun pointed at your heart. It was the sound of The End.

The fourth time the horn sounded it was joined by a chorus of bellicose brass, horns of war that wrung all will to resist from my body as the tiny spotlight that shone down on our home field widened suddenly, split the sky like a knife ripping open a wound, flooding the terrain with a rapturous, unflinching blaze as a host of seraphim in gold and white football jerseys poured down from the break in the clouds and stormed the field, a beautiful, thunderous stampede of infallible athletic ability with the greatest record of any school in the history of the universe. These were our opponents. This was Paradise High.

"We have to fight *Heaven* in our Homecoming Game?" I asked, totally flabbergasted. Across the field, a glowing body of halos and white robes filled the opposing stands.

"They've never been defeated," Art said and bit into a corndog.

"Why am I not surprised?"

"It ain't that bad, son," Roland offered. "It's like, this one doesn't count, you know?"

"Doesn't count?"

"Yeah, you know," Art said. "They can't be beat. Nobody's ever even scored on these guys. When God's sitting in the other team's bleachers, the bookies take the day off."

"Is that Genghis Khan looking through their playbook?"

"He's their head coach."

"But wasn't he, like, a bloodthirsty conqueror?"

"And a strategic genius."

"But wasn't he, like, a *bloodthirsty conqueror?*"

"Did the first-string linebackers at Harvard score 1600s on their SATs?" Roland asked.

I stared blankly down at the fetus.

"I don't *think* so," he answered as the whistle rang out for the kickoff.

I left when the scorekeeper lost count. The hometown crowd hadn't made a peep for the better part of three quarters. Whether we were too sorry to cheer for Middle Plain or too guilty to root against Heaven I couldn't say, but I supposed it didn't matter. My mind hadn't been on the game anyway.

I wandered back to the cemetery. Every grave was empty. Everyone had shown up to see their team get clobbered. I wondered why.

"You know, you're quite a unique young man."

I whirled around, surprised. I was going to school in the land of the dead, but a strange voice in the middle of a cemetery was still mildly alarming.

Ms. Needlemeyer, the Clown of Dachau, leaned against the wall of a mausoleum, trying to light a cigarette without the ability to inhale.

"Excuse me?" I asked.

"You're a very unique young man," she reiterated. "You are, after all, the only one who's ever been unhappy."

"Wha . . . huh? I don't get it."

"That's what you want to hear, isn't it?"

I stopped, looked at her with her painted skull and fallen stockings. She looked like a hooker who'd died propped against a lamppost and no one had noticed while she wasted away to nothing but bleached bones and a low-cut dress.

"No," I replied, softly.

"Here," she held out the as-yet unlit cigarette. "Little help?"

I plopped down on the tombstone beside her, lit her cigarette, handed it back.

"So what *do* you want to hear?"

I thought about that question, tried to look past the immediate thoughts of fame, money, sex. I thought about Ginger, and my 'rents.

Most of all I thought about how everyone on the planet seemed to kind of suck, in a general way, while I, clearly the only one who didn't suck, seemed to be the only one that was unhappy.

"I want someone to tell me it's going to be alright."

A dry chuckle sounded in Ms. Needlemeyer's throat, the sound of drumsticks on a pelvic snare drum.

"What?" I asked.

"You, young man, are the only person that can honestly say that to yourself. That's what growing up is, hon." She held the cigarette between her bare teeth, let the smoke float up into her eye cavities in a dead French inhale. "Becoming that person."

Mercifully, across the churchyard and over the last hill, the final whistle of the game blew. We turned and watched the sky tear open behind the school. The angels flew home quickly, whooping and hollering and cheering like a parade.

"Everybody always wants to be somewhere else," Needlemeyer noted. "Always making plans to be somewhere they'd rather be. I don't imagine it's any different in Heaven. I'd just like to know where they'd rather be."

I looked at the painted bag of bones, at the dirt caked on my shoes.

I had to keep my distance from Ginger at the Homecoming Dance. No one but our inner circle of friends knew how serious things had gotten between us and no one else *could* know, or there would be hell to pay. Literally. So I stood against the wall with Art while Roland danced on Missy's outstretched palm and Ginger boogied beside them. After a few songs he came back to catch his breath. Missy went to the bathroom with Ginger.

"What the dilly, son?" Roland asked. He sounded like a winded rubber squeaker toy. "You upset about the game? Don't let it get to you, bro. We *always* lose Homecoming."

"Huh?" I looked up from my feet. "Oh. Nah, I don't care about that shit."

"Then what's up?" Art asked.

"Nothing."

"Yeah, right."

"You love her?" Roland asked.

On the dance floor, Misty and Twisty and everybody else danced. Everyone danced differently. I wondered what it had been like, years ago, when nobody danced alone. You found a partner or you waited for one, looking for someone to ask.

"I don't know," I replied.

"That means *no*, son. When it comes to love, anything but *yes* means *no*."

I watched Ginger and Missy come out of the bathroom. Ginger looked for me across the dance floor, found me. I met her gaze, held it as I walked out to the dance floor and took her hand for a slow song.

"What are you doing?" she asked.

I made no response. We fit our bodies together and started to move.

"I think I love you," Ginger said after the first refrain.

She said it the way everybody says it the first time, when what they really mean is *I think I want to tell you I love you*. She looked at me, wanting me to say it back. I wanted to say it back, but I couldn't speak. All the blood in my body reversed its flow. I felt like I did in the cemetery, when Art, Roland, and Missy had played the prank on me, convincing me that I'd been dead the whole time.

"Aren't you gonna say it too?"

There was a pause between songs, long enough for someone to bet it all and lose; long enough for a plane to make an emergency landing; long enough for the next song to load, and begin.

"I, I—"

"I mean, if this isn't love, what is?" she asked, needing me to have the answer.

Again I found no words. I couldn't speak to her. Couldn't look at her.

"What are you thinking about?" she pleaded softly. She pressed her head against my chest, let the familiar cold of her tears soak through my shirt.

"Nothing," I replied, the old conversational parachute that worked more like an anvil tied to a ripcord.

"Please tell me."

I looked down at her, and for the first and probably last time, spoke with absolute honesty to a woman who I cared about:

I'd been thinking about my mother, about a certain Christmas morning when I was seven years old. It was our hardest holiday together. My father had been laid off before the previous semester had begun and it had plunged him into a crisis of being from which it seemed he might never emerge. He slept most of the day and haunted our house at night while we slept. Once, when I couldn't sleep, I'd gone down for a drink of water and found the old man standing in front of the open refrigerator, talking to the appliance's innards like a door-to-door salesman might present his product on some anonymous stoop, trying his damnedest to get his foot in the door. He'd sold vacuums door-to-door one summer when he was nineteen to save for the down payment on a car. He was brushing up the old pitch. I didn't know this at the time.

Months later, when Christmas came, my mother picked out my presents, spent hours poring over the discount bins at Toys "R" Us and JC Penney's looking for toys I might like that wouldn't break the bank. When the morning of December 25th finally came around, I found her asleep on the couch. She'd waited until late to bring out the toys and had fallen asleep wrapping them. When I saw what Santa had brought, I cried. I said they were stupid. I said they were awful.

Like everyone, I've done some shitty things in my life. I've hurt good people, most of the time without meaning to. And I've forgiven myself for those misdeeds, because like everyone, I convince myself that the things I do, I do because I must. But I've never forgiven myself for what I said that morning.

My mother had tried to explain, rapidly wiping tears from her eyes before I could see them. She said that there must have been a mix-up. Santa, she explained, had confused our house with someone else's. She said she was surprised it didn't happen more often. But all I could do was cry and whine and complain about how good I'd been all year.

"I know, sweety," she sniffed, comforting me, hugging me. "You've been so good. We'll write Santa a letter. We'll write him a letter and he'll clear everything up. You just have to give it a little time to get there."

By the following Christmas, I didn't believe in Santa Claus. Yet to this day, my mom still writes "From Santa" on a couple of presents every year.

"I don't get it," Ginger replied when I finished telling the story.

"That's what I think love is."

"But it's such a sad story," she explained. "What does that have to do with me?"

"I love you."

"I love you, too."

The second slow song ended. The DJ came on to announce that the next song would be the final slow number of the evening. I'd reason, years later, that neither of us really *loved* each other then. I'd also figure that it didn't really matter.

"I love this song," she said. It was a song about dreams, about having a nightmare that the singer's true love had died. "You know, I've never had a nightmare since I've been here. I don't think I've had a single dream."

I looked down at her, at the people staring at us with attraction and disgust.

"I love you," I said again, to the whiskers on her head.

"I love you too," she said as I pulled away, turned around, and began to run.

I found Paul in the gymnasium, trying to dribble a basketball and failing. As I approached, I watched him pick up a ball with both hands and drop it. He swatted at the bouncing thing and missed, waited for it to settle at his feet, then picked it up again. I looked at the floor around him, at the equipment he'd dragged from storage: dodge balls, footballs, soccer balls and nets, tennis rackets, swim caps, and racing hurdles. He was wearing a gym uniform. The shirt was inside-out. I picked up a metal baseball bat, felt the weight. I watched him pick up the basketball again. Outside, moonlight streamed in through the high windows. I held the bat over my shoulder, stood like a major leaguer. I thought about Ginger. I thought about Art's blood in his mom's ice cube trays. I thought about Christmas, and swung the bat.

They were asleep when I got home. The TV was on and the color bars watched over them silently. My father sat at the end of the couch with my mother sprawled out on the adjoining cushions, her head on Pop's lap. The old man's brow was creased, his throat moving and sounding, talking to someone in his dreams. His head ticked to the left and he spoke again, in his throat. His mouth opened suddenly, breathing in.

"Hey," I said quietly. I put a bloody hand on his twitching shoulder. "I'm home."

SONG OF THE SELKIE

Gina Ochsner

from Tin House

HAVING SWALLOWED TOO MANY BONES, THE SEA HAS A BAD CASE of indigestion. This sound of dyspepsia shatters the nerves and Erlen Steven knows that is why no one wants to live at the lighthouse. It doesn't help matters that three men died during its construction. When the mail boat ferries him to the docks this fact is just one of the many things Erlen knows to keep quiet about in the presence of the local coasties.

Which suits him fine. He is not in the business of making noise, but of making light. In water and at sea, life revolves around his light. And each evening before starting his watch, Erlen recites the Lightkeeper's prayer. A longish prayer—Erlen does not have it up by heart. Which is why the prayer is typed, framed, hanging at the landing at the base of the light tower. Erlen does not bother with the beginning, but the end holds salt: . . . *grant, oh Thou Blessed Savior, that Thou would join us as we cross the last bar and struggle for the farther shore, the lee shore of the land where the sun never goes down, and where there is no darkness for He who is the light of the world will be the light thereof.*

No one would accuse Erlen of being overly religious, but he isn't the type to stand in the way of it either. A prayer can't hurt here on the rock, he thinks when he climbs the steep sixty foot spiral staircase to the service room where the light is kept. The light, a first order Fresnel, stands nearly twelve feet tall and six feet wide. The lenses are composed of glass segments arranged in rings and stacked in concentric circles. When his father kept the light it used to take the young boy—and then later—the young man Erlen all of a day to clean the nearly one thousand pieces of glass. This left only a little free time to comb the rocks for pieces of the sea: sand-smoothed pebbles, razor clam shells, the spiraled dog whelks that house miniature tornadoes inside their fragile casings.

The shells held to his ear, the young man Erlen marveled that out of such dryness could issue the musical sound of water. And that the high tide could carry such items of fragility and strength (once—whole green and blue glass floats all the way from Japan) seemed a mystery intended for him to solve. Imagine his surprise when he found one day not a shell, but a woman, nude and shivering, washed up on the breakers. What could he do, but take her and that bedraggled fur coat tucked under her arm, into the lighthouse? What could he do but fall in love with and marry her? What could he do but get her with children—twins no less? And what could he do, being book-bound and a little forgetful, but lose her?

"I'm not surprised," Inspector Wilson said when Erlen delivered the news: Mrs. Erlen Steves, wearing nothing but that tattered fur coat minus the collar and a portion of the left sleeve, had jumped from the rocks. "This lighthouse has a history of driving its keepers mad." Inspector Wilson circled a finger at his ear, and then tugged on his jacket of his Coast Guard uniform.

Erlen searched his memory of all the logbooks he'd read. "I didn't know that."

"Well, you know it now." Inspector Wilson said, casting a long look at the girls, already toddlers and tethered to a laundry line—in accordance to the lightkeeper's safety manual.

"A selkie loves water," Astrid says.

    "—A selkie loves land" says her sister, Clarinda.

    "—A selkie walks on two feet,"

    "—whenever she can."

Jump-rope geniuses, Astrid and Clarinda sing out tandem rope rhymes and never miss a beat. At the Mt. Angel boarding school they are unusual girls—always have been, Mother Iviron thinks—and not just because they are twins. Skin pale, jaws strong, mouths flat, the girls have eyes a color of blue so reluctant they border on gray. The only way Reverend Mother Iviron can tell them apart is the way Astrid pushes out her lower jaw in the presence of uninvited pity, while Clarinda tears up and turns red.

United utterly, what one girl starts the other girl finishes: rhymes, riddles, math problems. A phrase in the mouth of one twin finds its completion in the mouth of the other. If Astrid feels the bite of nail, Clarinda cries out as it punctures the sole of her shoe. When Astrid slaps the girl who calls her creepy times two, it is Clarinda who makes penance with a spate of Hail Mary's, repetition being the heaven of duplicate things.

> *Hail Mary, full of grace, the Lord is with thee.*
> *Blessed art thou among women, and the fruit of thy tomb, Jesus.*

Fruit of the tomb? Mother Iviron, beyond girlhood puns, doesn't think twice when she makes the girls wear the hair shirts. Old fashioned, oh yes. But to tell the truth, they didn't seem to mind it too much. Equally suspicious to Mother Iviron is the way the girls prepare for bed. They slide their cots together and before climbing in, they line up their shoes, turning the points toward each other as if the shoes might continue an ongoing conversation.

"When a selkie drags you under"
"—she'll split your skin asunder."

When she hears this kind of talk, Mother Iviron stretches a hurting smile across her face. Far be it from her to stifle the imagination. And certainly tragic stories of the sea bear instructional value. But when the girls turn eleven and substitute sea chanties for prayers, Mother Iviron sends them home to their father with her regrets.

The lighthouse stands sixty feet high, tall as a castle. Ringed black, and white, the painted markings turn the light tower into layered cake, spun sugar. The staircase curves in a tight spiral, the corkscrewed architecture of a lightning whelk. In the lantern room, the girls crack open a window and take turns playing Rapunzel. All the lighthouse needs now is a resident witch.

The girls shout out into the wind: come find us! In the meantime they keep busy. The work: polishing brass and cleaning glass, doing all to bend and multiply light in its refractions and reflections. Special care must be given to the first order Fresnel and its catadioptric lens assembly. The bulls-eye lens rotates and magnifies the light as it swings. From a distance of twenty-six miles away the light appears as a flash over the water. At least, this is what their father's manual of operation says. But to the girls wearing their green safety goggles the lenses look like a gigantic transparent beehive. The rotating bulb behind the bulls-eye is the queen bee. Astrid and Clarinda, the custodians of the glass, are the confused dim-witted drones.

For the longest time they thought the light was meant to lure the ships nearer, yes right up to the rocks. Never did they imagine the light was meant to turn away every vessel except the mail boat or Inspector Wilson's tender, which would arrive in evenings without any warning and set their father scrambling. Astrid and Clarinda aren't quite sure what to make of Mr. Wilson, the Coast Guard's Aids to Navigation Inspector. When he comes with his high-powered nose lowered, Mr. Wilson always examines the kitchen first, tallying its contents and cleanliness down to every drawer and cupboard, each piece of cutlery. Astrid thinks he looks like a bloodhound on the scent of something turned sour. Clarinda thinks he looks like God wearing a dark uniform and white gloves. Only God would smile more often, Clarinda decides as she pockets two knives, a fork and spoon—just to throw the count off.

Bewildered. Erlen Steves is bewildered. Nobody told him how to raise girls. His many books about sea creatures, legend and lore have been no help at all. And nothing in the engineering texts or the lighthouse operation manuals explain how to ease the loss of a wife and a mother.

All of which to say, Erlen hasn't fully recovered. He knows this. Lulled by the changing moods of the water, its murmuration and roaring, it's hard not to think water, think salt, think tears. He knows it's unseemly to grieve for so long, but his sorrow is amplified, doubled on account of the girls. He is not sad for himself: he lost a wife he suspects he was never meant to have. But for the girls to lose their mother while still so young—it splits his heart in half every time he looks at them.

He tries to be strong. He kisses them each on the forehead. Astrid's skin is always a little cool to the touch, Clarinda's always a little warm, feverish even, and then he climbs the sixty feet to sit with the light. The night watch he spends alone in the service room, cleaning the glass, polishing the bull's-eye lamp, which turns and turns as regular and steady as the beating of a heart. That anything so large or so small as a bulb could whirl with such constancy brings a comfort to him, here, in the lighthouse where he knows nothing, not even water, should be taken for granted—neither the things the water carries away nor what the water might bring.

By day Sister Rosetta teaches the K-6 boarders at the Mt. Angel Parochial school. By night she writes a religious mystery novel and edits the *Convent Cloister Herald,* circulation thirty-eight. Thirty-seven after Sister Margaretta, God bless her, died peacefully in her sleep.

She's got a talent, that one, the other sisters say. A real way with the words, the way they never lock-step fail on her. And the way she can phrase a question: "Does Jesus still bear the wounds in his side and hands and feet now that he is ascended to the right hand of the Father?" A question so direct it unsettles the older sisters, Mother Iviron in particular, whose eyebrows stitch together at the scent of such mysteries. Such unanswerable questions ring with the hollow interior of the rhetorical. They make Sister Iviron's joints ache and her teeth throb. Sister Rosetta, blissfully unaware of what her words do to Sister Iviron, pokes around for the soft entrails, for the heart of faith, keeps poking with these questions in her nighttime dreaming.

Her dreams!

Sister Rosetta's dreams could fill an ocean. Will she ever stop? Honestly, Sister Iviron says. The way Sister Rosetta's frolicking queries keep the first year postulants up at night, roiling the calm rarified air within the stone walls of the convent—it's enough to drive them to distraction. *Why did Jesus heal some and not others?* Sister Rosetta asks in a dream, and the postulants and novitiates rise and bob in the gathering waters of Sister Rosetta's viscous questions.

It wouldn't be so bad, except Sister Rosetta is always the first to stir, waking with a shout and leaving the rest awash in her unnavigable dreams. Some of the postulants have signed up for swimming lessons. Others wear life jackets under their seersucker bedclothes and clamp plugs over their noses.

After too many nights left stranded in Sister Rosetta's dreams, Mother Iviron makes phone calls, drafts letters. In record speed, Sister Rosetta's resume makes the rounds.

A man fell in love with a woman.
But the woman was in love with the sea.

Their father's voice winds down the stair case from the service room, that furnace of green and light and heat grown thick with their father's singing. He is shaping his grief, casting sorrow line by line, limb by limb, into the figure of a woman they cannot remember. In the place of her body they have these weepy words Astrid and Clarinda know they were never meant to hear, but have long ago committed to memory. The same words that pushed Sister Iviron's determined smile askew, words that make the girls thirsty to know things. So many questions Astrid and Clarinda would love to ask their mother. So much about sky, skin, water, they would like to know. But their mother swam out to sea one day and forgot to return. "It was very strange—she being a champion swimmer," their father sometimes says.

When they cannot bear to hear their father sing they climb the steps, put on the safety goggles, and tug on his sleeves. They pull him down to the kitchen for dinner, for midnight snacks, for breakfast which is always the same fare: Spam on crackers or macaroni with caned tomato sauce.

"Tell us a story,"
"A sad, strange story."
"A strange, scary story."

Erlen tries. He collects and collates the strangest stories he can find. To date he has amassed two notebooks full of sea lore and legendry. As they eat their macaroni and Spam, he tells of lighthouse ghosts and large boats split to splinters on rocks like these, and small, mischievous sea creatures. He tells them about a mermaid who almost married a prince. But the prince married another and the mermaid came to him one night as he lay sleeping and killed him with a poisoned kiss upon the lips.

"That's not so sad," Astrid says, pursing her lip and whistling through a piece of uncooked macaroni.

"And it's not so strange," Clarinda adds. She holds a row of macaroni noodles between her teeth and makes strange music through her homemade harmonica.

"Then maybe you've heard about the Selkies, who look astonishingly likeseals. In their whiskers they carry magic. If they fall in love with a human—and they do this more often than you might think—then they will unzip their fur, tuck it into a bundle and hide it somewhere safe. Later, when they are tired of their human body, tired of human love, they simply pull their fur back on and swim out to sea."

The girls shudder. The pupils of their eyes dilate then pin-point as if their eyes themselves are breathing. Erlen likes to tell this story because it's the only story the girls sit still for. But certain parts of the story he doesn't tell. A wayward Selkie who has children with a human must come back for the children when they become women— otherwise those children will forever remain trapped in their human bodies. But this involves the changing of bodies and desires, and this isn't something Erlen likes to think about. He doesn't like change. To Erlen's reckoning, his girls will always be girls just as the lighthouse will always be their stronghold, their safety.

But one night he finds the girls in the lantern room, their long hair braided into knots and flung out the window as a ladder, their bodies leaning dangerously over the sill, and he realizes in a blink how thoroughly he doesn't understand them—how foolish he's been to hand them so many fictions to inhabit. He hauls them back in, too hard. His fingers leave a mark on Astrid's arm. But it's Clarinda who gasps and narrows her eyes. And he knows everything he will do to make it up from this point forward will be exactly the wrong thing.

In the waking world water is danger, water will drown them. The girls do not know how to swim. Though long off their lighthouse leads, they still cling to each other behind the rail, afraid of the seventh wave, the sneaker that might pull them over and out. At night they push their beds together. Two commas, if they lie on their beds, touch toes to toes, head to head, their bodies form a circuitous loop. Choosing one heart to live in, one body of dreaming to inhabit, in no time they drift into each other's dreams. Barefoot they clamber over shore rock and into the shallows where the limpets and starfish move so slowly it's as if in dreams, time sheds its hold over things born in water. Deeper they wade until they feel underfoot the velvet and buzz of the corals.

Farther out, the rock and sand shelf plunges and the water swallows them. It burns a little to take it in through the nose. But they've been practicing every night in their dreams and breathing under water comes easier than it used to. Overhead the sun blooms purple, blooms blue, a kelp bulb floating across their untroubled ceiling of liquid. When they wake to a waterless sun, the light carries edges and angles, slicing their room. Gone are the dreams, the very memory of the fact that they had, indeed, been dreaming. The only clues: salt rimming their eyelids and crusted under their fingernails, their night gowns wet and wadded up into a pile at the foot of their beds.

The girls are good readers, having scoured the lighthouse logs for any mention of their mother. And they've even memorized the lighthouse prayer in its entirety—no easy feat. But theirs is a lopsided education, and when the girls ask how to divide twins by twos—a problem of fractions if ever he's heard one—Erlen writes to Mr. Wilson, requesting a visiting schoolteacher and nanny.

In no time he receives a typed letter on heavy linen paper. It is from Mt. Angel Convent. A suitable candidate will be sent over immediately. Erlen scratches his head, sniffs the lily-white stationary in sheer amazement. He cannot recall actually mailing his request. The notion that God and Mr. Wilson might work in tandem and quicker than the Tuesday mail boat only adds to his bafflement. For there is Mr. Wilson's tender, nosing alongside the landing. All this on a Monday!

With a bellow from the fog horn, the boat hoves to and down Erlen goes, *clink, clink, clink*, his boots over the steps. The girls, eyes gray as stone, stand on the landing and clutch the rail. But it's the new teacher he's worried about, bobbing and pitching in Inspector Wilson's tender. Erlen ties off the boat and studies her. A stranger to water, he can see that her stomach is in her throat: her face is as pale as her starched collar and veil, and she's got a fine sheen of sweat above her upper lip. When he grabs for her hands, soft and pudgy like a child's, they melt to fit his. Erlen lifts her from the boat and his breath stutter steps in his throat. He realizes he had forgotten what a woman's hands feel like.

Sister Rosetta, a little queasy in Mr. Wilson's tender, surveys the lighthouse rock and her new charges. She spots the two girls standing at the railing. Hard telling where one girl begins and the other ends and Sister Rosetta understands why she's been sent: to care for them in the singular, to care for them in the plural. For it's clear in a glance that this land does not love these girls. Stick thin, chalky faced, their long brown hair whipped to tails, Sister Rosetta sees a picture of twinned longing, so raw and pure she has to look away.

Mr. Steves, the girls' father, reaches out and pulls her from the boat. His hand is rough against her skin and though his grip is completely appropriate, she feels flustered, can't help thinking that this is the perhaps the first and last time she will be touched by a man, any man.

The boat leaves with another blast. Mr. Steves strides ahead to the lighthouse with her suitcases. Sister Rosetta tips her head at angle and studies the girls whose fingers have turned white under the pressure of their grip.

"Are you all right?" Sister Rosetta asks.

"Seven," says the girl on the left.

"Cry seven tears at high tide and a selkie will cry with you," explains the girl on the right.

"Seven," Sister Rosetta says, "is God's number."

"Why?"

Sister Rosetta nudges her glasses higher onto her nose. "Because on the seventh wave what God has taken, He gives back."

"Our mother was swept away on the seventh wave. It was very strange—

"—she being a near champion swimmer."

"I'm sorry. I didn't know that," says Sister Rosetta, blinking fiercely behind her glasses.

"Well, you know it now," says the girl on the left, her jaw thrust out.

The girl on the right: nose red and snuffling, chin all a-tremble. It's going to be a job, Sister Rosetta knows, but the girls turn sweet, leading her by the hand up, up, up the winding stairs, throwing open the door to each room so that she can see for herself: the storage room, kitchen, sleeping quarters and bathroom, library, and at the very top, the service room. Sister Rosetta doesn't know about the green tinted safety goggles and looks directly into the heart of the light, into brilliance so fierce it's like looking at God in glory, a light meant to guide but viewed too closely would certainly blind.

Days pass, each one a crow-shaped stain falling from the shore pines. The wind kicks up, breaks brittle days into halves, throws Erlen's nose out of kilter. The lighthouse smells of metal, of wet copper, of pennies. It was his wife's smell: pure and elemental, edged and biting like salt. One afternoon Erlen leaves the lantern room, his nose roving in all directions, tracking the scent of skin and wet fur. His nose leads him to the library where the wind has snapped a windowpane. Sister Rosetta is there, a flurry of pages from the primer swirling around her. She stands on tiptoe reaching for the paper that curls out and away from her. She looks like a figurine in a snow globe. The sight of her, not at all a bad looking woman, provokes his heart to skip. And it's at that precise moment Erlen becomes a religious man, thanking God for this wind, for stirring things up.

The wind, Sister Rosetta, too, is thankful for. It howls through the lighthouse, inside Sister Rosetta's ears. But then Sister Rosetta, textbooks and papers in hand, stumbles. Her veil, caul, and wimpole fall. Her shaved head is bared. Where are her feet? She wonders, as the floor rises to meet her. And then Erlen is there, catching her. It's a surprise, the sureness of his grip. For even she doesn't quite remember where her elbows or knees are beneath the voluminous folds of the wool habit, and yet he knows exactly how to right her: an arm hooked around her rib, another anchoring her elbow.

Don't ever let go. That's what Sister Rosetta is thinking. What she says instead:

"Is there something you were wanting?" She is trying so hard to sound utterly unflappable, though she can feel herself blushing, yes, down to the roots of her shorn hair.

Erlen retrieves her glasses, hands over her limp headpiece. He is careful with her vestments, averts his gaze even as he helps her with the veil, the hem of which has come unraveled. But his nose can't quit. Erlen's arms go stiff, his elbows lock. He considers Sister Rosetta, points his nose at her neck. She's not the source of that scent he's tracking, he realizes.

"Give the girls a bath," Erlen whispers, his nose twitching, "with extra soap."

Sister Rosetta's religious mystery novel is not going well. The hardest question: *Does God really know what He is doing?* hasn't provoked a

quick answer. Not in her writing, not in her life. Equally uncoopera-
tive are the twins who do not want to shave their legs and underarms,
who do not want to bathe at all. The three of them sit on the rim of the
enormous metal tub and look at the water.

"Skin replaces itself," Astrid leads off,

"—cell by cell," Clarinda adds,

"—every thirty days,"

"—but hair replaces itself more slowly."

"Besides, we like being hairy—"

"—the hair keeps us warmer at night."

A smile starts on the left side of Astrid's face and travels from girl
to girl. Sister Rosetta shrugs. The truth is, underneath her habit, she is
a little hairy, too.

"I'll go first," Sister Rosetta says, hanging her habit and veil on a
hook. She soaps herself and shows them how to run a razor the length
of a leg, around the tricky points of the ankle. Her flesh hangs from
her body in doughy folds. Sister Rosetta wonders if they know how un-
moored she feels inside her own skin, this awkward transparent sleeve.
Can they even guess how badly she wants to turn the razor and make
a longitudinal incision, stem to stern, and step free of her body that
weighs on her, shames her?

But the girls aren't even watching her. Astrid bends to the tub,
trails a finger in the water. "Our mother liked baths."

"Took them on full moon nights like this one," Clarinda says, nodding at the window where the moon was a buoy in the dark sky.

"She's coming back for us," Astrid steps out of her pants. "She's
going to teach us how to swim." The girls climb into the tub and
no sooner have they settled in the water than they begin to bleed.
Simultaneously, of course: two scarlet threads unspool from between
their thighs. The girls are unnaturally calm, looking at Sister Rosetta
with their wide eyes.

Sister Rosetta helps them out, towels them off, shows them what a strange contraption the belt and hook, what good for girls becoming women such modern day conveniences are. Afterward, Sister Rosetta carries the bath water, pink and smelling of iron, in large pots down to the landing. Like carrying a comb to the sea, it's a risky thing to do but Sister Rosetta pours the contents of the pots over the railing anyway.

That night as Sister Rosetta climbs into bed, she considers the lighthouse lens turning silently. She thinks about Erlen with his hand at the light, true and shining. In no time at all, she is asleep, awash in a dream where she stands knee deep in the surf and unlocks a suitcase full of keyhole limpets, chitons, lightning whelks, and several specimen of spindled Venus Murex. *How wide are heaven's gates, how deep?* Sister Rosetta wonders. She is stringing a rosary made of these musings, each question another chiton or whelk, the surfaces asymmetrical in pattern and design. Meanwhile, the good nuns at the abbey, uncostumed and unrestrained, turn their gazes to the expanse of Sister Rosetta's borderless dreaming. They link arms and kick their heels together with glee as they rush for the water. Wearied of their rosaries worn down between fingers and thumbs, they are only too glad to wade in deep, exchange their smooth beads for the sharp points of Sister Rosetta's queries.

Sister Rosetta's snoring keeps Astrid and Clarinda from sleep. Boredom and insomnia provoke their curiosity. Though the ground floor storage room is strictly off-limits, with Sister Rosetta asleep and their father up in the lantern room, there's no one to stop them.

The storage room is black as tar. It's an interesting proposition, such darkness held in the belly of the lighthouse. For fun they do not light matches or shine flashlights. Instead they drop to hands and knees and crawl across the floor, ending up in a far corner, where they find fur: one long strip and a smaller crescent shaped patch. They tuck the scraps under their arms and race up to their room, where they survey the scraps over the bedspread.

The fur is shiny silver like a seal's. They know without speaking it aloud, the fur is from their mother's coat. Instinctively, Astrid drapes the long swatch of fur over her shoulder, where it adheres to her skin, stretching from tip of shoulder to point of hip. Clarinda fastens the collar of fur around her neck and the girls know: there isn't a shoehorn big enough, a crowbar strong enough to pry these strips loose now

Later that night the moon slips off its lead and a storm rolls in hard and fast. The wind whistles harsh lullabies that send the girls into unsettled sleep. Only their thin and flimsy human skin separates all that water outside from the water inside their bodies. They could drown—this has been the point of their father's stories, they know. But Sister Rosetta has taught them fractions and they now understand that they are two-thirds water, maybe more. They will float like the fish that swallowed the moon. They will rise buoyant and swim. All their lives it seems they've been practicing—in dreams, of course.

They know Sister Rosetta understands this. They know this because that very night they wade into each other's dreams: the girls into Sister Rosetta's dreams and Sister Rosetta into the combined dreaming of the girls. In their dreams nobody wears clothes, and so they swim naked—Sister Rosetta and Astrid and Clarinda—their fears and their terrible longings and their many questions bobbing beside them. And they show each other what they never could during day: Astrid's strip of fur that now girdles her waist and Clarinda's collar of fur, which has already spread as a cape over her shoulders. The girls are sloughing their cracked and flimsy skins and Sister Rosetta runs her fingers over their beautiful patchwork bodies in utter amazement.

And then Sister Rosetta reveals her raw heart, ready for something more than wind and salt. Something more than the threads of her veils binding her up or her many lesson plans. And the girls with their eyes grown so gray now they are nearly black, see Sister Rosetta's heart and know exactly what they are seeing.

"You take care of him," they implore in the singular and Sister Rosetta bolts upright in bed.

Midnight. The fur has spread, covering the girls from neck to knee. They turn their skins under and roll them down, as women do when stepping out of a pair of nylons. They tuck their skins under their arms and wind their way carefully down the stairs. Astrid trails a hand along the stone to steady them, while Clarinda bites her lip. With each step Clarinda thinks *right*, thinks *left*. Thinks *down*.

"Don't," Astrid whispers,

"be afraid," Clarinda replies. It's what their mother said, the day she swan-dived from the rock for the water. Now they know, now they remember. How to swim? That will come. But it's the land they must leave, once and for all, leave it for the water that will lift and carry them. *Water*, Clarinda thinks as she pushes the sky aside with her hands.

"C'mon," Astrid urges. "Hurry now." At the landing Clarinda hesitates.

"Don't—" Astrid says.

"—be afraid," Clarinda replies.

Don't be afraid.

When Astrid lifts her left foot over the ledge, Clarinda steps off with her right.

Erlen smells the girls. He leaps to his feet. *Slap, slap, slap*, down the stone steps. Above him the light turns behind the glass. You would think for all this light he might see something. But he doesn't, can't, the light shining miles and miles beyond him. By the time he gets to the landing, the girls are gone.

"Come back!" He shouts, knowing full well they can't hear him, having slipped beneath the water with their slick and oily bodies. Two transparent skins drape over the railing; two unzipped girl-shaped casings drip the color of fog.

Erlen, beyond bewilderment, fingers the skins. Next to him is Sister Rosetta, her lips moving silently. *Guide them*, she prays. Her prayers stand tiptoe to press against the invisible beating heart of God. *Guide us all*. She understands, looking at Erlen, looking at the skins he folds into halves, into quarters, that none of them have ever been quite right for this world, casting about in skins they aren't quite suited for.

Erlen turns to Sister Rosetta. "They're not coming back are they?"

Sister Rosetta peers out over the water. "No." She is crying hot oily tears. She will miss those girls with their luminous eyes and stories. She is sorry already they've gone. But she is not really worried. It's Erlen she's thinking of now. No, it's herself and Erlen—together—she's thinking of. She rests her palms flat and hard against her heart, her heart so full, she thinks it will burst from the pressure. Sister Rosetta smiles, can't help thinking this is another mystery, this hurt wrecking her, this full measure of sky she's swallowed, pressed and running over. So full in her lungs, she might drown on it.

Is it love? She wonders, considering Erlen leaning at the railing. Is this how love finds us even when we're sure it won't, finds us anyway, splits us wide open? It's an unforeseen plot complication and she's not sure what to do but offer thanks: thank you, parable. Thank you, rhyme. Thank you, unanswerable questions.

Erlen presses his hips against the railing. His daughters are gone, he can feel it as certainly as he feels his heart tumbling. Gone but not lost, he feels that, too. In the hills the dogs bark and bark, beyond reason, beyond logic, barking for the sheer joy of repetition. To see, perhaps, if the moon might wag its tail.

Erlen turns to Sister Rosetta. Her face glows beneath the moonlight. Her woolen habit is beneath Erlen's hand. Sister Rosetta is beneath the habit. From rib to rib his heart is a melon falling rung by rung down a long ladder.

"Sister Rosetta—"

"Rose," she says, slipping her hand in his. The wind whips her veil and caul from off her head. She doesn't have time to think: *catch it*. It tumbles past the breakers, caught now and carried, beyond the surf where it disappears into darkness.

A TROOP [SIC] OF BABOONS

Tyler Smith

from Pindeldyboz (online)

"Unruly gangs are raiding the expensive homes that line the spectacular coast of South Africa's Cape Peninsula, clearing out pantries, emptying fridges and defecating on the designer furnishings. It's baboon versus human in a string of wealthy ocean-front communities 30 minutes from the trendy center of Cape Town, a top tourist destination."
—*The Washington Post*, May 23, 2006

THERE WAS A TIME WHEN WE LIVED IN RELATIVE HARMONY WITH the baboons. You could call it a fragile armistice. But today, the people of the Cape Peninsula are besieged. Like any overwhelming calamity on a society, the baboon progression was insidious. I recall numerous picnics in Kruger National Park where we would take in a puppet show, munching on biltong and regarding our hirsute "friends" performing a scene from Anton Chekov's *The Cherry Orchard*. During the scene in which Lopakhin begins to tire of Mrs. Ranevsky's refusal to clear the orchard, we would always feel a strong sense of pathos when the Erik, the baboon playing Lopakhin, would storm off to the side of the stage and consume his own feces listlessly. I often mentioned Erik's technique during my lectures at the University.

There was a buoyancy, a lilt to those early days co-habitating amongst the baboons. Sure, occasionally we would find a few members of a troupe rummaging through our garbage or sneaking out the back of the public library with a copy of *Scaramouche* tucked under their naked muzzles. But the baboons always seemed to return to their refuge. And scathing irony, it is now we who must run to our refuge (an abandoned movie theatre on Adderley Street that shows screenings of *Critters II* every two hours on the hour) after being forced from our homes.

The real trouble started for my family and me when we came home from a week-long vacation in Malta and found around fifteen members of one particular troupe rehearsing *Die Fledermaus*. When I endeavored to shoo them off while explaining that Dr. Falke had been dressed not as an emu at the masked ball, as the baboons had played it, but as a bat, Rudy, one of the larger members of the troupe, and if I recall correctly, portraying the bumbling lawyer Mr. Blind, gnashed his teeth at me while my wife Kristin and a demure drill called Bobo had a heated exchange over the best way to fix our toilet. After my son Luke startled the troupe with a flare gun, they all filed out the front door and looked back at our family in haughty disgust. "You win this round," they seemed to say, "but we have the guile of a thousand Smerdyakov Karamazovs and you haven't seen the last of us . . . assholes."

Things ran smoothly for about a week. The only problem our family encountered was during a brief incident in which I discovered a baboon (Luther, we think) had stolen my identity along with a pair of my Dockers and an Oxford button-down and attempted to buy a used Volvo at a local dealership. The salesman, weary from "my" incessant grunting and roaring, called my wife to make sure nothing was fishy. After my wife assured him that I possessed neither a cynocephalus, nor tail, nor an out-of-the-ordinary quantity of red spots on my rear, the salesman retrieved my credit card as the ornery baboon sashayed, albeit briskly, out of the dealership humming the rondo from Mozart's Sonata in A.

With hindsight, the ensuing Götterdämmerung was to be expected. After the week of relative calm, our family was often visited by at least ten to fifteen baboons every night for a viewing of *Masterpiece Theatre* at which the baboons would chortle, whoop and guffaw at the (at least in my opinion) superb work of Olivier, Burton, Guinness, and Gielgud. "What a bunch of guano!" they indicated by throwing their own bowel contents about the room while aping (excuse the quasi-pun) what they obviously felt were inferior performances by some of true masters of stage and screen. Koko, one of the more puerile mandrills would, at the sight of the rape scene in *Titus Andronicus*, run to our liquor cabinet, down a bottle of sherry and then break wind in front of the television until the rest of the troupe howled with simian laughter. I decided I ought to take a stand. We entreated Luke to take the bus to his grandparent's house in the city. Then, on a warm Tuesday evening after the baboons had finished playing their *Madden 2006* tournament on my son's PlayStation, I crept up behind a few of them and, using a taser gun my wife had bought for protection (against humans, oddly enough), I zapped them with one hundred thousand volts. To my chagrin, I woke up two hours later in our Irish Setter's dog house. My head throbbed and I felt my teeth sweat, and out of my one good eye I was able to make out the baboons performing a scene from *The Glass Menagerie* in our back yard. At the moment Jim (played quite understatedly by a four-year-old mandrill called Sunny) tells Laura (played by my wife) that he is already engaged, Porky, the baboon technical advisor, administers a shock of one hundred thousand volts to my wife's nostrils, causing her to carom off of our barbecue pit and into the Namaqualand daisy garden. I pass out, myself, the pain so far up my ass it feels like an electric eel has set up shop in my colon.

After my wife and I convalesced over the span of the afternoon, I rushed to the back door, red with fury and found it locked. The same thing with the front door. When I knocked with a flurry of knuckle-rending jabs, a young, bluish baboon peered through the French door and gave me the middle finger. I felt, for the first time, truly defeated.

While camped out in our backyard that night, my wife and I discussed the viability of overrunning our now baboon-overrun abode with a surprise attack at dawn. We spent the night in agony, as we could see through the backlighted curtains a number of baboons in repose, sipping from a bottle of my Rustenburg Peter Barlow 1997, Stellenbosch and watching an instructional video on Kundalini yoga. The first hint of dawn inclined with the crow of a cock and I resolved to make one last valiant attempt at ridding my home of these pretentious, vile baboons. I tip-toed to the garage and undid the latch on my safe, removing my twelve-gauge. I motioned to my wife to "stay low" and mouthed the words "call for help if it looks like things are going awry." She shrugged her shoulders quizzically, crouched behind the dog house and blew me a kiss. The house, the yard, the sky were all dark, there was nary a sound save for the buzzing of a fluorescent light in the living room. I charged with all my might through toward our living room window, bracing myself for the cacophony, the shattering of glass, the ultra-violence.

I woke up two days later in the movie theatre, my wife rubbing a cool washcloth on my head. I had apparently been feverish and in and out of sanity for the last thirty-six hours and near death during the first twelve. My wife explained that the baboons had, at some point during our unconsciousness, managed to rig up a stage set from Ibsen's *Little Eyolf* and negotiate it over the back of our house. I had run full bore into the cedar-made backdrop (as I think on it now, you really only need a few chairs to stage *Little Eyolf*, but you've got to give the baboons points for meticulousness.) which had been, as far as my wife could tell, rigged up with one hundred thousand volts from the taser gun then run through a carbon allotrope blaster tube lined with graphite and here I was. Here we are! Defeated.

My wounds have healed for the most part and, along with the Stangenbergs, our family is making due here at the theatre. We are healthy, which is no small luxury, but we are bored. If any of us watches

Critters II again, I fear there may be rampant lunacy. But, then, there is the alternative. Last night, a promotional flyer was slipped under the door of the theatre with an eerie, almost primitive scrawl in crayon across the paper that read, after heavy deciphering: Baxter Theatre, 8:00 p.m. *Waiting for Godot*.

Typical, I thought. They've gone post-modern.

PIECES OF SCHEHERAZADE

Nicole Kornher-Stace

from Zahir

THE THOUSAND NIGHTS, THOSE WERE NOTHING. SHE WAS ONLY buying time. It took her three years to stave off the inevitable, to haggle her life back with what currency she knew: three years of tale-telling from dusk to dawn; three years of pacing, and fretting, from dawn till dusk. So passed the famous thousand, sieving like sand through her fingers. When no one was looking she tallied them, as prisoners will do, with pilfered ink and a needle, on the tender hidden arches of her feet. Her wounded pride couldn't settle for forgetting. Or so the evidence suggests.

And on the thousand-and-first night, though it was given out widely that she was pardoned, wedded, settled, and so remained thereafter in the palace as a favored bride (ridiculous, insult to injury: the woman was brimful with other people's adventures, spilling over with their ghosts: how could she be bought with such tepid promises, such a dull reconciliation?)—the truth is she vanished, she dissolved like sugar into water, like darkness into night.

So why didn't she escape earlier, we are driven to ask, before the marriage and the charivari and the ritual bedding ever took place? Why not make her bid for freedom before the thousand slave-nights had elapsed?

As for that, we will never know. After the humiliation of captivity, the lost years spent songbird-caged, she had dredged her brain to buy her life with story but one secret she had managed to retain. She ran with it and hid with it. And after a time (during which an impostor was cunningly transposed in the palace, and actors made of puzzled maids and children, to save face) she died with it. But it did not die with her.

When we found her she had nothing, only this.

We had been fortunate to find her at all, even more fortunate to find her as we did. It appears that when she ran she took little with her—enough food for a few days, perhaps, and water, not enough to be missed from the labyrinthine kitchens of the palace; also ink, it would seem, and the needle with which she'd counted her days. In the desert she found a cave, and walled herself up inside it. (This is at least what we deduce; it is unlikely she had had an accomplice.)

And she told her last story.

She told it to the sand and the stone and the night, and to the cast-off phantoms of what long-stale tales she'd conjured, once, to drive her death away. In her perpetual darkness she told it, and in the silence beyond the obsolescence of speech. She told it painstakingly and at great cost. It must have taken some time. But it was the only story she would ever tell on her own terms, in her own words, in her own way. So she wrapped herself in it and died in its arms.

Perhaps it was a lucky wind that drove the sand to cover her, once she had gone. Though the nature of the winds in that area are such that the cave should have been left clear of drifting—in fact *must* have been so, if she was to find it in the first place—she had been walled in by this time, and the sand had to have come from *somewhere*. It is a pleasant thought to think, that there are still such mysteries in the world.

Then again, perhaps she had foreseen this need. She had had a thousand days, after all, to prepare.

In any case the sand had covered her, had preserved her from decay, for such a time as upon reflection seems astonishing.

We uncovered her. Slowly, gently, with endless aching care.

And we read.

(Barring the theory of the accomplice, who is to say how she did this thing? In the cave neither mirror nor light could possibly have been provided; and as to how she succeeded in inking that precise tiny lettering into the small of her back, for instance, or on her eyelids, across her shoulder blades—the inks, long dried, were found beside her, shades of blood and jade and indigo, and the needle still clutched in her hand. Neither the corpse of an assistant nor the vessel of a jinn were anywhere in evidence.)

In no way could we presume to arrange the text either in the order of its writing or into any structured tale, familiar or otherwise. We must assume the dying author intended for her last words to be read as they were found, as we came to them, armed with tools to brush and peer and transcribe, and as the light fell across her antique skin we chronicled the variable timeline of their discovery. Or else, that the existence of these words could never possibly be realized, that living eyes would never be laid on them at all. It would not be the first secret the desert has kept, and probably not the greatest.

In any case find them we did, and we set them to paper as best we could, though it proved an endeavor beset at once by kismet, by chance, and by human subjectivity. Naturally, all errors of intention and translation are our own—but the words, the *words*, were only ever hers.

One cannot help but sense in them some unsounded bitter welling of regret, almost of apology, though she provides us with no clue as to who this might address.

[Item: blue ink, brow and temples, trailing off between the eyes]
Ever since she was a child, she's been guilty of treating life as a gift in paper too pretty to tear. Only in dreams has she honestly felt alive. The sort of dreams you wake from in a fury, a rage of loss.

This one most recurs:

[Item: green ink, cheekbones to lips]

If she dared to fall asleep for just a moment, he'd shake her into wakefulness. *The night's still young*, he'd say. *The telling's through?*

Half-awake she'd answer him, *Not yet. Be still and listen, and you'll hear—*

[Item: blue ink, both eyelids]

They told her she was witty and pretty and gentle and good.

And then they sent her away, because these things were all true.

[Item: red ink, jaw-throat-collarbone,
avoiding the jugular with surgical precision]

Once not so very long ago there lived a little girl. She was not like other little girls. She gathered stories to herself, crystalline ideas of the way the world should be: beautiful, terrible, endlessly adventuresome. When she was very small she fell into a deep state of disappointment because there were no monsters living under her bed. When she was older, the monsters still had not evidenced themselves, and her condition had not improved. When she was older still, her parents married her off to a man of great importance, and she moved from her lifelong home, leaving all the tracings of her aborted childhood behind. There were no monsters under her new bed, either. There was one in it, nonetheless; and that was quite enough for her.

[Item: red ink, back of neck, disappearing upwards into the hair]

"Which is the sweeter, losing or finding?"

"That must depend."

"On what?"

"On what is lost."

[Item: green ink, across the shoulders and down the length of the back]

What they say is that he travels, ever travels: his haunts are boundless and his guises many: he goes in coats of sparks or ashes, skins or leaves. All the ways and all the keys are his. When come upon the sea, he goes around. When come upon a mountain, he goes through. When winter rides the roofs he'll ride above them, or else walk on fallen towntops, in the snow. He has a little knife to prise out stars with, a little hammer to break the dawn with, a little sickle to cut forks of hazel with, which aid him as he seeks. Too, he has a feathered jacket, in which he flies unfettered, magpie-greedy, taking, here and there, such souls as shine. His finding-list is in the pocket sewn where he might instead have had a heart. He's brutal, beautiful, and fey.

They also say:

If he comes to you in dreams, that dream's your last.

[Item: red ink, upper right arm]

She was well aware what had in actuality befallen such brides as briefly warmed his bed for years before she herself was trundled in—with what etiquette, what strained and empty politesse—to share that phantom-haunted bed, and set her fate with theirs. She knew, and yet she went. Though she did not forgive her father, she did resign herself to whatever kismet, in its caprices, might choose to throw her way: she accepted all these awful unnamed mysteries with neither protest nor complaint. There were those, she knew, who wondered why. Ah, she could have answered, had they only ever thought to ask.

[Item: blue ink, upper left arm]

Sometimes, late at night, after he had dropped off into sleep, she'd stay wakeful for a time, taking quiet inventory of her head. By now she'd told him all the stories of the desert, the cunning pirates in their galleys and the jinn-lamps in their caves; she told him the borderless stories, familiar everywhere, of the faces in the stars and on the sun, and of the cyclic birth and death of years. She'd told, too, the tales of foreign lands, hauled up from memory: full of ashy riddling peasant-princesses, forbidden rooms, clever snakes and foxes, and things-that-

are-not-what-they-seem; of skin-switchers, of between-worlds-pris-
oners, of ever-ageless witch queens whose frozen hearts are missing
somewhere dark; of all the questing youngest sons, sent by default:
accidental wanderers, and by the will of another, and, upon return, lost
to all the world.

[Item: red ink, sides of ribs and waist to upper hips]

It was snowing. She had never seen snow, but knew it in her heart
through childhood stories brought from foreign lands, and so she could
not be surprised. In the snow she walked, under a wintry white sun,
side by side and hand in hand with he who had rescued her from the
lesser and greater tyrannies of the palace and its master. Through a
wood they went, ankle-deep in white, grafting their shadows to the
shadows of trees native only to distant, wetter lands. They walked until
they came upon the center of the wood, where stood a snug little house,
all nestled down into the wintering green: low-roofed and unassuming, with wooden walls and firelit windows, and a length of smoke
untangling from the chimney, like a silken veil tossed up into the air.
She knew the house at once to be her own, their own, and indeed it was
toward the front door that they headed. He led her and she went. There
inside the little house, it was warm, much warmer than the air without.
In one corner, a fire blazed. By a farther wall leaned a table, holding
milk and wine and honey and fruit and bread. Between the doorway
and the hearth there was a bed, thick with quilts and pillows, deep and
soft, already warmed by the heat of the fire. He led her there and lay
her down and kissed her top to toe and at that point, always just then,
she woke, and he, a ghost in light, dissolved.

[Item: green ink, between the breasts and down to the navel, spiraling there]

Fact: All tales have lessons.

　　Lesson. The key to the kingdom is the denial of the lock.

　　Lesson. Slay the standard-bearer. Always. First.

Lesson. Icarus had the right idea. There are too many prisons, not enough wings.

Lesson. Live each day as if it's your first. Live each day as if it's your last.

Lesson. Amidst atrophy, nothing's prettier than pain.

Lesson. Too much of a good thing is nowhere near enough.

Lesson. Perpetual disappointment leads to a state of zero responsibility.

Lesson. The only difference between a memory and a ghost is that one leaves scars as it passes (which only hurt more as they fade).

Lesson. To be blissfully ignorant is to be ignorant of bliss.

Lesson. Unattainability is the greater part of worth.

Lesson. We are no greater than the sum of our *discrepancies*—

[Item: green ink, girdling the hips]

Who ever asked her what she wanted? She knew enough to know not to tell what she was not asked; but this she could have told, asked for it or no, in detail and at length. She could have, even though they'd never understand. She did not want the palace and its trappings. She did not want the gowns. Neither the jewels nor the ornaments held her attention. The rich foods and fine wines stuck in her throat like stones. Beneath the layered finery, her entire person itched, like it wanted to jump clean out of its skin. Maybe it did. Maybe then she would have been free. Free of the clucking maids and the unwanted attention, free of the endless eyes on her, free of the invisible leash to which she was very actually tethered. Free of the courting king and his occasional tendernesses and his not infrequent cruelties; free of his smile, which ground on her like glass; free of his hands, which sought her and repulsed her and sought her still, even forced her, at times, at his whim. Free of the endless nightly telling, of the endless daily rummaging in her exhausted mind, of the endless looming need to make such draining payments against the keeping of her life.

Deep in her heart, none of these things had any claim. There, she was already free.

[Item: blue ink, right forearm and hollow of right elbow]

At one point, the princess was a child. Being a princess, she had lots of things that didn't really matter. Among these riches, her only prized possession was some piece of cheap jewelry, some clay beaded necklace or ring, some worthless something. She didn't know where she got it, only that she had it, and it meant the world to her. Maybe to her imagination it was quite valuable, and possession thereof made her terrifyingly rich. Maybe she fancied it had some hidden importance, some ability. Who knows. Who cares. The point is that one day she realized that this thing, this basis of her existence, was a piece of junk. It wouldn't help her in any way, wouldn't come to aid her in distress, wouldn't open doors to other worlds. She had built her life up around it and it was nothing. And so was she.

[Item: green ink, left forearm and hollow of left elbow]

His mistress, too, is a soul-shearer, of a kind—but her flayings of herself. Come thaw, she hangs her old skins in a tree, and when they're dried, she'll cut her dresses of them: they never fit, but serve to ground her. Her eyes are birds' eyes, and she rides the wind, astride a stand of thorn. Hunting, she walks backwards, on one foot, sweeping her prints from before her; returning, she skips, whirls, cavorts, heedless, in her skirts of skin. Her hat is hung with birdskulls, her boots beaded with the bones of baby hares. It's she who pens the finding-lists; she mends his ash-coat, spark-coat, coat of leaves. She follows and she leads. When he's lost, it's she who finds him, stuck up trees or down lakebottoms, searching sunken gravestones in the mud. He's bound to her, breath and bone: he rises to her cry.

And she, for her part, never tires, discovering, rediscovering, day by day, by night, all the dark unsounded deepenings that make him.

In short, she's in his blood. And he in hers.

[Item: green ink, back of right hand and fingers]

Sometimes the maids asked her little questions, because they found her answers amusing, and because they also found that amusement was hard for them, in that place, to come by. One day they came to her and asked her if she was afraid of death. She was a brave little girl, so she said no. She knew death well, she knew him from stories, she had hold of him by the name, and so she could hardly bring herself to fear him. But if they had asked her if she was afraid of life, with whose name she was acquainted, but whose face was still a stranger's—who knows what answer she'd have given?

[Item: blue ink, back of left hand and fingers]

It did not take her long to realize that the Greeks had told the story all wrong. To navigate the labyrinth you don't need weaponry (to slay the Minotaur) or the nymph with the golden thread (to lead you safely home). You need scissors, walking shoes, and a touch of wanderlust. And don't worry about the Minotaur. It was you all along.

[Item: red ink, inside of left wrist, veins again avoided]

Rather, she only ever wanted one thing, which, despite the riches, gifts, and finery, was nowhere on offer in the palace. More precious even than freedom was this thing. More precious even than the questionable privilege of winning back her life. What was it? Only this: for the truth of her existence to measure up to the fictions in her head. She ached for all the peace and all the adventure and all the happiness and victory and joy of countless empty tales to begin to appear, somewhere, if only on the margins, if only in their tracings, if only in the dreamtime of her small and stunted life. And there was no more for the asking.

[Item: blue ink, inside of right wrist, same]

Although everything beyond the city gates stood ruined, the king's heart was made brave by the untouched symmetrical fastnesses of his palace, the perfect whiteness of its walls, the perfumes of its sculpted gardens; and so he took to his balcony, and there, above the gathered people of the last unbroken city, declared a nationwide moment of silence: for foiled arson everywhere. For all the fires that might have been.

[Item: green ink, palms of both hands, following the lines prewritten]
Last night he came to her in a dream. He appeared to her in the form of a child; but by his coat of sparks she knew him, and by the divining-stick which had sniffed out her sleeping soul and drawn him down to it, to her, down there beneath the sand. He kissed her eyes to open them, and they opened, and she woke, and when she woke, she knew that it was time.

[Item: red ink, fingertips, microscopically]
Once there was, and once there wasn't, a great and legendary hero. On one day he was born. Over other days he grew. On another day he went adventuring. On yet another he returned. Over other days he aged and further aged. Then, one day, he died. They put him in the ground. The people came with flowers. And so?

[Item: red ink, inside of left thigh to knee]
Theirs is a twilight country, inaccessible by most, to most. The fleet of foot may reach it, if they spend a lifetime running. The deepest diggers may unearth it, if they tunnel through the world. But only by accident can it ever wholly be attained. It is a world of dawn and dusk, of silhouettes on violet skies, and of the shadows of shadows, which serve only to mislead. Here, roads lead back upon themselves; the buildings hang unfinished in midair; eyes like green sequins hide up every tree, and the flesh of every windfall's poison. The path does not exist that can be trusted to its end. Neither map nor compass will avail.

Just before the gates, those accidental travelers mill about, unlucky enough to reach them: as though people in a tale they pace a clockwork circuit, predescribed. Like ghosts wandering, seemingly at liberty, in a wood. But they are far from free.

[Item: green ink, inside of right thigh to knee]

This is what she would have said:

Words are handicapped by their given definitions. People are handicapped by their given names. Things are handicapped by their given uses. Explorations are handicapped by their given boundaries. Beliefs are handicapped by their given structures. Worlds are handicapped by their given rules. Lives are handicapped by their given expectations. All experience is handicapped by comparison. What it might, might not, surpass.

And so how could any of it suffice? It all pales so alongside its potential. The potential of worlds distant . . . planes unaligned . . . veils unlifted . . . songs unsung . . .

Or again she might have said:

Maybe she's only flung herself in the face of all she doesn't want to encounter for the simple sake of being flung in the face of *something—*

[Item: blue ink, hollow of left knee to ankle,
text tightly wrapped like a ribbon around the calf]

How many days had it taken? How many nights? How many vicarious triumphs, how many of some lucky other one's escapes? Too many, too many, and none of her own. Still, the stories were all she had to float her, in a way; and though they caused her to both envy and despair, they also raised her way high up above herself to a vantage point where she could clearly see. From there she saw much. She saw herself in miniature, locked as if in a portrait, smiling on the outside, nothing but glass underneath. She saw her patience and her desperation, and she saw that in all likelihood, neither one would save her. She saw these things and others, and also this: that something indefinable was changing in her. Something in her had hardened or only broken away. Something was weeping, raw as any wound. Perilous as the shock beyond the pain.

[Item: red ink, hollow of right knee to ankle, same]

For a time, while the stories were still young in her, she would reconcile herself to truth with speculations, she'd weave up little fictions with which she sought to justify her state. *They had no choice*, she'd tell herself. She'd say, *They'd already lost the war. How could they make peace with the enemy? Her father, the king, consulted his sages, and this is what they answered him: You must offer him your daughter in exchange for your city. What else could suffice to placate such a man? Ah, we see you hesitate. Think not of her safety: she will be safe. Think rather of the thousands whose humble houses will stay whole, whose possessions will not be ransacked, who will not themselves be forced to suffer the ravages of invading armies. Think of them who cannot depend on the mercy of their king's enemies, who cannot lean on the crutch of diplomacy, who have, in fact, only the beneficence of their ruler to comfort their minds when they wake to smell the wind-blown smoke, when they see the high fires on the horizon where yesterday the other cities stood.*

The truth is there had been no war. There had been no consultation of the wise. There had been a business transaction, a changing of hands, an exportation from one palace to another. What there was not was any consolation in truth. So she fell into fictions. For a while, anyway, she was more comfortable there.

[Item: green ink, top of left foot,
radiating in lines along the tendons to the toes]

There's an old superstition that will assure you that when you take off your shoes, if you set them down lengthwise in such a way that each one points in an opposite direction, toe to heel, heel to toe, aligned backwards, this is a surefire way to ward off demons. Well she for one has learned to set her shoes the other way, toes together, heels together, each to each. She needs more demons in her life. Or, at least, some new ones.

[Item: blue ink, top of right foot, same]

The hero never met the princess. How could he have done? He was always off adventuring, and she was forbidden to so much as set foot outdoors. Still, in a fairer world it might somehow have happened: he might have appeared one day to rescue her, to hammer down the gates and sweep her up and slay her monster for her, and take her away with him on his journeys to help slay monsters of his own. If she had lived a story, this all might easily have happened. But she did not, and it did not. The end.

[Item: red ink, sole of left foot, overwriting countless tally marks,
by now somewhat faded]

It seemed that by that time she had become very little more than this: a message in a bottle badly sealed, dead and waterlogged and host to mold and rot—a colony of real true life thriving battened on drowned words. She did not know when this transformation had taken place. Nor did she suspect it could ever be undone. In any case she'd been made, at times, to wonder: upon fusing oneself with innumerable fictions, is it a gain or loss of self that's precipitated? Both? Neither? And if the latter, then where had she gone?

Like dreams, like lives, like stories, to put this into words is to kill it, a little.

[Item: green ink, sole of right foot, same]

Behind every thwarted hero, you'll find a story crouching in his shadow. On the tongue of every dead man burn tales aching to be told. King and scapegrace prove themselves alike in this respect: what haunt us in death's waiting-room are all the things we've left unsaid. And when our names come first on his finding-list, and one day we glance toward the sky and see the silhouette high up there waiting, hovering, patient, somewhere between us and the sun, and when he lands before us, drops a bow, and curses at the newest rent in the feathered jacket that she'll now have need to mend, then turns to us and checks his list and nods and smiles, and, smiling still, holds forth one hand to take and lead us on and onward to his accidental country, we've nothing left to say to death but Wait—just a little while longer—such wondrous squandered truths I'd had in me to tell—but, somehow, never could quite find the way.

Next time around, death says, perhaps you will.

[Notably, it was neither starvation nor cold that claimed her, in the end. Autopsy reveals to us that when she died it was with a stable core temperature and food in her stomach. Rather what killed her was blood poisoning: all her veins running with calligraphers' ink.]

ORIGIN STORY

Kelly Link

from A Public Space

"DOROTHY GALE," SHE SAID.

"I guess so." He said it grudgingly. Maybe he wished that he'd thought of it first. Maybe he didn't think going home again was all that heroic.

They were sitting on the side of a mountain. Above them, visitors to the Land of Oz theme park had once sailed, in molded plastic gondola balloons, over the Yellow Brick Road. Some of the support pylons tilted or tipped back against scrawny little opportunistic pines. There was something majestic about the felled pylons now that their work was done. They looked like fallen giants. Moth-eaten blue ferns grew over the peeling yellow bricks.

The house of Dorothy Gale's aunt and uncle had been cunningly designed. You came up the path, went into the front parlor and looked around. You were led through the kitchen. There were dishes in the kitchen cabinets. Daisies in a vase. Pictures on the wall. Follow your Dorothy down into the cellar with the other families, watch the tornado swirl around on the dirty dark wall, and when everyone tramped up the other, identical set of steps through the other, identical cellar door, it was the same house, same rooms, but tornado-tipped. The parlor floor now slanted and when you went out through the (back) front door, there was a pair of stockinged plaster legs sticking out from under the house. A pair of ruby slippers. A yellow brick road. You weren't in North Carolina anymore.

The whole house was a ruin now. None of the pictures hung straight. There were salamanders in the walls, and poison ivy coming up in the kitchen sink. Mushrooms in the cellar, and an old mattress that someone had dragged down the stairs. You had to hope Dorothy Gale had moved on.

It was four in the afternoon and they were both slightly drunk. Her name was Bunnatine Powderfinger. She called him Biscuit.

She said, "Come on, of course she is. The ruby slippers, those are like her special power. It's all about how she was a superhero the whole time, only she didn't know it. And she comes to Oz from another world. Like Superman in reverse. And she has lots of sidekicks." She pictured them skipping down the road, arm in arm. Facing down evil. Dropping houses on it, throwing buckets of water at it. Singing stupid songs and not even caring if anyone was listening.

He grunted. She knew what he thought. Sidekicks were for people who were too lazy to write personal ads. "The Wizard of Oz. He even has a secret identity. And he wants everything to be green, all of his stuff is green, just like Green Lantern."

The thing about green was true, but so beside the point that she could hardly stand it. The Wizard of Oz was a humbug. She said, "But he's *not* great and powerful. He just pretends to be great and powerful. The Wicked Witch of the West is greater and more powerfuller. She's got flying monkeys. She's like a mad scientist. She even has a secret weakness. Water is like Kryptonite to her." She'd always thought the actress Margaret Hamilton was damn sexy. The way she rode that bicycle and the wind that picked her up and carried her off like an invisible lover; that funny, mocking, shrill little piece of music coming out of nowhere. That nose.

When she looked over, she saw that he'd put his silly outfit back on inside out. How often did that happen? She decided not to say anything. There was an ant in her underwear. She made the decision to find this erotic, and then realized it might be a tick. No, it was an ant. "Margaret Hamilton, baby," she said. "I'd do her."

He was watching her wriggle, of course. Too drunk at the moment to do anything. That was fine with her. And she was too drunk to feel embarrassed about having ants in her pants. Just like that Ella Fitzgerald song. Finis, finis.

The big lunk, her old chum, said, "I'd watch. But what do you think about her turning into a big witchy puddle when she gets a bucketful of water in the face? When it rains does she say oops, sorry, can't fight crime today? Interesting sexual subtext here, by the way. Very girl on girl. Girl meets nemesis, gets her wet, she just melts. Screeches orgasmically while she does it, too."

How could he be drunk and talk like that? There were more ants. Had she been lying on an antpile while they did it? Poor ants. Poor Bunnatine. She stood up and took her dress and her underwear off—no silly outfits for her—and shook them vigorously. Come out with your little legs up, you ants. She pretended she was shaking some sense into him. Or maybe what she wanted was to shake some sense out of him. Who knew? Not her.

She said, "Margaret Hamilton wouldn't fight crime, baby. She'd try to conquer the world. She just needs a wetsuit. A sexy wetsuit." She put her clothes back on again. Maybe that's what she needed. A wetsuit. A prophylactic to keep her from melting. The booze didn't work at all. What did they call it? A social lubricant. And it helped her not to care so much. Anesthetic. It helped hold her together afterward, when he left town again. Super Glue.

She'd like to throw a bucket of Kryptonite at him. Except that Kryptonite was expensive, even the no-brand stuff. And it didn't really work on him. Just made him sneeze. She could throw the rest of her beer, but he would just look at her and say why did you do that, Bunnatine? It would hurt his feelings. The big lump.

He said, "Why are you looking at me like that, Bunnatine?"

"Here. Have another Little-Boy Wide Mouth," she said, giving up. Yes, she was sitting on an anthill. It was definitely an anthill. Tiny superheroic ants were swarming out to defend their hill, chase off the enormous and evil although infinitely desirable doom of Bunnatine's ass. "It'll put radioactive hair on your chest and then make it fall out again."

"Enjoy the parade?" Every year, the same thing. Balloons going up and up like they couldn't wait to leave town and pudding-faced cloggers on pickup trucks and on the curbs teenage girls holding signs. We Love You. I Love You More. I Want To Have Your Super Baby. Teenage girls not wearing bras. Poor little sluts. The big lump never even noticed and too bad for them if he did. She could tell them stories.

He said, "Yeah. It was great. Best parade ever."

Anyone else would've thought he was being one hundred percent sincere. Nobody else knew him like she did. He looked like a sweetheart, but even when he tried to be gentle, he left bruises.

She said, "I liked when they read all the poetry. Big bouncy guy/ way up in the lonely sky."

"Yeah. So whose idea was that?"

She said, "*The Daily Catastrophe* sponsored it. Mrs. Dooley over at the high school got all her students to write the poems. I saved a copy of the paper. I figured you'd want it for your scrapbook."

"That's the best part about saving the world. The poetry. That's why I do it." He was throwing rocks at an owl that was hanging out on a tree branch for some reason. It was probably sick. Owls didn't usually do that. A rock knocked off some leaves. Blam! Took off some bark. Pow! The owl just sat there.

She said, "Don't be a jerk."

"Sorry."

She said, "You look tired."

"Yeah."

"Still not sleeping great?"

"Not great."

"Little Red Riding Hood."

"No way." His tone was dismissive. As if, Bunnatine, you dumb bunny. "Sure, she's got a costume, but she gets eaten. She doesn't have any superpowers. Baked goods don't count as superpowers."

"Sleeping Beauty?" She thought of a girl in a moldy old tower, asleep for a hundred years. Ants crawling over her. Mice. Some guy's lips. That girl must have had the world's worst morning breath. Amazing to think that someone would kiss her. And kissing people when they're asleep? She didn't approve. "Or does she not count, because some guy had to come along and save her?"

He had a faraway look in his eyes. As if he were thinking of someone, some girl he'd watched sleeping. She knew he slept around. Grateful women saved from evildoers or their obnoxious blind dates. Models and movie stars and transit workers and trapeze artists, too, probably. She read about it in the tabloids. Or maybe he was thinking about being able to sleep in for a hundred years. Even when they were kids, he'd always been too jumpy to sleep through the night. Always coming over to her house and throwing rocks at the window. His face at her window. Wake up, Bunnatine. Wake up. Let's go fight crime. You can be my sidekick, Bunnatine. Let's go fight crime.

He said, "Her superpower is the ability to sleep through anything. Lazy bitch. Her origin story: she tragically pricks her finger on a spinning wheel. What's with the fairy tales and kids' books, Bunnatine? Rapunzel's got lots of hair that she can turn into a hairy ladder. Not so hot. Who else? The girl in Rumplestiltskin who can spin straw into gold."

She missed these conversations when he wasn't around. Nobody else in town talked like this. The mutants were sweet, but they were more into music. They didn't talk much. It wasn't like talking with him. He always had a comeback, a wisecrack, a double entendre, some cheesy sleazy pickup line that cracked her up, that she fell for every time. It was probably all that witty banter during the big fights. She'd probably get confused. Banter when she was supposed to *POW! POW!* when she was meant to banter.

She said, "Wrong. Rumpelstiltskin spins the straw into gold. She just uses the poor freak and then she hires somebody else to go spy on him to find out his name."

"Cool."

She said, "No, it's not cool. She cheats."

"So what? Was she supposed to give up her kid to some little guy who spins gold?"

"Why not? I mean, she probably wasn't the world's best parent or anything. Her kid didn't grow up to be anyone special. There aren't any fairytales about Rapunzel II."

"Your mom."

She said, "What?"

"Your mom! C'mon, Bunnatine. She was a superhero."

"My mom? Ha *ha*."

He said, "I'm not joking. I've been thinking about this for a few years. Being a waitress? Just her disguise."

She made a face and then unmade it. It was what she'd always thought: he'd had a crush on her mom. "So what's her superpower?"

He gnawed on a fingernail with those big square teeth. "I don't know. I don't know her secret identity. It's secret. So you don't pry. It's bad form, even if you're arch-enemies. But I was at the restaurant once when we were in high school and she was carrying eight plates at once. One was a bowl of soup, I think. Three on each arm, one between her teeth, and one on top of her head. Because somebody at the restaurant bet her she couldn't."

"Yeah, I remember that. She dropped everything. And she chipped a tooth."

"Only because that fuckhead Robert Potter tripped her," he pointed out.

"He didn't mean to."

He picked up her hand. Was he going to bite her fingernail now? No, he was studying the palm. Like he was going to read it or something. It wasn't hard reading a waitress's palm. You'll spend the rest of your life getting into hot water. He said gently, "No, he did. I saw the whole thing. He knew what he was doing."

It embarrassed her to see how small her hand was in his. As if he'd grown up and she just hadn't bothered. She still remembered when she'd been taller. "Really?"

"Really. Robert Potter is your mother's nemesis."

She took her hand back. Slapped a beer in his. "Stop making fun of my mom. She doesn't have a nemesis. And why does that word always sound like someone's got a disease? Robert Potter's just a fuckhead."

"Once Potter said he'd pay me ten dollars if I gave him a pair of Mom's underwear. It was when Mom and I weren't getting along. I was like fourteen. We were at the grocery store and she slapped me for some reason. So I guess he thought I'd do it. Everybody saw her slap me. I think it was because I told her Rice Krispies were full of sugar and she should stop trying to poison me. So he came up to me afterward in the parking lot."

Beer made you talk too much. Add that to the list. It wasn't her favorite thing about beer. Next thing she knew, she'd be crying about some dumb thing or begging him to stay.

He was grinning. "Did you do it?"

"No. I told him I'd do it for twenty bucks. So he gave me twenty bucks and I just kept it. I mean, it wasn't like he was going to tell anyone."

"Cool."

"Yeah. Then I made him give me twenty more dollars. I said if he didn't, I'd tell my mom the whole story."

That wasn't the whole story either, of course. She didn't imagine she'd ever tell him the whole story. But the result of the story was that she had enough money for beer and some weed. She paid some guy to buy beer for her. That was the night she'd brought Biscuit up here.

They'd done it on the mattress in the basement of the wrecked farmhouse, and later on they'd done it in the theater, on the pokey little stage where girls in blue dresses and flammable wigs used to sing and tap-dance. Leaves everywhere. The smell of smoke, someone further up on the mountain, checking on their still, maybe, chain-smoking. Reading girly magazines. Biscuit saying, did I hurt you? Is this okay? Do you want another beer? She'd wanted to kick him, make him stop trying to take care of her, and also to go on kissing him. She always felt that way around Biscuit. Or maybe she always felt that way and Biscuit had nothing to do with it.

He said, "So did you ever tell her?"

"No. I was afraid that she'd go after him with a ballpeen hammer and end up in jail."

When she got home that night. Her mother looking at Bunnatine like she knew everything, but she didn't, she didn't. She'd said: "I know what you've been up to, Bunnatine. Your body is a temple and you treat it like dirt."

So Bunnatine said: "I don't care." She'd meant it too.

"I always liked your mom."

"She always liked you." Liked Biscuit better than she liked Bunnatine. Well, they both liked him better. Thank God her mother had never slept with Biscuit. She imagined a parallel universe in which her mother fell in love with Biscuit. They went off together to fight crime. Invited Bunnatine up to their secret hideaway/love nest for Thanksgiving. She showed up and wrecked the place. They went on Oprah. While they were in the studio some supervillain—sure, okay, that fuckhead Robert Potter—implemented his dreadful, unstoppable, terrible plan. That parallel universe was his to loot, pillage, and discard like a half-eaten grapefruit, and it was all her fault.

The thing was, there *were* parallel universes. She pictured poor parallel Bunnatine, sent a warning through the mystic veil that separates the universes. Go on Oprah or save the world? Do whatever you have to do, baby.

The Biscuit in this universe said, "Is she at the restaurant tonight?"

"Her night off," Bunnatine said. "She's got a poker night with some friends. She'll come home with more money than she makes in tips and lecture me about the evils of gambling."

"I'm pretty pooped anyway," he said. "All that poetry wore me out."

"So where are you staying?"

He didn't say anything. She hated when he did this.

She said, "You don't trust me, baby?"

"Remember Volan Crowe?"

"What? That kid from high school?"

"Yeah. He used to draw comics about this superhero he came up with. Mann Man. A superhero with all the powers of Thomas Mann."

"You can't go home again."

"That's the other Thomas. Thomas Wolfe."

"Thomas Wolfman. A hairy superhero who gets lost driving home."

"Thomas Thomas Virginia Woolfman Woman."

"Now with extra extra superpowers."

"Whatever happened to him?"

"Didn't he die of tuberculosis?"

"Not him. I mean that kid."

"Didn't he turn out to have a superpower?"

"Yeah. He could hang pictures perfectly straight on any wall. He never needed a level."

"I thought he tried to destroy the world."

"Yeah, that's right. He was calling himself something weird. Fast Kid With Secret Money. Something like that. Got kidnapped by a nemesis. The nemesis used these alien brain-washing techniques to convince him he had to destroy the world in order to save the world."

"That's really lame. I wouldn't fall for that."

She said, "Shut up. I hear you fall for it every time."

"What about you?"

She said, "Me?"

"Yeah."

"Keeping an eye on this place. They don't pay much, but it's easy money. I had another job, but it didn't work out. A place down off I-40. They had a stage, put on shows. Nothing too gross. So me and Kath, remember how she could make herself glow, we were making some extra cash two nights a week. They'd turn down the lights and she'd come out on stage with no clothes on and she'd be all lit up from inside. It was real pretty. And when it was my turn, guys could pay extra money to come and lie on the stage. Do you remember that hat, my favorite hat? The oatmeal-colored one with the pom-poms and the knitted ears?"

"Yeah."

"Well, they kept it cold in there. I think so that we'd have perky tits when we came out on stage. So we'd move around with a bit more rah-rah. But I wore the hat. I got management to let me wear the hat, because I don't float real well when I'm real cold."

"I gave you that hat," he said.

"Yeah. At Christmas. I loved that hat. So I'd be wearing the hat and this dress—nothing really revealing or cheap-looking—and come out on stage and hover a foot above their faces. So they could see I wasn't wearing any underwear."

He was smiling. "Saving the world by taking off your underwear, Bunnatine?"

"Shut up. I'd look down and see them lying there on the stage like I'd frozen them. Zap. They weren't supposed to touch me. Just look. I always felt a million miles above them. Like I was a bird." A plane. "All I had to do was scissor my legs, kick a little, just lift up my hem a little. Do twirls. Smile. They'd just lie there and breathe hard like they were doing all the work. And when the music stopped, I'd float offstage again. But then Kath left for Atlantic City, to go sing in a cabaret show. And then some asshole got frisky. Some college kid. He grabbed my ankle and I kicked him in the head. So now I'm back at the restaurant with Mom."

He said, "How come you never did that for me, Bunnatine? Float like that?"

She shrugged. "It's different with you," she said, as if it were. But of course it wasn't. Why should it be?

"Come on, Bunnatine," he said. "Show me your stuff."

She stood up, shimmied her underwear down to her ankles with an expert wriggle. All part of the show. "Close your eyes for a sec."

"No way."

"Close your eyes. I'll tell you when to open them."

He closed his eyes and she took a breath, let herself float up. She could only get about two feet off the ground before that old invisible hand yanked her down again, held her tethered just above the ground. She used to cry about that. Now she just thought it was funny. She let her underwear dangle off her big toe. Dropped it on his face. "Okay, baby. You can open your eyes."

His eyes were open. She ignored him, hummed a bit. Why oh why oh why can't I. Held out her dress at the hem so that she could look down the neckline and see the ground, see him looking back up.

"Shit, Bunnatine," he said. "Wish I'd brought a camera."

She thought of all those girls on the sidewalks. "No touching," she said, and touched herself.

He grabbed her ankle and yanked. Yanked her all the way down. Stuck his head up inside her dress, and his other hand. Grabbed a breast and then her shoulder so that she fell down on top of him, knocked the wind out of her. His mouth propping her up, her knees just above the ground, cheek banged down on the bone of his hip. It was like a game of Twister, there was something Parker Brothers about his new outfit. There was a gusset in his outfit, so he could stop and use the bathroom, she guessed, when he was out fighting crime. Not get caught with his pants down. His busy, busy hand was down there, undoing the Velcro. The other hand was still wrapped around her ankle. His face was scratchy. Bam, pow. Her toes curled. He's got you now, Bunnatine.

He said up into her dress, "Bunnatine. Bunnatine."

"Don't talk with your mouth full, Biscuit," she said.

She said, "There was a tabloid reporter around today, wanting to hear stories."

He said, "If I ever read about you and me, Bunnatine, I'll come back and make you sorry. I'm saying that for your own good. Do something like that, and they'll come after you. They'll use you against me."

"So how do you know they don't know already? Whoever *they* are?"

"I'd know," he said. "I can smell those creeps from a mile away."

She got up to pee. She said, "I wouldn't do anything like that anyway." She thought about his parents and felt bad. She shouldn't have said anything about the reporter. Weasely guy. Staring at her tits when she brought him coffee.

She was squatting behind a tree when she saw the pair of yearlings. They were trying so hard to be invisible. Just dappled spots hanging in the air. They were watching her like they'd never seen anything so fucked up. Like the end of the world. They took off when she stood up. "That's right," she said. "Get the hell away. Tell anybody about this and I'll kick your sorry Bambi asses."

She said, "Okay. So I've been wondering about this whole costume thing. Your new outfit. I wasn't going to say anything, but it's driving me crazy. What's with all these crazy stripes and the embroidery?"

"You don't like it?"

"I like the lightning bolt. And the tower. And the frogs. It's psychedelic, Biscuit. Can you please explain why y'all wear such stupid outfits? I promise I won't tell anyone."

"They aren't stupid."

"Yes they are. Tights are stupid. It's like you're showing off. Look how big my dick is."

"Tights are comfortable. They allow freedom of movement. They're machine washable." He began to say something else, then stopped. Grinned. Said, almost reluctantly, "Sometimes you hear stories about some asshole stuffing his tights."

She started to giggle. Giggling gave her the hiccups. He whacked her on the back.

She said, "Ever forget to run a load of laundry? Have to fight crime when you ought to be doing your laundry instead?"

He said, "Better than a suit and tie, Bunnatine. You can get a sewing machine and go to town, dee eye why, but who has the time? It's all about advertising. Looking big and bold. But you don't want to be too designer. Too Nike or Adidas. So last year I needed a new outfit, asked around, and found this women's cooperative down on a remote beach in Costa Rica. They've got an arrangement with a charity here in the states. They've got collection points in forty major cities where you drop off bathing suits and leotards and bike shorts, and then everything goes down to Costa Rica. They've got this beach house that some big-shot rock star donated to them. It's this big glass and concrete slab and the tide goes in and out right under the glass floor. I went for a personal fitting. These women are real artists, talented people, super creative, and they're all unwed mothers, too. They bring their kids to work and the kids are running around everywhere and the kids are all wearing these really great superhero costumes. They do work for anybody. Even pro wrestlers. Villains. Crime lords, politicians. Good guys and bad guys. Sometimes you'll be fighting somebody, this real asshole, and you'll both be getting winded, and then you start noticing his outfit and he's looking too and then you're both wondering if you got your outfits at this same place. And you feel like you ought to stop and say something nice about what they're wearing. How you both think it's so great that these women can support their families like this."

"I still think tights look stupid." She thought of those kids wearing their superhero outfits. Probably grew up and became drug dealers and maids and organ donors.

"What? What's so funny?"

He said, "I can't stop thinking about Robert Potter and your mother. Did he want clean underwear? Or did he want dirty underwear?"

She said, "What do you think?"

"I think twenty bucks wasn't enough money."

"He's a creep."

"So you think he's been in love with her for a long time?"

She said, "What?"

"Like maybe they had an affair once a long time ago."

"No way!" It made her want to puke.

"No, seriously, what if he was your father or something?"

"Fuck you!"

"Well, come on. Haven't you wondered? I mean, he could be your father. It's always been obvious that he and your mom have unfinished business. And he's always trying to talk to you."

"Stop talking! Right now!"

"Or what, you'll kick my ass? I'd like to see you try." He sounded amused.

She wrapped her arms around herself. Ignore him, Bunnatine. Wait until he's had more to drink. *Then* kick his ass.

He said, "Come on. You used to wait until your mom got home from work and fell asleep. You said you'd sneak into her bedroom and ask her questions while she was sleeping. Just to see if she would tell you who your dad was."

"I haven't done that for a while. She finally woke up and caught me. She was really pissed off. I've never seen her get mad like that. I never told you about it. I was too embarrassed."

He didn't say anything.

"So I kept begging and finally she made up some story about this guy from another planet. Some *tourist*. Some tourist with wings and stuff. She said that he's going to come back someday. That's why she never shacked up or got married. She's still waiting for him to come back."

"Don't look at me like that. I know it's bullshit. I mean, if he had wings, why don't I have wings? That would be so cool. To fly. Really fly. Even when I used to practice every day, I never got more than two feet off the ground. Two fucking feet. What is it good for? Waiting tables. I float sometimes, so I don't get varicose veins like Mom."

"You could probably go a little higher if you really tried."

"You want to see me try? Here, hold this. Okay. One, two, three. Up, up, and a little bit more up. Impressed?"

He frowned, looked off into the trees as if he were thinking about it. Trying not to laugh.

"What? Are you impressed or not?"

"Can I be honest? Yes and no. You could work on your technique. You're a bit wobbly. And I don't understand why all your hair went straight up and started waving around. Do you know that it's doing that?"

"Static electricity?" she said. "Why are you so mean?"

"Hey," he said. "I'm just trying to be honest. I'm just wondering why you never told me any of that stuff about your dad. I could ask around, see if anybody knows him."

"It's not any of your business," she said. "But thanks."

"I thought we were better friends than this, Bunnatine."

He was looking hurt.

"You're still my best friend in the whole world," she said, "I promise."

"I love this place," he said.

"Yeah. Me too." Only if he loved it so much, then why didn't he ever stay? So busy saving the world, he couldn't save The Land of Oz. Those poor Munchkins. Poor Bunnatine. They were almost out of beer.

He said, "So what are they up to? The developers? What are they plotting?"

"The usual. Tear everything down. Build condos."

"And you don't mind?"

"Of course I mind!" she said.

He said, "I always think it looks a lot more real now. The way it's falling all to pieces. The way the Yellow Brick Road is disappearing. It makes it feel like Oz was a real place. Being abandoned makes you more real, you know?"

Beer turned him into Biscuit the philosopher-king. Another thing about beer. She had another beer to help with the philosophy. He had one too.

She said, "Sometimes there are coyotes up here. Bears, too. The mutants. Once I saw a sasquatch and two tiny sasquatch babies."

"No way."

"And lots and lots of deer. Guys come up here in hunting season. When I catch 'em, they always make jokes about hunting munchkins. I think they're idiots to come up here with guns. Mutants don't like guns."

"Who does?" he said.

She said, "Remember Tweetsie Railroad? That rickety rollercoaster? Looked like a bunch of Weebelows built it out of Tinker Toys? Remember how people dressed like toy-store Indians used to come onto the train? I was always hoping I was gonna see them scalp someone this time."

He said, "Fudge. Your mom would buy us fudge. Remember how we sat in the front row and there was that one showgirl? The one with the three-inch ruff of pubic hair sticking out the legs of her underwear? During the cancan?"

She said, "I don't remember that!"

He leaned over her, nibbled on her neck. People were going to think she'd been attacked by squids. Little red sucker marks everywhere. She yawned.

He said, "Oh, come on! You remember! Your mom started laughing and couldn't stop. There was a guy sitting right next to us and he kept taking pictures."

She said, "Why do you remember all this stuff? I kept a diary all through school, and I still don't remember everything that you remember. Like, what I remember is how you wouldn't speak to me for a week because I said I thought *Atlas Shrugged* was boring. How you told me the ending of The Empire Strikes Back before I saw it. 'Hey, guess what? Darth Vader is Luke's father!' When I had the flu and you went without me?"

He said, "You didn't believe me."

"That's not the point!"

"Yeah. I guess not. Sorry about that."

"I miss that hat. The one with the pom-poms. Some drunk stole it out of my car."

"I'll buy you another one."

"Don't bother. It's just I could fly better when I was wearing it."

He said, "It's not really flying. It's more like hovering."

"What, like leaping around like a pogo stick makes you special? Okay, so apparently it does. But you look like an idiot. Those enormous legs. That outfit. Anyone ever tell you that?"

"Why are you such a pain in the ass?"

"Why are you so mean? Why do you have to win every fight?"

"Why do you, Bunnatine? I have to win because I have to. I have to win. That's my job. Everybody always wants me to be a nice guy. But I'm a good guy."

"What's the difference again?"

"A nice guy wouldn't do this, Bunnatine. Or this."

"Say you're trapped in an apartment building. It's on fire. You're on the sixth floor. No, the tenth floor."

She was still kind of stupid from the first demonstration. She said, "Hey! Put me down! You asshole! Come back! Where are you going? Are you going to leave me up here?"

"Hold on, Bunnatine. I'm coming back. I'm coming to save you. There. You can let go now."

She held onto the branch like anything. The view was so beautiful she couldn't stand it. You could almost ignore him, pretend that you'd gotten up here all by yourself.

He kept jumping up. "Bunnatine. Let go." He grabbed her wrist and yanked her off. She made herself as heavy and still as possible. The ground rushed up at them and she twisted, hard. Fell out of his arms.

"Bunnatine!" he said.

She caught herself a foot before she smacked into the ruins of the Yellow Brick Road.

"I'm fine," she said, hovering. But she was better than fine! How beautiful it was from down here, too. She felt like Kath on that stage, like she was glowing all over. Holy Yellow Brick Road, Bunnatine!

He looked so anxious. "God, Bunnatine, I'm sorry." It made her want to laugh to see him so worried. She put her feet down gently. The whole world was made of glass, and the glass was full of champagne, and Bunnatine was a bubble, just flicking up and up and up.

She said, "Stop apologizing, okay? It was great! The look on your face. Being in the air like that. Come on, Biscuit, again! Do it again! I'll let you do whatever you want this time."

"You want me to do it again?" he said.

She felt just like a little kid. She said, "Do it again! Do it again!"

She shouldn't have gotten in the car with him, of course. But he was just old pervy Potter and she had the upper hand. She explained how he was going to give her more money. He just sat there listening. He said they'd have to go to the bank. He drove her right through town, parked the car behind Food Lion.

She wasn't worried. She had the upper hand. She said, "What's up, pervert? Gonna do a little dumpster diving?"

He was looking at her. He said, "How old are you?"

She said, "Fourteen."

He said, "Old enough."

"How come you left after high school? How come you always leave?"

He said, "How come you broke up with me in eleventh grade?"

"Don't answer a question with a question. No one likes it when you do that."

"Well maybe that's why I left. Because you're always yelling at me."

"You ignored me in high school. Like you were ashamed of me. I'll see you later, Bunnatine. Quit it, Bunnatine. I'm busy. Didn't you think I was cute? There were plenty of guys at school who thought I was cute."

"They were all idiots."

"I didn't mean it like that. I just meant that they were really idiots. Come on, you know you thought so too."

"Can we change the subject?"

"Okay."

"It wasn't that I was ashamed of you, Bunnatine. You were distracting. I was trying to keep my average up. Trying to learn something. Remember that time we were studying and you tore up all my notes and ate them?"

"I saw they still haven't found that guy. That nutcase. The one who killed your parents."

"No. They won't." He threw rocks at where the owl had been. Nailed that sorry, invisible, absent owl.

"Yeah?" she said, "Why not?"

"I took care of it. He wanted me to find him, you know? He just wanted to get my attention. That's why you gotta be careful, Bunnatine. There are people out there who really don't like me."

"Your dad was a sweetheart. Always tipped twenty percent. A whole dollar if he was just getting coffee."

"Yeah. I don't want to talk about him, Bunnatine. Still hurts. You know?"

"Yeah. Sorry. So how's your sister doing?"

"Okay. Still in Chicago. They've got a kid now. A little girl."

"Yeah. I thought I heard that. Cute kid?"

"She looks like me, can you imagine? She seems okay, though. Normal."

"Are we sitting in poison ivy?"

"No. Look. There's a deer over there. Watching us."

"When do you have to be at work?"

"Not until 6:00 a.m. I just need to go home first and take a shower."

"Cool. Is there any beer left?"

"No. Sorry," she said. "Should've brought more."

"That's okay. I've got this. Want some?"

"I need a new job."

"You've already got like a hundred jobs, Bunnatine."

"Ski instructor, Sugar Mountain. Security guard, Beech Mountain. Lifeguard at the beach on Grandfather Mountain. Just applied for She-Devil of Mountain Mountain. Do you think that pays well? Lifeguarding was okay. I saved this eight-year-old's life last summer. His sister was trying to drown him. But I always end up back at the restaurant. Waitressing. Waitressing is my destiny."

"Why don't you leave?"

"Why go wait tables in some other place? I like it here. This is where I grew up. It was a good place to grow up. I like all the trees. I like the people. I even like how the tourists drive real slow between here and Boone. I just need to find a new job or Mom and I are going to end up killing each other."

"I thought you were getting along."

"Yeah. As long as I do exactly what she says."

"I saw your mom at the parade. With some little kid."

"Yeah. She's been babysitting for a friend at the restaurant. Mom's into it. She's been reading the kid all these fairy tales. She can't stand the Disney stuff, which is all the kid wants. Now they're reading *The Wizard of Oz*. I'm supposed to get your autograph, by the way. For the kid."

"Sure thing! You got a pen?"

"Oh shit. It doesn't matter. Maybe next time."

It got dark slow and then real fast at the end, the way it always did, even in the summer, like daylight realized it had to be somewhere right away. Somewhere else. On weekends she came up here and read mystery novels in her car. Moths beating at the windows. Got out every once in a while to take a walk and look for kids getting into trouble. She knew all the places they liked to go. Sometimes the mutants were down where the stage used to be, practicing. They'd started a band. They were always asking if she was sure she couldn't sing. She really, really couldn't sing. That's okay, the mutants always said. You can just howl. Scream. We're into that. They traded her 'shine for cigarettes. Told her long, meandering mutant jokes with lots of hand gestures and incomprehensible punchlines. Dark was her favorite time. In the dark she could imagine that this really was the Land of Oz, that when the sun couldn't stay away any longer, when the sun finally came back up, she'd still be there. In Oz. Not here. Click your heels, Bunnatine. There's no home like a summer place.

She said, "Still having nightmares?"

"Yeah."

"The ones about the end of the world."

"Yeah, you nosy bitch. Those ones."

"Still ends in the big fire?"

"No. A flood."

"I keep thinking about that television show."

"Which one?"

"You know. *Buffy the Vampire Slayer.* Even Mom liked it."

"I saw it a few times."

"I keep thinking about how that vampire, Angel, whenever he got evil, you knew he was evil because he starting wearing black leather pants."

"Why are you obsessed with what people wear? Shit, Bunnatine. It was just a TV show."

"Yeah, I know. But those black leather pants that he'd wear, they must have been his *evil* pants. Like fat pants."

"What?"

"Fat pants. The kind of pants that people who get thin keep in their closet. Just in case they get fat again."

He just looked at her. His big ugly face was all red and blotchy from drinking.

She said, "So my question is this. Does the vampire keep a pair of black leather pants in his closet? Just in case? Like fat pants? Do vampires have closets? Or does he donate them to Goodwill when he's good again? Because if so then every time he turns evil, he has to go buy new evil pants."

He said, "It's just television, Bunnatine."

"You keep yawning."

He smiled at her. Such a nice smile. Drove girls of all ages crazy. He said, "I'm just tired."

"Parades can really take it out of you."

"Fuck you."

She said, "Go on. Take a nap. I'll stay awake and keep lookout out for mutants and nemesissies and autograph hounds."

"Maybe just for a minute or two. You'd really like him."

"Who?"

"The nemesis I'm seeing right now. He's got a great sense of humor. Sent me a piano crate full of albino kittens last week. Some project he's working on. They pissed everywhere. Had to find homes for them all. Of course first we checked to make sure that they weren't little bombs or possessed by demons or programmed to hypnotize small children with their swirly red kitten eyes. Give them bad dreams. That would have been a real PR nightmare."

"So what's up with this one? Why does he want to destroy the world?"

"He won't say. I don't think his heart's really in it. He keeps doing all these crazy stunts, like with the kittens. There was a thing with a machine to turn everything into tomato juice. But somebody who used to hang out with him says he doesn't even like tomato juice. If he ever tries to kidnap you, Bunnatine, whatever you do, don't say yes if he offers you a game of chess. Try to stay off the subject of chess. He's one of those guys who think all master criminals ought to be chess players, but he's terrible. He gets sulky."

"I'll try to remember that. Are you comfortable? Put your head here. Are you cold? That outfit doesn't look very warm. Do you want my jacket?"

"Stop fussing, Bunnatine. Am I too heavy?"

"Go to sleep, Biscuit."

His head was so heavy she couldn't figure out how he carried it around on his neck all day. He wasn't asleep. She could hear him thinking.

He said, "You know, some day I'm going to fuck up. Some day I'll fuck up and the world won't get saved."

"Yeah. I know. A big flood. That's okay. You just take care of yourself, okay? And I'll take care of myself and the world will take care of itself, too."

Her leg felt wet. Gross. He was drooling on her leg. He said, "I dream about you, Bunnatine. I dream that you're drowning too. And I can't do anything about it. I can't save you."

She said, "You don't have to save me, baby. Remember? I float. Let everything turn into water. Just turn into water. Let it turn into beer. Clam chowder. Let the Land of Oz become an exciting new investment opportunity in underwater attractions. Little happy mutant Dorothy mermaids. Let all those mountain houses and ski condos sink down into the water, and the deer and the bricks and the high school girls and the people who never tip. It isn't all that great a world anyway, you know? Biscuit? Maybe it doesn't want to be saved. So stop worrying so much. I'll float like a bar of Ivory soap. Even better. Won't even get my toes wet until you come and find me."

"Oh good, Bunnatine," he said, drooling, "that's a weight off my mind"—and fell asleep. She sat beneath his heavy head and listened to the air rushing around up there in the invisible leaves. It sounded like water moving fast. Waterfalls and lakes of water rushing up the side of the mountain. Biscuit's flood. But that was some other parallel universe. Here it was only night and wind and trees and the stars were coming out. Hey, Dad, you fuckhead.

Her legs fell asleep and she needed to pee again, but she didn't want to wake Biscuit up. She bent over and kissed him on the top of his head. He didn't wake up. He just mumbled, quit it, Bunnatine. Love me alone. Or something like that.

She remembered being a kid. Nine or ten. Sneaking back into the house at four in the morning. Her best friend Biscuit has gone home too, to lie in his bed and not sleep. She had to beg him to let her go home. They have school tomorrow. She's tired and she's so hungry. Fighting crime is hard work. Her mother is in the kitchen, making pancakes. There's something about the way she looks that tells Bunnatine she's been out all night, too. Maybe she's been out fighting crime, too. Bunnatine knows her mother is a superhero. She isn't just a waitress. That's just her cover story.

She stands in the door of the kitchen and watches her mother. She practices her hovering. She practices all the time.

Her mother says, "Want some pancakes, Bunnatine?"

She waited as long as she could, and then she heaved his head up and put it down on the ground. She covered his shoulders with her jacket. Like setting a table with a handkerchief. Look at the big guy, lying there so peacefully. Maybe he'll sleep for a hundred years. But more likely the mutants will wake him, eventually, with their barbaric yawps. They're into kazoos right now, and heavy-metal hooting. She can hear them warming up. Biscuit hung out with some of the mutants at school, years and years ago. They'll get a real kick out of his new outfit. There's a ten-year high-school reunion coming up, and Biscuit will come home for that. He gets all sentimental and soft about things. Mutants, on the other hand, don't do things like parades or reunions. They were good at keeping secrets, though. They made great babysitters when her mom couldn't take care of the kid.

She keeps her headlights off, all the way down the mountain. Turns the engine off too. Just sails down the mountain like a black wing.

When she gets home, she's mostly sober and of course the kid is still asleep. Her mom doesn't say anything, although Bunnatine knows she doesn't approve. She thinks Bunnatine ought to tell Biscuit about the kid. But it's a little late for that, and who knows? Maybe she isn't his kid anyway.

The kid has fudge smeared all over her face and her pillow. Leftover fudge from the parade, probably. Bunnatine's mom has a real sweet tooth. Kid probably sat up eating it in the dark, after Bunnatine's mom put her to bed. Bunnatine kisses the kid on the forehead. Goes and gets a washcloth, comes back and wipes off some of the fudge. Kid still doesn't wake up. She's going to be real disappointed about the autograph. Maybe Bunnatine will just forge Biscuit's handwriting. Write something real nice. It's not like Biscuit will care. Bunnatine would like to crawl into the kid's bed, just curl up around the kid and get warm again, but she's already missed two shifts this week. So she takes a hot shower and goes to sit with her mom in the kitchen until she has to leave for to work. Neither of them has much to say to each other, which is normal, but her mom makes Bunnatine some eggs and toast. If Biscuit were here, she'd make him breakfast, too, and Bunnatine imagines that, eating breakfast with Biscuit and her mom, waiting for the sun to come up so that the day can start all over again. Then the kid comes in the kitchen, crying and holding out her arms for Bunnatine. "Mommy," she says. "Mommy, I had a really bad dream."

Bunnatine picks her up. Such a heavy little kid. Her nose is running and she still smells like fudge. No wonder she had a bad dream. Bunnatine says, "Shhh. It's okay, baby. It was just a bad dream. Just a dream. Tell me about the dream."

AN EXPERIMENT IN GOVERNANCE

E.M. Schorb

from The Mississippi Review

FOR SOME VERY IMPORTANT, AND TOP-SECRET, REASONS OF STATE, the people who decided policy desired a change in the thought processes of the people they ruled, so they brought back the rusty old rack and began to stretch anyone who could not change his or her mind fast enough to suit them. Members of the public entered the Ministry of Thought at their natural height and came out about two inches taller. At last, we have become competitive, cried one of the people who decided policy. We shall become the capital of fashion, for we have some of the tallest models available. The Eureka-like quality of this observation caused the people who decided policy at the Ministry of Thought to completely forget what the very important, and top-secret, reasons were that caused them to bring back the rusty old rack in the first place. It was our intention from the beginning, they said with one voice, to open an international modeling agency: and things looked very promising for the new democracy until the people began to shrink back to their natural height, shrinking cartilage pulled down by gravity, as it were, and the people at the Ministry of Fashion, which the Ministry of Thought was now called, searched everywhere for their original reasons for bringing back the rusty old rack, but found that their drawers and filing cabinets, originally stuffed with strategic schemes, were now stuffed with dress patterns, Butterick having infiltrated the Ministry, which had become little more than a rag-shop. Such are the pitfalls of governance.

THE NEXT CORPSE COLLECTOR

Ramola Ɖ

from Green Mountains Review

MY BROTHER ANWAR BRINGS THE MANGLED BODY IN WITH MY father. The red checked shirt is wet with blood, black cotton pant torn at the knees where the bones have slid through. They lay the body on the wooden bench in the courtyard, beside the one drumstick tree that is still standing. The arms hang down and they lift them. The left foot slips, they pull it back, close. They have already closed the eyes. They do not glance at each other. They stand and look down on the body.

It is no secret in our house that Anwar is the favored one, the one my father loves, whom my father looked, early, in the eyes and said, You will be the one who will carry on my work in your life. He meant the work of collecting corpses, from the hospitals and police stations, the bodies of those who lived on the streets, who had no one to sign their papers, dress their bodies for burial, take them to their final resting-place. My father did this for them. He waited outside the hospitals for the summons to pick up the body. With the help of the orderlies or the peons, he loaded the body into the rickshaw, put up the black vinyl cover, and cycled up to the Krishna Raja crematorium by the Krishna temple in Mylapore if they were Hindus or to the Inshallah cemetery in Kilpauk if they were Muslims. He avoided the main roads, seeking out the tight alleys and side-roads, past houses and small shops. He wanted to spare the living, but usually the body was well enough covered that it could pass for a sack of tapioca roots from the vegetable market, or, if reclined, like a sick person going to the doctor.

Sometimes he brought the body home to the house first. He laid the body out in our cramped courtyard, beside the two drumstick trees in the center, and washed and dressed it. He put clothes on them his mosque supplied as a service to the dead, clean white dhotis and long voile shirts on the men, cheap, colored Coimbatore cotton sarees on the women. My mother helped him then. And we did, too, Anwar and I, from very young, we were raised like this, among the living and the dead, it was not strange to us to wipe the whole, wet body down with a cloth, or to pull a comb through the matted hair of a corpse.

It is true the first time I saw one come through the wooden door and lie there in the sunlight on the cracked cement I was silenced. The round noon shadow of the drumstick trees by his foot was tight and dark on his skin. I know I was young, very young, how young I do not know. The shadows of things were large then. All bodies had weight. The house loomed around me like the inside of a giant shell. The walls were tall, the ceilings high. This was long before the house began to shrink into the toy shape it now holds, the cramped restlessness. I had never seen before such absolute stillness in any creature. It was like a sleep that was so deep and folded under itself it could not be touched.

And yet, he was human. I was afraid, because of this—he was a person, like any of us. He might wake at any moment, sit, open his eyes. But he was dead, he was not supposed to, it would be grotesque. He could make his face into a buffalo-demon mask or make his eyes go wide or reach out and squeeze our throats. Being dead all the time, and the horror held me still. My father beckoned me close but I hung back. I waited till they had begun to wash him before I approached. I saw a tuft of black curly hair first, smooth dark sheen to the skin, a layer of moisture on the face where my father had wiped it. A smell rose, sharp and strange, like Dettol, or the tight iron smell of new blood in a market. I came slowly close, held my breath. The eyes were lidded down, a wet sparkle of eye showing through the tight toothbrush lashes, mouth hanging slightly open. The bluish red tongue lolled to one side. It was a man, I saw, a young man.

So young, my mother murmured, as she brought a bucket of water to the body and sat beside him. His arms were thin, legs beneath the dhoti dark. I thought he might have been a rickshaw-walla, the muscles on his calf were tight and bulged. His body was splayed—arms out, legs out, everything spread, as if in defiance of us, the living. Or maybe just in completion, a natural arrogance a person acquires in the deep repose of such sleep, an unselfconsciousness. How did he die, my mother asked, rubbing a wet cloth over his chest. He drank himself to death, my father said. The Rampet police found him lying on his face right outside the toddy shop, in the side by the dustbin, where the pigs live. It's the toddy I smell, then, my mother said, taking her pallu across her nose and chin and tucking it into her shoulder.

I did not come too close. I saw the dry, chapped soles, bruise of bluish-green on the big toe, long, in-curved nails with the dirt under them. His body remained ordinary, alive. I was still afraid he might get up or open his eyes. My heart beat in my chest so loud, like a trapped moth lost in our room at night, I thought it might wake him. So I kept my distance.

But after that day I was not so afraid of the bodies that came to our house looking for that last wash, a hair-combing, clean bowels, and a fresh set of clothes to wear into the next world.

I watched from the door instead, while Anwar helped, and my mother cleaned, and carried away the waste in a closed pan, and my father went methodically over the tasks of pressing the lower abdomen to evict the waste, wiping, washing, clothing the person dead.

Fragments. I picked up fragments. Sometimes whole sentences. I would hear my father say to Anwar, see, this is how, and never leave the police station without this information. Always ask where the body was found, and by whom and how. Always note the time of death, this is important. Because the decay will start otherwise—you need to know when to be ready for it.

And the rigor mortis—you have to be able to move the limbs and push the muscles if you are going to clean the body.

My father never noticed me then, in those days. I hid behind a curtain or a door, trying to hear. It was like being in a school, but just outside the classroom. I ran my hands over the blue peeling wash covering the brick in the outside wall, sucked in the hot sun-smell of the courtyard, and kept still, so they would not know I was crouched there, listening. Anwar worked as if born to the act of service, pouring a bucket of water over the legs, hurrying around to the shoulder or the chest, wiping the face, smoothing the wet hair and fanning it with a dried palm-leaf fan. He was quiet and quick on his feet, which my father praised him for. Time is gold, he would say to him, in our profession, Time is of the essence. If Time is not on our side, we lose. If we spend our Time wisely, we win.

What do we win, he would then ask, like a schoolmaster. We win our fight against Death, Anwar would respond, mechanically. And I would watch them both half-lift, half-drag the body over to the rickshaw, and cover its face with the white cloth that signifies the dead, and tuck in the legs, out of the way of the wheels. My father would shoo the gaping, pointing street-children away. Anwar would squeeze in, beside the corpse's legs, and my father would slowly pedal down the street and into the main road, the clang-clang of his rickshaw bell resounding through the hot afternoon quiet.

I never saw Anwar complain about the work we did. He was a loyal son and he did what he was told. He seemed to have no feeling this way or that about any of it. I would have thought he would be pleased at how my father spent all that time teaching him. And how he brought him gifts: honey bananas, those small red bunches that grow only in the Nilgiris Hills, or yellow guavas from the fruit-man near the Durga temple, or fresh hot *mysore pak* from the next-door neighbor's sweet-shop on the main road. I would always get some too, but everyone, my mother and my father would say, Oh, let Anwar eat, don't bother him, you know he works so hard, he's the one who needs the strength! I took to stealing from the closed plate in the main room (which was our front room and eating-room and cooking-room) at night, it was the only way I could get my hands on the sweets especially, which Anwar loved. Sometimes *gulab jamun* thick with rose syrup, sometimes *laddus* fragrant with cardamom, the falling-apart kind rich with ghee-fried raisins and cashew nuts.

I was too late sometimes. Once, after my afternoon bath, I saw him finish eating something from a dried-leaf cup. He put the cup down and went toward the outside tap to wash his hands. I went toward the cup, put my fingers into the sweet sticky syrup lining the leaf and licked them. It was fresh syrup from a *gulab jamun* from the A One sweet shop, my father had bought this for him, as usual. I could sense Anwar turn, look at me. I scraped some more, I licked like a dog, I kept on licking, until only the taste of leaf touched my tongue. My eyes met Anwar's across the sunlit courtyard. He did not say a word to me. I knew he had not wanted to share the sweet with me. I kicked the cup with my feet and walked away.

My father would talk to me sometimes, here, Amir, go get a pillow for your father's head, or rub my calves down with oil, pa, or go help your mother with the vessels today! But he never taught me his trade as he did with Anwar, and I knew without telling what his heart wanted, and sometimes I would lie awake at night, burning inside like a forest.

I remember so well what happened then. First came the whole week of nights when I saw Anwar wake in the middle of the night and go to the courtyard. I would roll myself up to a ball and peer through the vertical bars of the low window in our room. He walked to the middle, under the drumstick trees where the bodies usually lay, and he pulled something out from his pocket. He scraped a match on the side of a box, lit a cigarette or beedi, I couldn't see what, and he smoked in the dark like any thief, waiting to ransack the house. He was fourteen years old. He finished his cigarette and lay down, right in the middle of the courtyard where every day, a body or two had lain. Sometimes he stretched his arms out wide, or lifted his legs, soles up, to the sky. He twisted slowly left and right, like a yogi practicing his exercises. He crossed his arms behind his head. I don't know if he closed his eyes. I don't know if he saw the moon or clouds float like *gulab jamun* in the blue syrup of that midnight sky. He lay there, motionless, face turned to the heavens.

I squinted upward from the window and imagined how his thoughts, which he shared with none of us, streamed silently out and rose with the wind to merge continuously with the far and sparkling, powdery river of stars. Every night he woke, for a whole week, and every night I woke when he woke and watched him. I fell asleep by the window, watching, slipping down my mat till only my head rested on the windowsill. In the morning I found him beside me in the room, steadily sleeping. My head still on the windowsill, sometimes an arm wrapped around a windowbar. I knew then he must have known I knew about his night-time waking, but he did not speak of this knowledge with me. In the daytime his face was carefully closed, a riverstone face he turned to me as to everyone else, I could not read his thinking.

The next week the cyclone they kept saying on the radio and the TV was going to hit us swept through the city, hitting us, and we had two days and two nights filled with wind and rain. Trees swayed back and forth and bent from the waist down, like bendable straw. Branches

crashed and thundered all night, you could hear only the screeching
and breaking, a floated, incessant howl, like cats fighting or an infant
without milk, unable to sleep. One drumstick tree in the courtyard
snapped in two and fell, as if one part of it wanted to go one way and
the other another. Constantly, leaves and bits of twigs from the neighbor's neem tree and the tamarinds up the street and the acacia clump
by the bus stop swept like rain into the courtyard and lay in a green
bed-blanket on the ground.

We were used to monsoon rain, but not wind and destruction like
this. Lightning flashed continually, and it was strange, sometimes in
colors, bright pink and green, Holi colors. Those two nights Anwar did
not wake and come outside. He lay on his mat as if asleep, although
each time I looked when the lightning flashed, his eyes were open.
It almost made me frightened, because his eyes were staring straight
ahead, as if, where the wall was, he could see something.

Once I said something to him like, hey, Anwar, look how crazy the
wind's getting, and he said, mumbling, as if he was talking to himself,
you only live once. He repeated this, then he said: afterwards, you are
dead.

This was the night before he vanished. Yes, it was still wind and
rain all around us, in the daytime clouds so thick sometimes, branches
flying in the wind, and the lightning yellow sometimes, green sometimes, when Anwar left the house. He was fourteen years old, and he
did not want to do this honorable work I do, my father would say, one
week later when they still could not find him, this honorable work of
preparing the unassociated dead for eternity. He meant the dead who
had no family, no family like ours to take care of you when you were
down or who let you down when you wanted to cling to them, pass
your future into their hands. But the day he left itself we knew he
was gone, there was a raw blistering certainty to the storm then, that
filtered to our bones. We sat on the kitchen floor tearing uselessly at
our hot *chapathis* with our hands, unable to eat, gazing hypnotically at

the small circle of flames on the kerosene stove where the rice was still cooking. My father's eyes in this light glistening with a watery sadness. Outside, the storm punished the trees, the sound of cracking wood loud in the air. The other drumstick tree was making a curious singing sound, bent nearly double to the ground.

When the rains stopped, everybody in the neighborhood looked for Anwar, even the street children, and the roast-groundnut vendor and the guava-lady and the plastic-bottle man who every day lined their carts at the end of our street, beside the Sitapet municipal school, where the bus-stop is, right next to the Durga shrine. They helped my father this way, as a matter of decency. They would expect we'd do the same if misfortune ever stopped at their doorstep. My mother came with us, sometimes, as far as the Sitapet market and the fancy-goods stores in front, she talked to herself, she was that distraught. But we did not find him. I felt foolish, because I did not expect we would. Why would he hide in the textile shops, or the liquor store, or the *maidan* four streets down where the rich-house boys played cricket or flew kites or sat around drinking? What street was long enough for him to lounge in, what rooftop could he possibly climb? My parents walked us in and out of the houses next to ours, tight-lipped and tight-muscled, peering into courtyards, behind zaried curtains, or up at flat roofs and terraces. I knew he had forever left us. He wanted not to be dead or to be with the dead, he wanted a life for himself. But I did not know why he had left his parents. Because it was clear to me all along they wanted him more than myself, it made me wonder what it was he hungered for, and how he could possibly have stepped away from them. I felt he must have wanted both to leave and not leave, there must have been struggle in his going.

Inside myself, too, there was a struggle, although I did not understand what I was feeling. The sadness I felt with him gone was more the sadness I imagined he must have felt, leaving, than anything else.

The time that came afterward was a silent time. My father relapsed into a stubborn melancholy, he could not laugh or joke as he had used to before, he could not bring himself to speak. He went to the mosque on Fridays as always to meet his friends, to worship, but he no longer returned calm and refreshed. My mother, who was Hindu, not Muslim like him, and had used to sing to herself in the evenings, as she lit the agarbathis before her god pictures and said her prayers in the small part of the main room she had set up as her puja room, lit the two kerosene lamps very quietly and did not sing. Her pink Goddess Lakshmi floating on a calendar lotus gazed down on her without kindness. Our god, Allah, whom my brother and I had been used to visiting in mosque occasionally on Fridays with our father, seemed equally determined to be distant. No amount of kneeling to face him in the East or reciting our prayers seemed to affect him.

The work of caring for the dead had to go on (for the dead wait for no auspicious moment to arrive among us), but there was no longer instruction. The work had to be learned by me now, but now my father was not going to teach, I had to pick up what I could. I followed his hands and eyes, I did everything they did. From the beginning I felt my brother was never coming back, and I worked because I believed this was my task now, my future, and my eternity. But in my house they believed the opposite. It might be today, they would think each morning. It might be this week, or the weekend, or the coming week. I silently washed and wiped the passed-away people's bodies and did not share my belief, that it might be never, if Anwar believed he could get away with it.

The secret was in Anwar, I knew. He had held that secret close to himself. The first day of that storm, when the wind had just started muttering and heaving like an old cow in the trees, a man had come to the shade of the drumstick trees in the courtyard whose life we could not imagine. This was because no cause of death could be found for him—no knife wounds or holes in his skin, no sign of swelling or infection, no blueness like gangrene to the limbs. His face was smooth and brown and shiny like a polished coconut shell. Every part of his body gleamed like this, as if he were made of a gleaming flesh-colored metal. The look on his face was calm, not tortured, as it might have been if he had consumed poison. No snake-bites or scorpion-holes in him. The doctors were baffled, my father said, they had released him with a certificate that said Cause of Death Unknown. When you looked at his body you were mystified. He was a man who worked, he had muscle. Yet his face showed refinement—he was well-shaved, his hair cut, fingernails clean. He was like a multiple contradiction. He looked both old and young, as if his age were incidental. Everything was smooth and closed into himself. Like he carried a secret all his life, and now he had died, he had taken it safe and whole away with him. The next day, after we understood Anwar was gone, this man's face kept coming back to haunt me. Once I even dreamed of him, floating in the air like a levitating yogi, closed and perfect in his sleep, under the drumstick trees.

I cannot begin to describe the way in which we lived. The days went by, the weeks, and then the months, Pongal, again, Muharram, Ramzan, Diwali, the monsoon season, the next hot season. Almost immediately it seemed the house had become a mirror of his absence. Between us a constant loss, as if the most necessary organ of the house, the live red throbbing heart, had been removed. And yet, if you can understand this, a whole year went by and we lived in the house as if Anwar was alive and lived with us.

This is how it was. There was always a plate laid out for him, and *chapathis* put on it, hot from the *thawa*, and rice, and yellow *dhal* with *jeera*. We ate as if he ate beside us even though his filled plate remained untouched. My mother filled his stainless-steel glass with water, same as always. The place behind his plate left bare, as if, any moment now, his body would fill it. After the meal my mother took his plate out, beyond the courtyard to the street, and laid it down in the ground for the street dogs. This she did every morning, every afternoon, every night, which is how a family of dogs came to live at our doorstep, and barked to guard our house at night, and wagged their tails when they saw us enter and depart. We became their sustenance. I do not know how my mother and father perceived this. They may have thought these were all ways in which they were helping Anwar, wherever he was. They were doing their part, laying out his food for him. It had become a bargain with God, a small hope that, alive, he was not ever in need, that someone, somewhere, would feed and clothe and shelter him.

And there were pomegranates still, and apples, and guavas, bought just for him. That I was still not allowed to eat, for now they would take the fruit, the day after it was bought, and give it to the poor—the beggar woman at the bus-stop or the man without legs who lived behind the Durga temple. Every now and then sweets would come to the house, but miniscule amounts—a small cone of layered *soam papad* from the street vendor, a single square of *mysore pak*, to be broken and crumbled into each of our plates, at breakfast.

And at night his mat would be unrolled, his sheet unfolded, his pillow fluffed up, a fresh glass of water laid by his pillow, in case he came back when it was dark and he needed to sleep. My mother lit a kerosene lamp and kept it out in the courtyard, so he could see his way in.

I lay in the room night after night and saw the empty mat in the corner, the sheets plain and flat, pillow soft and full. I thought often of how he would lie on his mat, hands folded behind his head, staring up at the ceiling. It was the last image in my mind before I slept. I did not think he would return. But I imagined, every night, his body in the room beside me. I felt, every night, his absence.

The days passed in a blur of routines. I concentrated on work, on helping my father with the bodies, my mother with the house. I lived the way I had always lived, and yet everything in my life was different.

Inside of me I felt the hardness already setting in, the smooth hardness of the muscles in the presence of death. My brother might still be alive, and yet, because he was not alive before us, he was no longer my brother. It was as if he had died and gone away, like any of the corpses who came to our drumstick tree to visit. I felt a skin begin to grow, a close leathery skin, over my feelings. It was I who had to work now for the two of us. I had to accompany my father to the hospitals first, then later in the day to the burning-grounds, where the stench of burning flesh, bleak as drying fish, fills the air for miles. Or to the Muslim cemetery where the diggers often threw me a shovel and made me dig. The days began to tumble headlong one into another, each the same as the one before, until I could no longer tell if there was any difference between sleeping and waking, working and being idle, morning and night.

But one morning I woke and without thinking started to walk down the street by myself to the local Sitapet market. It was a Sunday morning and all the shops were closed. I saw some families dressed in their church clothes heading for the Catholic church behind the Durga temple and I saw the old flower-seller threading jasmine at the corner beside the sweet-shop. I walked through the quiet streets, past the closed doors and sleeping windows, the slowly-waking people as they lined up at the street pumps with their colored plastic *kodams* for Corporation water, I walked past the staring slum women, the dogs sprawled in the loose debris of dustbins. I entered the market through the small alleyway by the side, near the subway and the fancy-goods store, I walked past the few slowly-opening stalls. I looked with glazed eyes at cut-open jewels of pomegranate, unruly heaps of blackening pink honey-bananas, flies already sizzling in the air above them, baskets piled with tiny white pearl onions. I took in the blue uneasy scent of sliced and bled flesh, I passed the sides and legs of goats hung upside down on iron hooks. At the masala store I smelled the high dry must of red chilies, the mountain tinder of black peppercorns. Men jostled against me, their muscles bulging and straining as they carried sacks of rice and groundnuts, going about their business. The boys helping with setting up stalls for the day, emptying boxes, arranging vegetables, paid no attention to me as I walked. I was a boy like them, and a boy unlike them, idle and wandering. Someone was playing a radio, and a woman singing Carnatic music, maybe it was Subbha Lakshmi, her voice kept going over and over the same sound—*aaahnh, aaaahnh, aaahnh*—over and over, each time a little higher. As if she were tuning in with the mridangam and veena behind her for the start of a song, just tuning in, not singing anything yet, but letting the singing go through her throat and out of it, over and over.

I do not know what I was thinking, where I was walking or where I was headed. I was moving as if something in my sleep had entered my mind and was propelling me, as if a dream were pushing me onward. On my feet were the black crossover rubber sandals my brother had used to wear, and before him, some dead person who had stopped in at our house for kindness. My father had taken the sandals to wash his feet and laid them aside, under the drumstick tree, and then, through some strange oversight, for he never overlooked such minute details, just forgotten them. Dressed, this person went barefoot to his Maker, and Anwar inherited the sandals.

He wore them for months, he wore them everywhere outside the house, each time he accompanied my father to the hospitals, each time he disappeared by himself, each time he rode on the rickshaw, before he discarded them. They were too large really, he said, and he went barefoot. So my father bought him soft white Bata slippers that fit better. The sandals then lay under the pile of sheets and mats in the corner of the main room until I found them one day, a full month after he was gone, and began to wear them myself. They fit loosely on my feet too and the heel squeaked each time my weight came down on it.

Because the sandals were loose, they slipped, once, when my foot slipped on tangerine seeds and custard-apple peel and into a ragged crack in the cement poured over the pathway between the stalls. One sandal pried loose, and it is this sudden break in my steady rambling that literally pulled me up short, made me realize what I was doing, where I was, and that people I did not know surrounded me.

That night my mother once more set out Anwar's food for the night, and fed it to the mangy, flea-bitten dogs, who had started to come into the courtyard, all their tails wagging. She spoke softly to the dogs, as if they were her children. Now, now, eat slowly, she would say. Or let that one eat, what's wrong with that. She petted their heads, and their tails wagged for her. Some even licked her hands as she touched them. Once she called to me. Amir, come, get fresh water for the dogs. Later that night, after the doors were closed and the kerosene lamp taken to the middle of the courtyard and turned down low so only a smudge of gold billowed around it, I lay in my room, eyes closed and trying to sleep.

But sleep did not come to me, only the sound of the strange going-over singing I had heard that morning, transmuted. It was no longer calm and practiced, a mature singer's careful rehearsal of voice or song, it felt like it hummed beneath the ground on which we slept and started to tremble as it rose upward into the air and kept rising in pitch and volume until the sound tore like a scream through the walls and the roof and went straight upwards in a burning steel flute into the starry river of sky. It felt as if the house itself was screaming, everything inside us we kept hidden, one from the other, was screaming, and only the sky, with its riven, glittering bodies shorn and distant yet forever burning, knew it.

The next day I walked away by myself again, in the middle of the day when my father was waiting outside the General Hospital by himself, and I was supposed to be waiting by the Sitapet police station, I headed in the direction of the Sitapet market but I went beyond it, toward Rampet. I walked past the St. George's boys' high school and the St.

George's Church and the glass bangle sellers, I walked down the street of household utensils, the rice vessels and milk vessels shining eversilver above my head, the brooms weeping upright where they stood and the new plastic dustpans sheathed safely in their plastic covers from the dirt of the street. The sun rose high in the sky. I felt the heat on my shoulders like a white-hot demon weight descending from the sky, growing larger. My shirt separated damply from the bones of my back and flapped as I walked. Tiny rivulets of sweat crept down the skin inside my shorts.

I stopped only when I came to the Shiva temple pond where they grow purple lotuses, where our mother had taken us once, to see the flowers. It felt like a long time ago. I stood on the narrow bridge linking the street to the temple, and searched through the stray violet blooms, here and there, as if I were looking for something. The temple seemed to float in a sea of large green leaves and spikes and blooms of lotus. I stared at the few intervening scoops of black water. I could not see a sign anywhere I looked. I had not known before I had been looking for one. Now I felt a gnawing achiness inside me, as if a live creature lay coiled inside my stomach and was slowly eating his way outside.

I stood on the bridge for a long time, staring at nothing in particular. Then I stared at the people coming into the temple, the people sweeping the veranda, the people bringing plantains for the gods, and sweet khal-khal and red kum-kum. I stared at the row of male and female flower-sellers sitting outside, weaving garlands of jasmine with their hands. I watched the boys across the street working on bicycles, blowing air into the tires, wiping the spokes with black oily cloths. I was both present to the place and absent in it. Only a part of me was standing there, foolishly watching all the activity around me, and yet this part, unconsciously arrived at this place, shielded by my own dumb confusion, felt furious and desperate to watch.

Those were my early excursions, and I began everyday to make new ones into the vast unknown that lay beyond my parents' house. I was not in school, for I was helping my father. I was not helping my father, for I was in a state of fascination with the world outside my father's house. Each day I craved a new direction, a new horizon. The smallest newness I found myself marveling at, even the sight of convent schoolgirls in their navy blue pinafore uniforms, or the sight of pink-skinned tourists in backpacks throwing bread to the ducks that lived in the Shiva temple water, among the lotuses. More and more I began to spend time away from the house, to sit for hours in various locations in the hot afternoon sun and watch other people going about their daily business. These people were alive, they had work to do, other work than cleaning the dead. Their work, I saw, catered to the living, whether rolling *paan* in betel leaves, cooking hot tea, tailoring sari blouses, or carrying newspapers to the offices. I sat among the ricksha-wallas or the fruit-men with the carts, I watched them.

It was not long, only a few days, before my father noticed this distraction in me, this physical distance I was unrolling between my life and his. My mother tried to protect me, but my father got angry. You are a wastrel, he told me one day, you are not like your brother, you have not a single drop of loyalty in your blood! I am your father, he said, you will do what I do, do what I tell you to!

He began to drag me with him forcibly in the mornings to the hospitals and the police station, he no longer entrusted me alone to one or the other. But now I knew I could wander away from his side, I could watch the doctors and the nurses, the people racked with coughs or bleeding from a knife wound, stationary in the crowded Emergency Room, waiting. Or the policemen talking on their pocket intercoms, jumping onto their motorcycles.

You are becoming dreamful and useless, my father said, as he arranged a man's body in the rickshaw, sitting up, the white sheet the hospital had given draped around his face and shoulders, while I stood by the front wheel, idly staring. Then he said it again, and I knew he was wrong about this: you are nothing like Anwar, such a good and hardworking son, you are not like your brother!

He stopped and twisted his hands, as if they pained him. He himself became upset then, because Anwar's name had been invoked, and in our house, the past few months, we had stopped saying it, even though we were still feeding the dogs in his name. There was too much pain in the syllables, too much loss in the summoning of his presence. We rode home in a sullen silence. I felt as if a cloud of smoke or rain had twisted itself around my tongue. I felt unable to speak out, defend myself. But that night as I first lay alone in my bed, then got up and went to where the stars and the round shivery moon shone in the courtyard, and lay where the bodies lay during the daytime, and stretched my limbs, up to the sky and twisting, first to one side, then to the other, I knew what my father did not know yet. I saw the tiny drumstick leaves cluster around the stars, I felt the hard cement beneath my spine, and I knew already I was becoming my brother.

I was even being mistaken for him. Once, at sunset as I sat at the edge of the *maidan* beside the rich-people's houses with gates and gardens, watching the rich boys play cricket, a tall boy in blue jeans and a loosely open white shirt came up and sat beside me on the wooden bench. He started to smoke, offered me a cigarette. Then he took it back, as if he must have seen how young I was. He stared hard at me, then he shook his head and left. I thought you were someone else, he said. You look exactly like someone I know. I felt a chill as he walked away. I wanted to speak. I wanted to say his name. *Anwar. You knew Anwar. He was here, like I am now, you knew him.* But the boy was gone. I sat for a while longer, watching the game, feeling the fluttering of my heart as if it were a live creature inside me. It got dark and I went home, dragging my sandals in the dust. I felt I was tracing his secret life with my feet, tracing his paths, his habits.

It was a few months afterwards that I left the house. It was the beginning of the monsoon season. We had already lined all our plastic buckets in the courtyard to catch the rainwater. All week we had to use plastic sheets to cover the bodies in the rickshaw, and we had to bring them inside, to the main room, to clean them. Every day we tried to ride them back, to the burning-grounds or the cemetery, but one evening it rained so hard and the water rose in the courtyard so my father said no, let us take him in the morning. The body slept with us, silent and alone in the main room, just a few feet from where I slept, as if he were one of the family. He was an old man, found dead in the gutter, beside a clutch of dead sparrows. They, the man and the birds, had all perished of food poisoning, of hotel food gone bad, a handout from the hotel. Other people who had eaten there had been rushed to the hospital. But an old beggar is easily forgotten.

I could not sleep that night. I remembered how my father cared for all the dead, as if they were all his family. This man he had made a bed of blankets for, as if his body could feel the underlying softness. My mother too had lit agarbathis in the room and left a kerosene lantern by his feet, so he could see the shape of the air in the room if he so wished. As if he were her own son, sleeping for the last time in his parents' house.

I felt a warm spreading sadness for my father and my mother. They had done the best they could, they had done everything they could for Anwar and me. And it was not enough, and they did not know it. They could not make a living thing out of a dead person, they could not work for the living. They were in the hands of dead people, and this is who they were turning me over to.

I stayed awake for a long time that night. I rose from my mat once to look in on the sleeping people. The dead man lay deeply dead, my parents slept against each other, curled into themselves. My mother's gold nose ring glinting, the specks of grey beard on my father's chin beginning to grow. In sleep they looked unguarded and peaceful.

I woke the next morning, very early, and left the house. It was dark and cloudy and raining. I put a piece of plastic over my head, I hoisted my bag of clothes over my shoulders, and I hurried out of the house and the courtyard. A dirty white dog ran up to me in the dark, in the rain, wagging his wet bottle-brush tail, making small whining sounds with his mouth. Shush, I said to him, go away. I walked into the rain and the dog followed me. But he stopped at the end of the street, his tail down, he stood looking at me, as if I were a traveler from a distant land he knew had come only to visit. I kept walking onward. Once I turned back. The dog still stood there, looking, his brownish white silhouette dissolving into the rain, and the whole street looking blurred and desolate, as if it was being washed away.

I hurried, for I knew exactly where I was going. I was going to the Shiva temple at the edge of Rampet, and beyond it, where I had seen the alleyways give way to open land and streets give way to railway lines. I was going to find the station down from those lines and I was going to board a train. I was going to go to a place I had never seen before, the next town, or a big city. I was going to find people I could live among, living people, and work from then on only for the living. Doing what I did not know, but I was going to find out.

And this is what happened, exactly how. I was half-walking, half-running, because it was still raining, and it was dark, and though the street lights were on, their yellow reflections in the pools of water in the street made the light confusing. No one was in the street but myself. No one, not a crow, a rat, a grey pigeon. Most people were asleep in their beds, intending to wake at a godly hour, and even the roosters were sleeping. But it was not daybreak yet, no light was making an appearance. The plastic over my head was not enough to cover me, water dripped down the edges and flew at me from the sides so I was wet in less than twenty minutes, water running warmly all down my body. My shirt and pants were soaked and clung wetly to my skin. I came to the Shiva temple, a shroud of rain over the gopuram, I climbed the bridge in front and stared at the giant sleeping lotuses being battered by rain, their large folded leaves as they shuddered, their billowy petals. I could smell the stale used air from a thousand *malais* of jasmine, a thousand offerings of rose petals, a thousand overripe bananas from yesterday's puja. A damp ferment of leaves rose from the water. No one was in sight. The rain made a swishy white curtain in front of the street light and fell frothily to the ground. I turned, I hurried onward.

It was after I had passed the closed tool shops I had never passed before, bicycle shops I had never seen, rows of tire shops and old garages, and was looking at the streets, wondering which one to try for the railway lines, when I stumbled into a doorway with a flat extended awning over it. I stood for a minute under it, wringing the water from my shirt. Then I decided to take shelter for a little while. Other people were already using this space as shelter. Two men rolled up in blankets were lying right up against the door. A fruit-vendor who had parked his cart on the cement apron in front lay curled under the cart like a dog.

I stood, watching the rain fall in streamers beneath the white mercury lamp across the street. It had become heavier and I shivered. It had also become colder. I slid down to my haunches. Then I sat in a lotus. Then I put my head against the rolled-down aluminium door, my bundle sliding down beside me, and inexplicably, for I had believed myself alert and wide-awake, I slept.

When I woke it was light and everyone was awake. The smell of fresh wet earth was strong in my nostrils. It looked like it might be about seven or eight in the morning. The rain had stopped. There were people walking about in the slowly steaming street. I looked around, pulled myself upright. The two men who had slept beside me had disappeared. The fruit-man had pushed his cart away from the door and wheeled it to the side. Now the pile of fruit covered the night before was exposed.

Bright yellow and orange mangoes rose in pyramids against each other. And beside the cart, seated on a small wooden stool, eating a mango, was Anwar.

A sprouting of beard and moustache obscuring the lean features I knew. His long hair curled down to his shoulders. The moment blurred, a shocked series of impressions, one after the other. Like looking at a ghost of someone you had known once, long ago, when you were both brothers in the same house, and had slept for years together, in the same room. It felt, remembering, like another life. His face still thin, eyes sunken, as if the sleep he had wasn't enough. But Anwar. It was Anwar.

He looked at me and bit into his mango, which he was holding in his hand so that the juice ran down his elbow and onto his shirt. My eyes traveled over him. His shirt was torn in about a hundred places and did not look like a shirt. Like a rag, rather, with holes that he had hung about his shoulders. His khaki shorts were turned black with dust. His feet were bare, and even from here, a few feet away, I could see the cracked skin on his soles climb toward his ankle.

It is telling that we did not speak in this first moment that we looked at each other and saw what the other was doing. I saw he was now a mango-man. He must have seen I was now a runaway, just like him. We observed these things for a few moments. Then he spoke.

You want a mango? He held one out to me.

I got up, walked over to take it. I did not say, that is the first time you have offered me something. Whose are they, I said.

The mango-man's, he said. I mind the cart for him in the mornings.

Was that you sleeping under the cart last night? I had seen the small curled figure and had not even imagined.

Yes. The mango-man lets me sleep with the cart. Since he doesn't need it.

I smoothed my fingers over the mango, catching the nub at the top. The mango was yellow with black sheared streaks and marks on it, as if it had been bumped about in a cart, or dropped to the ground. I tried to pull at the skin and Anwar handed me a knife. It was very quiet between us. It was as if all those months of his being gone had become walls and stood silently between us. I started to peel the rubbery skin with the knife.

How come he doesn't need it?

He has a house to go to, said Anwar. He has a family.

My eyes flicked toward him and away. His eyes were intent on the mango seed he was sucking at, he would not look at me.

I went back and sat down on the cement beside my bundle. I dropped the skin on the cement, started to eat the mango. He threw his seed away when he was finished. He arced it across the street to the gutter. Then he washed his hands with some water he took from a plastic bottle.

After a while he said, You should eat your mango and go home.

The words stung. Who are you to talk, I said, feeling the long kept-down anger start up inside me like an all-consuming burial fire. The sweetness of the mango dripping over my hands and my clothes. Are you going home, I taunted, now that you have finished yours?

He did not rush toward me and grab me by the throat as I half-thought he would. He did not move. He said instead, as if he were reciting his arithmetic tables from his school-going so long ago, I have no home.

I did not have to think before I answered. You have a home, I shouted. You have a family! You have a father and a mother who wait for you as if there is nothing else on earth to do! You have a hundred dogs who eat the food they put out for you everyday, who are all fed in your name! Something was twisting upward through me and choking me as I spoke. I dropped the half-eaten mango, grabbed my bundle, and started to go. But I had just woken, I was in a strange street, I was confused. I did not know which side to go. I saw I was in the middle of a street lined with shops which stretched in both directions. I was not sure which side to walk, to find the trains. I stood, poised to run, I did not know in what direction.

Then I heard it. Anwar's face had gone still, his eyes round, then he was shouting something back to me, but I was listening to what rumbled beyond him. Over his voice a slow rolling rumble of a sound. A train sound. I listened, it came closer. It was behind Anwar, it was that side. I started to run. Anwar caught me as I went past him, lunging at me. That's not the way home, he shouted.

You go home, I shouted back, it's your turn to be the only son! I started to run then, dodging bicycles, men with carts, scooters, mopeds. Anwar came behind me, shouting my name. Amir! Amir! All I wanted was to get away from him, the ghost he had become in my mind. I ran past the people staring, the shops, I came to an open space and now I could see, in front of me the street ending, the stretch of empty grass with rubbish strewn all over, and the railway tracks. My sandals clunked and squeaked and fell outside my feet as I ran. Anwar had abandoned the mangoes and was shrieking after me as if there was anything he could say that would turn me back. I ran, clutching my bundle. I ran, trying to remember what my plan was. To catch a train, or to find a station? To climb into a running train, or to follow the tracks somewhere?

I was in the middle of the train tracks now. The sound of that train coming was very loud in my ears. I looked up once and saw the round black engine of the train approaching. There were so many rail tracks. I tried to make out which track that train was on. The gravel piled on the tracks got into my sandals as I ran. Then my foot slipped. The sandal flew half off my foot and got wedged in a track. The other half of the sandal was wrapped firmly around my foot. I bent, struggled with it. The train was very close now. I could see the black round engine, the long curved plough in front. A siren blew, and the sound was in my ears like a shuttling, disjointed scream. I tried to unloose the sandal from my foot, my foot from the sandal. I saw the frantic horror on Anwar's face as he came struggling toward me, shouting. I saw the blue washed-clean sky above, a streamer of violet cloud. I saw the black grime of the train's face. Then it was upon me.

Everything in me jolted, pushed, tumbled outward. Everything black and screeching and grinding. Many-sided the everything, many-sliding. In the second that I felt the hurtling weight knife my bones and saw, simultaneously, the bright white exploding of the death light in my face, and was tossed, shattered, whole, down into the long tunnel of my death, there was a terrible confusion in my mind. I was not sure who I was, where I was. The present and the past got confused in me. The future compressed into that moment and pushed through my skin. I could no longer reach out and feel what I wanted. I felt myself both paralyzed and moving. I could not sense where I was going. I could not make myself get up, hurry onward, as I had, just a moment ago, when I fled from Anwar. I was being pushed through something by something outside me. I was being moved, not moving myself. It was disorienting, unbelievable. It was like being pushed from a dream of another life, where you were someone else, into a cloud of fog covering your memory. No longer capable of recognizing the world.

Afterward, it seems like a very long time afterward, although it is not, that I am calm, that I understand what has happened, where I am, where I am going, why the ground appears far below me, and I can see, not merely tracks, a train, scrub around, but a spread of city, silver rail tracks winding through it, tens of thousands of houses, the tops of palms, and everywhere a stream of people, in cars, bikes, on foot, moving, moving, moving. Far away the aqua fringe of ocean, white lace at its edge, so close to the city. Just below it seems no time has passed at all. The train has stopped and people stream out of the train on either side to come to the front, where the engine and what it has collided with stand, confused in their mutual spasm. A small knot of people stand directly in front. They make no effort to come closer, to touch the body. But Anwar, who knows with his hands the feeling of death, is close. He is touching the red checked shirt, the torn black pants, the broken foot in the broken sandal. He is weeping as if it is his own brother who lies before him now, mangled and public, a corpse already. He is putting the bones inside the clothes. Covered with blood, long before the ambulance arrives, screeching its own siren down the waking streets, his hands are pulling the body out from under the wheels. While I keep on rising through the shivering velvet of cloud into flicker of blue, and begin slowly to feel again. The tiny drops of moisture, almost jasmine-scented, of the cloud. The warm roll of sun, turning over on my face. The touch of my brother's hand, sweet as syrup on my skin, smoothing my quiet body.

VILLAGE OF ARDAKMOKTAN
Nicole Derr

from Pindeldyboz (online)

1.

M Y FRIEND WAS AN INTERESTING FELLOW. HE WARMED AND disarmed everyone with his brown hair cropped short, nicely tapered torso, chiseled face. We liked to keep Graham around because he looked so pleasant. He held your eyes with his translucent greens.

For the sake of this account, it would be easier to classify Graham as shallow and describe his personality as something vapid, plastic. The problem is, however, that we never got him. We never understood what his personality was exactly. When recounted, his dialogue seemed cast in a proverbial green light, smacking of the unreal.

"I joined because there's no better way to get in shape," Graham told me the first time we met. He smiled a sincere smile, but what does a sincere smile have to do with a statement like that? He joined us in the spring. A short man towed his monstrous valise, which we later learned contained carefully selected, expensive foods: real rarities. An even shorter man, balding and bespectacled, bore the even larger valise containing clothing and other so-called essentials. I often wondered how he circumvented customs, for surely he must have escaped them somehow. I heard bribery no longer works—I also know from experience.

Ardakmoktan at that time was staggering under a brutal drought that forced authorities to ration the water severely. Slashed cactus drained of fluid, decapitated and dumb, marred the horizon. Our mineral water was flown in from America in large barrels. Deliverymen unloaded the barrels from their trucks, while security guards in tightly laced boots surrounded them, keeping the desperate locals (Moktas) with chapped lips from attaching themselves to the barrels and draining them like leeches. Sometimes the occasional Mokta succeeded in penetrating the ominous security circle, throwing himself on a barrel, and stabbing it open with a pocketknife. After sating himself with water for the first time in many months, an anonymous guard would then shoot him in the back, relieving him of all fluids forever.

We watched our barrels of water from the trees. We found it entertaining when the locals were shot. Too hot to go around shooting people ourselves. Our base was secluded, secure, and lush. The government employed a botanist to maintain the foliage. Almost all of our free moments were spent languidly hanging from these trees, wiping our brows with thick leaves, sweating life and time through our large pores. "This base is a vacuum," Graham once quietly griped. He raked his tanned fingers through his hair and flashed a disarming smile. "No, just kidding. I like the purging qualities of this place," he added vaguely.

Because the trees would not thrive naturally in the climate of Ardakmoktan, almost half of our mineral water was used to water them. Cactus, we were told, is bad for the morale: too desolate. The sad cactus waved to us from afar with spiky mittens.

So, where was Ardakmoktan in relation to the rest of the world, you wonder? You don't know geography very well, do you? Probably not. Unfortunately, our schools value geography very little. No more maps to color in with thick crayon. Imagine Ardakmoktan as a blank slate. I still imagine it as a blank slate.

2

Graham bunked with me. Every morning I watched him drop from his bed like an Olympic diver, precise and slick. He hung the requisite picture of a buxom girlfriend on his wall. I never saw him look at the picture and he certainly never told me her name. For all I know, her picture was ripped from a magazine and framed. For all I know.

He frequently plied us with gourmet foods from his bottomless valise. "Here . . . try this . . . and this," he would say, sometimes putting morsels directly into our mouths without awaiting a reply. "Try this too." And we did. (Never bite the hand, you know.)

I noted his emaciated face, realizing that he rarely ate his foods: although he put plenty of food in his mouth—like a sandwich, for instance—he then reeled it back out, only masticating and swallowing a minute portion. I found it strange, but said nothing. Too hot.

3

One afternoon my favorite security guard stood legs akimbo in his tight uniform. His mustache spanned ear to ear, underlined by thick wet lips. He smiled goofily while watching the barrels, rifle resting on a padded shoulder. A local, tall and lean, darted by him with the stealthy movements reserved for virile youth. The boy's loose blue shirt rippled in the dry, hot wind. We watched him from the trees, reclining on branches thicker than both of my muscular legs combined. He struck at the right time, before the barrels had been unloaded from the trucks, but after the truck had been backed up against the ramp; in short, everything was just right.

The youth had no knife. He had no desire to affix his face to the barrel and drain it until the moment he himself was drained. Instead, he leaped onto the truck bed and tried to roll one of the barrels onto the ramp. I propped myself up on my branch in surprise. He was still alive and he wanted the entire barrel—our barrel—of water. Usually the Moktas reached such a fever-pitched level of dehydration that they only wanted as much water as they could consume at once. To steal an entire barrel! The guards rested the rifles against their shoulders and aimed. At least eight men pulled the trigger. I yawned. The heat made me drowsy; the suspense made me drowsier. I wanted an end to this and I wanted my water. The foie gras and gull wine left me parched. I hated the idea of losing water, of helplessly watching it seep into the ground. I moved the leaf that had drooped in front of my face.

"I can't believe he's trying to take the entire barrel. What disgusting greed," I told my friend Graham. I turned to receive Graham's lavished support but he was no longer in the neighboring tree.

The barrel traveled down the gentle ramp, increasing in momentum. Locals spontaneously surfaced to help the boy control the now-rampaging barrel.

"Why aren't they stopping them?" my throat cried out in thirst. The men around me rested silently on their branches. "Graham?" I couldn't see him anywhere.

The guards dropped their useless rifles and ran through the sweltering heat after the runaway barrel, giving more locals the opportunity to snatch the abandoned weapons. Outraged, I rested my head against the tree trunk and yawned. In such heat, yawns are uncontrollable. The heat, the yawning left a pasty taste in my mouth. I yawned again. Through crinkled eyelids, I glimpsed Graham navigating the wobbling barrel with his strong, agile arms, running at full speed with the Moktas.

I yawned in disbelief and shock. The heat was an impasse for the guards, who returned to the truck to unload the unscathed barrels. They slunk onto the truck bed with rounded, defeated shoulders. I watched Graham's silhouette recede into the distance surrounded by other silhouettes, all moving in joyful, radiant complicity.

4

The guards were reprimanded for not apprehending Graham. They pleaded sabotage (how effortlessly they were beguiled!). We got in trouble too for not bothering to drop from our respective trees and help. I didn't care. It was too hot. Later I returned to Graham's tree and found his small brown satchel teeming with rifle bullets (not gourmet treats like I'd hoped). I left the heavy little satchel in the tree instead of turning it in to the investigating officer. It was simply too hot to slide down the tree with a bag full of bullets, walk across the entire base, and explain the whole situation without incriminating myself. It was simply too hot. I camouflaged the bag under leaves nourished with mineral water—leaves thickened by tiny chrysalides sheltering a delicate growth otherwise out of place in such a supposedly depraved environment.

THE MAN WHO MARRIED A TREE

Tony D'Souza

from McSweeney's

I. The townsmen

ONCE THERE WAS THIS MAN, CAME ONE DAY TO OUR TOWN. Drank in the bar evenings, kept to himself. He had India ink tattoos of tigers on his forearms. Some people guessed he'd been a sailor, seen the tragedies that ocean faring men do, that's why he didn't talk. Got drunk one night finally, passed out with his boots on in the scrap of wood by the river next to the bridge where the trains run over it. Right there in the middle of things where everyone could see. Maybe it was a cry for help, who knows? The sheriff put him in the tank for the night and he mumbled about those tigers, and bad weather. Didn't go into the bar again after that. Must have sobered him up, settled his spirit here.

Ours is a good town. Trains come through a few times a day, hauling coal north and lumber south. They stop our pickups at the crossing and we contemplate the garish, foreign graffiti painted by angrier people than we are on the cars as they rumble by. Up on the mountain is a tower, but cellular phones don't work down here. Still, we know that times are changing. What's being said by all those invisible voices bouncing around in the sky? Tourists stop in for goods and gas, talking about this and that from the city, telling us how beautiful our home place is, then they go on. Our young people move on, too. We remain, our stories with us.

But that man who came, he built a quiet place for himself down past the south end; built the cottage by hand, sent some business the hardware store's way a while, then that was it; he lived out by the trees. Trees everywhere about that place; he spent his time among them. Grew corn and vegetables, it was said; he fished and hunted. Got to know those trees real well. Then he married one.

None of us went to the wedding; no one was invited. But it's said he wore a sharp military uniform of some foreign design, brown, with a saber at his side and a few polished medals on his breast. He wasn't young anymore at his wedding, though his beard had dark streaks of life in it, and the tree wasn't either, though she was lovely. Her limbs were long and lithe, black spiders spun gossamer webs about her crown for a veil. Now and again someone would catch a glimpse of her standing by herself back by their bend of the creek, her pinnacle bent like thinking, her leaves hanging over the water like long straight hair and her man not around. It was the water and the stones and the solitude of herself that did it, but she stood there like a Japanese poem. Didn't know how to feel just then: those who saw her spoke of embarrassment, of feeling like they'd stumbled upon a beautiful woman taking a quiet bath. She was a tree that made you consider other trees, the trees that cover the mountains around here in their green and silent multitudes. Trees, trees everywhere. A wide and unknown world of trees bearing down on you when you paused to think.

Even so, when the wedding was first getting rumored, some of the womenfolk got their feathers up. They complained about it at the Elks, at the Eagles. They said, "Now every Tom, Dick, and Harry is going to think he can up and run off with a tree." We just shrugged our shoulders and looked at one another over our beers. Even if in our hearts of hearts we wanted to, who's to say there was a tree out there for us? For a while after that, you'd hear about this fella or that going off for a long walk in the woods, about how his wife or girlfriend had marched out there to haul him back in. But as far as actually marrying a tree? Time went by and no one else ever did.

Maybe we should have, though no one ever says it. Maybe that would have shaken up the tired order around here.

II. The postman

After that queer character who married a goddanged tree got old as folk and died, his sister breezed into town, stayed a while in that heap of a cottage he'd tossed up. What was his disorder anyway? A lost zip, if you ask me. But she was a savvy, skinny number from the city, pretty sorta around the eyes, you could tell right away she'd seen her share: she smoked. She sat mornings in the rocking chair on the porch and rocked and smoked and looked out at the trees where they stood just beyond his garden. Never once was so much as a circular for that place, but I went by anyway when she came to town. I wore long pants those hot days, so she wouldn't see my chicken legs and count me out right away. I've been around long enough to know you never can tell what might arrive with the mail.

Three days running I went up to the gate, said as polite as can be, "Howdy-do, miss," then rummaged through my sack as though I might actually have something for that pathetic address. What a joke! But I've fooled enough lonely housewives in my day not to try. Then I'd shake my head at her and say, "Seems like sorry again, dear. Got nothing for you today. Go figure. Get twenty in a day and then nothing for a month." On the fourth day, she puffed a long plume of smoke out my way as I came up the walk, and before I could say word one, she said, "Ask your question, postman, and let's be done with it."

Well now. Well just you wait a minute now. But I'm too quick not to make the best of anything. I hung my old wrists on the pickets of that fence like it was any old day or place and it was time to chew the fat. I looked out the corner of my eye at some dandelions for courtesy, and then I said, "Since you put it that way. There's been rumors running around for a long while, rumors about your brother. It's said he was married here, but you never did see any wife puttering about the place."

"Oh he was married all right. Happily goddamned married. He married a tree. Didn't ask any of us neither. Just went off and did it. A common trash lot birch."

I leaned in then, said like whispering, "Seems like I'd heard that, yep. A birch. The white kind. But since you brought it up, I'll say it doesn't sound exactly trash lot to me. Understand me now, the water's clean back there, comes from the Soda spring. City folks same as you come up every now and again with bottles, take our water back with them. It's a pride for folk around here."

"Common here, common there, I've always said. A birch. Why not a maple or an oak? Why not something to make people proud? That was the problem with Henry. Always did do his own thing."

"You mean to say a thing like that didn't surprise you people?"

"Surprise? Henry? Henry never had eyes for anything but trees. You take a bar full of leggy blondes and a tree walks in, and the next thing you know, there would be Henry, buying her a drink, asking all sorts of questions and embarrassing himself. He got tangled up with a knotty old buckthorn when we were kids. Mother had to clip him out of her brambles, and then she beat him. Threatened to chop that tree right down. But Henry got down on his knees and hugged the skinny trunk and said, 'Mama, don't you chop this sweet buckberry down because she's the only thing I ever loved.' He wasn't even but eleven, twelve. We knew before then. When he was little, before he could talk, he'd stand out in the yard with his arms up and his eyes closed, stock still for hours, acting like a full grown sycamore, like he'd been charged with holding up the sky. I bet that's when that old buckthorn got her eye on him. Ruined him. Ruined him she did. What can you expect from an exotic? She so old and twisted, him like a shoot. It made us all sick."

She swung her eyes on me, let out a slow cloud of smoke the way old Chinese ladies used to do in pictures. She said, "Postman? Do you really want to know the truth? I'll tell you. I loved an elm. Loved him my whole life. He grew in the parkway beyond our sidewalk, and I spent hours peeking at him from my bedroom window. Loved him more and more with every beat of my heart. How strong he used to be, so serene and bold! But I never worked up the courage to tell him. I used to be shy. And I was scared. What if he didn't love me as much as I loved him? All that longing, all those years! The Dutch disease got him. They sawed him down, chipped him to dust. Wrecked my life. Wrecked it as thoroughly as anything."

Well then. Felt like someone'd slapped me. She looked at those trees, and I did, too. They stood at the edge of the yard like they were watching, like they'd been listening to what we'd said, like they'd been thinking about who we were as people. Gave me the creeps. Made me want to get out of that confusion and never go back. I tilted my cap to her and hurried down the way. Didn't look back neither. Made me think a second; made me think about all that paper folded in all those letters.

III. The hardware store guy

Didn't want nails, that one. Don't know if that's good or bad. Joined everything. That's finer work than using nails. So that's good. But money spent on nails would have been appreciated around here, so that's bad. Who in the world is supposed to know? But he knew his tools and what he wanted to do. Bought his chisels and mortar and lumber and glass and that was it, nothing spendy.

Thing is, lots of fellas don't like to talk, not wanting to talk can't tell you everything there is to know about 'em. Why one guy came in here for years buying shovels. Every couple of months he'd come in, pick out a shovel, pay for it, go. Just like that. Never so much as hello. The next thing you know he's got Fish and Game out there putting up "Wetland" signs. Built an eleven acre marsh out there. Dug it himself. By hand. A couple guys went out and saw it. Said the whole place was nuts with buffleheads and mergansers.

Them tigers, too. The pictures guys put on their arms only say so much. Seen stranger tattoos than them tigers. Saw one guy with a tattoo of a flying pig. Wondered about that one. Then somebody came in and said, "His old lady only'd let him wear shoes in the house when pigs could fly, on account of her carpet. He got old, and winter got to his ankles, and that was that."

In the end, we did sell that fella some nails. At least to his sister. She paid his expenses and they needed a bunch to tack the lid on the pine box they put him in. Know a lot of people around here, but didn't know him. Would have liked to, if he'd of had the mind for it. Would have passed the time.

IV. The sheriff

I may have been the only one in these parts ever did shake his hand. Was in the morning, wasn't it? Yes, when I locked him up that night for a 647-F, Public Intoxication. Sleeping in the wood by the creek. I knew he was there that whole time. Fine by me. Then some old lady or other phoned in, woke me from a nod. Don't mind nodding now and again since I lost my Mary. "Sheriff! Sheriff!" she whispered. "There's a drunk man making mischief by the creek. That old sailor. Let 'em run loose at night, sheriff, a lady's liable to have all sorts of sorrows come calling. Why, what if he gets up and starts over here on those big, thick legs of his? What could happen then? Him so brawny and all, and me just like a baby bird? I'll tell you. He could kick down my door like sticks. He could throw me on my bed like a ragdoll and force himself on me. Could you imagine it? Me all alone for the taking and him so strong? He could do just whatever he pleased with that big hulk of a body of his. Been watching him from my window for over an hour. He's a bad one, a bad one sure. Better do something quick before he gets on over here and takes advantage."

What can you do when the whole town signs your paycheck? I took up a pair of cuffs, my gun, the keys, the whole rigmarole. When I got down there, he was snoring like a baby with the low branches of those trees hanging down on him strange-like, like a blanket, like the trees had wanted to keep him warm. "Hey now, bud," I said to him and nudged his elbow with the toe of my boot, "can't sleep here, fella. Got a nice bed for you though if you come along." Took a while, but I roused him. Mumbled about the weather at first like an old drunk lost soul. They fall off the train. It's like one single man, over and over and over again. Something fundamentally wrong with the world when it breeds all these lost dudes. But he was polite enough when his eyes got to blinking. Got to his feet as best he could, wasn't ashamed to use my shoulder for a steady. Saw my badge, things came clear. Said to me, "Sorry, officer."

"It's sheriff. And there ain't no sorry in this world."

"I know it,' he said back to me, 'but I'll say it anyway."

Then he moved his feet as nicely as a kitten. Big fella, too, so I was glad for it. A clean one, clean hands, he smelled of the woods and pines. Didn't have any reason to put the bracelets on him.

Folk keep their eye on the new one in town. They could have said a word to him now and again on the street, in the hardware store, but you know folk. They call it, "Leaving a man to his business." For a while, they liked to talk about him in conversation, wondering who he was, his tattoos, his last night in the bar. Folk is always the same. Natural curiosity. Nothing much else to occupy them around here, liable even to craft a story or two; they'd do it to anybody. He built a reasonable place down past the south end, gave it a gabled roof, put in windows just as smart as a glazier. I swung by now and again to see that he complied with our ordinances. He did. I'd wave to him if he was around. That was it. Never had a problem with him again. Wish the whole valley could be like that. His passing touched me, I'll own to it. Always hate to see a good man go, makes you count your own time, even if you're ready.

I remember that morning, the morning I let him out. Sitting on the bed and waiting for me, his big hands in his lap just like his mama taught him. I gave him his pebbles back, the pine needles he'd had in his pockets. Then we shook hands. Felt the power in him, felt it right down through my bones. A strong man, and not just of the body. He could have made a fine man around these parts if he'd wanted. They say he married, so I reckon he did.

V. The spinster

No justice in this world, if you ask me. None. Nose to the grindstone since the day I was born. Nobody walked the line like me. Nary so much as a peep. Spend the whole of this life minding my own and walking the line and waiting for my ship to come in and then you hear about someone running off and marrying a tree. How's a body supposed to react to all that?

Why my younger sister Becky, you should have seen. Had everything, she did. Drinking and cussing all those years away in the city. Liked lights, being under them, guess she thought she was something of a movie star the way she sought them out. And then she came back worn and spent if you ask me, lines all in her face, not like mine from patient age, the worn out kind that come on a person all at once, make you look like a dried up apple forgotten in the yard. She smelled funny, too. But Papa acted like it was the day she was born. Then that train supervisor who hopped off here a while, he dallied with me, I'll tell you. All Aggie this, Aggie that. Those were days, all right. Felt like I'd eaten bugs, the way my stomach fluttered when he'd come up in the evening in his overalls, whistling like it was going to rain gold. I even thought it might, too, a while. "Gimme a kiss, Aggie. One sweet little peck." Dang near wrung me out with that. Next thing you know Becky shows up working her citified ways on him and he couldn't see me any longer the way you can't ever really look at coal. Just like that. Then he popped out with this tin ring like he'd found a quarter and put it in a gumball machine, and Papa was want to kill a calf and Mama sewed Becky a trousseau on the bias. Moved back to the city, those two did. Had seven kids. Their faces were always dirty, even in photographs. I bet they let them eat molasses.

When the man with the tigers came, I'd see him walking up to the bar from my window. Walked right by here every night: a clock on two legs. I'd watch him go by and then I'd sit down to my programs. I'd knit a bit and watch my shows, and then it would be time to see him go by again on his way home, to see if he was really as regular as he was making out. And for a while, he was. "A drinker, Aggie," my quilting ladies warned. I blushed and said, "Bet I could fix him." Even waved to him once. Just lifted up my hand on some crazy urge and waved it at him. He didn't even nod his head.

The next thing you know he's stumbling around in the bracken like any of them zombies fall off the train. So he wasn't what I'd made him out to be after all. Can't a man even acknowledge a lady when she condescends to lift her hand at him? Maybe he couldn't see me with the light out and me behind the curtain and all, but then again, shouldn't he of just felt it? Shouldn't he have simply known?

All these people in the world wanting a little something for themselves: he goes off and marries a tree. Could she cook? Could she clean? These are the questions I'd like answered. Against the way of things, if you ask me. The world so big and lonesome, and he marries a tree. Why that's a rejection of the way life is, a basic desire to not participate.

What's next? People marrying rocks? Mud? Did she ever knit him a pair of tartan socks? That's what I'd like to know.

A good man, that's what they're saying now that it's too late to say anything else. Simple enough for people to temper their judgments when a man's just passed on. But ask them when nobody's looking, ask them what they really think. A good man? Just go and ask anyone normal.

VI. The Soda creek

He was a good man, he left the fish alone. That is to say, he took one once in a while, without game or folly, the way bears do, ospreys. I liked running through the hair of his legs, his toes, he was clean even when he came to me to be cleaned. It's about the spirit of a man, cleanliness. I praise it in men as much as they praise it in me.

That first year, he took stones from my bed to build the foundation of his house. The deep spaces he left in me I filled, and the fish came to nest in those spaces in turn. He would come to me in the evening and smoke a cigarette and listen to me and mull over the things men like him have to. All he seemed to do at that time was think. Think and smoke and listen to me as he looked at the evening. What advice did I give him that I don't give to any man? Once in a while he would bury his feet in the dirt on the bank and close his eyes as though to grow, to become a tree himself, and I would eddy up and rinse the dirt away. If he had been a child, I would have had a heart for that. But he was old enough to understand well that it was his sentence to be a man. What would it be after all if the squirrels began leaping out of the tall pines as though they were jays, if the jays used their wings to climb? Up and down me the man would walk, thinking, smoking. He never seemed to tire of the advice I had to give.

And her? I knew her from a seed. Knew her whole stand, generations of them. Sturdy trees; they held and died and made that bank. A fire came through one dry year and we all had to learn that even when life has seemed to stop, it will start again. What a fine young tree she had been, standing in a riotous clump with her brothers and sisters, taut in the wind, graceful as a wand. After the fire, she was the only one who came back, hardened, possessing that mellow beauty only the wizened achieve.

He'd seen some things. She had seen plenty, too. She'd survived loggings. Men came and took the pines, every one of them, once, again, left her alone. So many memories were coiled in her heartwood. So many reasons not to go on, but she did. She is a daughter of mine. I have many, but she is my daughter.

Did I think that they'd make a fine couple? I washed his feet, her roots, watered them, in that way, both. I hoped for it a long time. Then it did.

It happened slowly, befitting their natures. This pleased me because what do I have but time? Though those first years he would not admit to himself his love for the tree, he came to sit at me where he could see her out of the corner of his eye. It was as though he wished at all times to know how she fared, without admitting to himself that he needed to know. He'd scratch his arm and look at me, as though she was just another stick to him. For her part, what was the man to her? What was anything? She had lost much: her kin before the fire, the landscape that had held her before the loggings. She had survived to see the mountains dressed again in sturdy trees she'd watched sprout. The man sat and smoked on the bank until he knew my lie, every stone that riffled my run, the new currents I'd form when I'd grow restless and shift. All the time he was looking at her without turning his eyes. He was wondering, I imagine, if he had the strength to approach her, to be turned away by her, too.

Who determines these things? Winters came and went. The turtles burrowed beneath my knowing to dream their winter dreams, emerging again after the ice had dripped from the tree branches and every part of me awoke. She was in full bud, glorious; of course he had seen it before. But perhaps he'd had a whisper of death that long winter, certainly he had streaks of winter in his beard. He approached the tree, finally, an evening when I was full of nymphs hatching into yellow clouds of newly winged damsels and causing the trout to leap from me as if for joy, and crossed that short expanse of stone and shade and soil that had separated them. He did not move on my bank in the stumbling, heedless stride of a buck, but in the measured pace of one with the age to know he cannot afford to fall again. With life awakening all about them in the world, he lay down at her roots and rested his head gently against her base. As simple as that. What a moment that was! I would have stopped myself in my eternal trickle if only to let them know how tense I was, how much I needed, then, to know. All the woods fell silent for everything in them, too, had all been waiting for this moment. It seemed, suddenly, that so much depended on this when we all knew that nothing depended on it at all: bird and otter and rock and moss. And as we held ourselves to see what she would do, even the wind paused her coursing. What did that tree do? What did that fine tree who had no need of anything from a man to prove the success of her stubborn existence do? She rustled her branches to cast her soft bud casings on him like down.

VII. The soil

Mountains fear me, rocks. The stones in the rivers that traverse me fear me. Plants fear me, trees. Men fear me. I am everything's afterlife.

I would like to speak with my cousins. But mountains separate us, deserts. All will crumble and fall. Time belongs to me. Everything becomes me.

My voice is baritone. Only the mountains pay attention to what I say. I have been brutalized by man for twelve thousand years and still I remain. Divided, transplanted, shoveled, sold, pumped full of chemicals, and, finally, salted, I can only laugh, in my undulations. Even sidewalks will return to me, once the current tumult has subsided.

My reaches have seen much, have seen at the north of my body a man who loved a tree. What is there to say but this: he warmed me with his body, the length of him upon me, lying at her roots. I knew what was happening and I did not care. Why should I? His body would return to me, and so would his tree.

But he walked upon me in his bare feet. And he lay upon me at her roots. Her roots were strong ones, like a web that wound through me, her smallest tendrils searching and holding onto her life. But after they had married, the man would come and lay his short expanse upon me, and I would warm, what choice or care did I have? And the warmth of him would warm and open her roots, and then she would take the minerals suspended in me. For twelve thousand years, man has worried about my development. But the man who loved the tree let his warmth seep through me. This opened her roots and insisted upon her growth. These vibrations between them I hadn't otherwise known. I haven't needed to; I am a being that eats everything. This between the man and the tree was a new thing to me: tender in its quietness; I will admit their love.

VIII. The red-tailed hawk

Marriage? No. But net me, feed me, love me for a time, and I will feed us both. Let me go. My love is for myself. Things revolve, as I see them. I don't condemn them, don't care to understand them. Wind in my feathers as I surveyed them from my perch; all of creation has its particular way.

IX. The raccoon, the possum, the pigeon, the skunk

We love men, could love the man who'd feed us.

X. The mountain

I've seen stranger.

XI. The forests

We've seen worse.

XII. The trout

Grub, grub.

XIII. The sun

I shine on everything, choice-less.

XIV. The moon

I shine on everything, but impart meaning, in shades.

XV. God

XVI. Telephone poles

If only. If only.

XVII. The Forest Service surveyor

Had to go out there, tagging trees. Had a hammer, nails, my uniform on, my badge. Had a plate. Number 5392. Just doing my job, surveying, been doing it for years. Sure, they'll use my work to make maps that they'll sell to the timber industry, but a man has to feed his family, put his kids through school, help his kids feed their kids and put them through school, and so on and so on. No way around that.

That's the way the world works. Still, working around trees all the time just seems to change your perception. Can't think of anything nicer than a tree.

Anyway, while I was back there looking at his tree, the man came charging out from nowhere. I knew him even if he didn't know me. Everybody knew him. That's what happens when you marry a tree. He says to me, "Can I help you, mister?" those tigers flexing on his arms like stretching, like waking up. I say, "I got to put this plate on this tree. Marking boundaries, you know." He gives me a good, hard, long look. He says, "Do what you've got to do. But understand something. That's my wife." We just looked at each other a while. Two months before my stinking retirement and I had to deal with that. What was I going to do? Have two old guys like us splashing around in the creek and fistfighting over a tree? I walked down and nailed that plate to an old cherry. Who cares, right? The line's still straight, more or less. Maybe they'll even leave that hollow alone for a while. But what I want to know is, what gave that one single guy the right to go and mess with the rules? We all love trees, don't we? Why couldn't he have married some tree on his own damned property?

XVIII. The author

My work for the day is almost done, for something has been almost said.

I wish I was the man who married a tree.

XIX. The author's mother (on the answering machine)

Anthony, where is this place you're living again? I'm having trouble finding it on the map. Are you making any friends out there? Are you supporting yourself? It seems like you're the only one of your friends who's not married. Anthony? Are you there? Anthony? Are you making any money?

XX. The coroner

The Hutchinson girl found him. Having trouble with that girl, her folks were, trouble keeping her out of the woods. Those woods seem to pull her in like a filing to a magnet. They made her lead me to where the body was at the tree's roots. The tree had shaken her leaves down to cover him and he seemed no worse for the wear. I had half a notion to let him lie right there. But the news had already gotten out and things aren't done that way around here. It took a handful of strong backs to lift him out. On the table I opened him up and found what I'd guessed: thrombosis.

I wear the mortician's hat in this little town, I'm also the undertaker. I put on my black coat and went to his cottage to have a look and see if I couldn't find a way to contact any kin. It was a windy evening, and there were leaves blowing all around the place. The door didn't even have a lock on it, and inside, there were hand painted pictures of all the birds of this region, and an easel, and quite a number of well thumbed books, in stacks. Just any sort of book you could imagine reading. How had he got them there? Where had he come from anyway? There was a letter stuck in one of them, old and yellowed, a hand written thing wishing him well, signed, "Your loving sister." That's how we found her. A pleasant lady, her brother's passing touched her the way it was supposed to.

"What would you like to do with the body?" I asked her an evening after some time had passed and she'd settled in. The priest and deacon had been nosing around, but she said he wouldn't have wanted any of that, he wouldn't have wanted anything. So we stood in that house surrounded by his simple things, not knowing what to do and looking at each other. It was one of those long moments when there's nothing you can do but look away at the wall and feel terrible for people you don't even know. Before I could ask the question again, there was a knock at the door. "Oh," she said, startled. "Who could that be? Maybe that idiot postman?" She opened the door to reveal a solemn gathering of townsfolk, the men thumbing their hats in their hands, the women in coats for the cold. The sheriff was before them all and he cleared his throat, looked up at her from where he'd been looking down, and said, "We know we've been lax about things, but we'd like to welcome you to our town, and offer our condolences."

"Thank you," she said simply, and I felt a welling up inside of me for the basic goodness of my own people. There were leaves falling on everyone's shoulders, and we all looked around and noticed it was autumn.

"We'd like to help you any way we can," he told her, and she nodded her head at them. That was all, the saying of the things that are supposed to be said, the acknowledgment of them. The moment passed and they turned to leave. She looked at me a second urgently as though something large had crossed her mind and then she called to them. "Wait! I don't have a place to bury my brother. It doesn't seem right to take him away, and the ridiculous law says I can't bury him here."

They came back in their dark coats, murmuring to one another, a crowd of people, people with their hearts turned in kindness. The sheriff cleared his throat again, said, "We'll take him. We didn't much know him, but then again, maybe we did. He lived here a long time. We'll put him in our cemetery as one of our own."

The service was simple, a few words from the sheriff, his sister read a poem about a tree losing its leaves. Instead of a marker, they planted a sapling, a willow. The sister went back to wherever she came from with his effects, and spiders got comfortable in his house.

One day, before the snows came, a feeling came over me, and I drove out to his place. Things were changing there, the grass was tall between the dried corn stalks, leaves were everywhere in piles. The land was taking the house and garden back. There was a worn path leading back to the creek, and I followed it, followed it back until I found her, his birch, standing in her height by the edge of the water. I cannot explain what came over me. An old feeling that had been lost inside me long ago in the course of this profession, I felt it suddenly looking at her loneliness. I took off my glove, placed my hand on her bark, and told her as honestly as I could, 'I'm sorry.'

I know it didn't mean much. Sorrow, death. What are any of us in the face of it? I stood there with her until darkness fell all over the face of the land. It was the least I could do. It comforted me.

A FABLE WITH SLIPS OF WHITE PAPER SPILLING FROM THE POCKETS

Kevin Brockmeier

from The Oxford American

ONCE THERE WAS A MAN WHO HAPPENED TO BUY GOD'S OVER-coat. He was rummaging through a thrift store when he found it hanging on a rack by the fire exit, nestled between a birch-colored fisherman's sweater and a cotton blazer with a suede patch on one of the elbows. Though the sleeves were a bit too long for him and one of the buttons was cracked, the coat fit him well across the chest and shoulders, lending him a regal look that brought a pleased yet diffident smile to his face, so the man took it to the register and paid for it. He was walking home when he discovered a slip of paper in one of the pockets. An old receipt, he thought, or maybe a to-do list forgotten by the coat's previous owner. But when he took it out, he found a curious note typed across the front: *Please help me figure out what to do about Albert.*

The man wondered who had written the note—and whether, in fact, that person had figured out what to do about Albert—but not, it must be said, for very long. After he got home, he folded the slip of paper into quarters and dropped it in the ceramic dish where he kept his breath mints and his car keys.

It might never have crossed his mind again had his fingers not fallen upon two more slips of paper in the coat's pocket while he was riding the elevator up to his office the next morning. One read, *Don't let my nerves get the better of me this afternoon,* and the other, *I'm asking you with all humility to keep that boy away from my daughter.*

The man shut himself in his office and went through the coat pocket by pocket. It had five compartments altogether: two front flap pockets, each of which lay over an angled handwarmer pocket with the fleece almost completely worn away, as well as a small inside pocket above the left breast. He rooted through them one by one until he was sure they were completely empty, uncovering seven more slips of paper. The messages typed across the front all seemed to be wishes or requests of one sort or another. *Please let my mom know I love her. I'll never touch another cigarette as long as I live if you'll just make the lump go away. Give me back the joy I used to know.*

There was a tone of quiet intimacy to the notes, a starkness, an open-hearted pleading, that seemed familiar to the man from somewhere.

Prayers, he realized.

That's what they were—prayers.

But where on earth did they come from?

He was lining them up along the edge of his desk when Eiseley from technical support rapped on the door to remind him about the ten o'clock meeting. "Half an hour of coffee and spreadsheet displays," he said. "Should be relatively painless," and he winked, firing an imaginary pistol at his head. As soon as Eiseley left, the man felt the prickle of an obscure instinct and checked the pockets of his coat again. He found a slip of paper reading, *The only thing I'm asking is that you give my Cindy another few years.* Cindy was Eiseley's cat, familiar to everyone in the office from his Christmas cards and his online photo diary. A simple coincidence? Somehow he didn't think so.

For the rest of the day the man kept the coat close at hand, draping it over his arm when he was inside and wearing it buttoned to the collar when he was out. By the time he locked his office for the night, he believed he had come to understand how it worked. The coat was—or seemed to be—a repository for prayers. Not unerringly, but often enough, when the man passed somebody on the street or stepped into a crowded room, he would tuck his hands into the coat's pockets and feel the thin flexed form of a slip of paper brushing his fingers. He took a meeting with one of the interns from the marketing division and afterward discovered a note that read, *Please, oh please, keep me from embarrassing myself.* He grazed the arm of a man who was muttering obscenities, his feet planted flat on the sidewalk, and a few seconds later found a note that read, *Why do you do it? Why can't you stop torturing me?*

That afternoon, on his way out, he was standing by the bank of elevators next to the waiting room when he came upon yet another prayer: *All I want—just this once—is for somebody to tell me how pretty I look today.* He glanced around. The only person he could see was Jenna, the receptionist, who was sitting behind the front desk with her purse in her lap and her fingers covering her lips. He stepped up to her and said, "By the way, that new girl from supplies was right."

"Right about what?"

"I heard her talking about you in the break room. She was saying how pretty you look today. She was right. That's a beautiful dress you're wearing."

The brightness in her face was like the reflection of the sun in a pool of water—you could toss a stone in and watch it fracture into a thousand pieces, throwing off sparks as it gathered itself back together.

So that was one prayer, and the man could answer it, but what was he to do with all the others?

In the weeks that followed, he found thousands upon thousands more. Prayers for comfort and prayers for wealth. Prayers for love and prayers for good fortune. It seemed that at any one time half the people in the city were likely to be praying. Some of them were praying for things he could understand, even if he could not provide them, like the waitress who wanted some graceful way to back out of her wedding or the UPS driver who asked for a single night of unbroken sleep, while some were praying for things he could not even understand: *Let the voice choose lunch this time. Either Amy Sussen or Amy Goodale. Nothing less than thirty percent.* He walked past a ring of elementary school students playing Duck, Duck, Goose and collected a dozen notes reading, *Pick me, pick me,* along with one that read, *I wish you would kill Matthew Brantman.* He went to a one-man show at the repertory theater, sitting directly next to the stage, and afterward found a handful of notes that contained nothing but the lines the actor had spoken. He made the mistake of wearing the coat to a baseball game and had to leave at the top of the second inning when slips of white paper began spilling from his pockets like confetti.

Soon the man realized that he was able to detect the pressure of an incoming prayer before it even arrived. The space around him would take on a certain elasticity, as though thousands of tiny sinews were being summoned up out of the emptiness and drawn tight, and he would know, suddenly and without question, that someone was offering his yearning up to the air. It was like the invisible resistance he remembered feeling when he tried to bring the common poles of two magnets together. The sensation was unmistakable. And it seemed that the stronger the force of the prayer, the greater the distance it was able to travel. There were prayers that he received only when he skimmed directly up against another person, but there were others that had the power to find him even when he was walking alone through the empty soccer field in the middle of the park, his footsteps setting little riffles of birds into motion. He wondered whether the prayers were something he had always subconsciously felt, he and everyone else in the world, stirring around between their bodies like invisible eddies, but which none of them had ever had the acuity to recognize for what they were, or whether he was only able to perceive them because he had happened to find the overcoat in the thrift store. He just didn't know.

At first, when the man had realized what the coat could do, he had indulged in the kind of fantasies that used to fill his daydreams as a child. He would turn himself into the benevolent stranger, answering people's wishes without ever revealing himself to them. Or he would use the pockets to read people's fortunes somehow (he hadn't yet figured out the details). Or he would be the mysterious, slightly menacing figure who would take people by the shoulder, lock gazes with them, and say, "I can tell what you've been thinking." But it was not long before he gave up on those ideas.

There were so many prayers, there was so much longing in the world, and in the face of it all he began to feel helpless.

One night the man had a dream that he was walking by a hotel swimming pool, beneath a sky the same lambent blue as the water, when he recognized God spread out like a convalescent in one of the hotel's deck chairs. "You!" the man said. "What are you doing here? I have your coat. Don't you want it back?"

God set his magazine down on his lap, folding one of the corners over, and shook his head. "It's yours now. They're all yours now. I don't want the responsibility anymore."

"But don't you understand?" the man said to him. "We need you down here. How could you just abandon us?"

And God answered, "I came to understand the limitations of my character."

It was shortly after two in the morning when the man woke up. In the moonlight he could see the laundry hamper, the clay bowl, and the dozens of cardboard boxes that covered the floor of his bedroom, all of them filled with slips of white paper he could not bear to throw away.

The next day he decided to place an ad in the classified pages: "Purchased at thrift store. One overcoat, sable brown with chestnut buttons. Pockets worn. Possibly of sentimental value. Wish to return to original owner." He allowed the ad to run for a full two weeks, going so far as to pin copies of it to the bulletin boards of several nearby churches, but he did not receive an answer. Nor, it must be said, had he honestly expected to. The coat belonged to him now. It had changed him into someone he had never expected to be. He found it hard to imagine turning back to the life he used to know, a life in which he saw people everywhere he went, in which he looked into their faces and even spoke to them, but was only able to guess at what lay in their souls.

One Saturday he took a train to the city's pedestrian mall. It was a mild day, the first gleam of spring after a long and frigid winter, and though he did not really need the coat, he had grown so used to wearing it that he put it on without a second thought. The pedestrian mall was not far from the airport, and as he arrived he watched a low plane passing overhead, dipping through the lee waves above the river. A handful of notes appeared in his pockets: *Please don't let us fall. Please keep us from going down. Let this be the one that makes the pain go away.*

The shops, restaurants, and street cafés along the pavement were quiet at first, but as the afternoon took hold, more and more people arrived. The man was walking down a set of steps toward the center of the square when he discovered a prayer that read, *Let someone speak to me this time—anyone, anyone at all—or else . . . .* The prayer was a powerful one, as taut as a steel cord in the air. It appeared to be coming from the woman sitting on the edge of the dry fountain, her feet raking two straight lines in the leaves. The man sat down beside her and asked, "Or else what?"

She did not seem surprised to hear him raise the question. "Or else . . . " she said quietly.

He could tell by the soreness in her voice that she was about to cry. "Or else . . . "

He took her by the hand. "Come on. Why don't I buy you some coffee?" He led her to the coffee-house, hanging his coat over the back of a chair and listening to her talk, and before long he had little question what the "or else" was. She seemed so disconsolate, so terribly isolated. He insisted she spend the rest of the afternoon with him. He took her to see the wooden boxes that were on display at a small art gallery and then the Victorian lamps in the front room of an antique store. A movie was playing at the bargain theater, a comedy, and he bought a pair of tickets for it, and after it was finished, the two of them settled down to dinner at a Chinese restaurant. Finally they picked up a bag of freshly roasted pecans from a pushcart down by the river. By then the sun was falling, and the woman seemed in better spirits. He made her promise to call him the next time she needed someone to talk to.

"I will," she said, tucking her chin into the collar of her shirt like a little girl. Though he wanted to believe her, he wondered as he rode the train home if he would ever hear from her again.

It was the next morning before he realized his overcoat was missing. He went to the lost-and-found counter at the train station and, when he was told that no one had turned it in, traveled back to the pedestrian mall to retrace his steps. He remembered draping the coat over his chair at the coffee-house, but none of the baristas there had seen it. Nor had the manager of the movie theater. Nor had the owner of the art gallery. The man searched for it in every shop along the square, but without success. That evening, as he unlocked the door of his house, he knew that the coat had fallen out of his hands for good. It was already plain to him how much he was going to miss it. It had brought him little ease—that was true—but it had made his life incomparably richer, and he was not sure what he was going to do without it.

We are none of us so delicate as we think, though, and over the next few days, as a dozen new accounts came across his desk at work, the sharpness of his loss faded. He no longer experienced the compulsion to hunt through his pockets all the time. He stopped feeling as though he had made some terrible mistake. Eventually he was left with only a small ache in the back of his mind, no larger than a pebble, and a lingering sensitivity to the currents of hope and longing that flowed through the air.

And at Pang Lin's Chinese Restaurant a new sign soon appeared in the window: "Custom fortune cookies made nightly and on the premises." The diners at the restaurant found the fortune cookies brittle and tasteless, but the messages inside were unlike any they had ever seen, and before long they developed a reputation for their peculiarity and their singular wisdom. Crack open one of the cookies at Pang Lin's, it was said, and you never knew what fortune you might find inside.

Please let the test be cancelled.

Thy will be done, but I could really use a woman right about now.

Why would you do something like this to me? Why?

Oh make me happy.

PREGNANT
Catherine Zeidler

from Hobart

I FIND HIM SWEATING UNDER A BURNED OUT STREETLIGHT ON THE Brooklyn Bridge, one cigarette hanging from his lips and one shaking in his hand. "It's whiskey," he says. "I'm going to sweat out the whiskey. I sweat whiskey, shit beer. Wine gets cried out. Rum gets fucked out. But this is whiskey.

"I left her. So what? Do I know you? I think maybe I do but how could I?"

"I know your face," I say. It's starved and shivering and moist and young. His face is a thunderstorm. "Can I get you anything?"

"Oxygen."

"Do you want to come home?"

"Please."

I take the cigarette from his hand; he collects papers and sneakers.

"Do you know what the first thing I remember is?" he says. "The first thing I remember is the glow of my mother's cigarette moving in the dark as she sits on the floor watching me through the bars of the crib."

I wake in the middle of the night and he's there, sitting on the windowsill stringing cigarette butts into a crown as if they were daisies. In the morning when I go to brush my teeth, he is scrubbing the toilet. I have a zit in the middle of my cheek and he stands to pop it for me. He watches from the bed while I dress, pulls me onto his lap so he can hook my bra. I hear his breath behind me on the stairs, and when I get to the door he is already there, holding it open. When I walk down the street he goes ahead of me, sweeping the sidewalk. He pays my bus fare and then steps back down the stairs; he stands under the glass watching the bus leave. From the window at work I see him down across the street, sitting outside Rite Aid—his chin propped in one hand, scratching his head with the other. Sometimes he is smoking, sometimes reading. Sometimes he is playing the harmonica. Sometimes, but not often, he line dances. Sometimes he plays jacks. Sometimes he is drawing with chalk on the sidewalk. Sometimes he feeds stray kittens, darns socks, whittles, gives massages, plays cat's cradle, attempts to give himself the Heimlich, cries, spins, pretends to get shot, lies perfectly still on the sidewalk staring up at the sky. When I get home he is inside me and it is bliss—furious, famished bliss.

"There are some things you can't hide," he says.

"Like what?"

"Like leprosy. Leopards are hard too, in the city. Lobsters you can hide in a pot but the smell soon gives them away."

We are in bed for days, flickering in and out of sex like fireflies. He huddles his head between my legs and kisses me as if I could kiss back down there. We are sore all over.

"I'm going to lock you in a little metal box," he says.

"You'll have to catch me first."

I roll off the bed and run around the apartment, leaping over the coffee table, grapevining up and down the hallway, skipping over the couch.

He shakes his head. "I can't."

I run back to him, stand just far enough away that he can't reach me. "You're out of luck then."

My heart is smiling and I laugh. I feel joy like a tumbling building—debris crashing and burying me so I can't breathe—joy rushing into me like a cloud of soot. Joy that scares me half to death.

He is burrowed behind the washing machine dry heaving over mismatched wool socks.

"I am so weak," he stammers—eyes trying to push out tears, throat trying to push out bile, fingers wedged between his toes—"I can't feel them. They're stumps and the washer is grinding into my hipbone but who cares?"

He laughs like a ship burning. I light another cigarette and throw the old butt into the suds.

I let my torso fall over the machine; my head and arms hang behind it. He is trembling. I want to steady him, and I could, my hands are close enough to the curve of his back. But I'm afraid if I do he'll stay there, soldered to me, and we'll shake with the bulk of the washing machine between us forever.

When the cigarette is done I pull him out, and he slumps against the wall. I crouch over him and wait for him to look up. He doesn't, so I take off my shirt and lift his hand to my breast. He opens his eyes and raises his head. He laughs again.

"Nice try," he says.

He is lying behind the television. I sit down and hold his feet in my lap. They are calloused and dirty, and I press them to my stomach. He curls his toes and I feel the untrimmed nails dig into my stomach a little. I lean down and kiss the veins going into his ankles. He takes one foot and reaches it under my slip.

"Do you think we ought to get married?" he says.

I laugh. I cradle his ankle with both hands as he wiggles a toe just barely inside me.

"You're all I've ever wanted," he says. "Are you happy? I am. Don't leave me. Please, say you never will."

I start to braid some of his ankle hairs. I feel his moist toe sliding up. I want to fuck his foot. I don't want to promise.

I tell him I'm happy. I am. I'm elated.

I come home, and he is waiting on the stoop.

"I'm pregnant," he says. "Can we keep it?" His eyes lift from his belly. He takes my hand and puts it under his shirt. "It's not kicking but I think you can hear its heart beating, unless that's my blood. Feel it anyway."

The sky is purple and about to collapse. His skin pulses quickly and gently under my fingertips, and I look at his hopeful eyes.

"Hush little baby, don't say a word," I sing. "Momma's gonna buy you a kiwi bird."

He is pulling the hairs from my scalp, one by one, stretching them out in front of the sunlight and then putting them in his mouth and sucking.

"Do you think," he asks, "if I swallow them baby will feel them? I want him to feel your hair. I want him to taste it."

Cold rushes to my edges. A pigeon walks in the window and over the couch onto my foot. It circles, its cold claws wet and dirty on my skin. One of its toes is lost and it pecks at the place where it should be, looking at me with its awful oily eyes. I look away and it flies out the window and over the street.

"I think maybe he feels it," he says. "He feels like he's happy."

The structure of birds is so precarious. They barely exist; you could crush them with one hand.

"You're right," I say. "I think he does."

Now he is cowering under the couch, building a cradle out of toothpicks.

"What's the use?" he mumbles. "It's not going to make it. I'm going to find its shredded bloody tissues in the toilet one day with my piss. And then it's going to cry to me with its awful voice I've always known echoing in the porcelain: Put me to bed. Tuck me in. Will you read me *The Giving Tree*? Can Mommy come sing to me just one more time?"

He looks up and sees me. He smirks and peels glue off his fingers.

"You're going to leave us aren't you," he says. "You're going to leave us and then it's going to be bye, bye baby."

"You don't know."

"I don't know that you'll leave, or that when you do baby will disentangle and the feathery bones and just forming veins will come collapsing out of me like waste, and I'll be all alone with the torn fetus and this stupid fucking gluey mess of a cradle? Which one? It doesn't matter. What's the use? Don't kid yourself, dear."

He has bitten my fingers down so much that they are all blood and holes. He has peeled my nails mostly off with his teeth. I can't touch anything without it digging into raw flesh. When they grow back they will be rough and strained and then I don't know who I'll be.

Today he is smiling, bouncing back and forth in the rocking chair quilting and thinking of names.

"Aloysius, Babe, Cal, Desmond, Ezekiel, Fred, George, Herbert, Indiana, Joe, Kirkpatrick, Leo, Mister, Ned, Orson, Peter, Quill, Rupert, Sam, Theodore, Ulrich, Val, Willy, X, Yogi, Zechariah.

"Today he kicked," he says, "for sure. He kicked and I think he had gas. You don't have anyone you'd like to name the child after, do you?"

"I'd like to name it Cleopatra."

"He's a boy, dear."

"How about Cleopat?"

"I'll consider it. He is mine, really, so I of course have the last word. I've been thinking about Baron.

"How was work? Do you have a headache? Put your feet up. Dinner will be ready at 6:30. Shall I get you the newspaper? A cocktail? Your pipe?

"So, I'm fairly certain he had gas so I'll have to pay better attention to what I'm eating. You know there must be something inherently superior about organic food but I'm sure I don't have a clue as to what it is but I ought to buy it anyway."

The rain comes down like it's judgment day, and the wind pours in and cradles our backs. We're eating hot dogs in front of the fireplace—hot dogs and root beer.

"There's something awful about you," he says. "You don't seem to care if baby lives."

There's lightning sharp and brutal all around. I throw the hot dog into the flames and crawl out the window onto the fire escape. I'm drenched straight through instantly, and my hair flattens against my face and shoulders. I close my eyes and thunder cracks through my body.

"I'm sorry," he's saying through the window. "I'm so sorry. Please. Come back. I'm sorry."

I am so hungry for him I salivate. I get sick with hunger. My whole body starves. When he is with me there is burning glee, but still the hunger and the cold. His belly gets bigger and we gather around it to listen to baby gurgle, and to feel its lungs going in and out, and its limbs forming. I put my chest against his stomach and my head on his heart, and I feel all three hearts beating, and I wrap my arms tight around him and fall asleep.

He has taken all the hair from my head and now he is working on my eyebrows. He tugs them out while I am sleeping and I wake with holes in them. He is swallowing the hairs, I'm sure. There is no trace of them anywhere. I look between the sheets and in his socks and under the stove. Nothing.

He walks through the door and sits against the refrigerator cross-legged, staring at the leg of his pants.

"I brought home a yellow-jacket. I found her lying on my pants, looking like she was trying to suck something out of them. I stared at her for a while and she stopped moving and I wondered if she was dead. I flicked at her with a pen, and she started to rub her head and then walked around a little. Then she rested again and brought a leg up to her backside. I saw the big hole there, no stinger, nothing, but she was trying to scratch it, and I felt so sad for her I brought her home."

I sit next to him against the linoleum and press my hand to baby. I feel the mass of hair snarling around in his belly through the shirt.

"It's going to drown," I say. "You're going to tie baby in knots."

"You don't know what you're talking about. I'm just putting hair on his chest."

I feel weak. I feel tired. Sometimes it is difficult even to raise my eyelids. My body is a landscape of jutting precipices and skin sagging around taut hollows. He is soft and plump. His chest even seems to have grown full in anticipation. The joy I feel when he holds me takes all my energy and makes even my bones ache.

I try to stay awake to guard my skin, my teeth, my blood, my insides. I have caught him with a speculum trying to scrape away at my cervix. The hair doesn't bother me anymore, but now he brings a washcloth to bed to soak up the sweat that pours out of me while we are fucking. He wrings it into his mouth when we are done, and then he folds it over the bulge, tucking baby in.

"Sleep well, son," he says. "Please sleep. Sleep while your brain is still just a muddle, while you can sleep without dreaming of soot, and your screams buried under flaming concrete, and your mother a torn apart face running into the dark, running away."

"You know I can't run anymore," I say.

The skin there begins to pull and stretch, and we walk down the street looking into the wide eyes of babies. He turns his head to watch them pass.

"If only he could ever look like that," he says, "even that last ugly one; that child was an imp—even if his skin was bubbly with acid, even if he had a shrunken head, even if he had tongues for arms and no dick, even if he died as soon as I saw him. I don't think I'll be able to make another."

The scalpel presses into my shoulder and I am jerked awake, frozen. I hear his breath hovering above me, and I say, "Please." He doesn't answer but breathes heavily against my breast. It pierces my skin and I look away, sobbing, the cold around me tight like saran wrap.

He says, "I love you," positioning the vial beside my arm to collect the blood and the wasted skin.

I pull away and huddle against the wall.

"Go sit in the corner," I say. "Go put on the dunce cap. Go jump off the fire escape. Go shove a fucking coat hanger in there for all I care."

He slinks away from me, his neck bent like a safety pin. He moves down off the bed and into the corner, scratching at his belly and muttering, "Oh, my dear, my dearest dear," over and over again.

"We only wanted a little," he says at last. "We're thirsty and weak."

The blood is warm; it falls slowly, branching down over my chest and into my armpit. He has dropped the vial, and it lies empty on the floor. I go to him, hold out my shoulder.

"Take it," I say. "Don't waste it."

His mouth is soft and gentle and grateful. He sucks like an infant hushed in the night by his mother's tit. When the bleeding has steadied he laps at the stain that runs down my chest with his rough tongue. I never feel teeth, just moisture and suction and tears.

"I'll get all of it," he says, "if it takes a week. I'll get it. Don't worry."

I wake without breath. All motion in my body seems to have stopped. I put my pinky in his nostril and he wakes with a start.

"What? What is it?"

I open my mouth and bring his hand to feel the stillness in my lungs. I point out the window.

"All right," he says. "I'll take you."

We take the subway to Coney Island. I sleep in his lap on the way out and he whispers in my ear that the people in the car are looking at us like we are incestuous teenagers running away from home. When I lift my head we are above ground, and I turn, peering out the window like a toddler, trying to see through the softening darkness. I make out clotheslines and empty lots, a naked man waiting for dawn on his roof, dark smoking youths playing soccer with a Coke bottle down in the empty street, trees and boarded up windows.

"Are you breathing?" he asks.

I shake my head.

When we get into the open air he walks me past the caged freak show and bumper cars and hot dog stands, past men strewn across the sidewalk like rubbish, the abandoned roller coaster before us on the horizon—weeds choking it like boa constrictors. Above the board-walk the gulls circle, screeching at the first glimpses of light, predatory and large to the point of deformity. Men cast their fishing lines from the pier.

We climb over the railing and onto the sand. He ties our shoelaces together and slings the shoes over his shoulder. I tell him to be careful of glass; he says it doesn't matter.

"I could fall into a shark's mouth and not feel it," he says. "I wish you wouldn't go."

The sand is cool and wet on our feet as they sink in. We walk through the plastic rings of six-packs, bottles, plastic bags, paper dishes splattered with ketchup, dirty magazines, umbrellas stretched inside-out, votive candles, popcorn, prize stuffed-animals forced to fight with strays and left for the birds to pick at. We sit enlaced—he leans against my chest and I wrap my legs around his belly—at the edge of the wavering skirt of the ocean. I can feel baby's breath against my calves in deep, even pushes as steady as the waves. Sitting inside each other, feeling the sun begin to push through the project towers in the east, we all breathe deep and fill our bellies with hope for each other. We are warm and fat and bubbling with it.

THE WAREHOUSE OF SAINTS
Robin Hemley

from Ninth Letter

> Too many blessings break a man apart
> —Tomaz Salamun

TODAY, WE DID INVENTORY, MY SON DOMENIC AND I: TEN SHIN bones belonging to St. Timothy. Sixteen tibias of Paul. Four skulls of John the Baptist. Three complete skeletons of Mary Magdalene. A jar of teeth simply labeled, "Assorted Saints." A cask of desiccated organs. Thirteen livers of St. Peter. The dried tongues of Judas Iscariot, Simon, and Thomas. Fingernail shavings of the great kings of France, including the entire big toe nail of Richard the Lionhearted. His entrails, too. The scapulas of Saints Catherine and Michael. Enough True Cross splinters to build a bridge from Chinon to Paris. God even sends us bones on His day of rest, and that confounds me. Are all other mortals deemed worthy enough to share in His rest, except us, His bone slaves?

"Does it concern you, my son, that Saint Peter had so many livers, and Mary Magdalene so many skeletons within her?" I have asked him this question and variations upon it before, but my son is clever, and I marvel at the many reasons we should revere God's contradictions. If God did not prefer the impossible to the possible, and the incomprehensible to the comprehensible, he would not have bothered to give form to the firmament and breath to the earth's confounding creatures. Domenic has reminded me of the loaves and fishes, of the water into wine, of the Holy Trinity, of Christ's body and blood.

"The Jews believe that ten thousand people heard Moses at Mt. Sinai," he says, combing his beard with a comb carved from the ribs of St. Batholeme. "Every Jew alive today has a piece of one of those souls co-mingled with his own. What the Jews believe is not what I believe, but I use this as an example. The sums of God are not our sums."

I am a simple man. Such faith inspires me—though there are times, I admit, that I doubt the good Domenic and I do. I named my son after Saint Domenic who appeared to me in a dream and cut off his index finger and gave it to me. He said, "Mathias, even the whitened bones of the saints clamor to do God's bidding." Yet, it took sixteen years before the true nature of Domenic's prophecy was revealed to me. In the early years, I sold herbs and potions concocted by my wife. Only after her death, when our future looked bleakest, did the bones and relics start to mysteriously appear at the mouth of our cave. Then I understood my true calling. In the two years since, Domenic and I have built our business into the largest inventory of bones and relics of saints in the Loire Valley.

Domenic bows his head and tells me that if the Lord's ways were not mysterious, they would not be the Lord's ways and there would be nothing He could do to inspire or impress us. Man should not try to explain everything in the world and beyond. Still, I wonder. That is my sin. Wonder. And from wonder sometimes doubt springs.

Our tufa stone cave is narrow but deep. Only six cows could fit side by side at its entrance, but a herd could be driven in and disappear within its belly. I have not explored its depths. I stay near the entrance where the light from the sun mingles with the candles we have placed within the niches and shelves we have carved into the soft stone. Domenic is a tall boy and although the ceiling is higher than his head, he often bends as though in reverence.

We live in a murderous region, my son and I, a place never to my knowledge visited by angels and saints. In Chinon, the Dauphin reigns in his chateau, though not unthreatened. His own mother would betray him to the English and says he is a bastard. In such a world, is it a surprise then that more travelers are murdered on the road to Chinon than make it through alive? Bandits are our true rulers, and the Dauphin, under whose protection we live, can neither stop a brigand from slitting my throat, nor a witch making a changeling out of me, nor the English making a mockery of the French monarchy. In my youth, things were much better. You could walk the streets of Chinon at night, no one locked his door, and everyone greeted his neighbor.

Even in our cave, we hear the rumors, and many believe that France is doomed, that before long an English king will rule over us all. A week ago, the Dauphin was visited by a girl who calls herself Jehanne from the village of Domrémy who said she was heaven sent to lead him to victory against the English. She speaks for God, the people say, and they brought her to see the Dauphin, but the Dauphin's advisors, fearing she might have been sent by the English to murder him, put an impostor on the throne. When she was led to the throne room, the impostor said, "I am the heir to the kingdom of France," but this girl ignored him and pointed to the Dauphin, hiding in the crowd. She knelt before him and said, "Gentle Dauphin, I have come, by the grace of the King of Heaven, to raise an army and see you crowned in Rheims." That she was not beset upon by bandits in the forest of Chinon on her way to meet the Dauphin had already convinced many that she was under God's protection, but what she said to the Dauphin, in front of scores of witnesses, has made even him willing to listen. I am not so sure I would call the Dauphin gentle. In Asay le Rideau, a few of the Burgundian guard once insulted the Dauphin and so he set the town ablaze and put to death hundreds of their number. Still, I prefer the Dauphin I know to the Dauphin I don't, and we must forgive him his outbursts.

This Jehanne, if she speaks for the King of Heaven, is not the first woman in this place to have God's ear. In Fontrevraud, it has been decreed that the head of the order will always be a woman—in this way, the men who serve under her learn humility. The present Abbess, Blanche D'Harcourt, is generous with the humility she doles out to the monks. Men at the Abbey eat no meat, only fish, and receive a daily ration of a quarter liter of wine to the nun's half a liter. If not for the problem of the wine ration, I could be a monk at Fontrevraud. I have no difficulty bending to the will of a woman. My own Genevieve spoke regularly with God, though He never told her anything grand to do. God gave her the ingredients to use when mixing her tonics and potions and taught her the language of chickens and wild boars. Useful yes, from time to time, but nothing that inspires reverence and awe. Still, she was able to foretell her own death when she overheard the chickens speaking of it one gray morning as she approached the henhouse.

Today, I have found a neat stack of bleached bones by the entrance to the caves. They do not always arrive so. They appear in the mornings, arriving from where I do not know. Heaven sent, Domenic says. Sometimes they arrive in sacks, sometimes moldered, sometimes with bits of sinew and clumps of hair and clothing attached, sometimes the individual bones, the smaller ones, are wrapped in sausage casings. Through divination, we come to understand to which saint the bones belong. Domenic is good at this. I have never been so good at divination, except for my dream of Domenic's finger.

Domenic and I often laugh about the first time I pulled a skull from one of these sacks and ran into the fields, staying until nightfall. "Father," Domenic called, "this is the head of John the Baptist. We are saved!"

"We are doomed," I called from among the wheat fields. "Where did this skull come from? It smells of earth and worms. We'll be hanged, drawn apart, and then, Mother of Mercy, excommunicated. You must bury it again—the crossroads of Fontrevraud and Couziers would be a good place. At midnight. And you must blindfold the skull so it will not find its way back to us. Then you must go to mass, have neither food nor drink, cease urination for four days, and spit whenever you hear the words, 'owl,' 'vagina,' or 'potato.' You must never speak to anyone of this." The words "owl," "vagina" and "potato" had formed unbidden in my mind, but why these words, I can't say. I only know that "owl" "vagina" and "potato" made me feel great foreboding and so I thought maybe this was a sign from God. And spitting never hurts.

"Father, it's the dream. Your dream," Domenic shouted. "We are saved, not doomed. We must tell everyone." Now we keep this head, our first saint, up in the front of the cave, by the money box in a special niche, for good luck.

"Good news, Father," he tells me now, appearing out of the dark where I do not like to go. "We can fill the order from the Abbess in Fontrevraud."

"An order from the Abbess?" I say, staring at a group of pilgrims making their way towards us from the river Vienne. "I don't remember such an order."

"It was only a week ago," he says "A large quantity of pelvis."

"Another miracle," I say, bowing my head in prayer.

We can hardly keep the pulverized pelvis of the Holy Virgin in stock—it's been out of stock for months. A spoonful mixed into the mortar of a church before consecration, chapel, abbey, or cathedral (proportions vary, depending on altitude) will ensure entry into heaven for all the congregants and their livestock. When mixed with the tepid breast milk of the mother of a stillborn boy infant with eleven toes, it is said to cure gout and taste delicious, but this I cannot verify.

"Domenic," I say, "God's mercy is great, is it not?" I meant to say this in praise, but my tone of voice was not the one I intended. I sound doubtful. I have dreams and visions I cannot understand. Angels with swords slitting the throats of Cathar children. Poisonous flowers fluttering from heaven. Last night, I dreamed of a field of dead popes, each of whom was disinterred to receive communion. One pope lay in his casket, blind, while a priest teased him with a communion wafer. Then the pope's tongue burst into flame. Why am I tormented with such undecipherable visions?

Domenic kneels beside me. He rarely answers a question without giving it great thought first. He swats some flies from my nose and lips. I crane my neck around him to note the progress of the pilgrims. Soldiers walk among them. Although I can't recognize any faces, the sun glints off the soldier's armor. One carries a staff bearing a strange seal.

"Father," he says. "Have you been thinking of the Albigensians again?"

"The wretched Albigensians," I say.

"The Albigensians were heretics," he says. "It is God who grants mercy, the devil who shuns it. If you pity the Albigensians so, why did you name me after the saint who wiped them from the earth?"

Domenic does not understand. It's not so much pity that plagues me as a nagging thought. I can't give voice to the thought, so heretical is it, and for this reason it keeps rising. Perhaps these thoughts were planted in my head by the devil. I know I would be burned at the stake if I told anyone of them besides Domenic. I think these thoughts, I believe, because I'm surrounded by the bones of the saints, and they talk to me. They whisper doubt to me, not faith. What if the Albigensians were right? What if man is evil as I've heard the Albigensians believed and the only way to redeem himself is to suffer multiple lifetimes? What if Pope Innocent and Saint Domenic did an evil thing in hounding and slaughtering the Albigensians by the thousands, and in so doing, eradicated our chance to redeem ourselves through their teachings? I'll never know, but maybe we're on the wrong path, not the right one. Is it possible Saint Domenic proved the Albigensians right by killing them?

Domenic stands and plucks a hair from his beard, examines it, and lets it fall to the dirt. He turns slowly as the wind carries the shouts of the group toward us.

At the head of the group of soldiers and townspeople rides a stout boy on a mare. The boy carries a white banner I've never seen: against a field of lilies are written the words *Jhesus Maria*, and underneath these words is a picture of Christ surrounded by two angels. The boy wears a black cap, boots, leggings, and a tunic that reaches to his knees. A coat of arms, red and gold, blazes from the tunic. We have had important visitors before, princes and bishops and cardinals, all drawn to this place to see what we have to offer. Some send their emissaries, but most choose to visit in person. Buying the bones of a saint is a delicate business—the buyer wants to know what he's getting, wants to see it, wants to heft its holy weight and hear it whisper its secrets and tell one's destiny if it wishes. One cannot send an emissary for that. But this banner the boy carries is such I've never heard of nor seen, and I feel a peculiar tingling in my toes, an ache as though my own bones were struggling to answer some invisible summons and rise bidden from my body.

A voice somewhere inside me speaks. "Jehanne," it calls. "Jehanne." I turn to alert my son, but he has already retreated into the cave. "Domenic, come out," I say. "You must see this."

"I saw it," he answers, his voice suddenly sulky.

"But I think it's that woman we keep hearing about, dressed like a man," I say.

"That's right," he says. "I have an intimation." The boy is always having intimations, often accompanied by a headache. And he starts to pray the special prayer to ward off women who dress like men.

"But Domenic. She carries a banner with our Lord's name on it."

He doesn't pause his prayer but only prays louder. Presently, the voices of the crowd gather at the mouth of the cave and one voice, surprisingly deep for a girl so young, sounds above the rest.

"Troglodytes!" she hails us. ""I wish to speak with you about the relics you trade in. We ride to Orleans soon to break the siege of the English."

The girl dismounts her horse. In the air, a faint whiff of honeysuckle wafts, the swish of her horse's tail, the nonsensical song of Jerome, the town imbecile, always lagging last in any procession.

"We're closed for inventory," Domenic shouts. "Don't touch anything." But they seem not to hear him. As if in a dream, they have already started milling about the shelves, picking up relics. Domenic stands among them, grabbing the relics from their hands and replacing them in the niches. Two men and one woman lie prostrate before the three skeletons of Mary Magdalene.

"Holy!" one murmurs.

"Preserve us," another says.

What's this?" Jehanne asks, picking up the lucky skull of John the Baptist.

"That's John the Baptist," I tell her. "Very rare. Our first saint."

"Look, it's the toe of St. Ignatius," a monk from Fontrevraud shouts to his brother.

"Put it back," the brother says. "What are we going to do with the toe of St. Ignatius?"

"What *can't* be done with the toe of St. Ignatius?" the first monk says. "Never was there such a versatile saint! Not only was he the child the Savior took up in his arms as described in Mark 9:35, but he was among the auditors of the apostle St. John and the third Bishop of Antioch, if we include St. Peter."

"Oh, there you go again," says the second monk. "The third Bishop of Antioch, *if* we include St. Peter."

"Oh, luckless bones, I hear your voices," Jehanne says. "This is nothing but the daughter of a farmer from Borgueil."

The anguish of her voice cloaks me like another skin and I look at my hands as though they hold my answer to her. But they do not. They are dumb and cannot speak. No part of me can speak with the certainty of this Jehanne. They cannot even speak the terror of my doubt.

I bring her a stool to sit on and walk to the well to give her something to drink. "No, it's John the Baptist all right," I say, my voice betraying me. "But he's not for sale."

"Where did you get these?" she says, sitting down with John's skull and looking into his sockets.

"Here and there," I say. "Domenic, do you want to tell her? It's really quite an amusing story! That very skull you're holding was our first relic, wasn't it, Domenic?" I laugh and turn to Domenic, who seems to be quaking. He stares at the girl. And I stop to stare at him. An excuse for him begins to form, that the dankness of the cave has made him shiver. But I cannot say this and believe it. This is my own son. How can I doubt my son? Even if he is wrong, I wish his certainty again.

"Borgueil?" he asks her, in the slightest voice I've ever heard from him.

Jehanne casts the skull in the dirt and produces a piece of worn leather from her robe. She holds the leather kerchief in front of Domenic. As she unwraps it, we strain to see what the leather holds, a bone small and curved like a rib, but brittle, covered by a thin red dust.

"Domenic," she says. "Tell me from whose body this was taken?"

Domenic stops shaking and peers at the bone, then carefully plucks it from its wrapping. She's so much smaller than him. She's a girl who looks like a boy and wears men's clothing. Maybe she's a witch. He looks into his hand as though he has never seen a bone before.

"More light," he says. "I need light," and one of Jehanne's followers, a boy wearing a tunic with Jehanne's crest crudely stitched onto the cloth, takes a torch from the wall of cave and brings it to Domenic.

He touches his beard and closes his eyes. He makes the sign of the cross and we all cross ourselves, even Jehanne who looks at him otherwise without emotion. He puts the bone to his nose and sniffs it, then breathes its scent deeply. He places it by his ear and listens to the voice of the bone. He places the bone to his brow and divines the thoughts of the bone, or its teachings if it belongs to a saint. He nods and nods again and the light of the cave trembles because the boy holding the torch has begun to shiver.

"This is a splinter from the ribs of the Savior Himself," he announces in his normal ringing voice, the voice of a prophet. "Do you remember the Roman soldier's spear in our Savior's side?" he asks those of us in the cave and there is a murmur, heads bowed. "From that blow came this splinter. Where did you find it?" he asks Jehanne, setting the bone back in its kerchief, his eyes bright with understanding and divine light. I want to shout at the return of such a light and strength to his features.

"In a chicken coop," Jehanne says. "From a cock who died in battle with another cock, a valiant but meaningless death."

She gathers up the leather kerchief from Domenic and shakes the bone onto the floor with a small laugh. "Grave robbers," she says. The monks, the children, the soldiers, even Jerome the idiot lose their looks of reverence and mill about us, the firelight dancing on the walls.

"Bastards," a soldier shouts and spits at me.

"Witches," says a boy and spits on Domenic.

"Devils," says an old woman and spits twice, once on each of us.

Spitting on heretics and blasphemers is one of the favorite pastimes in Chinon, but we're not heretics. Don't we do the Lord's work? Domenic has fallen on his knees, his eyes closed, tears streaming down his face. Now he reaches in his tunic and holds his hands outstretched to Jehanne, shouting, "Here, here. This is a true relic, a true relic."

Jehanne puts up her arm and silences the crowd. She moves to take what he offers, though his grip is strong and he almost forgets to let her take it. He finally opens his hands to reveal a small bone, one that I do not recognize. It is yellow with age, long and thin, a human finger. The bone whispers doubt to me, not faith.

Jehanne takes the bone and examines it. Then she crosses herself and mutters a silent prayer.

"Where did you find this?" she asks him.

"I don't know," he says, crying and shaking his head. "I don't know. It appeared. It was the first. But no more came after this."

She smiles at him and says, "A true relic. A powerful and holy relic I will take with me to Rheims."

"But whose?" I ask her. "How do you know?"

She doesn't answer, and this is what troubles me. I used to wonder how Dominic could be so certain of himself, when even the nuns in Fontrevraud recite the Holy Book without the slightest inflection, so afraid are they of adding their own interpretations to God's words. And how do the kings and queens of the world determine with such certainty the difference between God's voice and the voice of the serpent?

"Redeem yourself, Domenic," Jehanne says.

"Redeem them," one of the monks says with a sneer. "Redeem them both."

And that is all I hear except for a buzzing, growing louder and louder still until all other sound is drowned out. We're carried out of the cave by the crowd, and Domenic stumbles on a rock and falls. As he looks up, I graze his cheek with my hand.

Jehanne regards him, her face colorless, her lips as thin as a man's.

"Show him God's mercy," I say, lifting him up. Would that he could be borne to heaven now, but it is only I, Mathias, helping him to his feet.

"Redeem him," I beg.

"Redeem yourself," Jehanne says as she's helped up on her horse by the boy with the coat of arms stitched in his tunic.

Domenic looks at me tearfully. "She knows, she knows. We must follow her, father. She has been sent by the Lord to save us."

"You'll follow her, all right," says the boy, and there's laughter close to him and murmurs at the back of the group. "What did she say?

What did she say?" They think it was Jehanne who spoke, but she has no trace of mirth. She looks away, shifts on her horse and starts away.

Our hands are bound by soldiers. Her followers stuff our relics into sacks and tie these sacks by rope around our necks. And as we march into Chinon, the soldiers and townspeople sing, forgetting us. "Let each take his hoe, the better to uproot them. And if they do not wish to go, at least make a face at them. Do not fear to strike them, those big-bellied English soldiers, for one of us is worth four of them, or at least he is worth three of them."

Jehanne on her horse holds the finger of the saint, her prize, in one hand while grasping her horse's rein in the other. The bone seems like a banner, towering invisible in its power into the clouds.

A voice whispers to me, "Mathias, what have you done?" then says no more.

Jehanne circles back to me, regards me from her horse, and shows me the finger as if instructing me. But then she closes her hand around it and canters off. Did she show me this to torment me or to light the way?

"Show it to me, too," Domenic begs, as though he has never seen it before, though it has been in his possession for years.

Perhaps only our bodies imprison us as the Cathars taught, and in each material object the divine spark glows. From the bones of the saints, the glow is constant. But what of the bones of ordinary men? If even the bones of the saints lead us astray, then what good can they really be?

We stumble countless times as our bags of bones choke us when they stick on tree roots and rocks and brambles. But still, we drag them on, and they rattle and clamor as if they wish nothing more than to join in battle and in the songs of our redeemers.

Until I refuse to walk farther.

I wait in the dusty road, attentive to all sounds, all voices, a terrible thirst parching my throat. They walk on ahead of me, even Domenic, who joins Jehanne's followers in song as though one of them. I wonder if he truly believes now or if he sings to save his mortal self.

The boy in the tunic moves to drag me, but I am much too heavy, so he beats me in the face with a switch.

Samuel, when he heard God's voice, thought it was Eli calling to him for help. After being awakened by Samuel three times, Eli understood and told Samuel what to say when God spoke.

This is what I try to say through the furious lashes of this boy.

"Speak, Lord, for your servant hears your call."

THE LEDGE
Austin Bunn

from One Story

MOTHER, I HAVE SEEN SUCH MARVELS. LIKE THE OCEAN AGLOW at night with a cold green fire and a fish with a child's face and two fleshy whiskers. (No man would eat it. We blessed the creature and tossed it back.) I've seen a corpse with golden hair in a boat set adrift; his eyes were the slits on a newly born kitten. When the boatswain came-to after three days on the *garrucha* for the crime of sodomy—his wrists tied behind him and hoisted above the deck so that his arms tore and jellied—he asked, "Am I dead?" and soon he was. I looked to Diego, who dropped his dark eyes in shame, and I saw that too. Three hundred leagues into the Ocean Sea, we came upon a floating meadow, crabs and petrels tinkering along its dank branches and fronds. A palm tree had taken root there and I imagined, briefly, the coastline of Seville, of home.

But none of these compare to you mother, suddenly here, at the gunwale of this ship, soaking wet. Your hands are folded across your chest and you stare away, at the ledge. You look precisely as I left you six years ago, dressed in an immaculate cobalt shift, your long black hair damp and loose against your back and your bare feet white as salt. Around me, the crew and the others race to trim the *Elena's* sails in a westerly. The Captain is missing and I am full of questions. Are you a dream? Is this a fever or worse? I'm afraid to speak. And so I sit alone, in the shade of the quarterdeck, with my ledger and write.

The great Venetian who saw the court of the Kublai Khan wrote his *Book of Marvels*. I remember how I loved it as a young man. I stole into the *colegio* to read the manuscript pages, to teach myself the words. It took me a year to finish it, and when I was done, I started over again. At night, I dreamed of trader Polo's adventures: the falcons of Karmania, the silver tower of Mien, and the festival of wives . . . Marco Polo told his story from a Genoese jail. The *Elena* is now my prison. His stories saved his life. Perhaps so will mine.

This record begins three days ago, on the *Elena's* twenty-second day at sea. We sailed in search of the sea-path to India, driving a slant from the Canaries to the Azores into the blue-black unknown. For days, we had been mired in a meadow of sargassum. Captain Veragua, convinced it was the grass of a sub-marine ridge, ordered the crew to sound the waters on every watch. The bulb of lead, at the end of the fathom-long cordage, could never sink through the dense thicket. In boredom, the English conscript used a crossbow to hunt a petrel, resting on the carpet of weed, and succeeded only in punching it into oblivion. But on Sunday, the meadow miraculously began to break into patches and then lacy fingers. As it trailed into our wake, the crew sang psalms and *Salve Regina* with renewed (if not exactly pleasing) vigor.

Summoned by our good feeling, a group of dolphins assembled beneath the *Elena*. They moved together like a shadow, fracturing and collecting with astounding speed. They teased us playfully, the way children at the Magdalena city gate greet strangers. They leapt into the air and made an exuberant bird-like speech. I opened the navigation ledger and stared at our rhumb-line. It hung on the page like a gypsy's tightrope, fixed only at one end and one thousand leagues long. I wrote, "Sea like a river, new friends, new hope."

And then a cry came from the rigging. Diego, swung up in the web of mainsail rope, yelled a shapeless sound and pointed frantically off the side of the ship. At port, two iridescent coils, the height of three men, arched across our length. They moved as fast as a lash and seemed pure muscle, strong enough to splinter the *Elena* to matchwood. Their scales shimmered like cathedral glass, slick and brilliant. I froze with the ledger open on my lap. Before long, other sea serpents, large as the first, foamed the water in a frenzy. The ocean was a tipped basket of eels. The serpents coiled and, at once, lunged beneath the boat.

The men backed away from the gunwale. The waters went still and the air flashed with heat. No man moved. In short time, our wake ran red. Bits of pink meat floated and were snatched down.

Pinzón, our interpreter, clutched my arm.

"Where," he whispered, *"are we?"*

Every sailor knows the stories of seacats and mermaids with cadaver-cold breasts. St. Brendan told of sailing home to Ireland on the back of a whale. But in my six years at sail, as a scribe, men never died from stories. They reefed on fogged-out coasts. They wrecked on breakers off Cape Bojador, circled forever in the *mare tenebrosum*. Except now, new horrors brushed against our keel and knifed the water. We were eighteen men buoyed by forty feet of caulked and tarred oak, the thinnest wooden wall between our fate and us. My fingers found the western blank of my chart, the freefall of our rhumb-line, where lay the mapmaker's warning: *Here be monsters.*

Thirteen-year-old Marco, the ship's boy, squirreled up the mast, as high as he could go. The twin deckhands, Alfredo the Tall and Armando the Taller, fell to their knees and raced through the Lord's Prayer. Others rushed to the sail locker for armaments, but as an ocean exploration ship, the *Elena* is fast and weak. We carry no arms stronger than crossbows and a meager falconet mounted on the deck that spits scrap-metal. Against raiders—or worse—we have little defense.

Diego alone craned over the side and searched through the water. I wanted to go to his side, the safest place I know, but panic fixed me.

"What do you see?" said the conscript, his teeth clacking. Piss had spilled down his right legging and his swagger had gone with it. "Tell us."

But Diego didn't speak, didn't even look up. He has his tongue and his wit, but Diego is as mute as an African. Much as I feel for him, Diego has never spoken my name. Can you love something that you never name?

I was with the Captain when we found Diego grinning on the steps of the cathedral, a drunk Franciscan friar, tonsure gone prickly. A spray of freckles fell across the bridge of his nose and vanished beneath a black beard that ran up his cheeks. He looked like a wine cask, browned and wide-bellied. The friars said that he'd been silent since he entered their order as a young man and had never taken to cloistered life; he kept the garden full of flowers and birds and finally cats, until a plague of aphids brought it to ruin. The Captain asked him to join our expedition as a cook. In answer, Diego pointed down to the banks of the Guadalquivir and would not stop pointing.

How is it that some men inspire no feeling in me while others stir the deep waters? At the cathedral, I took his broad right hand, delicate as calfskin. He pressed his left against the outside of mine, so that my hand was held in warm, gentle prayer. I felt my blood rise up, the way a bulb of quicksilver feels in a pot of boiling water. He pointed to my ginger hair and made a flickering motion with his fingers: Fire. I smiled like an idiot. The Captain saw the meeting of new friends, but I felt found. And if Diego did not speak, his hands were more fluent than any words. He practiced a religion at the cook-box, the communion of salt-pork and sea fish, which was all that mattered. And at night, in shadows, those hands made other blessings. Now, at the bulwark, Diego looked eager and expectant. As if this encounter was his whole reason for coming.

The deck bell rang. Captain Veragua stood at the entrance to his quarters. In full daylight, he was plainly dying. He wore a brown hooded smock and a red cap to shield his burns from the sun. His eyes shone like marble knobs. On our second week at sail, the Captain had stupored on wine and a candle tipped in a swell, setting his bedclothes and doublet alight. He jumped overboard and when he was fished from the water, his left side looked like a hank of meat rescued from embers. It took two days for Diego to pare the seared cloth from his skin with a carving knife. Every command he gave to us now was curt and purposeful, trimmed to the minimum amount of gesture.

"Peralonso," the Captain asked me, "What is that sound?"

My attention went to the sails. The wind had wore out; the main and the fore drooped without breeze. The ship's planks creaked in complaint. The sea slapped lightly against the *Elena*. We had entered a white calm, the horizon crouched behind a mist. But as I listened, below all of this came a faint, wide roaring, like the rumor of a waterfall. It stretched the width of my perception.

"Land?" I answered.

The Captain ordered the deep-sea lead hove overboard. The first line, at one hundred fathoms, failed to find bottom. Armando and Alfredo recalled the line, spliced a second to the first, and sent that into the sea. Again, the lead drifted in the current. The sea here was too deep to sound.

Then the Captain called for the land-birds to be released. The two crows sat in their cage high on the mast; these birds hate travel over seawater. They sight land and fly there without pause. Marco scampered up the rope ladder and raised the cage. The birds circled higher and higher. They continued to loop until we could not make them out.

"*Listen,*" the Captain said.

Soon enough the drone was all I could hear. The *Elena* drifted in a minute current. Slowly, as the world reaches focus through a looking glass, the mist thinned and revealed itself as a great spume of ocean water. One league away, the curve of horizon straightened to a line, to a drop. Like the edge of an enormous table. Clouds bent over this line and disappeared.

Coralito, the *Elena's* frail navigator, crossed himself and went to the Captain, our sail chart spindled in his hand. He was an old and difficult widower, too vain to admit his fading eyesight. Long white eyebrows billowed from his face, like puffs of sweet weather. For weeks now, he had been unable to hunt the Polestar, and I took turns with him shooting our location with the cross-staff. But as aged as he was, Coralito was the *Elena's* will, our human compass. At the Talavera Commission in Salamanca, he watched flame-haired Queen Isabella decree, on a carpet of maps, that the world was a plate ringed by water. That to traverse this lip from Spain to the Indies would take three years. Under his breath Coralito had muttered, *What do priests and Queens know of science? The world is not flat. It is as round as a ball of wax and as knowable. You can leave a place, travel a line, and arrive where you began.*

"What did you say?" the Captain asked.

"I have failed you Captain," Coralito repeated. "I was wrong."

The crows returned and settled noisily on two belaying pins.

"We have reached the edge of the ocean," Coralito continued. "We can go no further. This is the fourth corner of the world."

Every man is born to his first corner. Mine was a pile of flour sacks in a house in the port city of Seville, in the year 1469, under the reign of King Ferdinand of Aragon. That year, my father, a blacksmith, was conscripted into the *armada marvallosa* in the English war and lost at sea. He returned to my mother as one thousand *maravedis* of wheat grain, the compensation for sacrifice. Desperate and poor, my mother bricked in his furnace, hand-ground her grief into powder, and opened a bakery.

Every morning, I rose to find her kneading the dough beneath the heavy rafters. I will always remember her ghosted with this fine white dust, cool and papery to the touch, haunting a passage to and from the oven. She was a striking, sad beauty, her hair gathered in a silver band.

Countless men needled me in an effort to get her attention and force a smile on her. But none could tempt her out of the downward stare of her solitude.

"You must never leave me," she would say, flattening my hand against her cheek. "One day you will want to. It will be a girl with gray eyes, or a distant shore. That day, you will count all the things that are keeping you here and they will not be enough. That day will be my last."

My mother gave me the gift of letters. When I was thirteen years old, she led me to a field of goldenrod and covered my head in a shawl. She told me I must study a new book and make new prayers. I asked, "Who are we praying to?" and she said, "To the God of Israel, your true people." That afternoon, I became two: a Catholic, the faith of my father, and a *marrano*, Jew by candlelight.

Soon after, the butcher came on afternoons to sit me on his lap and write the alphabet on a slate. He read each letter aloud while I repeated them. Sometimes he would whisper made-up words in my ear, or put my hand on his warm, furry belly to show me how breath worked until he sighed. I delighted in this and the heat of his lap, but my mother sent him away. "You're too old for such things," she said. I wept inconsolably for a loss I felt but couldn't bring into words. I chose then to give up on her faith, any faith that prescribed loneliness.

Over time, my mother's bakery grew to serve the harbor, preparing tack and meal for sea journeys to and from the Levant, the terminus of the spice road. It was my task to deliver the breads to the *barcas* and *naviculas* anchored in the river. I grew to love the crowded port, so dense with ships that I couldn't see the water. There were many familiar faces, salted in every crease, and crabs savoring the treacle on hulls, dry-docked on the sandbar. The port felt like a floating city of fathers: exuberant, bronzed men, barefoot and dressed only in trousers. They taught me knots, the mysteries of splicing and parceling the cordage, even as they pilfered my delivery breads. Many asked if I wanted to join their crews as a grommet, but only if I could assure that their hardtack would never worm.

I was tempted. The sailors spoke of the Spice Islands, the Moluccas, and their incomprehensible bounty. They had seen the moon dyed orange by wind-blown curries, palms scorched betel-red. Along the coastline, the air was so heavy with pepper you had to breathe through cloth. It seemed to me that these spice villages harvested delirium, and the lives there were surely made of pure color.

Once, the boldest I ever was, I stole into the hold of a returning caravel. Twenty barrels sat lashed to the floor. One barrel had been knocked open, revealing a sack full of a ruby-like powder. Mace, the fine netting on the nutmeg shell. I'd seen it in the market, a spice so treasured that a tablespoon is worth a week's labor. I tasted it with a finger. I felt that I was savoring a quality of light.

Just then, a mariner stepped from the shadows. He was broad-shouldered and grimy, as if he'd been swimming in the bilge. I stumbled back, afraid. The thief motioned for silence and slid closed the lid of the barrel. From the deck, I heard the mainsail catch in a gust and felt the ship pull.

We stayed that way, in stillness, until I broke free and launched myself out of the hold. Seville was already some distance behind us. The crew laughed at my terror—I'd never gone to sea. A hand shoved me overboard. That I couldn't swim only intensified their pleasure. I thrashed about. The shoreline disappeared under the water. I choked and sank.

Without warning, a thick arm wrapped around my neck and I found myself dragged to shore. On the riverbank, I vomited water into my lap. My rescuer, the thief, stared back at his ship as it coasted down river. Our bath in the water had transformed him, washed him clean. I saw how supple and pale his skin was, his hair straight and yellow like straw. He swung a bandoliered wineskin out from under his shirt. The cork had popped and the wineskin was swollen with river water. He poured it and the water ran clay-red—it was the stolen, ruined mace. He shook his head and tossed the skin into the current. We said nothing.

I brought him back to my mother's shop. My mother was gone and we lay together on my bed of flour sacks to dry. He held me tightly, his arm belting me from behind, as Diego has done, as if I was on the verge of falling. There are many ledges that split this world, between the known and the unknown, and we choose to go over. While the thief slept, I watched his pulse tick in a vein in his forearm, a single cord snapping taut then loose in neat, regular meter. I was more awake than I'd ever been. It is said the celestial spheres chime as they roll against each other. In just this way, my body vibrated against his. I knew then I would leave my mother and join his world, the world of men. Even after he left, I felt as a sail, sheeted full, faces a wind bearing what will be found.

The *Elena* drifted. We continued with the watches, four hours to a shift, all heads listening for the catch of canvas. But no breeze filled the sails, and a small, inexorable current pushed us toward the drop.

At evening, the hard sun sank behind the ledge. With the *Elena* hove to and sideways toward it, the English conscript took a cross-bow—he was now inseparable from it—and fired an arrow over. It dropped silently out of view. Alfredo told him he "had missed" and fired another. It too vanished.

At half a league's distance from the ledge, the Captain—from his bunk—ordered all the ballast dumped from the ship and the crew to mount the sweeps. We would row the *Elena* back into whatever trades brought us here. With our barrels of supplies adrift around us, the crew dug the oars in the water the entire night. I laid my quill in the ledger and joined Diego to pull. We sat next to each other on a bench and, in the darkness, he laid his hand atop mine. I took his warmth greedily.

Pinzón, the interpreter, was afraid the motion of the oars would call the serpents. We set torches along the gunwale, but spotted nothing. Perhaps even the serpents recognized the danger of the precipice, the way certain fish know to stop at the mouth of the Guadalquivir and go no further. Despite our hours rowing, the *Elena's* prow made no progress. The current towards the ledge was too strong.

The Captain called out to me. Inside his quarters, he lay dressed in a long, loose tunic, with Coralito, the navigator, kneeling at his side. From the hem, Captain Veragua's withered legs stuck out long and rigid as fork tines. He seemed to have lost half his weight.

"How far are we?" he asked. "Coralito cannot see the distance."

"I should think we will meet the ledge in two days' time," I said.

The Captain closed his eyes. In the faint light, I made out the spottings of blood and grease on his shirt. Beneath it, his skin healed in the fat that Diego applied to it as salve.

"Drop the sea anchors behind us," the Captain ordered. "And bring the longboat." The Captain lifted himself up and winced. "Dress me Coralito," he said. "Then take me to my men."

I did as I was commanded, though his intentions were unclear. I woke Alfredo and Armando to cast the sea-anchors. The broad canvas sacks hit the water and swelled immediately. They would slow our drift nearly to a stop, but the *anclas de salvacion* were a last resort. We would no longer be able to turn and sail. Next, I led the longboat that trailed the *Elena* up amidships. Without sail or mast, the longboat was designed for short islanding journeys. It was a glorified rowboat, shadeless and exhausting. Didn't the Captain know we were a thousand leagues from home? Or had his mind fevered past reason?

"You can't row that to Spain, Peralonso," the English conscript said.

"Not without miracles," Pinzón said.

Wincing in his officers' trousers, the Captain appeared on deck, a pouch in his hand. He began, "Let us give thanks to He who has thought us worthy to discover such a great wonder, this ledge." He shook the pouch. "In this sack are eighteen beans, representing the crew of the *Elena*. Among them are four marked with crosses, four great honors. I want each man to come and take a single bean. At dawn, those that pull a cross will strike out for the ledge and report back. I will go with you." He paused and finished, "Those who go, go with God."

The men eyed one another skeptically. Our Captain had admitted that our Great Expedition was folly. The countries we knew were the only countries. But what unimaginable vale awaited us over the ledge? What did it feel like to fall forever?

The sack was passed from man to man, and each fished among the beans. The English conscript went first. He sighed in relief; his bean was smooth. When Diego pulled his bean, he made no expression, but I felt the air rush out of me. I took his silence for luck. The steward Bartolomé, who picked an unmarked bean, cried out when his nephew pulled a cross; Bartolomé demanded to join him. The carpenter Ginés pulled the second and Pinzón the third. He rushed to the Captain.

"I am an interpreter," Pinzón said. "I'm not a seaman or have any skill with a bow. I will be a failure to the crew of that small boat."

The Captain rested his mottled hand on Pinzón's shoulder. "Every country, every animal speaks a language. When we return, you will tell with your best words what you have seen."

"But this plan is suicide," Pinzón continued.

The Captain said back, with slow force, "You have been paid to risk your life with me. You shall be rewarded. Or face the lashes."

I went last. On the surface of the final bean, I felt the markings of a knife.

The last cross.

The Captain asked, "Who is the fourth man?"

I looked at Diego. He must have seen the fear in me because, with a courage I would never know, Diego then stepped forward, casting his bean off the side. He would be the fourth. I would stay afraid and alive.

The Captain said, "We will leave at dawn."

As the crew scattered across the deck, sinking into their privacies, I felt a cutting mix of shame and loss. How could I let Diego take my place? How could I let him go? The men began to pray—Alfredo and Armando and Bartolomé and Gonzalo and gap-toothed Ginés and others—all the men praying for deliverance, for the opportunity to see their fathers and wives and children again, for an everlasting life that I could not understand. I knew only the ache of the present. I thought of my mother pulling a tray of *alfajer* from the oven, scored with the Hebrew letter for righteousness. "The world begins the day we are born," she told me, "and the world will end the day we die."

Under the torchlight, I found Diego alone on the forecastle, staring out at the drop. He looked calm and peaceful and welcomed me with a pat on the deck beside him. I sat and began to cry, as quietly as I could.

"Why Diego?" I whispered. "Why did you save me?"

His eyes were gentle. To my amazement, he took the ledger from my hand and lettered slowly. I had never seen him use a quill. For the first time, I heard his voice on the page and, in shock, my tears stopped.

YOUNG, he wrote and pointed at my chest. MORE LIFE.

"But you have life too," I said. "Why are you not afraid?"

He took up his lettering again. SOMEONE I WISH TO SEE.

He pointed out to the ledge. A shudder traveled along my spine. Then Diego clutched me, generously, openly, and I felt a finality, as if he were trying to give over whatever part of him I hungered for. He felt solid and strong and then he was gone, crossing the deck to the cook-box. Until dawn, he stoked the fires, preparing a breakfast of breads, served with the Captain's jars of prunes and jam. I came to him. "Diego," I began and stopped, unsure of how to shape into words an ocean of feelings.

He pressed his pinched fingers at my lips. The last time I felt him alive. Powdered cinnamon dusted my mouth and exploded into a rounded, delicious silence.

At dawn, the crew mounted a torch to the prow of the longboat and cinched the long fathom line to an oarlock. The line would run from the longboat to the *Elena*, to keep it tethered in case of rescue. When the preparations were done, Diego and Ginés lowered the Captain into the boat and set him in the bow. In his hand, he held the Queen's Letters of Introduction. At the stern, Pinzón pleaded upwards. (He'd spent the night writing long letters to his wife. At dawn, he burned them all and wrote one to his mistress in Madrid, a letter he sealed with wax and swore me to deliver.)

The sun rose as they set out, oars slapping into a waveless ocean. The hemp line uncoiled in lazy jerks. The Captain peered out from the bow, his eyes fixed on the approaching ledge. Diego rowed and rowed, never looking back at me though I yearned to share some last secret contact. On the *Elena*, no one spoke as the longboat shrank into the distance. When the second knot on the line passed over the gunwale, Alfredo called out, "Two fathoms gone!"

In an instant, the line unwound ferociously and the longboat vanished over the ledge. We never heard their cries. The crew jumped on the rope and found themselves nearly propelled over the side. I grabbed the final length of line and knotted it around the base of the main-mast. When it uncoiled completely, the rope, three-fingers thick, sprang taut. The mast howled under a massive weight. The crew crushed forward to regain a purchase, but could not pull the line back. We were strung tight; the fathom-line ran from the *Elena*, through the air and over the ledge.

A monstrous pull tilted the ship sidelong and dragged her towards the drop. Everything on deck slid to one side.

Alfredo drew his knife and leapt onto the fathom-line. He began to cut. But my courage alit inside me. I couldn't let him release Diego and the others to their death. If there is only this life—and nothing after—then it must be defended.

I met him at the line, his blade already biting in.

"You'll kill them," I said.

"They're lost already," he said. "We'll go with them!"

I grabbed the knife from his hand and tossed it overboard, Alfredo looked at me as if I were mad. In an instant, I felt another blade across my throat.

"Cut the line," the English conscript called out from behind me.

Armando came to his brother's side and continued the sawing with his own knife. The fathom line opened like a tendon. But then my eye caught something out at the ledge: Diego, pulling himself up along the rope, hand over hand, back to the *Elena*.

"Look!" I cried.

Armando stopped when he saw the survivor climbing back to us. The crew gathered at the line and heaved. And this time, the line began to yield. We managed to reclaim it, until it was clear that we were pulling a weight far greater than just Diego. With a final heave, the tension on the line dropped and then we could see the longboat itself crest back through the spume and come to rest on the ocean surface. We had gaffed Diego back onto the deck—he rolled on his back and sank into a stupor—before I noticed the longboat was not empty.

A lone figure sat inside it. A woman.

She sat primly on one of the benches, in a high-waisted dress with flared sleeves and a heart-shaped hat. She was old and frail and dripping wet. Her skin looked as pale as boiled bone.

"Where am I?" she called to us. "I'm frightened."

I knew the *Elena's* bilge could inspire delusions, awash with rotting food, piss, the human slurry of a long voyage. Ethers from below-decks had been known to poison sailors with mirages, even throttle them in sleep. You could be surrounded by fresh sea air and your own ship could suffocate you. But we all saw this woman. Could every man be taken with the same dream?

Coralito peered out, his face blanched. His eyes hunted through his blindness. "Who is there?" he asked. "I cannot see."

"A woman," I said. "From beyond the ledge."

"What is your name?" Coralito called out.

The woman swooned. "The sun is burning my skin. I must dry and get out of this heat."

"What is your name!" Coralito called again. "Your name!"

The woman looked back oddly. "Coralito?"

Coralito gasped and staggered back. He crossed himself.

"This cannot be," he said. *"She has been dead for six years.* We must not allow her onto the ship."

"Tell us your name," I called out. "And we will help."

The woman flapped her hat in her face. "My name is Isabela Hernandez Coralito, wife of Fernando Mancuello," she said and cast a glance over her shoulder.

"Please," she said. "There are so many others waiting."

We kept her in the longboat. All day she cried out, demanding shade and water. Her voice was so human, so frail and chilling. She tried, fruitlessly, to paddle forward. When the sun continued to rise in a rinsed-clear sky, she grew more urgent and pained. If she had been alive, truly alive, our treatment—watching an old woman wilt—would have been torture. Instead, as Coralito swore, his wife had passed away. He set her tombstone himself.

At dusk, Diego gathered strength, though he was now ashen, his skin drained of color. I caved a blanket around him while he stared into the bowl of his hands. They were red and badly cut, one wrist disjointed and swollen where he'd twisted it up in the line as he climbed back. He rehearsed his grip, opening and closing his fingers. I sat beside him, holding the ledger.

"Write," I said. "Tell me. What did you see?"

I noticed, then, his wound: a deep gash at his right wrist that ran through to the other side. Inside, the tissue was gray. Every time Diego rotated his hand, the flesh opened like a mouth and did not bleed. He looked at it queerly.

His letters were feeble and wrong-handed. DEAD?

I felt a kick to my leg. "What'd he write?" the English conscript asked, peering on the page. "What're those letters?"

"He's weak," I answered. "We need to leave him alone."

The conscript sized me with cold eyes. "You're not very good at that, are you Peralonso?" he said and leaned down to me. His tongue flickered at the end of his mouth. "You think I don't see how you are together, but I see," he said. "I served ten years for my crime. And you, for yours?"

At the sound of oars in the water, I pushed him off. I stood to see Alfredo and Armando in the fishing dingy. They approached the woman with a small skin of fresh water—their Christian duty—and a crossbow aimed at her chest. Coralito joined them. The dory held still at thirty strokes from the longboat.

"Fernando, why do these men hold their weapons at me?" she called out, nervously.

"Where have you come from?" Coralito asked. "I buried you."

She stood, her hand on her chest. "What?"

"You died in our bedroom in Aragon, in my arms," Coralito said. "We fell asleep and when I awoke you were gone, Isabela. This was six years ago."

Isabela collapsed.

"I don't remember, Fernando, I don't remember any of that," she said.

Then, at Coralito's sign, Armando and Alfredo rowed the dory closer and closer until it knocked the side of the longboat. They dropped the crossbow and Coralito stepped over to attend to his wife.

She was fed and given a swath of tarpaulin for shade. While Coralito comforted her, Alfredo and Armando rigged a small shelter with a split-bunk post and cord fixed to the prow. They left Coralito and rowed back to the *Elena*.

"I felt her breath," Armando whispered. "It was cold, like a winter draft."

"But her pain is real," Alfredo added. "As real as any."

By nightfall, Coralito called for the dory. Back on ship, he steadied himself at the mast. "She is no dream," he said.

"What does she know of the Captain, of the others?" I asked.

He shook his head. "Nothing."

"Where did she come from?" Armando asked.

"It is a peculiar story," Coralito began, chewing his nail. "She told me that one day, she awoke on a shoreline, crowded with people. The sea there was tideless and still. Inland, trees loomed over the shore, a forest so dense it seemed like a wall. People there wandered along this shore as far as she could see, men and women of many ages, colors, costumes, speaking in bewildering tongues. Each appeared to travel alone, and they often stopped her and begged things, but she was afraid and pulled away. Eventually, she said, she began walking too. She never saw the same face twice.

"At one moment, a moment that she could not separate from other moments, Isabela moved into the sea, knee deep. She had never thought to enter the water before. But something called to her.

"The water pooled at her feet, like stepping into the face of a mirror, she said. From the mist, the longboat drifted into her sight. She got in. The crowds from the shore saw and rushed at the water. The fathom line snapped taut and she found herself pulled out to sea. She held tight as a mist enveloped her. The sound of the voices faded until it was replaced by a rumble and a vertiginous turn. The next she knew, she could make out the *Elena*."

Coralito stopped and ran his hand across his face, wiping the disbelief from it. Armando the Taller crossed himself. "Dear God."

"I asked for her hand and made a cut along her finger," Coralito continued. "Her blood is as red and as real as ours."

The English conscript spat back "Lie. She doesn't bleed. Just like the mute." He gestured to Diego. "They're both wraiths now."

The crew stared at Diego. He did not look up.

"What do we do?" Alfredo asked.

"We'll let Coralito have the night with his wife," I said. "But come morning, we return her to the ledge."

Coralito tugged his tunic taut against his chest. "Then I go with her," he answered. "I will not leave my wife alone."

"Diego must go too," Armando said.

His twin brother stepped toward him. "But what if there are others, abandoned over the ledge? Are we to leave them in purgatory?"

Armando shook his head. "Anything else would defy God's will."

Alfredo's face lost all of its softness. He seemed to rise up his whole length and stand, finally, taller than his brother. "You speak of God's will Armando?" he shot back. "Was it His choice to take our brother? Or was it yours?"

The twins leapt on each other and wrestled to the deck. They fought, equally matched, like a man with his reflection. If no one stopped them, it was because we felt we were watching the war within us playing out. Each man aboard—Coralito, the conscript, Diego, Marco and the other grommets and deckhands—understood that the ledge was now among us. We could pass over the edge or we could plunder it, but we couldn't escape. We watched in silence until the two brothers sat across from each other, exhausted and bruised. A rivulet of blood ran down Alfredo's face from a nostril. His brother massaged his jaw.

"I remember him," Alfredo said. "I will always remember him. He was our brother. And if he is still alive, I will go and get him myself."

That night, there was no reversing of the sand-clock, no order to the *Elena*. Coralito boarded the dory and was rowed out to his wife. The men drained the wine casks and fired all the supplies in a noisy, reckless feast. Diego stood at the prow, ignoring me, and looking even paler, like alabaster. He paced, the way a wife grooves a path of anticipation on a widow's walk, and stared out at the ledge. I could find no consolation in the riot around me and the chill air had me missing the simple heat of my mother's bakery. Why had I ever left? Why is it that men are always leaving? What is this hunger for what we can't see? I ached for the Calle de la Mar, for the sounds of the fruit carts jostling, and to see one more time my mother at the doorway and smell her honey cakes rolling out into the street. I called to her in a prayer. I wanted to see her face again and feel blessed, but I could not summon the whole of it. It remained blurred and opaque, like smoked glass, and the knowledge that I had forgotten it filled me with a clawing emptiness. The night wore on. The crew's exuberance faded into melancholy, and they keened for their families and home cities, for those they would never see again. I fell asleep alone, in a curl of loose sail.

I woke to a jerk, the *Elena* tugged in the water. Under the first kindling of clouds, the fathom line was already strung out to the ledge. Alfredo, Diego and others guarded the rope and, with a great cry, they pulled together.

"What are you doing?" I asked. None turned to answer me.

Armando shoved his way forward, shouting, "This is blasphemy!" But before he could fight, the longboat returned over the ledge and came through the spray, laden with three new figures.

"Armando?" one called back, standing. "Is that you? I felt you calling me!"

Armando's anger disappeared. He dropped his hands from the rope and took a step back, shocked. His brother ran to the gunwale.

"Brother!" Alfredo called back eagerly. "We're both here! Come to us!"

The longboat knocked alongside the *Elena*, and Alfredo lifted the young man to the deck with a stevedore's strength. This new man looked identical to the twins, only he stood tallest of the three and appeared years younger. His skin had no pigment. He hugged Alfredo with genuine pleasure.

"You seem so *old*," the new arrival said. "Have you been away?"

"No no," Alfredo said beaming. "It's *you* who left *us*."

Armando, terrified, made the sign of the cross.

"You are dead Antonio," Armando said. "I took your life."

A laugh shot out of his brother. "Come," Antonio said and clutched to his brother. "You took nothing."

A boy followed up the rope ladder, unkempt, in tattered trousers. He was not more than five or six years old, and a swollen lump rested at the base of his neck. It had been years since I'd seen a mark of the plague. The boy stood still, bewildered by the unfamiliar faces, until the ship's gimbaling startled him and he began to shake and cry. Diego pushed his way forward to face the child, who then threw himself at the older man. Diego collapsed around him, choking with sobs.

"My son," he said. "My son."

Diego's voice. The sound of it shattered me. So rich and sorrowful, the deepest chime of the closest, celestial sphere.

When the final figure boarded the *Elena*, holding her head down in humility, I knew that I had called her. Those who crossed the ledge did so because we summoned them with yearning. The familiar cobalt shift was so soaked with water it was black. The shawl lay on her shoulders, a damp rag giving no warmth, though none was needed. When she looked up, I understood why the crew had mutinied: Death is the tyranny. To conquer the ledge was a conquest over this. The greed of time.

My mother stood before me, wet and shivering in her resurrection. Her black eyes studied me in a bloodless face.

"Peralonso?" she asked in disbelief.

I embraced her and as I did, I noticed the odd twist in her body. Her neck was stretched. An angry, red indentation wrapped around her throat. My fingers sought it out and ran these ridges where a rope had once been tied tight.

"I told you to never leave," my mother said.

My strength left and I buried myself in her hair. "Forgive me," I said. I remained there until I felt a lock of it brush against my face in a breeze.

From where I sit, I watch the crew busy with lines. Every one is now strung over the ledge. In time, each snaps taut and the deckhands pull first the longboat, then a handful of crude rafts around the ledge, heavy with people. Soon, the *Elena* is crowded with men and women, in all kinds of dress and colors, my mother lost among them. I write in the ledger, "Many new souls."

By afternoon, the crew sends the longboat one last time over the drop. This time, they cut free the sea anchors and raise the mainsail for a broad reach. A westerly favors us, and even before our sails are half-raised, the *Elena* heaves forward with life. An enormous weight drags on us and the *Elena* groans beneath it. Hemp lines split, some tear from their braces.

Finally a Portuguese galleon crests through the spume, with dozens of people clutching to its deck. The *Elena* has towed it over. The white faces look as if they have survived a squall, as if they are amazed to be alive. Eventually the men of the galleon set its sails and drop more lines back into the roar.

They pull over a strange ship, this one low and open and driven by oars, with a high wooden dragon head fixed at its prow. The two ships repeat this, and before long, the sea here becomes busy with boats, many unknown to me, and far outnumbering the *Elena*. The water carries the noise of weird cries and tongues. This motley army of the dispossessed, recovered from the ledge, soon fills the ocean as far as I see. At evening, we depart east together, sails bellied in the new wind.

LAZY TAEKOS
Geoffrey A. Landis

from Analog

ONCE THERE WAS A BOY NAMED TAEKOS WHO LIVED ON A heart farm.

His parents were hardworking people: they grew new hearts for old men, and tiny hearts for babies; they grew strong hearts to plant into young men who had crashed their air-scooters and needed replacements; and they grew rugged working hearts for androids who were grown in a vat.

But Taekos didn't want to live on the farm. He was lazy, and wanted to do something that was more fun and less like work.

One day he slung his pack over his shoulder and told his parents he was off to seek his fortune in the big city. He hitched a ride with a passing businessman driving an old-fashioned one-wheeled gyro-car, and in a few minutes he was in the big city.

In the big city he apprenticed himself to a robot builder, but his robots were built all askew, and didn't want to work, but just sat and wrote poetry all day. No one would pay to buy a robot to sit around and write poetry, and so after a week, he was let go.

He apprenticed himself to a bioengineer, but he was too lazy to sculpt DNA, and spent the day programming the micro-robots to play croquet with each other, using xenon atoms as balls. And then, when he was bored with that, he programmed them to gather all the atoms of one kind together—copper, he decided, he will make them gather copper atoms—and link them together in a sheet, until the floor shone with a molecule-thick plating of copper. But no one would pay to hire a bioengineer who would not splice even a single DNA strand, and so after a week he was let go.

He apprenticed himself to a spaceship pilot, but he just flew his ship in great lazy swirls around the sky. The businessmen who were to be ferried to the seven moons refused to pay him, and so after a week he was let go.

And thus it was, when he had used up all his prospects, and no one in the city would take him on as an apprentice, he sat in the park. He sat by the river of floating flowers, singing nonsense songs to himself and giving names to each of the clouds that passed in the sky. He was braiding together great kjill blossoms to make kites, and releasing them one by one to drift in the sky, when he saw a girl watching him.

After a while he saw one of his blossom kites float through her, and he knew she was a projection. Ah, he thought. If she didn't eat and didn't need to pay to enter an entertainment, it would cost nothing to take her out. She was the perfect girlfriend for him.

"Will you be my girlfriend?" he asked.

"Certainly," she answered. As they talked together, he discovered that she had a dowry of ten trillion pretty rocks from her grandfather, but until the day she married, she told him, her stepfather controlled it, and she could not spend any of it, not even a single rock, except for what her stepfather allowed.

Her stepfather was crafty, and did not want her to wed, and take away his fortune. He had locked her away in a titanium crystal castle, and the robots who controlled it would only let in the man who would marry her. Her stepfather could not forbid her to marry outright, but he had sworn an oath.

"She will marry a man who has never been born, who is wearing a cloak that has never been worn, whose shadow is silver and nothing of gold, who can sleep in a fire and never get cold," the girl (whose name was Phoevus) quoted to him. "And that is the only way I shall marry."

"That," Taekos observed (as he knotted together the stems of a hundred kjill blossoms into a great braid in the shape of a Moebius strip) "doesn't make any sense at all."

"No," she said sadly. "I will never marry. But he can't prevent me from projecting."

Yet I myself was never born, he thought to himself; I was grown from a seed, like all of the sons of farmers he knew. And he wondered at the silly ways of the city people, who never heard of growing a child from a seed, like any sensible farmer would.

"Can you not weave me a cloak that has never been worn?" he asked her.

"Indeed," she said. "I will instruct my robots to weave a cloak. But if you wear it, it has been worn, surely you know that."

"Leave that to me," he said.

And so he made an appointment to come to marry the girl, and on the appointed day he arrived at the titanium crystal castle, and presented himself.

"My step-daughter is very beautiful," the stepfather told him, "and I love her very much. She is so beautiful that she can only marry a man who has never been born, and so you must leave and go away, for you cannot marry her."

"But I myself was never born," Taekos observed. "I was grown from a seed, and here are my identity papers to show it." And indeed, when he showed the sheet of molecule-thin poly-ply that was his identity papers, the word "BORN:" on the sheet of poly-ply was followed by a simple "NO."

The stepfather's face darkened as he saw this, and Taekos thought that his face was like a storm cloud, but the stepfather merely said, "My stepdaughter is very delicate, and I love her very much. Because she is so delicate she must only marry a man who wears a cloak that has never been worn, and so you must leave and go away, for you can never marry her."

"But I myself am wearing a cloak that has never been worn," Taekos observed, "for it was woven by your daughter's robots this very morning, and you can verify that, if you like, by asking any one of them."

But the stepfather only smiled wickedly, and said, "You are yourself wearing it, and so how can you say it has never been worn?"

"This?" Taekos asked, and passed his hand through it. "This is only a projection. The cloak itself is in your daughter's room, and has surely never been worn."

The stepfather's face darkened further as he saw that he had been tricked, and Taekos thought that his face was like a storm cloud that is all swollen up with lightning, ready to burst into electrical fury, but the stepfather only said, "My step-daughter is very intelligent, and I love her very much. Because she is so intelligent, she must only marry a man who has a shadow of silver, and nothing of gold, and so you must leave and go away, for you cannot marry her."

But at this, Taekos said nothing at all, only gestured with his hand down at the floor. And the stepfather looked down, and with great surprise noticed that Taekos' shadow in fact reflected with a silvery sheen. The stepfather brought out a light, and moved it from side to side, but to whichever side he moved, the silvery sheen appeared on the opposite side, a shadow of silver.

"Robot!" he called out, and a robot appeared at his side. "Robot, what color is that?" he said, and pointed at the shadow. "Master, that color is silver," the robot answered, and Taekos smiled.

Taekos' smile was a smile of relief, for robots are very literal, and the robot answered the question that was asked. Had the stepfather asked what the shadow was made of, the robot would surely have answered aluminum. He had tried to instruct the handful of micro-robots that he had spread behind him to gather silver atoms, but there were not enough silver atoms in the molecules of the ground, and instead he had to settle for telling them to gather aluminum atoms, which were also shiny and silver.

But the stepfather called his robots together, and had them go into his vast treasury and fetch gold dust by the handful. The stepfather's robots sprinkled gold dust on the shadow, but as fast as they sprinkled gold dust, the micro robots (which Taekos had borrowed from the DNA engineer before he'd left his apprenticeship) plated them over with a thin veneer of aluminum atoms, so that they shined silver and nothing of gold, and the stepfather knew that he had again been tricked.

The stepfather's face darkened, and Taekos thought it was like a great storm of a gas giant, ready to expand out across the planet until the whole surface was engulfed in turbulence, but the stepfather only said, "My step-daughter is very rich, and I love her very much. Because she is so rich, she will only marry a man who can sleep in a fire and never get cold, so you must leave and go away, for you can never marry her."

But Taekos only laughed, and said, "Why, certainly I can do that, and so indeed can any man, for if one sleeps in a fire, surely he will get hot, and not cold. And so, sir, please step aside, for I wish to go inside to marry your step-daughter, and you are in my way."

But the stepfather only smiled now, a wicked and triumphant smile, and he said softly, "No, Sir Trickster, clever you are, but indeed you may not pass. For you may say you can sleep in a fire, but indeed, I will not credit your boasting until I see it myself. Come back, sir, in seven days. I will make a fire, and you will sleep in the fire I have made myself, with none of your trickery, and when I have seen that, then you will marry my stepdaughter.

"But until then, you must go away, and not come back."

"I will go away," said Taekos, "and not come back for seven days."

And when he had gone away, and sat in the park by the river of drifting blossoms, the projection of his girlfriend came to him, and said sadly, "Oh, Taekos, how will you meet the challenge of my stepfather?"

And Taekos had no answer. He had expected to pass based on clever words and brazen courage, but he had never really had a plan. Nor, for all that he wracked his brains for ideas, could he think of one.

But then, he had seven days. And he was, after all, a very clever lad. Surely he would think of something.

And indeed, the next day, as he slept in the shade of the tijiell trees in the park (it was necessary to sleep in the shade, because the seven moons beamed down light in a wonderful, but not at all restful, array of colors), a most remarkable thing happened to him. The old stepfather came up to him. It took him a moment to realize that this, too, was a projection, and not the real man, but still, it surprised him.

"Sir Trickster," the projection of the stepfather. "You are a cheat, and a thief, and I wish you to have nothing to do with my step-daughter. I will offer you a thousand pretty rocks, and with those pretty rocks you may go as you please, wherever you like, as long as you never again come back to ask for the hand of my step-daughter in marriage."

This is very interesting, thought Taekos, very interesting indeed, but all he said was, "I think not."

And the next day, the same projection came to him, and said the same thing, but this time offered him two thousand pretty rocks. And again, Taekos thought, this is very interesting, but replied only, "I think not."

Each day of the seven, the stepfather offered a higher price, and each day, Taekos thought, this is very interesting, but replied only, "I think not."

For this was the thought which Taekos found most interesting: why would the stepfather offer him a bribe to give up a suit that he could not win?

And so he sat in contemplation, braiding his flower kites, and planning.

On the seventh day, the very image of Taekos showed up at the castle of titanium, all resplendent in the finest of feathers and braided spider-silk. And the stepfather, surrounded by his robots, did not seem surprised to see him, but Taekos said only, "I am here to claim the hand of your step-daughter in marriage, for she is very beautiful, and I love her."

The stepfather said, "Well indeed, but I do not believe that you are here at all." Turning to the robot on his left side, he said, "Robot!" and the robot aimed a counter-projection projector and turned it on. With that Taekos vanished—for of course it was only a projection—and the stepfather said, loudly so all the robots could hear, "Since the suitor has not shown up, he has forfeited the challenge, and shall not marry my step-daughter."

But Taekos stepped out from behind one of the robots, and said, "Not so, for here I am." He was no longer so resplendent (for he could afford only the projection of finery), but now only dressed in an ordinary working-class cloak, such as a heart-farmer's son might wear, and he thought to himself, it was a pity that the projection trick would not fool him twice.

"Well indeed, then," the stepfather said. "I have here a fire, and I will very much enjoy watching you sleep in it." And he turned to the robot on his right side, and said, "Robot!" and the robot opened a door. Through the door was a room, and inside the room was a nuclear furnace, with a door just large enough for a man to crawl through. Taekos noted with some interest (for he had once been a spaceship pilot's apprentice, and knew what the engine for a spaceship looked like) that the inside of the chamber would be at an even, cheerful heat of one million degrees.

"I apologize," Taekos said. "But I have brought with me a dictionary," and he rubbed the activation of the dictionary, and murmured to it, "fire." At his word, the dictionary said, in its clear, cool voice, "FIRE is a form of combustion, releasing heat by the combination of a fuel with oxygen."

"This chamber of yours is certainly a fine engine," Taekos said, "but it is not a fire. Shall I call a magistrate, and we shall see if he, too, has a dictionary?"

"Very well, Sir Trickster," said the stepfather, "there is no need for a magistrate." He bid the robot close the door, but at the same time gestured another robot to open a different door. Through this door there was a chamber, and in the chamber was a very large pile of wood. The robot entered and set the wood to burning. "I believe even your dictionary will accept this as a fire."

"Indeed, this is a fire," Taekos said, and walked into the room, swirling his cloak.

"One moment first, Sir Trickster," the stepfather said. "With your pardon?" And with a word from the stepfather two robots stepped to him, and sprayed him with a light mist, one spraying his left side, one his right. "It appears that your skin had been infested with a swarm of micro-robots," the stepfather said.

Taekos was taken aback, for indeed he had his microrobots with him, several trillion of them or so (he did not know exactly, for he was too lazy to count them all) and he had carefully instructed each of them in how to turn infrared photons away from his skin. For of course heat is nothing except infrared photons, and if the robots caught each photon by its tail and turned it around to run the other direction—well then! Well indeed! But the mist had set the micro robots into sleep mode, and it would take him many hours to reboot each one of them.

But Taekos had one more trick to play, and this he did. He had a few of his robots left, this time just very simple and stupid ones, and they sprayed water onto the fire, just enough to put it out. He then pulled a sack from his cloak, and from the sack he poured iron dust into the empty fireplace, and then stepped in and went to sleep in the dust. His laziness was indeed famous, but yet he had this one skill, to go to sleep anywhere and at any time.

After some time sleeping, he yawned, and stretched, and rose, saying, "I'm not cold at all. I win, I slept in a fire. And I'm not cold."

"You have to sleep in the fire while it's burning," said the stepfather.

"Really?" said Taekos, wide-eyed as if this thought had never occurred to him. "Who says?"

"I say this, and in this castle my word is law," said the stepfather.

"Well, fine enough," Taekos said. He produced his dictionary again. "A fire is combustion," he said. "Even as I was sleeping, the iron was slowly rusting, and rust, of course, is nothing but oxidation, or, as we can call it, combustion."

"But it is not hot," said the stepfather, scowling.

"And who is it who says that fire has to be hot?"

"I do."

"And I don't," said Taekos. "Here is a dictionary. I win. I claim my prize, and if you do not agree, I shall call a magistrate."

"No, not a magistrate!" the stepfather said. "I will concede to you half of my step-daughter's wealth. Do not call a magistrate, and we shall both be rich!"

Why is he afraid of magistrates? Taekos asked himself, and with that thought, he called one.

The magistrate robot arrived. "Your dictionary, sir," the magistrate said to him, "is evidently quite faulty. I have consulted the archive of dictionaries, and the compact (although low-cost) model you own should tell you, fire is a form of combustion resulting in visible flames."

"Humph," said the stepfather. "As I said."

"And who are you?" the magistrate asked.

"I," stated the stepfather, "am the legal guardian of this girl, Phoevus, and the trustee of her fortune and of her person."

"No," said the magistrate, "you are not. You are a projection of a recording of a certain Phineas Nator Zond, a sapient personage whose existence has been discontinued seventeen years, seven months, three weeks, two days, eleven hours and thirteen seconds before this moment. A projection cannot be a guardian, nor a trustee, of a sapient person."

"But this is my step-daughter, and I love her very much," the projection of the former sapient personage known once as Phineas Nator Zond said. "And if I am not to guard her, and be the trustee of her fortune and her person, then who is to protect her from fortune hunters, and from the evils of the world?"

"She is a sapient personage," the magistrate said. "If she wishes to be guarded, she must see to it herself." And with that, the magistrate robot turned the projection off.

After a while, when the magistrate had left, and the robots that the stepfather (or his projection) had brought to guard the titanium crystal castle showed themselves to be unresponsive, Taekos said, "Phoevus, my love, your stepfather no longer is in our way, and so we may marry."

And the projection of Phoevus came down, and said, "Taekos, you are charming, and amusing, and clever, but only a foolish girl would marry such a lazy rogue and schemer, and such a foolish girl certainly would come to no good end."

Taekos contemplated this. "What will you do?" he asked.

"I have been here in this titanium castle for long enough. I will be off on my own adventures." And as her parting words to him, she added, "but thank you for dealing with my stepfather."

And with that she was gone. The robots, left behind, began to disassemble the titanium crystal castle, and in very little more than no time at all, it, too, was gone.

And so, Taekos thought, here I am, and left no better than I was.

But then again, no worse, he observed, and went forth to seek his fortune.

FOR THE LOVE OF PAUL BUNYAN

Fritz Swanson

from Pindeldyboz (online)

S HE WAS TENDER. SOFT AS A SAND DUNE AFTER A WINDSTORM. Back in the before days, she would wake up and stretch those arms out across the sky, her left hand arched over the Baffin Islands, her right curled up under her jaw, her elbow casting a swaying shadow over the Jack Pine Forests of Saskatchewan. She was a tangle of stretching and yawning, and I would let slip a quiet sigh from where I lay, snuggled down along the south shore of Lake Erie, my head pillowed up on the Adirondacks.

Clouds would cling to her ears, and if she got lost in a bit of work, say weeding the plains of Iowa or cleaning gunk out of Old Faithful, she could get a whole murder of crows caught up in her crazy black hair. Sometimes, if she needed the room, she would gather up a flock of wheeling starlings in her cupped hands. Gentle as any mother bear, she would carefully move them down into the belching swamps of Cuba out of her way, or off into the air over the blue-calm seas of the Grand Banks in June. God, how she cared for things . . . polishing the mountain ice in winter, scrubbing the granite shoreline of Maine come spring. And the soup she could make, cooked up in a hot-spring kettle in the heart of Yellowstone . . . The rich aroma of creamed potatoes and apples clouded the air back then.

But she wasn't all cherries and milk, either. Once, in a fit after we had fought she tripped me and I came down hard on my left hand and dug out a huge print in the mud. And one time she kissed me like a river so hard I didn't come around again until the glaciers had retreated and little men were all abroad in the land stalking the bigger cats (that is, the ones big enough that I could scare her with one by hiding it in the toe of her boot). And the land looked transformed after a while, and then I realized that she was gone.

But I think now that everything in the before days was a fuzzy cloud of mists and rains and sweet fruit. It was like moss and green sprouts and black loamy earth. But that cloud of tender is also a shroud of regret, free floating, for I cannot remember where our fight started, or over what, and worse I have the sense that my own . . . my sense of that time was of laying about and consuming.

Her absence is a great mystery to me now, in this smaller time where the bears roam and I feel that I have become so much less. I wonder about her rage, and I find myself constantly wandering the woods around that great hand print of mine which, I suppose, has grown so much larger than me. The mud-print pushed up a pile of dirt, which became a hill, then a mountain, then a great land amongst lakes.

Finally, I found myself raging in the woods as the trees rose up around me. The trees loomed and the shadow of my life filled the air, amongst a closing cave of teeth and obscurity. And I knew quickly that as things were going, soon, I wouldn't be able to even see the next county, let alone all the way to the sea, and how are you supposed to find a woman in this damn world if you can't see both seas at once? If she isn't on one coast, she could be on the other and you would have to walk all that way just to check. Her space is huge and hidden and covered in so many layers of shadow . . . I feel that it was just a little thing that we fought over. Something small. But she made me feel so large, and in amongst all that, the little things seem fuzzy and I cannot see . . . I felt . . . and she . . .

That was when I started cutting. Hacking. Sawing. Beating. Tearing down. And now I find that the little men have grown a bit and they need cutters and I *need* to cut, to clear, to make open and plain the whole of the land so that I can see, god let me see far.

AN ACCOUNTING

Brian Evenson

from ParaSpheres

I HAVE BEEN ORDERED TO WRITE AN HONEST ACCOUNTING OF HOW I became a midwestern Jesus and the subsequent disastrous events thereby accruing, events for which I am, I am willing to admit, at least partly to blame. I know of no simpler way than to simply begin.

In August it was determined that our stores were depleted and not likely to outlast the winter. One of our number must travel east and beg further provision from our compatriots on the coast, another must move further inland, hold converse with the midwestern sects as he encountered them, bartering for supplies as he could. Lots were drawn and this latter role fell to me.

I was provided a dog and a dogcart, a knife, a revolver with six rounds, rations, food for the dog, a flint and steel, and a rucksack stuffed with objects for trade. I named the dog Finger for reasons obscure even to myself. I received as well a small packet of our currency, though it was suspected that, since the rupture, our currency, with its Masonic imagery, would be considered by the pious Midwesterners anathema. It was not known if I would be met with hostility, but this was considered not unlikely considering no recent adventurer into the territory had returned.

I was given as well some hasty training by a former Midwesterner turned heretic named Barton. According to him, I was to make frequent reference to God—though not to use the word, *Goddamn*, as in the phrase "Where are my goddamn eggs?" "What eggs are these?" I asked Barton, only to discover the eggs themselves were apparently of no matter. He ticked off a list of other words considered profane and to be avoided. I was told to frequently describe things as God's will. "There but for the grace of God go I" was also an acceptable phrase, as was "Praise God." Things were not to be called "Godawful" though I was allowed to use, very rarely and with care, the term "God's aweful grace." If someone was to ask me if I were "saved," I was to claim that yes indeed I was saved, and that I had "accepted Jesus Christ as my personal Savior." I made notes of all these locutions, silently vowing to memorize them along the route.

"Another thing," said Barton. "If in dire straits, you should Jesus them and claim revelation from God."

So as you see it was not I myself who produced the idea of "Jesusing" them, but Barton. Am I to be blamed if I interpreted the verb in a way other than he intended? Perhaps he is to blame for his insufficiencies as an instructor.

But I am outstripping myself. Each story must be told in some order, and mine, having begun at the beginning, has no reason not to take each bit and piece according to its proper chronology, so as to let each reader of this accounting arrive at his own conclusions.

I was driven a certain way, on the bed of an old carrier converted now to steam power. The roads directly surrounding our encampment—what had been my former city in better days—were passable, having been repaired in the years following the rupture. After a few dozen miles, however, the going became more difficult, the carrier forced at times to edge its way forward through the underbrush to avoid a collapse or eruption of the road. Nevertheless, I had a excellent driver, Marchent, and we had nearly broached the border of the former Pennsylvania before we encountered a portion of road so destroyed by a large mortar or some other such engine of devastation that we could discover no way around. Marchent, one of the finest, blamed himself, though to my mind there was no blame to be taken.

I was unloaded. Marchent and his sturdy second, Bates, carried Finger and his dogcart through the trees to deposit them on the far side of the crater. I myself simply scrambled down hand over foot and then scrambled up the other side.

To this point, my journey could not be called irregular. Indeed, it was nothing but routine, with little interest. As I stood on the far side of the crater, watching Marchent and his second depart in the carrier, I found myself almost relishing the adventure that lay before me.

This was before the days I spent trudging alone down a broken and mangled road through a pale rain. This was before I found myself sometimes delayed for half a day trying to figure how to get dog and dogcart around an obstacle. They had provided me a simple harness for the cart, but had foreseen nothing by way of rope or tether to secure the fellow. If I tried to skirt, say, a shell crater, while carrying the bulky dogcart, Finger, feeling himself on the verge of abandonment, was anxious to accompany me. He would be there, darting between my legs and nearly precipitating me into the abyss itself, and if I did not fall, he did, so that once I had crossed I had to figure some way of extricating him. Often had I shouted at him the command "Finger! Heel!" or the command "Finger! Sit!" but it was soon clear that I, despite pursuing the most dangerous of the two missions, had been disbursed the least adequate canine.

Nevertheless, I grew to love Finger and it was for this I was sorry and even wept when later I had to eat him.

But I fear I have let my digression on Finger, which in honesty began not as a digression but as a simple description of a traveler's difficulty, get the better of my narrative. Imagine me, then, now attempting to carry Finger around a gap in the road in the dogcart itself, with Finger awaiting his moment to effect an escape by clawing his way up my chest and onto my head, and myself shouting "Finger! Stay!" in my most authoritative tone as I feel the ground beginning to slide out from under my feet. Or imagine Finger and I crammed into the dogcart together, the hound clawing my hands to ribbons as we rattle down a slope not knowing what obstacle we shall encounter at the bottom. That should render sufficient picture of the travails of my journey as regards Finger, and the reason as well—after splicing its harness and refashioning it as a short leash for Finger—for abandoning the dogcart, the which, I am willing to admit, as communal property, I had no right to forsake.

Needless to say, the journey was longer than our experts had predicted. I was uncertain if I had crossed into the Midwest and, in any case, had seen no signs of inhabitants or habitation. The weather had commenced to turn cold and I was racked with fits of ague. My provisions, being insufficiently calculated, had run low. The resourceful Finger managed to provide for himself by sniffling out and devouring dead creatures when he was released from his makeshift leash—though he was at least as prone to simply roll in said creature and return to me stinking and panting. I myself tried to eat one of these, scraping it up and roasting it first on a spit, but the pain that subsequently assaulted my bowels made me prefer to eat instead what remained of Finger's dog food and then, thereafter, to go hungry.

I had begun to despair when the landscape suffered through a transformation in character and I became convinced that I entered the Midwest at last. The ground sloped ever downward, leveling into a flat and gray expanse. The trees gave way to scrub and brush and strange crippled grasses which, if one was not careful, cut one quite badly. Whereas the mountains and hills had at least had occasional berries or fruit to forage, here the vegetation was not such as to bear fruit. Whereas before one had seen only the occasional crater, here the road seemed to have been systematically uprooted so that almost no trace of it remained. I saw, as well, in the distance as I left the slopes for the flat expanse, a devastated city, now little more than a smear on the landscape. Yet, I reasoned, perhaps this city, like my own city, had become a site for encampment; surely, there was someone to be found therein, or at least nearby.

Our progress over this prairie was much more rapid, and Finger did manage to scare up a hare which, in its confusion, made a run at me and was shot dead with one of my twelve bullets, the noise of its demise echoing forth like an envoy. I made a fire from scrub brush and roasted the hare over it. I had been long without food, and though the creature was stringy and had taken on the stink of the scrub, it was no less a feast for that.

It was this fire that made my presence known, the white smoke rising high through the daylight like a beacon. In retrospect cooking the rabbit can be considered a tactical error, but you must recall that it had been several days since I had eaten and I was perhaps in a state of confusion.

In any case, even before I had consumed the hare to its end Finger made a mournful noise and his hackles arose. I captured, from the corner of an eye, a movement through the grass, the which I divined to be human. I rose to my feet. Wrapping Finger's leash around one hand, with the other I lifted my revolver from beside him and cocked it.

I hallooed the man and, brandishing my revolver, encouraged him to come forth of his own accord. Else, I claimed, I would send my dog into the brush to flush him and then would shoot him dead. Finger, too, entered wonderfully into the spirit of the thing, though I knew he would hurt nobody but only sniff them and, were they dead, roll in their remains. There was no response for a long moment and then the fellow arose like a ghost from the quaking grass and tottered out, as did his compatriots.

There were perhaps a dozen of them, a pitiful crew, each largely unclothed and unkempt, their skin as well discolored and lesioned. They were thin, arms and legs just slightly more than pale sticks, bellies swollen with hunger.

"Who is your leader?" I asked the man who had come first.

"God is our leader," the fellow claimed.

"Praise God," I said, "God's will be done, the Lord be praised," rattling off their phrases as if I had been giving utterance to them all my life. "But who is your leader in this world?"

They looked at one another dumbly as if my question lay beyond comprehension. It was quickly determined that they had no leader but were *waiting for a sign*; viz, were waiting for God to inform them as to how to proceed.

"I am that sign," I told them, thinking such authority might help better effect my purposes. There was a certain pleased rumbling at this. "I have come to beg you for provisions."

But food they claimed not to have, and by testimony of their own sorry condition I was apt to believe them. Indeed, they were hungrily eyeing the sorry remains of my hare.

I gestured to it with my revolver. "I would invite you to share my humble meal," I said, and at those words one of them stumbled forward and took up the spit.

It was only by leveling the revolver at each of them in turn as he ate that each was assured a share of the little that remained. Indeed, by force of the revolver alone was established what later they referred to as "the miracle of the everlasting hare," where, it was said, the food was allowed to pass from hand to hand and yet there remained enough for all.

If this be in fact a miracle, it is attributable not to me but to the revolver. It would have been better to designate said revolver as their Messiah instead of myself. Perhaps you will argue that, though this be true, without my hand to hold said weapon it could not have become a Jesus, that both of us together a Jesus make, and I must admit that such an argument is hard to counter. Though if I were a Jesus, or a portion of a Jesus, I was an unwitting one at this stage, and must plead for understanding.

When the hare was consumed, I allowed Finger what remained of the bones. The fellows who I had fed squatted about the fire and asked me if I had else to provide them by way of nourishment. I confessed I did not.

"We understand," one of them said, "from your teachings, that mankind cannot live by bread alone. But must not mankind have bread to live?"

"My teachings?" I said. I was not familiar at that time with the verse, was unsure what this rustic seer intended by attributing this statement to me.

"You are that sign," he said. "You have said so yourself."

Would you believe that I was unfamiliar enough at that moment with the teachings of the Holy Bible to not understand the mistake being made? I was like a gentleman in a foreign country, reader, armed with just enough of the language to promote serious misunderstanding. So that when I stated, in return, "I am that sign," and heard the rumble of approval around me, I thought merely that I was returning a formula, a manner of speech devoid of content. Realizing that because of the lateness of the season I might well have to remain in the Midwest through the worst of Winter, it was in my interest to be on good terms with those likely to be of use to me.

Indeed, it was not until perhaps a week later, as their discourse and their continued demands for "further light and knowledge" became more specific, that I realized that by saying "I am that sign" I was saying to them, "I am your Jesus." By that time, even had I affected a denial of my Jesushood, it would not have been believed, would have been seen merely as a paradoxical sort of teaching, a parable.

But I digress. Suffice to say that I had become their Jesus by ignorance and remained in that ignorance for some little time, and remain to some extent puzzled even today by the society I have unwittingly created. Would I have returned from the Midwest if I were in accord with them? True, it may be argued that I did not return of my own, yet when I was captured, it is beyond dispute, I was on the road toward my original encampment. I had no other purpose or intention but to report to my superiors. What other purpose could have brought me back?

In those first days, I stayed encamped on that crippled, pestilent prairie, surrounded by a group of Midwesterners who would not leave me and who posed increasingly esoteric questions: Did I come bearing an olive branch or a sword? (Neither, in fact, but a revolver.) What moneychangers would I overturn in this epoch? (But currency is of no use here, I protested.) What was the state of an unborn child? (Dead, I suggested, before realizing by unborn they did not mean stillborn, but by then it was too late to retrace my steps.) They refused to leave my side, seemed starved to talk to someone like myself—perhaps, I reasoned, the novelty of a foreigner. They were already mythologizing the "miracle of the everlasting hare"—which I told them they were making too much of: were it truly everlasting, the hare would still be here and we could commence to eat it over again. They looked thoughtful at this. There was, they felt, some lesson to be had in my words.

The day following the partaking of the hare, serious questions began to develop as to what we would eat next. I set snares and taught them to do the same, but it seemed that the hare had been an anomaly and the snares remained unsprung. It was clear they expected me to feed them, as if by sharing my hare with them I had entered into an obligation to provide for them. I tried at times to shoo them away from me and even pointed the revolver once or twice, but though I could drive them off a little distance they were never out of sight and would soon return.

But I am neglecting Finger. The men sat near me or, if I were walking, dogged my footsteps. I found my hunger banging like a shutter and had no desire so strong as to abandon their company immediately.

Soon they began to beseech me in plaintive tones, using phrases such as these:

Master, call down manna from heaven.

Master, strike that rock with your stave [n.b. I had no stave] *and cause a fountain to spring forth.*

Master, transfigure our bodies so that they have no need of food but are nourished on the word alone.

Being a heretic, I did not grasp the antecedent of this harangue (i.e. my Jesushood), but only its broader sense. Soon they were all crying out, and I, already maddened from hunger did not know how to proceed. A fever overcame me. Perhaps, I thought, I could slip away from them. But no, it was clear they thought they belonged with me and would not let me go. If I was to rid myself of them, there seemed no choice but to kill them.

It was here that my eyes fell upon Finger, he who had shared in my travails for many days, the cause of both much frustration and much joy. Here, I thought, is the inevitable first step, though I wept to think this. Divining no other choice, I drew my revolver and shot Finger through the head, then flensed him and trussed him and broiled him over the flames. He tasted, I must reluctantly admit, not unlike chicken. *Poor Finger*, I told myself, *perhaps we shall meet in a better world.*

Their response to this act was to declare I came not with an olive branch but with a sword, and to use the phrase *He smiteth*, a phrase which haunts me to this day.

It is by little sinful steps that grander evils come to pass. I am sorry to say that Finger was only a temporary solution, quickly consumed. I had hoped that, once sated, they would allow me to depart in peace, but they seemed more bound to me than ever now and even offered me tributes: strange woven creations of no use nor any mimetic value which they assembled from the tortured grass: crippled and faceless half-creatures that came apart in my hands.

I thought and pondered and saw no way out but to sneak away from them by night. At first, I thought to have effected an escape, yet before I was even a hundred yards from the campsite one of them had raised a hue and cry and they were all there with me, begging me not to go.

"I must go," I claimed. "Others await me."

"Then we shall accompany you," they said.

"I must go alone."

This they would not accept. *I cannot stop them from coming with me,* I thought, *but at least I may move them in the proper direction to facilitate my eventual return to my camp.* And in any case, I thought, if we are to survive we must leave this accursed plain where nothing grows but dust and scrub and misery. We must gain the hills.

So gain the hills we did. My plan was to instruct them in self-sufficiency, how to trap their own prey and how to grow their own foodstuffs, how to scavenge and forage and make do with what was at hand and thereby avoid starvation. This done, I hoped to convince them to allow me to depart.

We had arrived in the hills too late for crops, and animals and matter for foraging had grown scarce as well. We employed our first days gleaning what little food we could, gathering firewood and making for ourselves shelter prone to withstand the winter. But by the time winter set in with earnestness, we discovered our food all but gone and our straits dire indeed. I, as their Jesus, was looked to for a solution.

We have reached that unfortunate chapter which I assume to be the reason for my being asked to compose this accounting. Might I say, before I begin, that I regret everything, but that, at the time, I felt there to be no better choice? Were my inquest (assuming there is to be an inquest) to take place before a group of starved men, I might at least accrue some sympathy. But to the well-fed necessity must surely appear barbarity. And now, again well-fed myself, I regret everything. Would I do it again? Of course not. Unless I was very hungry indeed.

In the midst of our suffering, I explained to them that one of us must sacrifice himself for the others. I explained how I, as I had not yet finished my work, was unable to serve. To this they nodded sagely. And which of you, I asked, dare sacrifice himself, by so doing to become a type and shadow of your Jesus? There was among them one willing to step forward, and he was instantly shot dead. *He smiteth*, I could hear the men mumbling. What followed? Reader, we ate him.

By winter's end we had consumed two of his fellows, who stepped forward both times unprotesting, each as my apostle honored to become a type and shadow of their Jesus by a sacrifice of his own. Their bones we cracked open to eat the marrow, but the skulls of all three we preserved and enshrined, out of respect for their sacrifice—along with the skull of Finger which I had preserved and continue to carry with me to this day. Early in Spring I urged them further into the hills until we had discovered a small valley whose soil seemed fertile and promising. In a cave we discovered an unrefined salt. I taught them to fish and how as well to smoke their fish to preserve it, and this they described as becoming fishers of men (though to my mind it is more properly described as fishers of fish). We again set snares along game trails and left them undisturbed and this time caught rabbits and birds, and sometimes a squirrel, and this meat we ate or smoked and preserved as well. The hides they learned to strip and tan, and they bound them about their feet. I taught them as well how to cultivate those plants as were available to them, and to make them fruitful. When they realized it was my will that they fend for themselves, they were quick to learn. And thus we were not long into summer when I called them together to inform them of my departure.

At first they would not hear of this, and could not understand why their Jesus would leave them. *Other sheep I have*, I told them, *that are not of this fold*. Having spent the winter in converse with them and reading an old tattered copy of their Bible, I had become conversant in matters of faith, and though I never did feel a temptation to give myself over to it, I did know how to best employ it for my purposes. When even this statement did not seem sufficient for the most stubborn among them, who still threatened to accompany me, I told them, *Go and spread my teachings.*

By this I meant what I had taught them of farming and clothing themselves and hunting but, just as with Barton, it would have served me well to be more specific. Indeed, this knowledge did spread, but with it came a ritual of the eating of human flesh throughout the winter months, a ritual I had not encouraged and had only resorted to in direst emergency. This they supported not only with glosses from the Bible, but words from a new holy book they had written on birchbark pounded flat, in which I recognized a twisted rendering of my own words.

It was not until I had been discovered by my former compatriots and imprisoned briefly under suspicion and then returned to my own campsite that I heard any hint of this lamentable practice. It was enquired of me if I had seen any such thing in my travels in the Midwest. Perhaps it was wrong of me to feign ignorance. And I had long returned to my duties, despite the hard questions concerning dog and dogcart and provisions that I had been unable to answer, before there were rumors that the practice had begun, like a contagion, to spread, and had even crossed from the Midwest into our own territories. I had indeed lost nearly all sense of my days as a midwestern Jesus before the authorities discovered my name circulating in midwestern mouths, inscribed in their holy books. If when I was again apprehended I was indeed preparing to flee—and I do not admit to such—it is only because of a fear of becoming a scapegoat, a fear which is in the process of being realized.

If I had intended to create this cult around my own figure, why then would I have ever left the Midwest? What purpose would I have had in abandoning a world in which I could have been a God? The insinuations that I have been spreading my own cult in our own territories are spurious. There is absolutely no proof.

There is one other thing I shall say in my defense: What takes place beyond the borders of the known world is not to be judged against the standards of this world. Then, you may well inquire, what standard of judgment should be applied? I do not know the answer to this question. Unless the answer be no standard of judgment at all.

I was ordered to write an honest accounting of how I became a Midwestern Jesus and to the best of my ability I have done so. I regret to say that at the conclusion of my task I now see for the first time my actions in a cold light. I have no faith in the clemency of my judges, nor faith that any regret for those events I unintentionally set in motion will lead to a pardon. I have no illusions: I shall be executed.

Yet I have one last request. After my death, I ask that my body be torn asunder and given in pieces to my followers. Though I remain a heretic, I see no way of bringing my cult to an end otherwise. Let those who want to partake of me partake and then I will at least have rounded the circle, my skull joining a pile of skulls in the Midwest, my bones shattered and sucked free of marrow and left to bleach upon the plain. And then, if I do not arise from the dead, if I do not appear to them in a garment of white, Finger beside, then perhaps it all will end.

And if I do arise, stripping the lineaments of death away to reveal renewed the raiment of the living? Permit me to say, then, that it is already too late for all of you, for I come not with an olive branch but a sword. *He smiteth*, and when he smiteth, ye shall surely die.

ABRAHAM LINCOLN
HAS BEEN SHOT

Daniel Alarcón

from Zoetrope

WE WERE TALKING, HANK AND I, ABOUT HOW THAT WHICH WE love is so often destroyed by the very act of our loving it. The bar was dark, but comfortably so, and by the flittering light of the television I could make out the rough texture of his face. He was, in spite of everything, a beautiful man.

We'd lost our jobs at the call center that day, both of us, but Hank didn't seem to care. All day strangers would yell at us, demanding we make their lost packages reappear. Hank kept a handle of bourbon in the break room, hidden behind the coffee filters, for those days when a snowstorm back East slowed deliveries and we were made to answer for the weather.

After we were told the news, Hank spent the afternoon drinking liquor from a Styrofoam cup and wandering the floor, mumbling to himself. For one unpleasant hour he stood on two stacked boxes of paper, peering out the high window at the cars baking in the parking lot. I cleaned out my desk, and then his. Things between us hadn't been good in many months.

Hank said: "Take, as an example, Abraham Lincoln."

"Why bring this up?" I asked. "Why tonight?"

"Now, by the time of his death," he said, ignoring me, "Lincoln was the most beloved man in America."

I raised an eyebrow. "Or was he the most hated?"

Hank nodded. "People hated him, sure they did. But they also loved him. They'd loved him down to a fine sheen. Like a stone polished by the touch of a thousand hands."

Lincoln was my first love, of course, and Hank knew the whole story. He brought it up whenever he wanted to hurt me. Lincoln and I met at a party in Chicago, long before he was president, one of those Wicker Park affairs with fixed-gear bikes locked out front, four deep to a stop sign. We were young. It was summer. "I'm going to run for president," he said, and all night he followed me—from the spiked punch bowl to the balcony full of smokers to the dingy bedroom where we groped on a stranger's bed. He never stopped repeating it.

Finally, I gave in: "I'll vote for you."

Lincoln said he liked the idea: me, alone, behind a curtain, thinking of him.

"I don't understand what you mean," I said to Hank.

"Here you are with me. Together, we're a mess. And now the wheels have come off, Manuel."

"Like Lincoln?"

"Everything he did for this nation," Hank said. "The Americans had no choice but to kill him."

I felt a flutter in my chest. "Don't say that," I managed.

Hank apologized. He was always apologizing. He polished off his drink with a flourish, held it up, and shook it. Suddenly he was a bandleader and it was a maraca: the ice rattled wonderfully. A waitress appeared.

"Gimme what I want, sugar," Hank said.

She was chewing gum laconically, something in her posture indicating a painful awareness that this night would be a long one. "How do I know what you want?"

Hank covered his eyes with his hands. "Because I'm famous."

She took his glass and walked away. Hank winked at me and I tried to smile. I wished he could have read my mind. That night it would have made many things between us much simpler.

"The thing is," Hank said once he had a fresh drink, "there's a point after which you have finished loving something, after you have extracted everything of beauty from it, and you must—it is law—discard it."

This was all I could take. "Oh Christ. Just say it."

There was a blinking neon sign behind the bar; Hank looked over my shoulder, lost himself in its lights. "Say what?" he asked.

"What you want to say."

"I don't know what I want." He crossed his arms. "I never have. I resent the pressure to decide."

Lincoln was a good man, a competent lover, a dignified leader with a tender heart. He'd wanted to be a poet, but settled for being a statesman. "It's just my day job," he told me once. He was sitting naked in a chair in my room when he said it, smoking a cigarette and cleaning the dust from his top hat with a wooden toothbrush. And he was fragile: his ribs showed even then. We were together almost a year. In the mornings, I would comb out his beard for him, softly, always softly, and Lincoln would purr like a cat.

Hank laid his hands flat on the table and studied them. They were veiny and worn. "I'm sorry," he said, without looking up. "It wasn't a good job, was it?"

"No," I said. "But it was a job."

He rubbed his eyes. "If I don't stop drinking, I'm going to be sick. On the other hand, if I stop drinking . . . Oh, this life of ours."

I raised one of his hands and kissed it.

I was a Southern boy, and of course it was something Lincoln and I talked about. Hank didn't care where I was from. Geography is an accident, he said. The place you are born is simply the first place you flee. And then: the people you meet, the ones you fall for, and the paths you make together, the entirety of one's life, a series of mere accidents. And these too are accidents: the creeks you stumble upon in a dense wood, the stones you pick up, the number of times each skips across the bright surface of the water, and everything you feel in that moment—the graceless passage of time, the possibility of stillness. Lincoln and I had lived this—skipped rocks and felt our hearts swelling—just before he left Illinois for Washington. We were an hour outside Chicago, in a forest encroached upon by subdivisions. Everywhere we walked that day there were trees adorned with bright orange flags, trees with death warrants, land marked for clearing, to be crisscrossed by roads and driveways, dotted with the homes of upright American yeomen.

Lincoln told me he loved me.

"I'll come with you," I said. I was hopeful. This was years ago.

That morning he'd gone to the asylum to select a wife. The doctors had wheeled her out in a white gown and married them on the spot. Under the right care, they said, she'd make a great companion. Her name was Mary Todd. "She's very handsome," Lincoln said. He showed me a photograph, and I admitted that she was.

"Do you love her?" I asked.

Lincoln wouldn't look me in the eye.

"But you just met her today."

He answered with a sigh. When he had been quiet long enough, he took my hand. We had come to a place where the underbrush was so overgrown that the construction markers seemed to get lost: everywhere were mossy, rotting tree trunks, gnarled limbs and tangled vines that hung over the trail. Lincoln kept hitting his head as we walked.

"This forest is so messy," he complained.

I said, "You're too fastidious to be a poet."

He gave me a sheepish smile.

It's true I never expected to grow old.

Back at the bar, Hank was falling apart before my eyes. Or pretending to. "What will we do?" he pleaded. "How will we pay the rent?"

It was a good question. He slumped his shoulders and I smiled at him. "You don't love me," I said.

He froze for a moment. "Of course I do. Am I not destroying you, bit by bit?"

"Are you?"

Hank's face was red. "Wasn't it me who made you lose your job?"

It was good to hear him say it. Hank had been in the habit of transferring his most troublesome callers to me, but not before thoroughly antagonizing them, not before promising that their lost packages were only the beginning, that they could expect far worse, further and more violent attacks on their suburban tranquility. Inevitably they demanded to speak to a manager, and I would be forced to bail out my lover. Or try to. I wasn't a manager, I never had been, and the playacting was unbearable. The customers barked insults and I gave it all away: shipping, replacements, insurance, credit, anything to get them off the line. Hank would be listening in from his cubicle, breathing a little too heavily into the receiver, and I knew I was disappointing him. Afterward, he would apologize tearfully, and two weeks might pass, maybe three, before it would happen again.

It took Accounting months to pin it on us.

Now Hank sighed. "It sure was hot today," he said. "Did you feel it? Pressing up against the windows?"

"Is that what you were looking at? The heat?"

"What would you have done without me anyway? How could you have survived that place?"

I didn't answer him.

We emptied our pockets, left the bar, and walked into the night. It was true that the heat was never-ending. It was eleven-thirty or later, and still the desert air was dense. This time of year, those of us who were not native—those whom life had shipwrecked in the great Southwest—began to confront a very real terror: summer was coming. Soon it would be July, and there would be no hope. We made our way to the truck. Hank tossed me the keys and I caught them, just barely. It was the first good thing that had happened all day. If they'd hit the ground, we surely would've spent hours on hands and knees, palming the warm desert asphalt, looking for them.

"Where to?" I asked.

"You know."

I drove slowly through downtown, and then under the Ninth Avenue Bridge, and out into the vast anonymity of tract homes and dry gullies, of evenly spaced streetlights with nothing to illuminate. We had friends who lived out here, grown women who collected crystals and whose neighborhood so depressed them they often got in their car just to walk the dog. Still, beneath the development, it was beautiful country: after a half hour the road smoothed out, another ten minutes and the lights vanished, and then you could really move. With the windows down and the hot air rushing in, you could pretend it was a nice place to live. A few motor homes tilting on cinderblocks; an abandoned shopping cart in a ditch, glittering in the headlights like a small silver cage; and then it was just desert, which is to say there was nothing at all but dust and red rock and an indigo sky speckled with stars. Hank had his hand on my knee, but I was looking straight ahead, to that point just beyond the reach of the headlights. With an odd job or two, we might be able to scrounge together rent. After that, it was anyone's guess, and the very thought was exhausting. I felt—incorrectly, it turns out—that I was too old to have nothing again.

Lincoln and I spent a winter together in Chicago. He was on city council, and I worked at a deli. We couldn't afford heat, and so every night we would curl our bodies together, beneath a half-dozen blankets, and hold tight, skin on skin, until the cold was banished. In the middle of the night, the heat between us would suddenly become so intense that either he or I or the both of us would throw the covers off. It happened every night, and every morning it was a surprise to wake, shivering, with the bedclothes rumpled on the floor.

I'd made my way south by the time he was killed. It had been eleven years since we'd been in touch. For the duration of the war I had wandered the country, looking for work. There was a white woman in southern Florida who had known my mother, and when I wrote to her she offered me a place to stay in exchange for my labor. It seemed fine for a while. At dusk the cicadas made their plaintive music, and every morning we rose before dawn and cleared the undergrowth and dug canals in an endless attempt to drain the land. There were three men besides me, connected by an obscure system of relations stretching back into the region's dim history: how it was settled and conquered, how its spoils had been divided. There was a lonely Cherokee, and a Carib who barely spoke, and a freed black who worked harder than the rest of us together. She had known all of our mothers, had watched us grow up and scatter and return. She intended to plant orange trees, just as she'd seen in a brochure once on a trip to Miami: trees in neat little rows, the dull beauty of progress.

But this land was a knot, just a dense, spongy mangrove atop a bog. You could cup the dirt in your hands, squeeze it, and get water. "It'll never work," I said one afternoon, after a midday rain shower had undone in forty-five minutes what we had spent a week building. She fired me then and there, no discussion, no preamble. "Men should be more optimistic," she said, and gave me a half hour to gather my things.

It was the freed black who drove me to the bus station. When he had pulled the old truck out onto the road, he took his necklace from beneath his shirt. There was a tiny leather pouch tied to it.

"What is it?" I asked.

"It's a bullet." He turned very serious. "And there's a gun hidden in the glade."

"Oh," I said.

He barely opened his mouth when he spoke. "That woman owned my mother, boy, and that land is going to be mine. Do you understand me now? Do you get why I work so hard?"

I nodded and suddenly felt a respect for him—for the implacability of his will—that was nearly overwhelming. When I had convinced him I understood, he turned on the radio, and that's when we heard the news: Ford's Theatre, the shooting, *Sic semper tyrannis*. The announcer faded in and out; we found a place with good reception and without having to say a word both agreed to stop, though I would miss my bus because of it. The radio prattled breathlessly—the assassin had escaped—no, they had caught him—no, he had escaped. It was a wretched country we were living in, stinking, violent, diseased. I listened, not understanding, and didn't notice for many minutes that my companion had shut his eyes and begun, very quietly, to weep. He closed his right fist around the bullet and with the other gripped the steering wheel, as if to steady himself.

I've been moving west since.

That night we were fired, Hank and I made it to the highway, headed south, and then everything was easy. Along the way I forgot where we were going, and then remembered, and then forgot again. I decided it was better not to remember, that something would present itself, and so when the front right tire blew, it was as if I had been waiting for it all night. Hank had dozed, and the truck shook violently, with a terrific noise, but somehow I negotiated it—me and the machine and the empty night highway—in that split second, a kind of ballet. Hank came to when we had eased onto the shoulder. I was shaking, but alive.

"What did you do?" he asked, blinking. "Is this Mexico?"

It seemed very real, what I felt: that truck had, through mechanical intuition, decided to blow a tire for me, to force me to stop. I turned on the cabin light. "How long has it been since you stopped loving me?"

"Really?" he asked.

I nodded.

"What month is this?" Hank said desperately.

I didn't budge.

"Are you going to leave me here?"

"Yes," I said.

He smiled, as if this were a moment for smiling. "I'm not getting out. I paid for this truck."

"No you didn't," I said.

"Still," he shrugged, "I'm not getting out."

Which was fine. Which was perfect. There was a spare in the back, but it was flat too. If one must begin again late in life, better to do so cleanly, nakedly. I left the keys in the ignition. Out here, outside our small city, the air had cooled and I breathed it in. Life is very long. It had been years, but I recognized the feeling immediately. It wasn't the first time I'd found myself on a dark highway, on foot, with nowhere to go.

BIT FORGIVE
Maile Chapman

from A Public Space

THIS MORNING I RECEIVED A LETTER OSTENSIBLY FROM MY
friend Niklas Nummelin, fifteen years almost to the date since
the accidental sinking of his ship and his presumed death by drowning
somewhere off the Finnish coast of the Bay of Bothnia.

The letter doesn't contradict the version of events we all heard long
ago from the single crewmember who survived by reaching (if indeed
he was not incarcerated in) the small punition boat towed behind the
Bit Forgive; criminal or not, we believed him when he described his
drowning comrades shouting and gurgling through flooding mouths,
pulling at him in the endless cold water with heavy, sharp fingers. And
we forgave him for what we knew he must have done—fighting off the
drowning men who reached his tiny boat, who would have sunk him
under their combined weight. We believed and forgave because no one
else from that ship came back to our harbor, neither alive nor dead, and
surely we needed him, because we needed to see the proof preserved on
his back, shoulders, and cheek in the form of five-fingered scars from
those who did not survive.

Over time, and through human nature, the story has become romantic through retelling. Public grief is still extravagant and downtown on the anniversary of the sinking it is not uncommon to hear
toasts to the memory of drowned friends, beloved family members, and

neighbors. People laugh and cry easily to the words of a lilting, mournful song made popular in the aftermath.

I am not unmoved but I find the song inappropriately pretty. Instead of drinking and singing along I light beeswax candles in the cathedral, placing them in sight of the miniature wooden ship which hangs in midair as a tribute. And in private meditations I have accepted that life here has fallen into two chronologies: before Niklas and the others were lost, when seemingly all was straightforward and retrospectively optimistic; and now afterwards, when it isn't.

I have concealed my interest in the letter from my wife, Ninne, for obvious reasons.

> *Dear Bennet,*
> *I send greetings. From under the sea. Dear Bennet. You were my closest friend. I want you remember me and our conversations. I want you to know that you were wrong when you argued, with no reason except bad temper, that death is the end of the individual.*
>
> *You think this is a joke. I know because I know you. And you know me and you know I only sailed on the* Bit Forgive *because I wanted time and air. I had the story of my uncle sailing at my age. A trip at sea. A way to mark my graduation. I can tell you details no one alive can repeat. The crew were afraid of fire—flooding the decks, spreading stinking wet cattle skins on the wood. They posted a law that any man starting a fire on board would be used to snuff it out. But every man on board smoked tobacco and every man carried the makings of fire in his pockets. Below decks in the galley they cooked on an open fire. There were gratings in the deck to let the smoke rise and all the time I smelled it and sometimes*

I felt panic, thinking we are on fire . . . *mostly it was only the preparation of pork and peas. But then someone smoked above. In the rigging, on the main top, I'm speculating, I don't know what happened. There was smoke. The smoke choked us suddenly and then the ship fizzed like a match-head on the water. They were frightened and they panicked, looking for someone to punish while the fire spread. I climbed the rat-lines to a platform and saw flames moving deep below the gratings . . . it was hot, and there was no chance to escape . . . I remember the blackening deck. I did not guess that they had a military cargo until it blew: pitch-rings wrapped in hemp and dipped in tar, and fire-rings, each with a mortal blow of shot and gunpowder . . . I never would have sailed, had I known what the hold contained.*

In the midst of fire I saw the final explosion blossom up through the grating. It took forever. But there wasn't even time to urinate in my pants.

Then I saw the heavens of the sea, sparkling.

That was the end, Bennet. No one could have survived. But I did. I came back like waking up with alcohol poisoning. Nauseated and with the taste of smoke. I felt cold water moving my limbs. I felt cold water chilling every crevice. When I got my eyes open I didn't know whether I was just above the water or just under it—the surface looks the same from either side. Then I saw below me the illusion of a road, growing out of the sea floor: a weal of black stones like scabs on an old injury.

Don't laugh, Bennet. Don't disbelieve. I was slow and
numb. The tips of my shoes scraped the road's crustaceous
surface. Pulling and scraping. There was a silence so
heavy and full that I thought my eardrums would tear.
I was afraid that I was drowned; I knew I was under-
water because of the silence, and the gloom. The quivering
green obscurity. The stones were clear, but everything else
was clouded by floating particulates, a slurry of pulver-
ized rock and plankton. Then I felt light touches on my
hands and saw in the silt a cloud of flickering fry. They
were so small that I would have mistaken them for dust
shaking out of my clothing. Except they moved with in-
tention. And this, Bennet, this visitation of the fry was
my first proof that although I felt alive, I was floating
under the sea.

At this point I put down the pages.

Years ago, there was a popular fad for letters "from" the *Bit Forgive*. Written anonymously, they were printed in newspapers and framed in pubs, these letters in which the departed offered wisdom and comfort to the living. "Open Letter to a Sailor's Daughter," for example, can still be purchased in stationery shops. But those letters were maudlin, extremely sentimental, often with a religious undertone, and intentionally broad enough to appeal to anyone who read them.

I looked at the envelope for clues about how the letter had arrived and who had written it. The first envelope was blank. The second envelope inside was addressed to me in familiar handwriting. It wasn't from Niklas, I knew. I might wish it could be, but that is only a response of the mind under an old pressure of grief, reaching for impossibilities.

*Bennet, (*the letter continued*) I am out of the habit of ordering my thoughts coherently. I am ready to try. But when I think of how quick we were, the debates we had, I feel sad. All my sharp edges have been blunted. For peace of mind I will assume you are much blunter now too.*

My story should hold your interest. You know what I mean. My belief in the afterlife and your flat denial. Remember the physiology books. The philosophies of death and human nature? Bennet, you were wrong on some points. I still exist. But you were right about others. The afterlife holds no greater opportunity than actual life. I wish I had taken the chance to be more alive when I was alive and dry. I remember you with the medical school girls. Kissing their bleach-tainted breath. Sharing their severe preoccupations. Seducing them over dinners. Swallowing fishbones and gristle to impress them. Your appetites. Now I agree that appetite is the engine of life.

But Bennet, you wasted a lot of time in the last months of my life. Your research, voles and the birds that eat voles . . . who cares about the voles? The specimens, the shriveling, the tricks to make the dead voles look alive again? Why were there reconstructed voles stuffed with cotton on your bedside table? I have admitted that appetite is good. And I have admitted that you had a good appetite for life in your way. Please see my point and answer. What was wrong with you? Why did you let yourself stink of preservative? I feel angry, Bennet, remembering how much valuable time you wasted in the last year of my life in your selfish academic pursuits.

Still I would live that year forever. Because we met Ninne then. Her two black eyes like antique coins. Ninne came and saved me from you, your life of taxidermy, my brief encounters with the camisoles of your discarded medical school girls.

Ninne came and it was normal that she and I would be together. She pinched me to the point of blood and I pinched her too. We shushed in my room—did you know? Your days were full of killing, then instilling the illusion of life back into your voles. I wasn't leaving her when I sailed, Bennet. I was leaving you. I was eclipsed by you even though I was smarter than you. There wasn't much proof of it then.

But now I have survived. I have proven myself strong, and smart, and resourceful. I have triumphed.

At last I have bested you, Bennet, albeit in strange ways.

Naturally I continued reading. It was disappointing, but not unlikely, that any letter purporting to be from Niklas should contain some element of anger. Everyone knew that he was unpredictable. That aspect of Niklas in my memory is still painful, contracting and convulsing against itself, making me ashamed to remember it now that he is gone and incapable of changing for the better.

But contrary to the letter, it is absurd to think that Niklas would wish he'd followed his appetites more. For years we went together to all the student suppers and all the dances and I introduced him to every girl I met. And invariably I would then see him near the musicians, dancing bonelessly, dancing suggestively, lifting up the slim, spatulated fingers of one hand to disguise the other drawing closer and closer to a new girl's bare upper arms, the neckline of her dress, reaching for her hair, which he would try to pull as a prelude to affection. And on the way home, if he'd been drinking, he would often fall backwards out of his unlaced evening shoes. I was always sober enough to walk home but I couldn't always pull or carry him along, not when he took my arms to drag me down with him. Once when he was very drunk he bit my arm through the sleeve of my dinner jacket, leaving a distinct bruise in the shape of teeth which I made him acknowledge every day until it faded.

One typical evening we had been for several hours at our preferred café in the Esplanadi, drinking schnapps on the yellow velvet sofa in a side room with a view of artificial flowers. We'd brought Ninne—this was before women were permitted in the cafes unaccompanied—and she was sitting just beside me. She liked the music. She tapped her foot first against my leg, and then against Niklas', and every few minutes she stole a sip of my drink and swallowed a whole mustard herring from a shining silver dish. Her sleeves were lace and fitted well, exceedingly snugly from the neckline down over the palm of each hand, and her stockings, which I saw when she tapped my leg, were lace as well. Through the lace I could see, when she pressed close, the pattern of fine golden hairs growing along her skin.

"What do you think?" she asked, leaning against my arm, her breath metallic, her lips plump and silky with oil. "Will I end up with you, or with Niklas?" She leaned in and blinked, slowly, touching my cheek with her eyelashes. "How can I possibly choose?"

I pushed her back, gently, for her own good, but she resisted. She was, in some ways, very like Niklas even then.

"You live together," she said, speculatively, and touched the side of my face with her unsmiling tongue.

I did not particularly wish for fish oil on my face. "You're an evil girl," I said pleasantly, pushing her again; looking up I saw in the mirror that something had happened. Niklas held a napkin to his face and the white towel on the arm of the barman was stained with his blood.

I took him outside and examined him under the streetlight. He'd cut his lip drinking from a broken glass, which he tried to demonstrate for me.

"I drank like this!" he said hoarsely, pantomiming with his arm and moving his head too quickly so that the blood started again and his eyes rolled back, but he was looking at me the whole time, and I knew he had seen Ninne offering me her tongue.

"Hold still," I said, but he put his fingers to his face again.

"I don't care how you did it," I said, pressing my handkerchief over his mouth to shut him up and hide his bloody teeth. "At home you'll sit in the kitchen and let me stitch that lip and if you complain I'll stitch your mouth shut."

He dropped his arm and put his head to one side, staring, unsteady on his feet. Behind us Ninne came to stand in the doorway, watching over the fur collar of her coat.

"Thanks," he said curtly. He leaned on my shoulder and I turned to find a cab. I lifted my hand but before the driver stopped Niklas laughed in my ear and buckled his knees, taking me down with him on the cobblestones and ice, cracking my elbow so that I was not in fact able to stitch him up, and to the end of his life there was that scar under his lip, which I knew to be the charming evidence of his urge for self-sabotage.

Even if the letter did not come from Niklas, still, as it always is with letters, I could hear a voice speaking through it, and the voice sounded like Niklas. But I do not say this was pleasant. There is a tension between the past and the present. It is a cruel fact, easily recognizable whenever someone now picks up the unfinished work of someone who has gone before, completing it in their absence.

Anyway, Bennet, listen. I want you to imagine how lonely I felt drifting through the silt. I want you to think of it like this: You remember when for graduation we took the brassy elevator in the Hotel Ja Visst up to see the woman who gave colonic purges to the foreign students? Remember the cramping that made you relive every feeling of emotional pain in the history of your life all at once? She told us that the body always remembers. That memory lives in the muscles, and some of the organs. And then we talked of our viscera for weeks. The floating gave me that pain again and I hung my head and saw between my feet a mark in the water, a line of blood floating out of my pants. I knew then that my life and my blood were draining out into the silt. The cramping went on and on mercilessly and I was afraid I would lose an organ out the bottom of my pant leg.

Are you still reading? It is hard to pay attention to someone else's pain. I don't expect you to enjoy reading this. Except I know you're some kind of clinician now, and you have always had a tolerance, albeit an ethnographical one, for distress.

But I will spare us both. I will skip over those details to describe how, much later, after I floated to the end of that black stone road, emerging out of the silt into a better-lit place, I began to live in half of the shipwrecked Bit Forgive *which I found floating eerily upright on the sandy bottom. The water was thick enough to encourage part of the hull and, ironically, the reinforced stone firewall of the galley to stay propped together and I lay there on the cook's wooden bench for days, without a pulse to* give satisfaction to the pain. I didn't realize until then why the silence—it is not too much to say—terrified me. My ears were dense with pressure, but I couldn't hear my heartbeat.

The sun, when it rose, was watery and distant. When my pain finally lightened, my surroundings were less frightening.

Yes, Bennet, I am telling you a story of transformation. I became empty and flexible. My belly was without bulk, without function. My skin got looser and looser until when I touched myself my flesh kept the imprint. When I got up from the bench I drifted with bent knees, swallowing mouthfuls of the fry and poking at the occasional dissolute sea-vegetables. I did not feel tired at night. Day and night were hardly distinguishable. I half-slept only to escape what now seems obvious: the fact that I was already dead.

Another current came and carried me towards the rocks on the horizon. I was worried. I did not want to leave the Bit Forgive. It was the one tie I still had to the world above and without it I was alone with the weight of leagues or miles of water pressing down on me . . . Once the wreck was out of sight I realized I could not inflate my chest, that I'd been fighting off the feeling of suffocation for days. I lost my buoyancy. I sank and crawled towards the nearest pile of rocks. I wanted shelter in that bland dim landscape and when I got to the rocks I forced my head inside a crack. I stayed there for days with my head hidden and a new, final ribbon of blood dispersing in the water . . .

Imagine how much I must have wanted some news of Niklas, that I could continue to read even such terrible details of a fabricated humiliation.

From habit I glanced to the window to see how Ninne looked. She was as usual sitting in the white metal chair in the back yard, surrounded by the two banks of blue hydrangeas that I suggested to the gardener. Her sunhat was tied on and her back was to me. It was unlikely that she would be coming indoors before I could put the letter out of her sight; to keep her peaceful, I have always avoided bringing up the death of Niklas, though I knew that with the anniversary approaching she was thinking of him too.

Today it is nice to see that she sits, instead of getting up to hide in the trees, or to worry the locked latch of the gate.

> *Bennet: this was another turning point. When I came out from under the rocks I saw something on the horizon, something so ordinary that words don't describe it's dizzying oddness. It was a house, Bennet, as out of place as the upright wreckage of the* Bit Forgive. *I went to it, dogged by the ribbon of blood stretching out behind me, and I believed I was hallucinating because it was the house of the parents of Ninne. And in that hallucination I made myself go into the rooms where I had been uncomfortable during visits—Dr. and Mrs. Gunderson never liked me, because of you; they compared us unequally, they liked your studies of anatomy better than whatever I might have wanted in life.*

> *The house was intact but different like a dream of a place you don't know well enough to reproduce exactly. I can't swear that these were the real walls of the large red staircase, I only know that in this house the par-*

ents of Ninne had hung their pretensions on those walls, portraits in ersatz gold and ivory frames, photos stiffly posed, painted over with a layer of sticky oil to make them look valuable. Ninne's mother in a hat and veil, holding the bridle of a horse, but with the horse cropped out of the photo. Had there ever really been a horse? If I hadn't been eviscerated I'd have laughed at the empty bridle hanging in a photographer's studio. Nearby was her husband the doctor standing as if beside a gamey pile of dead pheasants, and with a gun over his shoulder . . . but again cropped, no birds visible. And there were some of Ninne which were too difficult to look at because I believed then that she was lost to me forever. I put my hand over a photo of her sitting on her knees, reaching to stroke a nest of kittens not pictured. No! I said; I even tried to say it out loud.

And further up, the humid and abandoned bedrooms, coverlets and pillows reset for sleeping, clothing swaying on hangers, all the products of my imagination. Ninne's room at the corner, whose windows I'd seen from the yard. And on her bureau, a framed photo of myself, unbloated and alive.

You can imagine the investigations, my curiosity about their life in that household. But I was respectful. I was reverent in Ninne's closets, desk drawers, jewellery boxes. It hurt when I touched her belongings. But I rediscovered her in my memory. And then I left the house.

You will ask, why not claim the house and stay there?

Bennet, you would have entered that house and been content to hover lifelessly forever. But even here I am not, like you, a creature of compromise and conformity. My dislike for Ninne's parents was strong and I was able to take their house for granted in this undersea incarnation, and to reject it. And then I was able to pass by without feeling obliged to enter. I felt power in recognizing that I no longer need to sleep in a bed, at such a point of extremity as this.

I filled my time elsewhere. There was a place behind the house where I began to find objects from the shipwreck appearing with quiet consistency: spools of twine, pewter bottles, clay pipe-stems like the ribs of birds half-buried in the sand. There were more floating fry there and I sometimes opened my mouth and let them in by the thousands as I kicked at the compacted dunes, believing that life must eat, persisting in the illusion. I was drifting like this past the Gundersons' house with my mouth open, half-walking and half-floating, when I saw something that made me feel the ghost of a cramp of horror. Through the large front window I could see, newly, one angle of a previously hidden interior wall, and the wall was painted a deep hammy pink, weirdly refractive and tinting the whole inside of the house. This warmth even spilled out of the windows . . . but more startling and more alarming than this . . . there was a cuckoo clock on that exposed pink wall, and the hanging weights beneath it were in motion.

This was the first regular motion, the first human activity or evidence of human activity that I had seen since the belated bucket-line at the burning of the Bit Forgive. *Though I was alone on my undersea plateau, this movement was a sign that change was not impossible. After this, I was not afraid to hope.*

Bennet: I know that only the cold dark waters of the wormless Baltic have preserved me, meaning that I cannot ever leave.

I will make this place my own to the extent that I can. I began with the totemic red marble stairs, the petrified gullet of that house. With a sledgehammer salvaged from the ship I broke the steps into small pieces. It took a long time with my waterlogged muscles, but I destroyed the steps and I paved the interior of the house with their remains. All is open now. And I have caused to grow around the house the red trees that I miss from home, whose twigs look like slim fingers holding peppery white blossoms. I want to tell you these things, Bennet. I want you to know that I have made the house a museum of my death. With the remains of the ship-carpenter's grease-box and the sledgehammer I drove oakum into the walls, between every board I could uncover, to waterproof the house and live again, as humanly as possible, inside. Do you find that funny? It is not funny. It is difficult for a dead man to rebuild a house, especially when he knows that this house can only be a tribute to a life I wanted and was denied by the sinking of the Bit Forgive.

I wanted her, Bennet. I wanted Ninne and in time I would have married her and built a real house and we would have had black-eyed children, and water decently contained in ponds, and I would have stocked my property with beautiful imported wild turkeys for the pleasure of seeing her father pretend to want to shoot them, and I would have said: These are the pets of my children, and you are an artificial sportsman. I would have put a horse there too. And I would have put my hands on Mrs. Gunderson's waist and I would have forcibly lifted her high into the saddle, to judge for myself what kind of horsewoman she might really be.

I have been brave. I have been strict, even in my loneliness. I emptied the closets, sent the Gundersons' garments to float away, so that the shapes of their bodies would not be my only companions. And to fix that emptiness I filled the closets with what I found from the ship: felted woolen caps, corpselike leather boots, patchwork mittens with a pile extra thumbs, all black, hard, dead, shattering. For the dresser, the contents of hypothetical pockets: tin buttons, a lead sinker, and fourteen copper coins. And on the floor, the pitiless horror of a single footless shoe.

This was the world I thought I wanted when I sailed on the Bit Forgive, *reproduced in pieces. I remade and briefly accepted the environment. But after this, Bennet, I had a glorious realization: I was ready for company.*

And then: when I saw Ninne, as I had so strongly expected to see her—standing in the kitchen against the flesh-pink wall, staring at the wooden handle of a broken fork—for one overwhelming moment I could not feel the proper reaction of hope, love, and exultation. But then directly

after, I did. Emotion did not desert me, and Bennet, I
swear that I have these feelings still.

At this, whatever my own feeling for Ninne I stood and went to the
window again to see how she looked and where she was. She is ordinar-
ily easy to find now. A few years ago I had the fence built in order to
keep her in sight. And because I am not completely insensitive, I had
the gardener plant soft shrubs at intervals to disguise the fact of her
unfortunate captivity, and I hoped in this way to reconcile her to staying in the yard in a peaceful way. The hedge however was slow to grow
together, and for some time there were interstices of board visible between the leaves. I would often find her standing in these blank spots,
with her feet between the roots, facing the boards, which she could just
see over, staring at the harbor.

If she had been peaceful, as I wish she could have been for her own
sake, this would have been enough containment. But I had to ask the
carpenter, with the approval of Ninne's parents, to add another three
feet of height to hide the harbor and so stop her from scratching, from
climbing, from bloodying her mouth and damaging her teeth against
the wood. It worked, but I still find her in the hedge. Facing the boards,
waiting, as a cat faces a door and waits to be let out.

When I looked she was sitting peacefully on the bench. But then
slowly she turned her head towards the house and she looked at me.
And customarily she did not blink; she stopped blinking naturally some
long time ago. At night and many times during the day I or someone
else must remember to drop a gummy glycerin mixture into her eyes
to save her sight. The drops probably blur her vision, unfortunately, but
she will not say, and we can't be sure.

She misses you a little, Bennet. She's told me all that hap-
pened. She says that she waited, and then eventually she
gave in to the pressure from all sides, and that she mar-

ried you but never loved you as much as she loved me, and because I know this I can accept your years of excruciating intercourse with Ninne as a result of my apparent death, and I forgive you both for that.

But: she is with me now. She is here, sitting in a burnt chair that I carried from the galley of the Bit Forgive *and placed behind the house. The rayon of her dark dress is thick and stubborn in the water and she moves slowly along inside it. She will hardly speak, but opens her mouth sometimes to let the fry in. While resting she sometimes shakes herself awake, a seizure of the muscles originating in her dead belly . . . but this happens less and less often.*

Bennet? Did you notice she was gone?

She and I, we are not a living couple, there is no decent possibility of physical expectation between the dead. We accept the circumstance and are grateful to be together now, so late after the burning of the Bit Forgive, *and so late after you took her and convinced her that I was gone. Now we have made a household together. And although we are complete as we are, nonetheless we both have a persistent feeling that you will be coming through the region of silt towards us sometime soon.*

I have caused this much to happen, that the house appeared, and was changed, and that Ninne has arrived, and stayed. I do not know whether this is objective reality or if this is my afterlife . . . what else could it be? This is the best I can hope for, after the ruptures that happened. Now we are deciding, Ninne and I, how to accept you here with us. We want to be generous. Maybe we want you to see how it should have been. Maybe this sounds cruel, but Bennet, you will die sometime, and I don't believe you want to be alone afterwards. What if you never got out of the silt? Wouldn't you rather be here with us?

Bennet, listen. I was almost lost completely, aware of my death with fondness and with regret, but without attachment: but I was strong. I have not disappeared and it is only by force of will that I am still here. And I have written this letter to prepare you for your future. I want you to remember what I say and to have courage in the coming ordeal. I believe I have bested you. But that does not mean I want you to disappear entirely. So you see, I am not as capricious, not as selfish as you believed.

After writing this letter I am reasonably content. Take heart, Bennet, and beware. We three can be together here as need arises. And all that I will miss then are the animals, the birds, even the voles of long ago. But perhaps you can bring these with you.

Your friend,
Niklas

I would have liked a moment alone in which to simply think of Niklas, to simply think of him without resorting to comparisons of who he was when his life ended, and who I have continued into, and who he might have become.

But wearily I see that here now is Ninne outside at the window standing with her feet no doubt in the border of deep blue flowers. She is watching me. And she has seen the letter though naturally I will not let on that I have read it, or that I am affected.

She breathes and stares and the condensation of her breath builds on the glass.

Suddenly I say: "Ninne! Did you write this letter, Ninne?"

I squeeze up the pages. It does not matter because regardless I will burn the letter later when the fire in the fireplace has been lit. And now with the rod I slide the curtain shut because she is still watching, and opening her mouth, the color of burgundy against the glass . . . but even when invisible beyond the curtain I know that she is there, red-eyed, breathing, still alive, and continually staring without mercy.

THE END OF NARRATIVE
(1-29; or 29-1)
Peter LaSalle

from The Southern Review

> "Unpicturable beings are realized, and realized with intensity almost like that of hallucination. They determine our vital attitude as decisively as the vital attitude of lovers is determined by the habitual sense, by which each of us is haunted, of the other being in the world."
> —William James, *The Varieties of Religious Experience*

1. Of course, there were many reports, as might be expected in a case like this.

2. Some say narrative ended with Borges. I sometimes believe that, and though the business of online blogs and the lovely young woman in New York with emerald eyes and lustrous auburn hair who kept a very personal one figures into much of this, as good a proof as any of the larger phenomenon of narrative's ending, still, there's no avoiding Borges on the matter.

3. Interestingly enough, a fact exists about him, documented by several sources, but not contained in any of the several available biographies, in English, anyway.

Which would include: Emir Rodríguez Monegal's *Borges: A Literary Biography*, New York, 1978 (quite good, actually, well-researched and heartfelt, even if it is dated, written by a Uruguayan who knew and understood the man, was even on a first-name basis with Borges' rather stuffy mother who largely controlled her bachelor son's life and so much longed to have her lineage recognized, have her son be thought of as an Argentine aristocrat); and Woodall's *The Man in the Mirror of the Book,* London, 1996 (also surprisingly good, with a lot of zip to it, as you might expect, it being written by a British journalist, and he catches some of the many slips in a first biography like Rodríguez Monegal's, little things, such as the fact that Borges always claimed that when Perón took over in 1946 and Borges lost his modest position that supported him—a job as an assistant at a branch library in a leafy but grim Buenos Aires suburb—he was transferred as a cruel joke by the thugs of ever-grinning, golden-haired Eva Perón herself to a position as chief inspector of Poultry and Rabbits at the Calle Córdoba Marketplace, when in actuality, the post that Borges was assigned to—and, naturally had to refuse, therefore losing any means of support—was simply Chief Inspector of Poultry, B. adding the "Rabbits" in embellishment and that suddenly becoming fact in itself, picked up by commentators on the Argentine master for many years); and Williamson's recent *Borges: A Life,* London, 2004 (truly terrible, written by somebody who is identified on the otherwise handsome jacket provided by the publisher—a bold aqua and yellow border, encasing a sepia photo of an aging Borges in a fine British-tailored suit and looking in his blindness suitably metaphysically startled, as the camera catches him staring up from a big writing desk—yes, Williamson, identified there as the "King Alfonso XIII Professor of Spanish Literature at the University of Oxford and Fellow of Exeter College," delivers the plodding and almost too-detailed account of the life, spanning nearly six hundred pages and sounding like a lot of academic criticism nowadays, more or less a massive sophomore lit paper gone somehow wrong through the usual earnest drudgery of beating to death some flimsy thesis, in this case arguing that Borges' short stories, which were, in fact, anything but autobiographical, were, in fact, very autobiographical and largely the product of his sexual frustration, biographer Williamson obscenely going on and on with it in turgid, fully laughable line-by-line analysis in that vein, though what was very entertaining was David Foster Wallace's brilliant review in the *New York Times Book Review* bombing the biography, frankly calling it essentially dishonest, and then a whiny and typically testy letter of the sort you would expect from anybody called the King Alfonso XIII Professor of Spanish, pompously defending himself and personally attacking Wallace and his own actually fine fiction; the letter was printed in the *NYTBR* the next week).

To repeat, one important and often referred to fact of Borges' life turns up in none of those three books, though so many people, orally and in print, speak of it in so many places elsewhere.

4. Simply enough, Borges could never sleep in a bed from which he could see a mirror. True, the Argentine master's lifelong fear, bordering on phobia, about mirrors has been well documented, and how often it is indeed found in the poems, essays, and stories, the way he suspected that the ultimate horror of mirrors was that they tossed back our watery, surely ghostly sense of self, or repeated us to the point that we didn't know who exactly we were, if, as it turns out, we are anybody at all. To avoid this problem at his own home, the apartment where he lived most of his long life as a bachelor with his widowed mother on Calle Maipú in Buenos Aires, was quite simple. Actually, Borges' room was the smaller of the two bedrooms in the place, what photographs of the apartment show as almost a monk's cell with a tiny iron framed bed with a cross over it and a single dark-wood bookcase, no mirror, of course, in that chamber, while the lavish master bedroom with fine antique furniture and oriental carpets and certainly more than one mirror was not only his mother's room during her long lifetime, but the same even after she died; Borges kept it exactly as she had left it, seemingly a shrine to her, as he himself, aging and increasingly going blind, ivory-handled walking cane in hand, would enter the apartment after an evening out and in the dark never fail to say aloud, "Mother, I'm home." No, the problem with the mirrors wasn't a matter of his life at home, but it was entirely a matter of so much of his later life spent travel-

ing, as at last the world discovered him; suddenly in the age of jet travel, Borges was celebrated on a global scale as no serious writer had ever been celebrated before. Tokyo, Cambridge (Mass.), Paris, Mexico City, San Antonio, Texas, Jerusalem, Madrid. It made no difference where it might be, and the blind Borges would be escorted into a good hotel room by the bell captain in a maroon uniform with gold epaulets, let's say, Borges would poke around a bit with the cane and ask where the mirror was, and then have that captain summon several more bellboys in maroon uniforms with gold epaulets, let's also say, to wrestle and yank with the big tortoiseshell furniture, until they had the configuration right.

Without the mirror visible, Borges could sleep in whatever foreign city he found himself in—horns blaring lonely in the black night the way they do in a foreign city, strange voices overheard hauntingly in the nighttime hallways of a hotel, the way they are overheard in the hotel of a foreign city—sleep very comfortably after lecturing or simply being, indeed, internationally celebrated once more, knowing that he could not see a mirror from his bed, and, more so—because, after all, he *was* blind—knowing that the silvery slab could not see him.

5.   Or, to put it more exactly, so the mirror couldn't see him *dreaming*, dreams being a mirror of reality, and mirrors being somehow a dream of unreality.

6.   Take a moment and think about it. It was then that the idea of narrative ended, no?

7.   But there are other reports, other theories.

8.   I mean, think some more about the whole topic yourself. There was a time you saw a stranger on the street who reminded you of somebody you had never known, and narrative for all intents and purposes ended.

9. Or, there was a nail puzzle—chromed ten-penny nails, twisted to-gether—and you held it in your hands and got ready for your most nimble dexterous assault, staring at the thing and studying it hard, before starting what you were sure was going to be a complicated project—and then it just loosened as easily as that, one chrome ten-penny serpentine nail with a round flat head in one hand, and another chrome ten-penny serpentine nail with a round flat head in the other hand, and you were quietly startled, half jarred, to see them come apart without even any working to render them free, shed like faded petals dropping from a withered blossom, and you said to yourself, yes, "Narrative has ended."

10. Also, before going on, I myself have been thinking about that business with Borges. I have been thinking that what he certainly knew was very true: that mirrors in waking life are one thing, where as protected and at least relatively safe as you try to believe that you are in the blue-skied, cloud-tumbling sunshine (be careful not to step on your dark shadow, always knock on mahogany), the old routine of the so-called routine, the rumored day-to-day, straightening your tie to look OK with a brave face, checking that the slip isn't showing beneath the hem of your best dark green silk dress, yes, in waking you always know, or knew, as Borges knew, that all that fragile—and supposed—safety is nothing and it simply disintegrates when up against the utter horror of a mirror watching you sleep, or, as said, dream. For Borges that was ultimately it: the whole undermining of narrative was there in dreaming itself, the netherworld we inhabit when sleeping, stories each of us drifts through that, in truth, are not stories at all, are not the recounted or narrated, because while dreams are actually transpiring they are as real as any-thing else, and to think of a tarnished, purple and gold iridescent mirror with its own reality watching that, questioning all of that, mirroring the mirroring that actually isn't mirroring, if you will, and ... and ... but enough of that tack, except to say, what Borges knew was that narrative had no other choice but to, well, end.

11. OK, look at it another way.

12. Once, this guy sitting next to me on a stool was looking at me in a bar.

It was somewhere around Ninth Avenue or possibly close enough to it, the Theater District proper. (I don't want to be too specific here, so take your pick: It could have been the sleek, crisp-table-clothed West Bank bar, downstairs in the orange high-rise that offers subsidized housing for theater people, a lot of pals of mine living there—some job-to-job actors and one struggling playwright—and even if the West Bank is pretty upscale, those theater people who just get by financially do often tend to drink in the place; or it could have been the dump just down Ninth Avenue, Rudy's, free hot dogs grilling behind the bar and duct tape on the upholstered booths, the glowing jukebox playing such loud sixties and seventies stuff, like the theme from *Shaft* or whatever; or it could even have been Sardi's with its famous rust-red walls splattered with black-framed pen-and-inks of theater notables, maybe there in the cozy separate bar at the front, where the sunlight late in the afternoon in winter comes through the slatted old venetian blinds in zebra stripes, dust motes suspended like little stars in the all but empty nook, and the bartender Gus from Flatbush in his proper white jacket knows that it's good that at least a few everyday people like me come into otherwise legendary Sardi's, and a bottle of beer actually isn't any more than what you'd pay most anywhere else in the Theater District.) I was sitting there, at the bar in one place or the other, and the guy kept glancing over at me, a guy in good shape and probably in his late thirties, with longish dark hair, wearing a tweed sport jacket, open-collar dress shirt, and jeans; he finally just said to me, almost as if I knew what he was thinking, or at least would be interested in what he was thinking.

"It threw me for a loop, you might say," he pronounced aloud.

"Excuse me," I said.

"It really, really threw me for a loop."

That's how it began. We talked a little as we drank at the bar, exchanged lines on routine stuff, and then he got back to what he really had to say.

"She was something else, coming along just when I had nearly given up on any relationship with any woman ever working out well. I paint, have had some luck with it, and there were always plenty of women, sort of artists' groupies, and there was one marriage, but none of it worked out, as I said, very well."

The way I think I understood it was that the affair started rather randomly, a chance meeting. It happened on the subway platform when he helped her pick up some books and such she had in a loop-handled shopping bag, yellow, that broke (he was specific about the color of the bag), and they got to talking and laughing, and she gave him her cell phone number in the course of it. Before she even got a call from him, she apparently had gone to a gallery in Chelsea to see some of his paintings, and when they did meet for drinks and dinner, they were so enamored with one another that there was lovemaking back at his place that very evening, just before he had to go to London to help set up a public gallery exhibit with his work. While he was in Europe for that week, there were some long distance calls, each of them saying how much he or she missed the other, each of them saying how much he or she had never met anybody quite like the other. He explained she was somewhat younger than him, only twenty-seven, but he wasn't so much older that there was anything really off about it, it was all within reasonable range, a dozen years; he said he was thirty-nine. And he emphasized it wasn't just her attractiveness, but other things too.

"Not to play down the fact she was attractive," he said. "Tall and with good posture, slim and small-breasted, with that lustrous auburn hair, like I said, and really emerald eyes, skin very white. Even if her teeth were a bit buck, or the front two of them sort of hinging toward each rather than flat so you noticed that, yet that, too, was somehow right, sort of a poutily Nordic overbite, really nice when she smiled. And she smiled a lot, beamed, really, with a such a lovely white smile, sort of nodding her head as she did it, sort of seeming like she was more or less happy as all hell. Which was wonderful, buoyant, but even that wasn't it. It could just have been something shared at first, and now that I think of it, maybe it was that we had Africa in common."

"Africa?" I asked him.

"I had put in a confused couple of years in the Peace Corps in Sierra Leone, which, if nothing else, is where I learned I really wanted to paint. Just the whole visual explosion of beautiful Africa, color like you have never seen before, the sheer wallop of the oozing honey sunshine making everything in Africa, no matter how shabby it is—the rutted red dirt roads, the spilling green vegetation, the scruffily happy people sometimes in close to rags of all sorts of wild colors—that sunshine put it all somehow in too-clear focus, entirely beautiful. Just seeing it convinced me I should pursue my painting seriously when I returned home. She had lived in Africa herself, Cameroon, and her father was a career man in the foreign service and was stationed there in Cameroon the longest. Her mother had died when she was only seven and she, like her sister before her, was sent to a swank boarding school in Switzerland, not because she was rich, but because tuition payment was a perk her father got for being in the foreign service. Nevertheless, she always spent summers in Africa, loved it, told me that she loved how I obviously had loved Africa too. She made me remember things about Africa. She talked to me of how the political thugs in Cameroon bought cheap splashy-print dashikis with a photo of the strongman head of state silk-screened on the front, the way thugs in every sub-Saharan African country—including Sierra Leone—always bought dashikis like that to try to play up to whatever strongman head of state there was in their own country at the moment, and how she and her sister used to wear them themselves as kids just because they thought the big things were ultra cool. She talked to me about trips she and her sister would take on their own to villages far from Yaoundé, the Cameroon capital, back-packing together in the summer, and she laughed to remember how the women who were prone to motion sickness and rode with you in those so-called mammy wagons, the little Toyota vans painted crazily and what passed for long-distance transportation in Cameroon, those women always brought their lidded old cocoa tins for any journey, to politely regurgitate into them for an entire sweating, twelve-hour trip through the winding hillside roads, that itself a something wonderful about Africa too. I had seen the same in Sierra Leone, how polite the women were about it, how also entirely dignified they were about it, ladylike, and she made me remember that. I will be honest. I missed her terribly when I was in London. We laughed a lot on the phone, and we laughed a lot when I got back from London overseeing the setting up of the exhibit and I got put up at the Commander Hotel."

"On Forty-eighth Street?" I asked him.

"Exactly. Right there on Forty-eighth, across from the Longacre Theater."

"And you were in love?"

But he didn't quite answer that, only said:

"You know, I didn't like the fact that she smoked, and not to get too far ahead myself, but that could have been the clue, or what pro-duced the clue signaling the mess that ensued. And I'll get to what happened in the deli when I was with her buying a simple six-pack of plain old red and white cans of Budweiser and she did what she did regarding the pack of cigarettes, which maybe was a *very* big clue, or maybe it's all I have to go on now, I suppose.

"Anyway, she would come to see me at the Commander Hotel af-ter she got out of work in the Fashion District, where she copy-edited for fashion ads and catalogs, which was probably why she dressed as well as she did, chic and quietly classy clothes. I guess I should have filled in the fact that for her senior year she went to a prep school in Philadelphia, again on the state department tab, an Episcopal operation that she loved, her taking the last year there to make college application easier, rather than doing it from the boarding school in Switzerland. Then she did her undergrad work, an English major, at the University of Arizona in Tucson, which she said was sort of an ongoing vacation, not very academic whatsoever, and she admitted that she should have spent a little more time thinking about where to apply. She said she went there only because a bunch of kids from the prep school in Philadelphia had gone or were going there, probably seeking some sun and escape from the Northeastern deep freeze that she really didn't need to escape, having spent so much time in Cameroon. Anyway, you know how that is, it would be comfortable for her because she would have friends there."

"Of course," I said, wondering where he was going with this. "Of course."

I mean, what else could I say?

I ordered another beer, and I did let this guy go on—and *on*, I suppose.

13. It seems that while he had been in London, the landlord for the apartment he leased in one of those blood-red brick tenements of which some still do exist on Ninth Avenue, not yet falling prey to the vicious yuppification of the whole old Hell's Kitchen neighborhood, had to start tearing walls out to go after a gas leak. The landlord had insurance that would put the few residents up in hotels for a while, and this guy at the bar who was entirely enamored with the young woman (listening, I thought that was good word for it, "enamored") decided to just go over a couple of blocks on Forty-eighth Street to the Commander, a good yet older midrange place where he got one of the rooms high up on the fourteenth, a corner one on the Eighth Avenue side, with a balcony, no less. And from that balcony he could see, then in summer, clear over the office buildings and the tenements, plus the puffs of feathery green treetops here and there, right to the Hudson, even see the

huge, top-heavy white cruise ships easing in and out of the couple of piers still used by cruise ships there. He would paint in his studio in a converted industrial garage over on Eleventh Avenue, then come back to the room high up in the Commander, take a nap with the windows and the doors to the balcony wide open, the sounds of taxis honking and trucks grinding through gears far enough below that it was almost distant and lulling.

"You know what I mean, the noise being rather pleasant," he said to me.

"I suppose I do," I said, "kind of like distant surf, or maybe a thunderstorm rumbling a couple of towns over in a town in the suburban hills, distant noise can be lulling."

"That's it exactly." He looked right at me. "You seem to be following me on all of this."

I nodded.

"Let's say I painted well that day," he said. "Let's say I felt good, and taking a nap like that, the drapes almost breathing in and out in the easy cadence of it all, it was all a most pleasant matter of sleeping some and waking some, still dressed and stretched out on the maroon floral print of the bedspread, knowing that soon enough I would hear a knock on the door, knowing that soon enough this tall, beautiful woman would materialize, smiling, softly laughing. We would sit around at the Commander and talk, usually out on the balcony, have dinner somewhere, sit around and talk at the Commander some more later with maybe a few beers bought at a delicatessen, soon enough making love and then relaxing and just lying around in bed some more after that, talking and talking still some more, which was always the very best part. We were well beyond that first stage in a relationship where you savor what you have in common, like Africa, basking in that, and now we basked in talking about everything. We talked about small things, art we liked, movies we liked, books we recently read. We talked about serious things, like the big sadness of my own divorce, which I survived, and the bigger sadness, surely, of her own mother dying of cancer when she was only seven, it happening when her father had been assigned to Jamaica. She told me, very seriously, that at first it seemed to have had more of an effect on her sister, eleven then, than on her at seven, and she herself had been really too young to realize the import of it, not knowing then that for her it would mean a life of being sent away to schools, and not knowing then that she would have the predictable teenage warfare when her father remarried later and she had to adjust to having a step mom, especially after she and her sister were used to having had their father all to themselves for so many years. Once, lying there naked together, the view from the bed and through the open balcony doors showing only big piled-up summer clouds igniting in all unheard-of pastels for a sunset there above what must have been New Jersey, she admitted how she had finally realized, years later, that maybe her mother dying so young probably had more of an effect on her than she had any chance of knowing when a kid, and even lately she kept having the same dream that she had had for years, what really told the story. In it she repeatedly found herself seven years old again, wandering out of the bungalow her father was given as a consular section staffer there in Kingston, Jamaica. She simply kept looking at the flowers, maybe cascading bougainvillea and giant, fleshy wild orchids, she kept staring at the sea, no sense of her mother gone but knowing, 'The flowers don't look the same anymore, I wonder why? The sea doesn't either.' I was always and very simply *happy* to be with her there in the Commander Hotel, happy to the point that for me it was half unreal.

"In truth," he said, "it reminded me of that often quoted line from Borges—you see, I do a lot of reading myself, have always liked Borges—that line where he says that we accept reality so easily, so readily, maybe because we suspect that nothing is real."

"Borges?" I asked him.

"Yeah. Like I said, I'm a painter, but, like I also said, I read an awful lot too."

I got a little nervous thinking of trying on him what I did try on him next, but it was as if I had no choice:

"Do you know that thing about Borges and mirrors in his hotel rooms?"

"What?"

He spoke that as if to imply, What the hell are you talking about?

"Forget it, OK," I told him, "and to get back to what you were saying, that you were in love, right?"

14. But again he balked on answering that directly, and after so much buildup from him, what did eventually happen, the pivot, came rather fast, the way he filled everything in for me there at the bar.

Apparently, for the month or so this relationship went on in New York, it was mostly a matter of weekday evenings together. Very busy, he was painting as hard as he could because they wanted a few more canvases for the gallery exhibit in London, were expanding it. Also, there was the matter of geography, and with her living over in Williamsburg in Brooklyn—as the latest influx into the city of people that age, twenty-somethings, inevitably live in Williamsburg, think it defines hipness, the urbanly exotic for them, I guess—that meant that most of their time together was spent there around the Theater District, with her sometimes staying the night at the hotel and walking to work down around Herald Square from the Commander in the morning. In short, he really didn't know much about her life over there in Williamsburg.

And not to preface it anymore myself, what eventually happened was that he discovered she had a blog on the Web, a *very* personal one, to put it mildly.

It seems he was in the very same bar in which I was sitting next to him now (the more I think about it, I think I can say it *was* the West Bank), and he ran into an old pal of his who was a literary agent. As the painter told the old pal about what could only be called, as said, his current enamorment, talked about a girl who grew up all over the world and went to boarding school in Switzerland and now lived over in Williamsburg, commuting from there to her job in Manhattan as a fashion copy editor, the young woman he was currently seeing, the agent said to him, "Man, if that ever doesn't sound like this blogger who goes by the online name Kiddlet." Yes, the situation was that this agent—always looking for new literary talent and hopefully the chance to rescue himself from his own problems with alimony from two marriages, dig himself out via a trendy blockbuster sale to some huge and typically mind-less conglomerate-owned publishing house that was only interested in another trendy blockbuster sale—this agent lately had his young assistants in the office keep tabs on the Web on some of the better personal blogs they got word on. Apparently, a very successful, re-ally big-time agent had discovered a young writer who recently got a huge book contract on the basis of her confessional blog that had developed a wide Net following, and every other agent was trying to cash in on the phenomenon, coattail it. The more the agent told the painter about what he had read from this so-called Kiddlet, the more it did, in fact, sound rather all too familiar to the painter. Not that the agent had thought the stuff would work as a book when he did see it himself, even if it did have verve, he said, or an engaging offbeat voice, wonderfully observant; the agent said that his assis-tants, young people and all Internet junkies, showed him so many of these diary blogs, and he still hadn't found one with the right writ-ing or material that would make him want to contact the person to see if there might be a novel or book of some variety in it.

"Actually, I had to fly back to London to finish setting up the exhibit," the painter said, "and it was the night before I left that I talked to the agent friend. And later that night, back at the hotel, the Commander on Forty-eighth, I typed in the words 'Kiddlet'—an in-vented word in itself, so it was entirely unique—and 'blog' into Google, and I came up with it. I mean, how should I put this, *sure enough* I came up with it."

He shook his head, troubled.

14. For the painter, it all got pretty painful.
(*Note: The numeral 14 has just been repeated here, but considering that numeral 10 got x-ed out—a bit muddled, that section—it seems to me that an extra numeral and section need to be inserted to make up for it, not so much a tribute to narrative consistency as just adherence to basic chronology, no?*)

15. "I've never been much of a computer guy," he confessed, "especially as a painter protecting my space and lately refusing to deal with even having e-mail, even a cell phone, if you can believe it. If somebody has to get in touch with me I have my dealers and gallery people to handle it. I don't think I've ever lost anything by not having all that noise assaulting me all the time. In fact, I think I've gained a whole lot, protected that space well. I can get in touch with whoever I want, but it's tougher for anybody to get in touch with me—the proverbial worn, orange Spalding basketball solidly in my court, if you know what I mean. I didn't even know much or care much about these so-called blogs, yet I suppose I knew there were political blogs and literary blogs and sports blogs, most bloggers playing sort of an online game, I guess, getting a measure of celebrity with a made-up name, like an old CB radio handle, or, more exactly, getting a pretend or virtual celebrity, at least among the couple of dozen or so blogger pals who read their posts, comment on them, chat-room style. But these personal blogs, maybe lifestyle blogs, I guess were the strangest, and quite popular, and I read around and found others that Kiddlet's linked me to. But that was later, and that night I just clicked the mouse, looked at the screen of my overpriced silvery Mac PowerBook G-4 laptop set on the little faux mahogany dresser/desk

in the pink-wallpapered room high up in the Commander—there was an AirPort-card wireless connection there, very reliable—and I got Kiddlet's blog. It had graphics pretty sophisticated, all done in white text on dark, dark blue, the letters themselves sort of stars in the sky, Kiddlet's blog itself titled, 'The Now of the Now of It,' which could have come from Beckett, I'm not sure. To put it mildly, or frankly, I can tell you there was no doubting that this was the woman I was seeing, I mean, it didn't take any detective work, computer forensics, and the agent buddy was smack on target with the admittedly very chance association."

"You sure you never thought about Borges," I asked him, "not just that this sounds Borgesian, but especially that thing he had about mirrors in hotel rooms? You've heard of that, no?"

He just looked at me, a bit confused again.

"Or nail puzzles that solve themselves," I said, "or a stranger on the street who reminds you of somebody you never have known?"

"Can I buy you a beer?" was all he said, as he ordered a next one for himself.

"Sure," I said.

16. Apparently, he started reading entries, documentation of Kiddlet's life as a freewheeling twenty-seven-year-old woman in the city. And it wasn't so much that she had been dishonest about anything with him, and they had spent enough time together already that they had talked a lot about their past, exchanged intimacies, but this was all too intimate, all too revealing. Just a few recent entries, without even dipping into the archives that were cataloged with little white roman numerals below on the achingly glowing dark blue page (he was very specific, definitely the painter in him) was enough to convince him that he had merely imagined who she was, maybe the way he wanted to envision her, be enamored with her, and her real life in Williamsburg and environs was obviously dramatically different. He said the whole

thing would have been comical, almost another lousy TV sit-com episode premise, a giant laugh, if it wasn't so absolutely painful, for him,
anyway.

"I'll confess, I had fallen in love with her, the way you do fall
in love without ever daring to say it, let alone to the other person
but even to yourself, and you just have certain attitudes that suggest
the utter airiness, the total selflessness of love. I suppose I already
cared about her the way you do when you do truly love someone,
and, I mean, even if she wasn't sure just how much she had been
affected by her mother dying like that when she was seven, I knew
that whenever I was with her that that fact itself, how she had been
left alone at that age, broke my heart, to think of her as a child being sent off on her own to schools from whatever country her father
was assigned to at the time, and I wanted to protect her from all
of that sort of pain in the world. With me always there with her
now, I told myself, she would never be alone again, which is what
love is all about, isn't it? The selflessness, the concern. That and the
truth that William James has argued for in that wonderful tome of
American tomes, *The Varieties of Religious Experience*, such a dark,
revealing book, such an essentially haunting and ultimately tran-
scendent book. One of his chief arguments for religion itself in the
chapter called 'The Reality of the Unseen' poses that to understand
how the visionary and half-hallucinated can be, in essence, very
real, is to call to mind the state of being in love, when you think of
the other person all the time, when you have them in mind when
apart, picturing them, hearing them, surely touching them in the
imagination, to the point that any distinction between the real and
the unreal melts, or maybe evanesces is the better way of describing it, because a word like 'melt' entails too much suggestion of the
physical. I pictured her all the time, even pictured myself protecting
her as a child all the time, and it was real."

I looked at him, he looked at me.

"I just saw that quote somewhere," I said. And I think I had. "Or a passage close to exactly that from James. I'm not kidding. As an epigraph on a short story or something."

He casually adjusted the lapel of his sport jacket, ran his hand through the thick, longish dark hair.

"It's a great observation, though isn't it?" was all he said.

Granted, for a painter he was definitely a reader, also not the usual sort of citizen you run into in idle conversation at any bar, even the sophisticated West Bank. But just as when I brought up the Borges business, or the ideas on strangers and nail puzzles and such, he didn't seem to respond, didn't make much out of my recognizing the William James quote either, when I mentioned having recently encountered it. He simply went on with the whole painfulness of discovering the blog called "The Now of the Now of It," the discovery happening the night before he was to fly back to London.

Actually, the evening before discovering it, he had been on the phone for a full hour with the young woman, saying their good-byes, and he sensed she was a little drunk, returning his call on her cell phone from a midtown bar where she had spent some happy-hour time with some people from work. Apparently, she whisperingly said in that conversation how much she missed him already, would miss him while he was away, how she really wished he didn't have to go. She purred that she just wanted to spend forever and ever with the windows thrown wide open and the balcony doors thrown wide open way atop the clutter of Eighth Avenue—everybody hurrying in and out of the theaters, the handsome Hudson beyond—in the Commander Hotel. She said all of that on the phone, and now at his computer, the painter saw how the most recent entry in the blog covered that very evening before and how later that night (she made absolutely no mention of him, the painter, in the entry), true, later it seemed that after they spoke on the phone and she did take the L-train back to Williamsburg, she, as the hip voice of Kiddlet would have it, stopped by the apartment in Williamsburg of a friend named Alex "to smoke a quick bowl," then headed out to a Williamsburg club called Catastrophe with him, to hear a blasting rock band that had some of his pals playing in it, the whole gang of them talking, laughing, talking all night, till after four in the morning when, totally drunk, they all had nightcaps behind closed doors after the place shut down, snorted a few lines. Who knows what happened with said Alex after that, and the painter explained that there was a highlight whenever the name "Alex" appeared in the text and you could click there to link to his own blog, which the painter did, to see a "Blogger Profile" photograph up top of a rather retro Mr. T. sort of guy, as the painter would have it, "right down to the muscle T-shirt, stiff Mohawk, and enough heavy body jewelry to sink an aircraft carrier." The painter didn't read on, he couldn't read on, but as maybe the aforementioned Beckett would have it, he *did* read on, he couldn't help himself, checking other recent entries, other adventures in the big city of Kiddlet, fashion copy editor in midtown by day and also—by night and on weekends, anyway—chain-smoking, pool-playing, bar-hopping wild child, yes, Kiddlet, semi-notorious among her blogger pals, all of whose sites you could link to on her site. Kiddlet liked to booze and do drugs (not just some pot, and there seemed to be a lot, truly an awful lot, of cocaine, always called "blow"), and Kiddlet liked a lot of sex (yes, she had told the painter about her early brushes with lesbianism, what had seemed just dalliance to him and understandably happening when she was at the all-girls boarding school in Switzerland, perhaps some of it lingering into college in Arizona, but he had never expected that it was still very much part of a wholeheartedly bisexual menu, and there was an entire entry in the archive, a mini essay, about what she had been discussing with her "Chick of the Moment" on the innate sensual beauty of the melodically polysyllabic word "cunnilingus," which Kiddlet held not enough people used anymore; there was one very excited—and for the painter painful—recent entry on some energetic gymnastics with the "Two Croatian Guys" she had met in a club one evening, "an awesome, awesome, *awesome* nite even by the standards of your not-so-humble correspondent Kiddlet!" and an equally enthusiastic series of posts on her short-lived, but very satisfying, affair with a shy and quiet eighteen-year-old, "Beautiful Boy," who she moved in on slowly, stealthily, as soon as she sighted him at a pool table at a Williamsburg bar, a first-semester freshman at NYU who, she sighed, was "tall, very tall, handsome enough at that delicate age to make you wince" and presumably no slouch in bed, "Children, do you know how to say *great*!" being the direct quote, the punch line, on that aspect of his CV.) There never seemed to be any real continuing relationships. Maybe ultimately worst—because, after all, booze and drugs and sex of whatever variety are surely a person's own tastes and preferences, the painter said—was what appeared to be emerging as a markedly sleazy side to much of it, how she and one of her bar-hopping pals, another young woman who regularly prowled around with her, would cadge drinks while sitting at the bar, let's say, at 3:00 a.m. from a bartender at a classier SoHo place, a guy who thought he had a chance with one or even the kinky twosome of them, how she and all her bar-hopping female pals liked to talk about how they regularly and drunkenly played plenty of other guys along at a lot bars for free drinks and drugs, that kind of thing.

17. "I remembered too many things," he said, "the two of us sitting there outside on the hotel balcony, or in the same room where we had whispered such fragile intimacies so often, in the bruised purple dark, and after reading enough of that blog that night, I felt like a confirmed chump, not to put too fine a point on it.

"I started thinking about that scene in the delicatessen, when I stopped with her after dinner to pick up a six-pack of Bud, and that was early on in the relationship. I remembered the way that when I walked up to pay in the cramped, yellow-lit place with all its bananas and all its canned peanuts there on Eighth Avenue, she simply said, offhand, that she needed cigarettes, she told the guy behind the counter who was ringing up the beer to give her a pack of Doral Lights, and she made some phony gesture of opening her shoulder bag as the clerk asked me if it was all together, with her then looking at me, saying, 'Oh, do you need money?' to which I told her of course not. Yes, there was something about how she just expected me to pay for her cigarettes, or simply thought if she acted fast enough in the shuffle there at the deli counter, I would end up paying for them, sleazy. I couldn't get that out of my mind now, and it made me think of other things, the way she kept saying that she would love so much to be with me in London during my opening, that she really didn't have the money for a ticket, but she would love so much if the two of us could be together there, for her to share with me the whole experience. She said she knew that already there was some buzz about the London exhibit, that I would be, well, celebrated somewhat when I eventually went back a third time for the opening, and she said again how much she would like to go, that she had already checked the prices of air tickets online. When I joked to her that it might be great to do exactly that, she purred some more about how she did really, really wish she had the money to do it, and asked outright if I could pay for the trip for her. In fact, I knew she made pretty good money on that job she had, and when I joked that she didn't want me to degenerate to being a sugar daddy altogether, she responded by tightening her case more or less automatically, as if she was used to flatly saying it: 'There's nothing wrong with a guy paying when he invites a girl somewhere, is there?' But I hadn't really invited her. And that seemed sleazy too. OK, OK, maybe I was reading into it, but it all compounded in my mind, beginning with the cigarettes episode, it all made a strange kind of sense, now that I had read her blog. She became something altogether different in my mind, whether she was in reality different or not, no longer the prize I had made her out to be. And I felt taken, all right, I felt stupid, and, admittedly, I also felt more than a bit heartbroken, but having that other information about her, I knew where I stood, if nothing else.

"So I decided that the trip to London would make a good way to cut it all off naturally enough. I didn't call her from there this time, and I didn't return any of her calls, the messages she left at the hotel where I was staying, so it seemed she got the idea. And before long, in my apartment again on Ninth Avenue, I was back with a former lady friend, who I had much more in common with, anyway. I decided I would work to make that relationship work, and now I know how important hard work like that is in a relationship. No, she's not all that much older than Kiddlet, but there's a whole lot more depth there, or what you might call lifestyle depth. She's a lawyer who spends most of her own free time and money with a group of other young lawyers who fly down together from New York to the Texas-Mexico border together, working pro bono to cut through the red tape to allow street kids in places like Nuevo Laredo and Matamoros and Juárez get legal immigration status and then eventual adoption by American couples. She's really brave about it, standing up to the Mexican police and government thugs, putting herself in real physical danger down there, and I've come to realize how important, even altogether sexually attractive, social concern and rare bravery like that are in the world."

18. But he still wasn't finished. Because then *"the other thing"* happened.

19. He started to get scared of all the narrative that was out there, he said, those thousands and thousands of blogs, everybody talking, everybody crying the story of their lives and bellowing their opinions, everybody maybe lying, but who cared, because that was what narrative was all about, anyway. And he admitted that the break with the young woman wasn't as clean as he had portrayed it, and he did, in fact, when in London, go online to see what was in her latest blog entries. He knew, however, from the Web site for his own painting, which somebody had helped him set up, that anybody with a site could check

who was visiting by using a simple tracker/counter or sitemeter, so he made sure that he protected against that. He read by accessing only Google's cache pages, never her site itself, which meant he was only entering Google's site and couldn't be tracked. Or—a safer method, he soon decided—he typed into Google as search words "Kiddlet" along with the date, to see if there was an entry that day, then he actually kept reading the best he could without visiting the site by incessantly typing into Google as search words the last few words of a sentence from the brief Google display of the hit, which would produce in a search the next few words of the next sentence, the painter reading that and then typing in the last few words of that sentence to produce in a search the next few words of the next sentence, the goofily frilled Google logo that touted some concocted holiday—red, yellow, blue, and green, with the big G—hovering atop the page and somehow belly-laughing at him. Reading like that—even if he felt sneaky doing it, obsessional and half stalkerish, out of character for him—he was constantly scared to see what he would find next, as he constructed the narrative, struggled with his own narrative force against the larger and prevailing anti-narrative force, bit by bit, hit by hit. He was scared, too, when he entered in the Google search window "Kiddlet," "The Now of the Now of It" and various search words that turned up in the mind, representing his worst fears, or close to that, that might be lurking there in the archives of Kiddlet's past posts. Using quotes, he imagined more and more scenarios: he typed in "Kiddlet," "The Now of the Now of It" and "drunk" and saw seven Google search result pages and 68 hit entries; he typed in "Kiddlet," "The Now of the Now of It" and "screwing" and saw a bigger list of fourteen pages and 136 entries (removing the "ing" led to, among other things, "screw buddy," what appeared to be a variation on "fuck buddy," and in the same sentence there the term—apparently describing said companion, most glowingly—"super-hottie" showed a full three times); he typed in "Kiddlet," "The Now of the Now of It" and not "coke" but that more colloquial "blow," and there were eleven pages and 110 entries, the noun turned up in her blog archives that many times, all right. But, to repeat, he *never* actually entered—officially visited—the site again, he certainly didn't want her to know he was scouring it. And, no, it wasn't a question of his passing judgment on her. He repeated to me that her lifestyle was her own business, and he said you could argue there was a certain freewheeling exuberance that continued to speak an electric, youthful don't-give-a-damnism, very honest and very humorous and with an undeniably alluring urban hipster voice, as the literary agent had observed; though it was also true that reading enough about such an iconic—or over the top—sex-and-the-city persona, with so much casual sex and so much drugging and sloppy drunkenness, complete with the occasional passing-out episode tossed in for good measure, could soon turn into a matter of dealing with what's usually and maybe not too kindly known as just a—one has to utter it, but probably he himself was being spitefully mean in his hurt, the painter said—"bar skank." The painter emphasized that I had to understand that this was somebody he had once been fantasizing about *marrying*, having *children* with one day.

"It was just that it was *all* not what I had expected," he said, "and just typing in words like those in my searches, or composing the sentences secretively, phrase by phrase, my gut would jump, suddenly nothing but a den of slithering baby grass snakes."

He also admitted to thinking back to the two of them together at the Commander, and he admitted he got sad. And sometimes he remembered something as simple as her smile and her happy laugh, those giant emerald green eyes, the prettily pouty overbite, and he got more than sad. But nervous and rattled all the while, too, to the point that he kept thinking more about blogs in general, he was *overwhelmed* with narrative, not just her escapades, but, again, all those stories of everybody out there, those thousands and thousands of bloggers, no, millions of bloggers, and he not only couldn't read her blog or other blogs, he couldn't read or think of reading *anything* for a while. Who

knew anymore what was real writing, narrative had ended, and there
was no story, no valid revelation in the world, only too much to be read
for any of it to have any consequence, only absolute meaninglessness.
He tried rereading his favorite books and couldn't get past ten pages,
Kerouac's *On the Road* or Bellow's *Humboldt's Gift* or James Agee's
Let Us Now Praise Famous Men, and the words on the page all looked
laughable, each book just another extended blog, leading nowhere, or
if it did lead anywhere it would be the ultimately frightening destination, all right, where narrative must go, "Which *was* nowhere," he said.
And . . . and . . .

20. And I might as well admit it, I myself had gotten to the point that
I couldn't read much of anything I tried either, so for me "*the other
thing*" had happened too.

21. Narrative had ended.

22. The furniture had been rearranged, so to speak, no mirror could
mirror life, *or* dreaming, for that matter.

23. I might as well *really* admit it.
    The painter's case was just one case, mine, actually.
    And I don't think of the young woman much at all now. I am a
writer, and making the writer a painter here, and making it all transpire in the course of a forced conversation in a bar, were attempts at
narrative legerdemain, what a writer like me does, even if it did get
clunky here with my having to do so much really forced explaining on
why my painter was such an avid reader, why he could execute so many
(way too many?) literary allusions. However, like the painter, I myself
did meet this twenty-seven-year-old woman when her yellow shopping
bag broke on the subway platform, the young woman a.k.a. Kiddlet in
her blog. I myself am thirty-nine years old, was in the Peace Corps in

Sierra Leone, and it was there, after Dartmouth on a baseball scholar-
ship, that I made the firm decision that I wanted to be not a painter but
a writer, of course. I live now in what used to be Hell's Kitchen, had
to fly to London a few times (a rare chance to teach a writing seminar
there and give what turned out to be a well-received public reading
of my fiction, then the rarer chance to talk twice to a British publisher about reissuing some of my stuff), and though I was also actually
displaced from my apartment on Ninth Avenue and, at my landlord's
expense, had to stay for a stretch in the Commander Hotel—so often with her, after she got out of work as a fashion-industry copy editor—even truths like that are deceiving, facts to be manipulated for not
always honest purpose, just more evidence of how vanished narrative
is, how, let's face it and as already asserted, it goes nowhere, is nothing,
doesn't even have the chance of telling us anything significant because
anybody is nobody, or nobody is anybody—or, yes, this is it, a beloved
isn't what you imagined she was, and be careful of mirrors, when either waking or surreptitiously sleeping; I suppose even my planting the
quote from William James at the starting gun's pop as an epigraph and
then having it referred to in the supposed (*don't laugh*) narrative here,
was and is more evidence of the ruinous duplicity afoot.

And it seemed as if for the world, not just me or the imaginary
painter (i.e. me), yes, for the entire world narrative had ended, those
smug French nihilists with their ton of language theory, any one of
them pontificatingly lecturing while puffing a Gitane on the dais of
the amphitheater filled with other attentively listening French nihilists
seated in the galleries and also puffing smelly Gitanes in that fine buff
stone bastion of supreme nihilism, the Collège de France on Rue des
Écoles there in Paris (lavender rain in Paris, strikingly brilliant sunshine in Paris, what does it matter?), they were right all along.

24. Narrative had ended. There was heard the quiet, restrained, ever-
so-smugly condescending patting of Gallic applause.

25. Narrative had really ended, imploded and then some.

26. Until something strange began happening. It took some time, but it happened.

On beaches, beaches all over this big, beautiful planet of ours—this place where the whole trick is to never lose sight of how special it all is, how it is all a matter of just so much precious oxygen, a finite amount, to be gulped and appreciated in these several dozen years any one of us is allowed, at best, to inhabit it—on beaches everywhere people would be walking alone, possibly in winter on the empty sands, admiring the ocean, admiring the waves. Waves that kept rolling in sets.

Mesmerizing waves, the glassy rise of the blue crests veined with foam, the building and building and building, one after another, arching in sets, each wave getting higher and higher, promising the final explosion, the beautiful and thundering and half-heavenly sudsy crescendo of it all, waves that seemed to say things full of promise, such as, "That observation in Rodríguez Monegal's biography of Borges is interesting, how Borges' mother longed for acknowledged aristocratic standing, *tell* me more," and, "That way that Borges embellished his own misfortune, saying that he was made inspector of Poultry *and* Rabbits, as addressed in Woodall's biography, is very interesting, *tell* me more," and, "Granted the recent Borges biography by Williamson, the King Alfonso XIII Professor of Spanish at Oxford, is a prototypical flat tire, still, nevertheless, that whole tale of Williamson attacking David Foster Wallace in the *NYTBR* is interesting in itself, please, please tell me *much* more." Which is to say, the waves all over the world, on sandy beaches everywhere as stared at by lone figures, did promise so much as they built—they hadn't, in fact, lost much of their essential power, inherent puissance.

27. The waves kept coming and coming.

28. Or, to put it yet *another* way, maybe narrative hadn't ended, which is to say, *hasn't* ended.

29. And, again, I can honestly say I don't think of her anymore.

I don't except once in a while, when I *do* still remember that trading of stories we did, often after lovemaking, especially early on and about the marvels of dreamy Africa, what I knew and what she knew and what was quite special for both of us, something shared. I suppose I was *hopelessly* in love for at least a while then. I mean, I speak fluent French, and (French intellectual nihilism aside) I don't know if I had ever been in an intimate relationship with a woman who could do the same—I guess I forgot to mention that sometimes we would speak French for a while just for fun, a little thing like that can become very important. Also, I can say what really scared me was that there was never any mention of me in *any* of the blogging, during the *whole* while we saw each other and she reported faithfully on other events. It was as if I and my own being weren't there, for all intents and purposes didn't exist in *her* narrative.

I was merely a reflection of a, well, mirrory reflection, I suppose, as in that repeatedly mentioned business of Borges and his having the furniture moved around so he couldn't see a hotel room's mirror, which is, of course, something I made up, a completely fabricated fact constructed out of the thinnest of thin verbal air for the narrative (or constant struggle to assert narrative? attempt at the classic narrative, a very true love story?) that I offer you here.

THE END

KISS

Melora Wolff

from The Southern Review

A THIN MOON TIPS ABOVE THE BEACH, AND FISHERMEN SLUMP IN sling-back chairs, waiting. Each fisherman keeps a lamp near his feet. The fishermen don't speak, though they are only a few yards from one another along the shore, and the night is passing, and they have sat here together through years and they are lonely. These men bring their wooden chairs and their lamps down to the beach every midnight so that something will happen in the darkness, where nothing much happens anymore but minutes and hours and the slow crawl of starfish through sand. Several churches sank into the encroaching sea a long time ago. On a low rock, one church spire remains amid a congregation of stones. Behind the fishermen, and beside a young girl, a man walks toward that spire.

The man feels old, stiff limbed and without the confidence of his youth, which he first noticed was gone only a few nights before, after he brushed his teeth and sank into his bed. But this night he walks through the fine sand with a girl who could be his granddaughter, he thinks, but is *not* his granddaughter, he also thinks, because he plans to kiss this girl, that's all, after he has pointed out to her the thin line of spilled ink where the water and sky are drawn together, after he has sung for her the steady B-flat music of the spheres and held the note for her to taste inside his mouth. But the kiss, when it happens, disappoints him. A cold air gusts across the water to meet him, fills his lungs, and stuns him as the inevitable, long-held final note of hymns once stunned him, and winded him, when he was a boy singing in church.

The fishermen, who have been dozing to the rhythms of the tide, waken to the kiss. They feel a strange, urgent tugging on their lines. The man does not know that the fishermen have dreamed. The fishermen themselves do not know that they have dreamed. How is it that they have caught all the drowned churches in their nets? The churches rise slowly from the sea, streaming and shining, lurching and plunging in the surf, and the bells of the churches swing, green with time. The old fishermen call out to one another, their first deep, wakeful cries in what seems to them centuries of solitude, their voices overlapping in waves, in octaves and descents. The men pull the churches toward the shore, or themselves toward the sea, using all their will, all their desire, all that's left of their rapture and grief.

CONTRIBUTOR NOTES

Chris Adrian is a pediatrician and divinity student in Boston. He is the author of two novels, *Gob's Grief* and *The Children's Hospital*, and his stories have appeared in *Best American Short Stories 1998*, *The New Yorker*, *The Paris Review*, *Zoetrope*, *Ploughshares*, and *Story*.

Daniel Alarcón is the associate editor of *Etiqueta Negra*. His collection *War by Candelight* was a finalist for the 2006 PEN/Hemingway Award. His first novel, *Lost City Radio*, was published by HarperCollins in February 2007.

Kevin Brockmeier is the author of the novels *The Brief History of the Dead* and *The Truth About Celia*, the story collection *Things That Fall From the Sky*, and the children's novels *City of Names* and *Grooves: A Kind of Mystery*. His work has appeared in *The New Yorker*, *McSweeney's*, *The Oxford American*, *The Georgia Review*, *Granta*, *The Best American Short Stories*, the *O. Henry: Prize Stories* anthology, and *The Year's Best Fantasy and Horror*. He is the recipient of an NEA Fellowship, three O. Henry prizes (one, a first prize), and the Borders Original Voices Award. He lives in Little Rock, Arkansas.

Austin Bunn has worked as a book ghostwriter, game designer for reality television, boat carpenter, and (primarily) as a magazine journalist. His non-fiction has appeared in the *Best American Science and Nature Writing*, *The New York Times Magazine*, *Wired*, other magazines now dead to him, and in the anthology *From Boys to Men: Gay Men Write About Growing Up*. He is the co-author, with independent film producer Christine Vachon, of *A Killer Life: How an Independent Film Producer Survives Deals and Disasters in Hollywood and Beyond*. He is a graduate of the Iowa Writers' Workshop.

Maile Chapman is a Schaeffer Fellow in Fiction at the University of Nevada, Las Vegas. "Bit Forgive" was written following a Fulbright year in Finland devoted to visiting sanatoria and other functional public buildings. She has lived in Ireland and Germany, and has an M.F.A. from Syracuse University.

Daniel Coudriet lives with his wife and son in Richmond, Virginia, and in Carcarañá, Argentina. His poems have appeared in *Verse*, *Denver Quarterly*, *American Letters & Commentary*, *Crazyhorse*, *The Iowa Review*, *Harvard Review*, *Conjunctions*, and elsewhere. His translations of the Argentinean poet Oliverio Girondo have appeared in *American Poetry Review*, *Massachusetts Review*, *Fascicle*, and elsewhere. His contribution to this anthology first appeared in an issue of *Mississippi Review* devoted to the Prose Poem.

Ramola D's fiction, essays, poems, and writer-interviews have appeared in *The Writer's Chronicle*, *Prairie Schooner*, *Indiana Review*, *Agni*, *Northwest Review*, *Small Spiral Notebook*, *Hyper Age*, *Literal Latte*, *Indian Express*, and other publications. Her collection of poems *Invisible Season* was published by Washington Writers' Publishing House in 1998. She is the recent recipient of a National Endowment for the Arts award in poetry (2005). She has worked as a technical writer and trainer, writing instructor, and freelance journalist, and currently teaches creative writing at George Washington University.

Tony D'Souza has contributed fiction to *McSweeney's*, *The New Yorker*, *Playboy*, *Tin House*, the *O. Henry Prize Stories*, and elsewhere. His first novel, *Whiteman*, a tale of identity, sex, and love, set in West Africa, debuted last year. *Whiteman* won the American Academy of Arts & Letters Sue Kaufman Award for Best First Fiction. His second novel, *The Konkans*, the story of an Indian man's love for his brother's white wife, releases in February 2008. Tony has received a 2006 NEA fellowship, a 2007 NEA Japan-Friendship fellowship, and a Lannan Foundation residency.

In addition to *Pindeldyboz Online*, where "Village of Ardakmoktan" originally appeared, **Nicole Derr**'s work has appeared in *The 13th Warrior Review* and *Words on Walls*. She holds a B.A. in German Studies from Washington College, where she studied Kafka's relationship to minor literature. Currently she reside in Allentown, Pennsylvania.

Julia Elliott's fiction has appeared in *The Georgia Review, Conjunctions, Puerto del Sol, Mississippi Review, Fence, Black Warrior Review, New Delta Review* and elsewhere. She also has a story forthcoming in *Tin House*. She lives in Columbia, South Carolina.

Brian Evenson is the author of seven books of fiction, including *Altmann's Tongue* (Knopf 1994), *The Brotherhood of Mutilation* (Earthling 2003), and *The Wavering Knife* (FC2 2004). His most recent novel, *The Open Curtain*, was listed by *Time Out New York* as one of the ten best books of 2006 and was a finalist for an Edgar Award. He is a recipient of an NEA Fellowship and two O. Henry Prizes. He serves as a senior editor for *Conjunctions* magazine. He directs the creative writing program at Brown University and lives in Providence, Rhode Island, with writer Joanna Howard and their dog Ruby.

Elizabeth Hand is the author of eight novels, including *Generation Loss*, and three short story collections, the most recent of which is *Saffron & Brimstone*. She is a longtime contributor to the *Washington Post Book World, Fantasy & Science Fiction Magazine*, and *DownEast*, among many others. "The Saffron Gatherers" is the final tale in "The Lost Domain," a story sequence examining obsessive love. Hand lives on the coast of Maine.

Robin Hemley is the author of seven books of fiction and nonfiction, and the winner of numerous awards for his fiction and nonfiction, including two Pushcart Prizes and first place in the Nelson Algren Award for Fiction from *The Chicago Tribune*. His work has recently been anthologized in *New Sudden Fiction, The Touchstone Anthology of Contemporary Nonfiction, Modern Love, 20 Over 40*, and his work has appeared recently in *Fourth Genre, Creative Nonfiction, 9th Letter, Columbia, The New York Times*, and *The Chicago Tribune*. His most recent books are *Turning Life into Fiction* (Graywolf) and *Invented Eden* (Bison Books, Nebraska). He is the Director of the Nonfiction Writing Program at the University of Iowa.

Nik Houser graduated from Wesleyan University where he won the Dorchester Prize for fiction. He lives in Northern California and is at work on two novels.

Nicole Kornher-Stace was born in Philadelphia in 1983, moved from the East Coast to the West Coast and back again by the time she was five, and currently lives in Saugerties, New York, with one husband, two ferrets, and many many books. Her short fiction has appeared in *Zahir* and *Rhapsoidia*, is forthcoming in *Fantasy Magazine*, and has been nominated for this year's Pushcart Prize. While she is currently looking for a publisher for her first novel, *Desideria*, she is at work on two others. Information on her work can be found at www.nicolekornherstace.com.

In his day life, Dr. **Geoffrey Landis** is a meek and mild-mannered scientist. During 2006 he was the Ronald E. McNair Visiting Professor of Astronautics at MIT, the institution where he received his undergraduate degrees in Physics and in Electrical Engineering. His scientific work includes being a member of the science team on the Mars Exploration Rovers mission and working on advanced technology for space flight at NASA Glenn Research Center. Dr. Landis writes under the name "Geoffrey A. Landis." An award-winning author, he has written 75 short stories, which been translated into 23 languages. His books include the novel *Mars Crossing* (Tor Books) and the short story collection *Impact Parameter and Other Quantum Realities* (Golden Gryphon). More information is available on his website at www.sff. net/people/geoffrey.landis.

Peter LaSalle is the author of four books of fiction. The latest is a story collection, *Tell Borges If You See Him: Tales of Contemporary Somnambulism* (forthcoming, fall 2007), which includes "The End of Narrative (1-29; or 29-1)." His work has appeared in many magazines and anthologies, such as *Paris Review, Agni, Tin House, Best American Short Stories, Sports Best Short Stories, Best of the West,* and *Prize Stories: The O. Henry Awards.* He is the recipient of the Flannery O'Connor Award for Short Fiction and the Award for Distinguished Prose from the *Antioch Review,* and has taught at universities in this country and in France, where in 2006 he was a visiting faculty member at Université de Paris, Sorbonne Nouvelle. He currently divides his time between Austin, Texas, and Narragansett in his native Rhode Island.

Kelly Link is the author of two collections, *Stranger Things Happen* and *Magic for Beginners.* Her short stories have appeared in *The Magazine of Fantasy and Science Fiction, Conjunctions,* and *Best American Short Stories 2005.* With her partner, Gavin J. Grant, she runs Small Beer Press as well as producing the zine *Lady Churchill's Rosebud Wristlet.* She and Gavin co-edit the fantasy half of *The Year's Best Fantasy and Horror* (St. Martin's). She lives in Northampton, Massachusetts. She owes Christopher Rowe and Josh Lewis for the conversation about evil pants.

Meghan McCarron's stories have appeared or are forthcoming from venues such as *Strange Horizons, Twenty Epics,* and *Lady Churchill's Rosebud Wristlet,* and her work has been longlisted for the Tiptree and Million Writers awards. She is a recent graduate of Wesleyan University and currently teaches film and English at a small boarding school in New Hampshire.

Sarah Monette grew up in Oak Ridge, Tennessee, one of the three secret cities of the Manhattan Project. Having completed her Ph.D. in English literature, she now lives and writes in a 101-year-old house in the Upper Midwest. Her novels—*Melusine* (2005), *The Virtu* (2006), *The Mirador* and *Summerdown* (forthcoming)—are published by Ace Books. Her short fiction has appeared in many places, including *Strange Horizons, Alchemy,* and *Lady Churchill's Rosebud Wristlet.* She was nominated for both the Crawford Award and the Campbell Award in 2006. Visit her online at www.sarahmonette.com.

Gina Ochsner is the author of two collections of stories, *The Necessary Grace to Fall* and *People I Wanted to Be.* She has won the Flannery O'Connor Award for Short Fiction, the Oregon Book Award for Short Fiction, and the PNBA award for short stories, and her work has appeared in *Tin House, The New Yorker, Black Warrior Review,* and elsewhere. Ochsner lives in western Oregon with her husband and four children.

Sumanth Prabhaker is twenty-four years old and lives in Wilmington, North Carolina, with his wife, Emily. He's currently studying for an MFA in creative writing at the University of North Carolina Wilmington, and working as the designer and fiction editor for *Ecotone,* UNCW's literary journal. He worked previously as a caregiver for adults with developmental disabilities at a non-profit organization called Little Friends, Inc. His stories have been published in *Identity*

Theory and *The New Pantagruel*. Sumanth can be reached at suprab-haker@yahoo.com.

Eric Roe is a native of Toledo, Ohio. He migrated westward from there, living in Wisconsin and Oregon, before bouncing over to the opposite coast in North Carolina. He has worked as a packing plant sanitation worker and as a legal assistant. His short stories have been published in *Fugue* and *Redivider*, and he has received several awards for both fiction and essay writing. He received his B.A. in English from Oregon State University, and in 2006 he began his M.F.A. in creative writing at North Carolina State University. He is currently working on a collection of short stories about packing plant workers, a collection of metafiction stories, and a novel spanning three generations of a family and the wars of their times.

E.M. Schorb's work has appeared in *The Southern Review, The Sewanee Review, Southwest Review, The Yale Review, The Chicago Review, Carolina Quarterly, The Virginia Quarterly Review, The Texas Review, The American Scholar, Stand* (England), *The Notre Dame Review, Rattle*, and the *New York Quarterly*, among many others. Schorb has published over two hundred poems and prose poems. His novel, *Paradise Square*, was awarded the Grand Prize for Fiction from the International eBook Award Foundation at the Frankfurt Book Fair. His verse collection, *Murderer's Day*, was awarded the Verna Emery Poetry Prize and published by Purdue University Press. He has won Fellowships in Literature from the Lannan Foundation and the Provincetown Fine Arts Work Center, the Arts Council of North Carolina, and the Ludwig Vogelstein Foundation.

Tyler Stoddard Smith is a freelance writer based out of Houston, Texas. He holds a B.A. from Rice University and received a Masters degree in Creative Writing from the University of Colorado at Boulder.

His works of fiction, non-fiction and poetry have been featured in *Barrelhouse, The Big Jewel, Box Car Poetry Review, The Bullfight Review, Identity Theory, McSweeney's, Monkeybicycle, Pindeldyboz, Twixt, Word Riot*, and *Yankee Pot Roast*, among others. He also edits a political satire website, www.demockeracy.com. He is currently at work on a novel. To his knowledge, he is the only person ever to beat Allen Ginsberg at "Frogger" on the Atari 2600. Learn more at www.stoddardsmith.com.

Ann Stapleton is a freelance writer from southeastern Ohio with a B.A. in English from Ohio University and an M.A. from Syracuse University's Creative Writing Program. Her novella *The Honor Farm* was published in *Alaska Quarterly Review*, and her poems and criticism have appeared in the Scottish-American poetry magazine *The Dark Horse*. She writes regularly for the University of Liverpool's *The Reader* and *The Weekly Standard*. After years as a housebound agoraphobic, she recently fell in love and took a trip to Scotland, where some mute swans had a word with her, and where she discovered the world is indeed a very nice place that she would recommend to anyone. She thanks William James for her new motto: "Reject nothing" and sends thoughts of encouragement and hope to anyone reading this who might need them.

Fritz Swanson is a member of the Poor Mojo Collective, where he writes for the august and long-running Ask the Giant Squid column, and where he helps edit the weekly 'zine *Poor Mojo's Almanac(k)*. Swanson teaches at the University of Michigan, and his work has appeared in *Pindeldyboz, The Mid-American Review, McSweeney's* and *Spork*. He lives in Manchester, Michigan, with his wife Sara and their son, Oscar.

Melora Wolff writes prose and poetry and lives in upstate New York. Her recent work has appeared in publications that include *The Southern*

Review, Green Mountains Review, West Branch, Fugue, and *Cimarron Review.* She teaches on the English faculty of Skidmore College, and is at work on a collection.

Catherine Zeidler's fiction has appeared in *Hobart* and *Smokelong Quarterly,* and has been nominated for a Pushcart Prize. She holds a B.A. from Barnard College and an M.F.A. from the University of Michigan. She lives in Brooklyn and is learning (slowly) to play the theremin. You can find her online at catpatz.com.

RECOMMENDED READING

The editors would like to call special attention to the following stories published in 2006.

"Stab" by Chris Adrian
Zoetrope, Summer

"Dominion" by Calvin Baker
One Story no. 75

"The Creation of Birds" by Christopher Barzak
Twenty Epics edited by David Moles & Susan Marie Groppi

"Inheritance" by Jedediah Berry
Fairy Tale Review, The Green Issue

"The Duel" by Tobias Buckell
Electric Velocipede no. 11

"The Life of Captain Gareth Caernarvon" by Brendan Connell
McSweeney's no. 19

"The Paper Life They Lead" by Patrick Crerand
Ninth Letter, Fall/Winter

"The Alternative History Club" by Murray Farish
Black Warrior Review, Fall/Winter

"Night Whiskey" by Jeffrey Ford
Salon Fantastique (edited by Ellen Datlow & Terri Windling)

"thirteen o'clock" by David Gerrold
Fantasy & Science Fiction, February

"Lucky Chow Fun" by Lauren Goff
Ploughshares, Fall

"Letters from Budapest" by Theodora Goss
Alchemy no. 3

"Galileo" by John Haskell
Public Space, Spring

"The Marquise de Wonka" by Shelley Jackson
Sex & Chocolate edited by Lucinda Ebersole & Richard Peabody

"Irregular Verbs" by Matthew Johnson
Fantasy Magazine, Fall

"The Mysterious Intensity of the Heart" by Jeff P. Jones
Redivider, vol. 4 issue 1

"Bainbridge" by Caitlin R. Kiernan
Alabaster

"A Secret Lexicon for the Not-Beautiful" by Beth Adele Long
Alchemy no. 3

"A Change in Fashion" by Steven Millhauser
Harper's, May

"Robert Kennedy Remembered by Jean Baudrillard" by Gary Percesepe
Mississippi Review Online, Summer

"The Man with the Scale in His Head" by Eman Quotah
Pindeldyboz, August 23

"Magnificent Pigs" by Cat Rambo
Strange Horizons, November 27

"Swimming" by Veronica Schanoes
Lady Churchill's Rosebud Wristlet no. 18

"Mountain Man" by Heather Shaw
Long Voyages, Great Lies edited by Christopher Barzak, Alan DeNiro, and Kristin Livdahl

"Snow Blind" by Bridget Behzer Sizer
Kenyon Review, Spring

PUBLICATIONS RECEIVED

In addition to online sources and printed materials sought out by the guest editors and series editor, the following websites, journals, and anthologies sent stories and publications to *Best American Fantasy* for consideration.

A PUBLIC SPACE
323 Dean Street
Brooklyn, NY 11217
apublicspace.org

ALASKA QUARTERLY REVIEW
University of Alaska, Anchorage
3211 Providence Drive
Anchorage, AK 99508
aqr.uaa.alaska.edu

ALCHEMY
P.O. Box 380264
Cambridge, MA 02238

ALICE REDUX
Paycock Press
3819 N. 13th Street
Arlington, VA 22201
gargoylemagazine.com

BLACK WARRIOR REVIEW
University of Alabama
Box 862936
Tuscaloosa, AL 35486
webdelsol.com/bwr

BORDERSENSES
4228 Hampshire Lane
El Paso, TX 79902
bordersenses.com

BRIAR CLIFF REVIEW
Briar Cliff University
3303 Rebecca Street
P.O. Box 2100
Sioux City, IA 51104
briarcliff.edu/campus_info/bcu_review/home_bcu_review.asp

CALYX
P.O. Box B
Corvalles, OR 97339-0539
calyxpress.com

CHANGE
12 Curtis Road
Natik, MA 01760
not-one-of-us.com

CHELSEA
P.O. Box 773
Cooper Station
New York, NY 01276-0773

DARK WISDOM
P.O. Box 389
Lake Orion, MI 48361-0389
darkwisdom.com

ELECTRIC VELOCIPEDE
P.O. Box 5014
Summerset, NJ 08873
electricvelocipede.com

FAIRY TALE REVIEW
Department of English
University of Alabama
Tuskaloosa, AL 35487
fairytalereview.com

FANTASY & SCIENCE FICTION
P.O. Box 3447
Hoboken, NJ 07030
fsfmag.com

FANTASY MAGAZINE
9710 Traville Gateway Drive, #234
Rockville, MD 20850
fantasy-magazine.com

FICTION
Department of English
City College of New York
Convent Avenue at 138th Street
New York, NY 10031
fictioninc.com

FLYTRAP
1034 McKinley Avenue
Oakland, CA 94610
tropismpress.com

GARGOYLE
3819 N. 13th Street
Arlington, VA 22201
gargoylemagazine.com

THE GEORGIA REVIEW
The University of Georgia
Athens, GA 30602-9009
uga.edu/garev

GLIMMER TRAIN
1211 NW Glisan, Suite 207
Portland, OR 97209-3054
glimmertrain.org

GREEN MOUNTAINS REVIEW
Johnson State College
Johnson, VT 05656
greenmountainsreview.jsc.vsc.edu

HARRINGTON GAY MEN'S FICTION QUARTERLY
10 Alice Street
Binghamton, NY 13904-9981
haworthpress.com/web/HGMFQ

HAWAII REVIEW
Kuykendall 402
1733 Donaghho Road
Honolulu, HI 96822
english.hawaii.edu/journals/journals.html

HOBART
P.O. Box 1658
Ann Arbor, MI 48103
hobartpulp.com

THE KENYON REVIEW
Kenyon College
104 College Drive
Gambier, OH 43022-9623
kenyonreview.org

LADY CHURCHILL'S ROSEBUD WRISTLET
176 Prospect Avenue
Northampton, MA 01060
lcrw.net/

LONG VOYAGES, GREAT LIES
Velocity Press
P.O. Box 28701
St. Paul, MN 55128
taverners-koans.com/ratbastards

MCSWEENEY'S
826NYC, 372 Fifth Ave.
Brooklyn, NY 11215
mcsweeneys.net

MISSISSIPPI REVIEW
University of Southern Mississippi
118 College Drive, #5144
Hattiesburg, MS 39406-0001
mississippireview.com

MYTHIC
3514 Signal Hill Ave NW
Roanoke, VA 24017
mythicdelirium.com

NEW ENGLAND REVIEW
Middlebury College
Middlebury, VT 05753
go.middlebury.edu/nereview

NEW GENRE
P.O. Box 270092
West Hartford, CT 06127
new-genre.com

THE NEW YORKER
4 Times Square
New York, NY 10036-6592
newyorker.com

NINTH LETTER
University of Illinois at Urbana-Champaign
234 English Building
608 South Wright Street
Urbana, IL 61801
ninthletter.com

NORTH CAROLINA LITERARY REVIEW
East Carolina University
Department of English
2201 Bate Building
Greenville, NC 27858-4353
ecu.edu/nclr

NOT ONE OF US
12 Curtis Road
Natick, MA 01760
not-one-of-us.com

ON SPEC
P.O. Box 4727
Edmonton, AB
Canada T6E 5G6
onspec.ca

ONE STORY
P.O. Box 150618
Brooklyn, NY 11215
one-story.com

OXFORD AMERICAN
201 Donaghey Avenue
Main 107
Conway, AK 72035
oxfordamericanmag.com

PARADOX
P.O. Box 22897
Brooklyn, NY 11202-2897
paradoxmag.com

PARASPHERES
Omnidawn Publishing
1632 Elm Avenue
Richmond, California 94805-1614
omnidawn.com

THE PARIS REVIEW
62 White Street
New York, NY 10013
theparisreview.org

PHANTOM
9710 Traville Gateway Drive, #234
Rockville, MD 20850

PLOUGHSHARES
Emerson College
120 Boylston Street
Boston, MA 02116-4624
pshares.org

POLYPHONY 6
Wheatland Press
P.O. Box 1818
Wilsonville, OR 97070
wheatlandpress.com

PORCUPINE
P.O. Box 259
Cedarburg, WI 53012
porcupineliteraryarts.com

REDIVIDER
Emerson College
120 Broylston Street
Boston, MA 02116

REALMS OF FANTASY
P.O. Box 527
Rumson, NJ 07760
rofmagazine.com

ROSEBUD
N3310 Asje Road
Cambridge, WI 53523
rsbd.net

SALON FANTASTIQUE
Thunder's Mouth Press
245 W. 17th Street, 11th Floor
New York, NY 10011
thundersmouth.com

SEX AND CHOCOLATE
Paycock Press
3819 N. 13th Street
Arlington, VA 22201
gargoylemagazine.com

SHIMMER
P.O. Box 58591
Salt Lake City, UT 84158-0591
shimmerzine.com

SOU'WESTER
Department of English, Box 1438
Southern Illinois University, Edwardsville
Edwardsville, IL 62026-1438
siue.edu/ENGLISH/SW/

THE SOUTHERN REVIEW
Old President's House
Louisiana State University
Baton Rouge, LA 70803
lsu.edu/thesouthernreview

SUBTERRANEAN
P.O. Box 190106
Burton, MI 48519
subterraneanpress.com

TIN HOUSE
P.O. Box 10500
Portland, OR 97296-0500
tinhouse.com

TWENTY EPICS
All-Star Stories
1640 Hearst Avenue #C
Berkeley, CA 94703
allstarstories.com

ZAHIR
315 South Coast Highway 101
Suite U8
Encinitas, CA 92024
zahirtales.com

ZOETROPE
916 Kearny Street
San Francisco, CA 94133
allstory.com

PUBLICATION HISTORY

THE EDITORS

Guest Editor **Ann VanderMeer** has been a publisher and editor for over twenty years. She currently serves as fiction editor for *Weird Tales*, North America's longest-running fantasy magazine. Books published by her Buzzcity Press include the IHG Award-winning *The Divinity Student* by Michael Cisco. In addition, she has been a partner with her husband, Jeff VanderMeer, on such editing projects as the World Fantasy Award winning Leviathan series and the Hugo finalist *The Thackery T. Lambshead Pocket Guide to Eccentric & Discredited Diseases*. A *Best of the Silver Web* is forthcoming from Prime Books. Currently, she is also co-editing the following anthologies: *The New Weird, Fast Ships, Black Sails, Steampunk, Last Drink Bird Head,* and *Love-Drunk Book Heads*.

Guest Editor **Jeff VanderMeer** has twice won the World Fantasy Award and is the author of several surreal/magic realist novels and story collections, including *City of Saints & Madmen,* and *Shriek: An Afterword*. His fiction has been published in 20 countries. VanderMeer's most recent books have made the year's best lists of *Publishers Weekly, The San Francisco Chronicle, The Los Angeles Weekly, Publishers' News,* and *Amazon. com.* He is the recipient of an NEA-funded Florida Individual Artist Fellowship for excellence in fiction and a Florida Artist Enhancement Grant. His nonfiction has appeared in *The Washington Post Book World* and *Publishers Weekly,* among others. His Modern Word essays on Angela Carter are considered essential reading for anyone interested in Carter's work.

Series Editor **Matthew Cheney** has published fiction and nonfiction with *One Story, Strange Horizons, Locus, Rain Taxi, Failbetter,* and others. He has served on the jury for the Speculative Literature Foundation's Fountain Award, and his weblog, *http://www.mumpsimus.blogspot.com,* was a finalist for the 2005 World Fantasy Award. He lives in New Hampshire.

THE COVER ARTIST

"I have been tremendously influenced by the teachings of Joseph Campbell. One of his main themes was that 'God is an intelligible sphere whose center is everywhere and circumference nowhere.' He also insisted that the function of mythology and religion is to put the human spirit in accord with its environment and the artist is the symbol maker and the visionary in tune with both."—Scott Eagle

The cover artist for the inaugural volume of Best American Fantasy is **Scott Eagle**. Eagle serves as Associate Professor and Area Coordinator of Painting and Drawing at East Carolina University in Greenville, North Carolina. His artworks have been exhibited and reproduced internationally. Publications featuring his artwork include *The Oxford American, The New York Times, and the Cleveland Plains Dealer.*

"In the often harrowing, dreamlike world that Eagle conjures in his art, humans are perpetually at the mercy of forces beyond their control. They're beheaded, attacked by sharks, menaced by tornadoes, sent tumbling through space and otherwise rendered powerless, while mysterious events unfold around them.

Eagle's work aptly reflects the uncertainty and frequent perils of corporeal existence. It's a timeless theme, but one that seems particularly relevant during troubled times."
—*Tom Patterson, Winston-Salem Journal*

"Perfectly capable of capturing the essence of his art historical sources, Eagle develops his borrowings into intensely personal statements, dense with implications. This introspective man, casting a wide net in his search for answers that ultimately come from within, distills what he has learned into accomplished paintings that glow darkly with a complicated commentary on these complicated times."
—*Huston Paschal, Curator of Contemporary Art at the North Carolina Museum of Art*

For more information on Eagle's art, please visit his website at: http://www.scotteagle.com.